"Heroine Adele Bonny leaves no stones unturned in her quest to find the Anne Bonny/Calico Jack treasure: A fun and exciting read."

—NBC News Denver

"Wendy Wilkinson has made a seamless transition from *New York Times* Best Seller non-fiction writer to a compelling and entertaining fiction author, with her debut novel *Pirate's Plunder*. Rich in historical detail and sense of scene, she has created fully developed characters coupled with a page-turning story."

—Ron Seggi, *Ron Seggi* syndicated radio show

"Having lived in Florida for most of my life, tales of pirates Anne Bonny and Calico Jack Rackham abound. Wendy Wilkinson has expertly blended historic pirate adventure with modern day piracy, with the journey of a contemporary woman on a quest to find her stolen family fortune and heritage!"

—Stephanie Toote, *IslandScene* magazine

"Wilkinson draws you into the world of pirates . . . then and now . . . along with spinning the story of a woman's journey to self-reliance and her pirate relative's journey to find redemption . . . a real page-turner from start to finish."

—Richard Randall, KVOR radio

"Wendy Wilkinson's fast-paced, irreverent style sweeps us across the ocean and into dangerous water, but along the way we fall in love with Adele as she recovers not only her lost treasure, but her true self. Terrific women's fiction with plenty of humor and delicious plot twists."

—Best-selling author Mara Purl

Pirate's Plunder

OTHER WORKS by WENDY WILKINSON

FICTION

ARGHH! Being the Vexing Letters from Pirate Anne Bonny to Her Secret Sister (Bellekeep Books)

NON-FICTION

with Cynthia V. N. Peck:
PARENTS AT LAST: Celebrating Adoption and the New Pathways to Parenthood (Clarkson Potter)

with Jill Rappaport: *New York Times* Best Seller
PEOPLE WE KNOW, HORSES THEY LOVE (Rodale)
[featuring Jeff Bridges, Richard Gere, Gisele, Robert Redford, and others]

with Donna Lee and Morgan Freeman:
MORGAN FREEMAN & FRIENDS: Caribbean Cooking for a Cause (Rodale)
[featuring Ben Affleck, Orlando Bloom, Kenny Chesney, Katie Couric, Daisy Fuentes, Tom Hanks, Alicia Keys, and others]

Pirate's Plunder

An Adele Bonny Adventure

Wendy Wilkinson

Bellekeep Books

This is a work of fiction.
Names, characters, places and incidents are the product of the author's imagination or are used fictitiously, and any resemblance to actual persons, living or dead, events or locales, is entirely coincidental.

For information address: Bellekeep Books
29 Fifth Avenue, New York, NY 10003
www.BellekeepBooks.com

Covers by Nick Zelinger, NZ Graphics ©2013
Copyediting, Design, and Typesetting by Jean Laidig
Author Photo by Don Jones

ISBN: 978-0-9855685-1-1 (paperback)
ISBN: 978-0-9855685-4-2 (e-book)

Publisher's Cataloging-In-Publication Data

Wilkinson, Wendy (Wendy Ann), 1954-
Pirate's plunder / Wendy Wilkinson.

p. ; cm. -- (An Adele Bonny adventure ; [bk. 1])

ISBN: 978-0-9855685-1-1

1. Women pirates--Bahamas--Fiction. 2. Piracy--Bahamas--Fiction. 3. Mercenary troops--Bahamas--Fiction. 4. Voyages and travels--Bahamas--Fiction. 5. Bahamas--Fiction. 6. Adventure stories. I. Title.

PS3623.I55 P57 2012
813/.6

Published in the U.S. by Bellekeep Books, New York www.BellekeepBooks.com
Distributed by Midpoint Trade Books, New York www.MidpointTradeBooks.com
10 9 8 7 6 5 4 3 2 1
Printed in the United States of America

To my wonderful husband and fabulous daughter
who have shared my love of the Caribbean
and my journey to bring Pirate's Plunder *to life*
over the last four years.
Also a special thanks to the lovely
Morgan Freeman,
for sharing my passion for all things Island.

Acknowledgments

I would like to thank my publisher Eric Kampmann and Midpoint Trade books, as well as Margot Atwell and Tara Goff at Bellekeep Books. Thanks to my gifted editorial team, which includes Jean Laidig, my tenacious and meticulous editor / proofreader, and Nick Zelinger for his creative and spot-on front and back cover design.

In addition I'd like to thank Susan Griswold of Wilkinson Brown for her work on and support of the book; Sharon House, partner in Much & House Public Relations, and especially to best-selling author Mara Purl for her advice and mentorship.

It is frequently said, "It takes a village to raise a child"; and it is also true that it takes a dedicated and professional team to create and produce a book! Thank you, team, for all that you have done.

WW

"I am sorry to see you here, but if you had fought like a man, you needn't be hanged like a dog."

— Anne Bonny to "Calico Jack" Rackham
in prison after his surrender

Prologue

Adele Bonny had no idea she had married a liar and thief when she painfully limped through the front door of their luxurious Cable Beach condo. Her husband, Curtis Albury, greeted her inside with a loofah and an open bottle of lavender massage oil. Helping her to the living room couch, he removed her flip-flops, examining her red and swollen right ankle. He then opened the oil and carefully poured several drops onto the natural fiber sponge and began to stroke her ankle and foot.

"You're late, Boots," he said.

"I know, and school sucks. Had to stay after the bell and teach Audrey's Thursday ballet class. Thank God Christmas vacation is in a week. I can really use the break. The students cared more about texting than their turnout position, and the only thing I know about toe dancing is what we saw in *Swan Lake*."

"Not good for the ankle. The swelling's pretty bad today."

"I know," Adele repeated. "Guess it's the cool, wet weather." She tried to make light of her pain. "My hair's been as curly as Little Orphan Annie."

Tousling her wild curls, Curtis continued his massage and she fell back on the couch with an arched spine and a sigh of sensual pleasure. She still had her messenger bag hooked tightly across her shoulder. It had been more than two months of Thursdays since her husband had greeted her after work in this special way. *Maybe things are getting better*, she hoped. *Maybe we're getting our magic back.*

He murmured that she was both the white and black swan,

and although that didn't seem to make sense he was sweet to say it; she sighed again happily.

But even as he went through the motions, Curtis admitted to himself that he couldn't fake the love tonight. Kissing her throat and upper chest, he took the opportunity to finger the necklace he'd given her for their first anniversary—a beautiful combination of light pink conch-shell tips and deep purple freshwater pearls. *And valuable. Beautifully valuable.*

Luckily Adele broke away first, mumbling, "I have to pee really bad," and headed for the bathroom.

When she was out of sight, he went to a small desk and took out an inventory sheet reading "Romantic Relics of the Caribbean." Staring at the paper for several seconds, his gaze landed on the description of one particular item: "Exquisite Eighteenth Century ceremonial sapphire and ruby encrusted 9-inch dagger pistol. Dagger blade intact and original, pistol mechanism restored to working order. From the Anne Bonny/Calico Jack Rackham Collection. Value: to be determined." He replaced the list where he'd found it and decided to keep his game going for a little bit longer.

In the bathroom, Adele pulled off her lightweight, dull blue sweatshirt and let it fall to the floor. Looking into the mirror, she fluffed her glossy shoulder-length red curls, smiling at her dark green eyes. *Not bad for thirty-eight*, she encouraged herself. She yanked off her necklace and shabby yellow bra, dropping them both on the sink shelf on her way to the bedroom. Opening her bag, she began to throw hundreds of pink plumeria petals all over the bed—their gorgeous but underused California King.

Then, as seductively as she could manage, she limped into the living room and captured Curtis by the arm, cuddling up against him. "Shut your eyes, I have a sweet surprise for you," Adele purred. As she pulled off his Ralph Lauren polo shirt, she couldn't help noticing the little stomach paunch he'd developed. *Oh, well, for better or worse. . . .* Leading him into their bedroom, she pushed him onto the plumeria-covered bed.

"Wait—"

"It's okay, it's not roses," she assured him, gentling him back onto the bed and caressing his rounded tummy. *Really, it's not so bad. He puts up with my ankle. It just means he's comfortable being married, right?* She reached up to kiss him, but it got awkward when he turned away from her between kisses. First one sneeze, then another.

Curtis opened up his eyes in horror. "Oh, my God, the pollen!" He scrambled up from the bed, but not before his perfectly shaved back was covered by an angry red rash.

"I'm so sorry, honey," she cried in a panic, wondering when her marriage had become so hard. "I thought tropical flowers would be safe. Will a cold compress help?"

Ignoring his wife, he rushed into the bathroom, turned on the shower, and let the cold water soothe his now blistering body.

Listening to the sound of the shower drone on and on, Adele abandoned the bedroom with its sad trail of crushed flower petals and decided to camp on the couch. Looking across the room at a photo of her and Curtis sailing a small Sun Chaser, she remembered the day he'd given her the nickname Boots. *He called me that tonight.* She smiled with renewed optimism. *He must still love me.*

She called out to Curtis when she heard the shower stop, but he did not answer.

He was too busy stuffing her valuable necklace into his shaving bag.

Chapter 1

It was Friday at two p.m. Adele was tired and tense when she left the ultra-chic private Island High School Academy. The unseasonably cool and wet week had been bad for both her soul and psyche, and working overtime didn't help her mood either. Always the good sport, she had agreed to take over the ballet class of a coworker who was on extended maternity leave. *I've only been teaching here for eighteen months and have already lost my joy. What's really getting me down? Is it teaching that's such a drag, or the seven dance classes a day with students who plod through the hour with no passion or heart?* Pulling off her high-heel sandals and rubbing her red, chafed feet, she slid into her lime green Volkswagen Bug with the darling daisy wheels, and reached for her bright red leather Day Planner before slinging her messenger bag into the back seat. She opened the notebook to December 9, where she had joyously written "School's out for Christmas" in the heading. Adele started to read—the next item was "Have Bug checked for funny noise"—but suddenly dropped the book to the floor and clutched her ear lobes. Pulling them gently, she tried to get rid of the ringing that had now been bothering her for weeks. Just yesterday the ringing had intruded at an even more critical time—in the middle of a swan dive into her condo's pool—resulting in a piercing pain radiating up to the front of her forehead. The water had been cool, but not nearly cold enough to cause a brain freeze. *I really must go see a doctor about my hearing*, she noted to herself.

Then there was her husband, Curtis. She'd been blaming him for not being more sympathetic and supportive. Perhaps her own bouts with pain, both in her head and ankle, caused her to be more irritable than usual. Maybe these mood swings were the reason for their recent marital problems. She'd thought there was light at the end of the tunnel last Thursday night, but her plans had been cut short by the plumeria incident.

Today, she had a mission. *The initiative will be mine. I'll entice Curtis with a great Pinot and tantalizing truffles.* She smiled to herself. *Maybe chocolate is only a Band-Aid, but I won't care tonight.*

Picking up the Day Planner, she thought about her three p.m. Exotic Dance Class and drinks two hours later with Curtis. *It'll be nice to be the student for a change.*

A ray of sun finally peeked out from behind the clouds. It was starting to be a beautiful day in the Cable Beach area of Nassau on the island of New Providence. The largest city in the Bahamas island chain, Nassau was where the rich and famous played and sailed, and Adele drank in the lush atmosphere of affluence as she slowly pulled up to The Rendezvous, an expansive and exclusive resort where she was meeting Elaine Jacobs for their class. Jogging into the spa, she saw that her friend had already changed.

"These last ten weeks have been so hard," complained Adele. "Seven hours of dance class every day and I don't have the toes of a twenty-year-old anymore. When did the joy of teaching dance become such a chore? You don't know how lucky you are, not having to work."

"I guess," Elaine said wistfully. "But you've always loved hard work. I remember when we first met in Florida and you were teaching non-stop in that cute little studio."

"Maybe I'm just tired." Adele started to change into her bright pink leotard and green tights. "I'm really looking forward to spending some down time with Curtis on my boat. He's spent weeks retrofitting the *Bonny* for our getaway weekend. Should be clear skies and smooth sailing by tomorrow." Once dressed in her leotard, she straightened her single-pearl necklace.

"The trip sounds fabulous and I want your life," asserted Elaine enthusiastically. "When do you leave and do you need a boat girl? I'd be glad to volunteer."

"Thanks for the offer but we already have our boat girl, Gracie, who'll be taking good care of us. I just want several days of solitude with Curtis, and am looking forward to previewing his work tonight over a very good Pinot and private anniversary celebration."

"Your husband is such a jewel," Elaine sighed. "And looking like a young Robert Redford doesn't hurt either. It always amazes me how blond some Bahamians are. I've thought about browsing the net to find my own Curtis, but I'm way too much of a chicken."

Playing her insecurities close to her chest, Adele did not reveal her rising angst about her husband, suggesting that they limber up before class.

"You're so motivated, Adele. You've gotten everything you've wanted ever since we've been friends."

"I'm not sure what you mean." Adele stretched down to the ground.

"Your condo has the best view of the water and the *Beautiful Bonny* is totally awesome."

"How quickly you forget," chided Adele. "I used all my dance dollars for furniture when I moved into Curtis' condo. It was one giant closet in those days. And it's taken me two years of swearing and sweat to get my abandoned *Bonny* back to seaworthiness." She looked into the skeptical eyes of Elaine. "As you know, I have to *work* for it."

Elaine thrust out her lower lip. "I know you do. And I'm just a useless, pudgy trust fund baby."

"Hey, don't be so hard on yourself." Adele reached a hand out to touch her friend's arm. "Our dance classes are really starting to tone you up. And maybe I envy *your* lifestyle just a bit."

The two women heard the music signaling the next class, so

they headed in for Exotic Dance—a mixture of Belly Dancing, Aerobics, and Strip Tease Pole stretches. Walking into class, Adele passed a very feminine looking, middle-aged Creole man, with obviously dyed black hair, and patted him on his shoulder. This was Reginald "Smee" Stocking the Third and he was wearing fluffy, bright blue pirate pants.

"Hi, Smee," said Adele. "Looking forward to learning some new moves?"

"Can't wait, my dear." He smiled brightly.

Adele then began to move side-by-side with Mandy, the nineteen-year-old instructor. Mandy Amore was a bit of a brainless beauty. The product of a mixed-race marriage, she was truly gorgeous, with tightly curled auburn hair, mocha-colored skin, and a natural grace to her movements. She was totally compelling—until she opened her mouth and revealed her Bronx accent. Adele looked at the rock-hard breasts protruding high above Mandy's rib cage. *Every woman in the room knows that these are not the pair you were born with, honey.* She was trying to teach the group of twelve local and resort guest women, and Smee, how to get in touch with their own "inner goddess," by showing them moves their partners would thank them for tonight.

Adele had a lean and lanky dancer's body—incredibly agile for a thirty-eight-year-old—except for what she called her bubble butt. *Curtis thinks it's one of my most appealing features.* Never quite good enough to go pro, she had a good reason why. At the age of nine she had broken her right ankle in modern dance and it never healed properly. A difficult jump could cause Adele to lose her footing and land in a crumple on the floor; a sharp turn frequently resulted in a searing pain up her calf.

In fact, it was when she was at a physical therapy appointment that she met Curtis. He was suffering from a severe groin pull, and after a vigorous session he kindly helped her to her car where they exchanged their 4-1-1 in the parking lot.

Missing a step now, she shook her head as if it would help

her stop thinking about her husband . . . and that sore ankle of hers. She brought her gaze to the mirror and moved her belly gracefully before going on to the pole stretches.

Two poles away, Elaine watched her friend and tried to mimic the moves, but her back was not nearly as flexible. After a cracking noise the whole class heard, she stood up wobbly, using the pole for support.

Mandy, who was wearing a rhinestone-encrusted purple leotard with leg warmers and lipstick to match, tried to bend Elaine's torso forward, none too gently. Though she made a show of helping her client, all the while she stared pointedly at the large ruby hoop earrings adorning Elaine's ears. Definitely raised on the wrong side of the tracks, Mandy loved everything bright and shiny, especially jewelry, and she knew the difference between a rock and a gem.

"Did you get those earrings from Schaffer's or Maxwell's?" she whined in her best Bronx voice.

"Neither," responded Elaine. Adele had to suppress a laugh as Elaine stuck her tongue out at Mandy, who was now walking in Adele's direction. She stopped, observing while Adele used her pole as a brace to help her move into the full splits.

"Way to move it, Adele," Mandy said, while Smee beamed with approval at the next bar.

"I kinda like the way you play with the pole. It looks kinda like you can pull it outta the floor and juggle with it."

Thinking about what Mandy had just said, Adele stopped stretching. "I don't get that, Mandy. Juggling involves throwing objects up in the air and keeping them in play so they don't drop to the ground."

"Really? I thought juggling was what those cute knights did with poles when they were fightin' over hot girlfriends."

Elaine stopped moving and started to laugh. "She means jousting."

"I do?" asked Mandy, looking perplexed.

At this Adele giggled, too. Mandy's offended expression just fueled their hilarity, and soon she and Elaine were laughing so uncontrollably that they had to leave class and head for the changing room. Collapsing on the benches, the two friends tried to regain control.

Adele wiped tears from her eyes. "Oh, there's nothing like a good laugh to clear the cobwebs."

"My sides!" Elaine gasped. "I bet I just lost two inches around my waist!"

"Listen, I better make a quick call to Curtis," Adele said when her voice was back to normal. "I should tell him I'm running a little late."

"Sure. I'll go into the Quiet Room and make a call too." Both ladies left the floor and Elaine called her father. "Hi, Daddy. Yes, I'll be there in an hour for dinner. Thank Mommy for making my favorite fish stew. Love you too."

Adele placed the call to their condo, but it immediately went to voice mail. Next she checked their voice mail but the only message was one he'd left yesterday. "Hi, Hon. Listen, I advise you not to buy those new captain's chairs for the *Bonny*. They cost eight hundred dollars each! With you being on Christmas break for three weeks, you're not bringing in a paycheck, you know. Love ya." *Always a bit of a control freak, he has to leave me a piece of advice.*

Maybe the third time will be a charm, she thought, dialing his cell phone. He answered on the third ring. "Hi, Boots, Happy Anniversary . . . but I may be late for our celebration—still trying to balance the books."

Sighing a bit, she reminded him to pick up her conch-shell necklace from the jewelers. "It shouldn't take a whole week to fix a clasp." She heard a vaguely agreeable murmur from Curtis. "A 2009 Pinot is waiting with me," she coaxed, trying to excite him.

She then walked into the changing room for a quick shower. Though she'd reassured herself earlier that she was looking good, she wasn't alone in the shower room and the comparison didn't boost her confidence level. Adele couldn't help but notice the bodacious Mandy and the raven-haired yoga teacher Melissa, who both stepped into the stall next to her. With those perky points and prominent pubic bones, Mandy's figure could truly stop clocks. As if to confirm Adele's observation the teenager stepped out of the water, shaking both her freshly washed bod and booty.

Melissa and Mandy grabbed each other playfully and the young yoga teacher whispered into her friend's ear. They started to giggle. Mandy glanced over at Adele, looked down at her large princess cut diamond wedding ring, gave her a smug smile, and after a brief towel dry wiggled into her thong. Opening her locker, Mandy took out her iPhone and started to text, but, stubbing her toe, dropped the phone onto the dressing room bench. Adele instinctively picked it up and noticed the beginning of the text: "Hi C, will meet you at the BB. . . ." before Mandy snatched it out of her hand.

"Pleeease, a little privacy," she hissed.

Something familiar about the initials gave Adele pause before she slipped into a new black sundress and headed to the parking lot, leaving Mandy to continue to admire any and everything that moved on her own body.

Driving several miles away from the fashionable resorts, she parked in front of an old warehouse and slipped silently through the side door of a small dance studio. She stopped for a moment to watch a lovely young dancer, the only one there on the scarred, wooden floor, practicing several ballet moves—including a perfect *plié* and then rising up to point on her toes where she fluttered ever so elegantly. After an enthralled sixty seconds, thinking back to when her students actually cared about how they moved their bodies, Adele made herself known.

"Hi, Rachel, how you've improved during the last eighteen months!"

The young dancer turned towards the opened door with a start and landed hard on flat feet. "Oh, hi, Mrs. Albury. I didn't hear you come in."

Walking with a slight limp towards the side of the room,

Adele slipped into an alcove housing twenty old lockers. "Guess it's about time to empty out my locker. Just keep practicing and don't mind me. Rachel, when did you switch from modern to ballet?"

Rachel followed her into the back room. "Just nine months ago. You know, Mrs. Albury, you were the best teacher I've ever had."

"I saw your potential," said Adele softly.

"Thank you," Rachel replied as she went back to the floor, but not before giving Adele a quick hug across the shoulders.

Looking at the locker line, Adele grasped the combination lock in front of number 13 and dialed right, left and then right again. After a solid tug it opened slowly, releasing a waft of ginger from an old scented candle. Two years of memories were tucked tightly inside. Adele pulled out an old, bright pink leotard and two pair of sexy black lace thongs—blessedly she'd taken her dirty laundry home long before—and held the leotard close to her. *This was the first gift Curtis ever bought me*, she thought. *He was so generous then.* Next she picked up a photo album and started riffling through it. The pages were full of images of dance students, all displaying different attitudes and poses. Adele, wearing the pink leotard and fuchsia tights, was depicted around the class, straightening legs and righting posture. A handsome and fit man, wearing black bicycle tights and black sweater, was seen in many of the images, smiling at Adele, and even participating in a yoga class. *Oh, that Curtis, he was so fit then and loved coming to class.*

A feeling of extreme sorrow choked her as she emptied the locker, stuffing her candle, clothes, photo album, and dance memorabilia into her messenger bag, and headed for the door. *God, I miss this place.*

Heading through downtown Nassau, Adele decided to turn down a small side street where she came face to face with a huge mural painted on the wall of The Provocative Pirates of the Bahamas Museum. The giant painting made her wince. On display was the over-sized image of a buxom female pirate with red hair similar to Adele's, wearing flashy purple pantaloons and a green, low-cut, open-tie blouse with mounds thrusting suggestively. Right next to her, striking a manly pose, stood a male pirate in black and white striped pants and flowing figured shirt. The man was brandishing a huge ax and the woman a cutlass—a large sword with a curved steel blade that swept into a graceful point. Adele shuddered and hit the accelerator, leaving the mural behind her.

Arriving at the Nassau marina, Adele breathed in deeply for the first time all day at the sight of so many gorgeous sailboats coming into view. She parked her Bug and hurried down a dock, stopping at the sign for the *Beautiful Bonny*. The slip was empty. Was she at the wrong dock? Confused, she headed down to the left side of the Marina. But the *Bonny* was not docked there either. Getting frantic, Adele started to run towards the dock master's office.

Adele's boat neighbor Grant, a literal man in his late 50s, approached her from the end of the other dock. "The *Bonny* is down here, Adele. Curtis wanted the western facing dockside breezes to dry her faster. He seemed very excited about tomorrow's trip."

"Thanks, Grant," called Adele. "How sweet," she said more quietly, softening up at the thought of Curtis preparing thoughtfully for their impending sweetheart sail.

Hurrying to the end of a colorfully painted dock, she took in the sight of the spectacular rose-gold sunset bathing her magnificent 42-foot Hunter Passage in a pinkish-purple light. A worker was feverishly painting a nautical blue stripe around the hull, eight inches above the water line. She jumped aboard her precious *Beautiful Bonny*. The fifty-foot-tall mainmast was still draped in white canvas, protecting it from blowing sand until the bleaching completely dried out for tomorrow's trip. Her boat was freshly repainted an eggshell white, and the worker made the final brush strokes on the double navy blue striping before leaving Adele to a very promising evening. She patted her boat's side approvingly, just as a proud mother would do, seeing that Curtis had polished the walnut wood to a cinnamon glow. Adele pulled up the skirt of her voile dress and gently rubbed the black fabric over the wood, not gathering a hint of dust.

Greeting her with a persistent *meow* when she opened the cabin hatch was a huge solid black cat with golden eyes and a perfect V-shaped cut in his right ear, snug and comfortable on a berth cushion. This was Gilligan, Adele's live-aboard pet for more than two years now. Coming to greet her, Gilligan slid up her leg and a soft purr replaced the insistent meow. Pulling out a small brush, Adele started to stroke him gently with it, trying to remove as much hair as possible. *And just think, Gilligan almost ended my marriage. When I introduced him to Curtis, the poor guy sneezed at least six times and blew his nose for a half hour!*

Only a promise to keep Gilligan aboard the *Beautiful Bonny* kept her husband from taking him to the Humane Society.

Going into the boat's head to fluff up her hair and empty the cat brush before her husband's arrival, she inhaled the scent of his fruity cologne, then found a bottle of lavender-vanilla massage oil and a new loofah on the counter. With renewed hopes for a great evening, Adele smiled and rubbed the oil on her hands and small décolletage.

Opening the cramped closet, she found a man's navy blue Burberry jacket and slacks draped perfectly on the one hanger. A floral cotton sundress, with the tags still attached, lay carelessly on the deck. Picking up the dress, Adele looked at the tag. It read "Size 6." *Oh, that Curtis,* she thought. *I'll never tell him I'm a size 10.* Going into the galley, she saw it was stocked with gourmet goodies and fine wine. Adele then popped the cork on a 2006 Pinot Noir, breathed in the rich aroma and poured herself a glass. She settled down into a comfy plush nautical blue silk chair with Gilligan snoozing on her chest. The marine clock read six-thirty p.m., so she started to browse through *Sailing Style* magazine. The publication had always been a favorite read of hers and, thumbing through its pages, she noticed a three-page spread on the most comfortable captain's chairs. She found one that'd be a perfect replacement for the two wooden chairs stationed at the helm of the *Bonny.* But, gasping at the price of the plush blue leather pair, she decided to look for an online bargain. In this case, it seemed, Curtis' advice had some merit.

At seven p.m. Adele brought out her laptop computer and began to Google captain's chairs, but nothing caught her eye. She then reached for her glass, took another sip of wine, and opened up her Facebook page. Scrolling through several images, she stopped at the one of her and Curtis dancing on the bow of the *Beautiful Bonny.* He was holding her tenderly and both were clearly having a wonderful time together. *He's always been so supportive of my dancing, paying for my continuing education and even taking some of my classes. What a great team we made.* Continuing to go through her Facebook, she opened up a short video she and Curtis had made at their dance studio. Out of focus and choppy, the last few seconds captured what could have been a bad fall, but somehow Curtis managed to catch Adele before she landed on the hard floor. They both smiled into the freeze frame.

Curtis has always been sympathetic to my pain, while Babs, a.k.a. Mom, always told me to "power through it," Adele thought bitterly. *No wonder she's never liked him.* Continuing down memory lane, she remembered Babs had never been a very sympathetic person, even after the *incident*, when she abandoned both Adele and her other daughter Alli.

I have an idea. Bending over a wooden side panel above one of the silk cushions, she pulled the fabric away from the bulkhead. Pushing a concealed button, she held it down for twenty seconds. The panel popped open and slid to the side, revealing a hidden cubbyhole a foot long and six inches deep. Taking the black lace thongs out of her messenger bag and enjoying the whiff of scent from her locker's candle, she tucked them into the open space, and didn't quite close the panel. *For later tonight and I want easy access.*

The night belongs to Curtis and me. Looking at her watch, she was surprised to see it read eight-thirty. Where was Curtis? Grabbing the phone, Adele tried Curtis' number, but heard the all too familiar voice-mail: "Ahoy, Matey. I'm off to find my fortune, so please leave a message."

And Adele did. "Where are you, Curtis? The wine's almost gone and I'm starting on the Godiva chocolates." Slamming down the phone, she reflected that Curtis was, indeed, always off to seek his fortune one way or another. But tonight was supposed to be Time Out! She opened the box of extra dark chocolate truffles, stuffing two raspberry-filled delights into her mouth at once.

Choking a bit, she heard a noise on the deck overhead. *Is he finally here? About damn time.*

As a pair of male feet descended into view, she did her best to wipe the chocolate from her mouth and straighten up her black dress. But when the head appeared, it wasn't Curtis standing there, ready with a glib, well-thought-out apology for being late. It was her boat neighbor Grant. "Well, hi there," she said. "How about joining me in some wine?" She burst out laughing.

He seemed to stand there a long time without saying anything. Finally he asked, "Where is Curtis?"

"Cha-ching! The sixty-four thousand dollar question, Grant. Where *is* Curtis?"

"Oh, boy."

"You look so uneasy, Grant. Why not pull up a bench and chew on a chocolate?" She managed to snag the box of truffles and waggle it under his nose.

Grimacing, he pushed it away. "You're hammered, Adele. I don't think it'll help."

Looking at Adele with obvious discomfort, Grant spun on his heels and ascended the ladder to the main deck, leaving Adele with nothing but the sound of his retreating footsteps, until she heard him toss back, "Have a good night, Adele."

Chapter 2

It was anything but a good night for Adele as she started to doze off. Waking up with a start nine hours later, she removed her now very wrinkled black dress. She didn't notice or care that it was another beautiful day at the Marina as the sun was just rising bright crimson over the water. Gilligan had taken a giant dump in his litter box and, using a small scooper, she threw the smelly poop into a plastic bag, making a mental note to dispose of it in a dockside trash can. Wincing a bit at the glorious sunrise, she angrily started to clean up the red wine stains and chocolate wrappers strewn across the bow of the *Beautiful Bonny.* Her head throbbing and eyes watering, she considered the most effective ways to overcome her wicked hangover. After quickly downing four aspirin, she crept into the head and under an ice cold shower. With hair sopping wet, she then put yesterday's workout clothes back on her damp body and angrily moved into several yoga positions on the bow of her boat.

Damn, she suddenly remembered, *I've got to head home now. Babs sent the loot by Brinks Security for a.m. delivery and I'm sure she's inventoried every piece. I need to get the treasure insured here on the island before the exhibit.*

Babs Bonny was a neat little piece of work from West Palm. Despite being the mother of two grown daughters, she was more than well-known on the islands for having partied on New Providence every New Year's Eve between husbands for over twenty-five years.

But, despite the steady flow of men in her life, her true passions were Anne Bonny and Calico Jack Rackham. She spent months at a time on the islands trying to find out more about their adventures. For the first twelve years of her life Adele had endured Babs' lectures about the importance of lineage and constant reminders that, as "indirect descendants" of Anne Bonny, they were related to the most famous pirate pair to sail the Caribbean. Studying both pirate fact and fiction at a local night school, Babs knew everything about Anne and Calico Jack during their three-year reign of terror across the Caribbean. Wearing a tightly laced corset and colorful pantaloons, Babs was usually dressed more like a wench than a swashbuckler when attending one of the gulf region's "Dress Like a Pirate" days. She even took "Bonny" as her permanent legal surname to honor her connection to the famous pirate—but also, Adele was convinced, because Babs must be tired of changing names every time she changed husbands. *Not exactly something to be proud of*, Adele frequently told herself.

For over twenty years Adele had downplayed her connection with the pirate Anne Bonny who, with her lover Captain Calico Jack, pillaged and plundered the shipping routes in the Bahamas from 1718 to 1722. This was during the heart of the Golden Age of Piracy and Nassau was at its core. Full of coves and inlets, the topography of the Bahamas area was ideal for pirate ships to hide in and then drive an unsuspecting merchant or military ship into the shallow shoals where the buccaneers could board quickly and commandeer both the ship and its treasure. Major trade routes linking the Spanish Main, the Caribbean, Florida, the Carolinas and Europe were all close by, giving the cutthroat crews a steady supply of victims.

Disguised as a man, because women on pirate ships were thought to bring bad luck, Anne was as brave and dangerous as any male pirate at sea—cursing and swearing with the best of them, and never cringing at the sight or cause of murder.

Adele found the obsession with these outlaws on the island

way over the top. She rarely revealed that she was the niece, thirteen times removed, of the most famous female pirate in history. The fewer people who knew about it the better.

With way too much to think about, Adele left the Marina and drove back to Resort Row and the beautiful Cable Beach area of Nassau, where her condo was located. As she headed for the entrance she spotted Otis, the maintenance man, performing yet another surgery on a wandering tile on top of the pool cabana. A pile of broken tiles sat under his ladder and Adele couldn't resist making a snide remark.

"Otis, that cabana roof is only fourteen by eighteen feet, what's the hang-up?" Adele unloaded on him with pent-up frustration. "This isn't the Sistine Chapel."

"Your sister is what?" asked the somewhat dim Otis. "I'm almost done."

"Great," responded Adele under her breath. "Hurricane Irene touched down months ago and you're still troweling those tiles."

"Have a great day, Mrs. Albury." Otis smiled. "Your condo's been awful busy this morning. First those armed guards, and then. . . ."

"They've already been here?" Adele interrupted.

"Yes, ma'am, and that husband of yours sure knows how to begin the morning right. After those men left, that foxy little fitness girl came by. Didn't even take the elevator. Maybe they be doing those butterfly stretches my Mavis saw on late night TV."

"Listen, Otis, I'm not Mrs. Albury, I'm Ms. Bonny, and I don't know what you're talking about. Curtis hasn't exercised in more than a year and would probably break or pull something if he started up again. Are you sure you didn't just see our boat girl, Gracie, taking those steps two at a time? She can't seem to wait too long to pick up her check."

Not waiting for an answer, Adele rushed inside and hopped the lobby elevator to the eighth floor. Looking at herself in the mirror as she always did, she took stock of her slim waist and high, firm "bubble butt," and once again nodded in self-approval.

With a little bounce in her step, she opened the door to 813. What she saw deflated her mood and stopped her in her tracks, terrified. *Oh, my God! The place has been ransacked. . . . But how could burglars have broken into the eighth floor of a high-rise? Unless this was an inside job.*

The living room was in a total state of disarray with wrapping paper, ripped cardboard boxes, and broken glass scattered across all four hundred square feet of an area overlooking spectacular ocean vistas.

"Curtis?" she screamed. "Are you here? Are you okay?"

At first running from room to room like a frantic sailor on a sinking ship, she then stopped and took a deep breath. Whoever did this could still be in one of the bedrooms. Adele backed out of the area and into the hallway. She punched in numbers on her cell trying to call Otis, but all she got was a busy signal as he was way too much of an island boy to have call waiting.

She kept quiet for a good ninety seconds, listening for any sound that might betray whether the prowler was still in the condo. But, when all she heard was silence, she gathered her courage and crept cautiously back inside. Now it was obvious to her, whoever had done this was long gone. She stepped over to the remains of the biggest box—labeled "From Babs Bonny" and stamped "FRAGILE." The box had been battered and broken into, and it was now as empty as a ghost town. Seeing Curtis' signature on the delivery slip, Adele sadly realized Brinks was not liable for the theft.

Searching the bedroom, she found only disheveled dresser drawers, a dirty red thong with tiny rhinestones imbedded on the tiny sides, and one ancient pieces-of-eight coin invitingly lying in rest. The panties were definitely Mandy's MO.

"Shit," shouted Adele as she picked up the coin. She now painfully had a clear confirmation that Curtis was having an affair and had ransacked their condo. The thought blew through her head like an island hurricane.

Stripping off her workout clothes, she pulled on a pair of shorts and message t-shirt appropriate to what she was thinking—"I'm the Booty!" Adele rushed out the door.

Furious and hurt, she raced down the eight flights of stairs and into the parking lot. Finding her Bug and yanking the door open, she started up the engine and went from park to fifth gear in just thirty seconds. *This is a serious theft. I need to report it to the police immediately. Can you get a speeding ticket if you're on the way to the police station?*

Arriving at a local police substation, she jumped out of her car and ran up to the front door. The daily duty sign read "Sergeant Cantrell—Officer on Duty"—not a name she was familiar with. Trying to calm down a bit, she told the Sergeant about the break-in and theft. *My good-for-nothing husband is suspect number one.* After taking her statement, Sergeant Cantrell assigned an officer to follow her back to the condo. Within minutes after the yellow "Police Line—Do Not Cross" tape was tied across her front door, Otis arrived with a stun gun and can of mace.

"This ain't my fault, Mrs. Albury," he cried. "Did that foxy female kill your husband?"

The police officer pushed Otis out of the way, but not before Adele's neighbor opened her front door. "My God, is someone dead?" she screeched. "Murder, murder, murder. . . ."

"No one's dead," said the officer, placing his hand over her mouth. "Now please go back inside."

"No one's dead yet," mumbled Adele as she tried to climb under the tape.

The officer stopped her with a firm hand. "This is police business now, ma'am, and I'm afraid you'll have to wait outside."

Waiting was not one of Adele's strong suits so she got into her Bug and peeled rubber away from the parking lot and rammed through the gears as fast as traffic would allow. She grieved for the gallant car as she heard it struggling, but maintenance was not a top priority just now. *Where am I going? Someplace I can think!* Not surprisingly, she ended up at the ruins of Fort Montagu with its view of miles and miles of the beautiful Atlantic. This had long been her favorite spot for dreaming and scheming, a place where she could think about her dad and get away from Curtis' constant *advice.* Yet it was a place of history too—her own family history. Legend said that this area of shallow coastal waters was the final resting place of the *Treasure*, Jack Rackham's beloved ship.

When her car rolled to a stop, she killed the engine and pulled out her Day Planner from the rear seat, flipping the pages to the Notes section. She began to vent, writing furiously.

"Today is almost the worst day of my pathetic life. Curtis stole my family treasure and ran off with my wretched little aerobics teacher. I married a worthless horn dog and he needs to pay for what he did!"

Adele keened the words out loud as she was writing them down. "He needs to pay!"

How could I have been so stupid? So what did I love? I loved his kindness and compassion in those first three years . . . the way he noticed every little thing about me . . . even the bad things. He made me feel special, understood, different, unique. Not only that, he embraced my quirky stuff . . . like tolerating my love of all things t-shirt. The fact that I love to dance, even the weird dances. The fact that I have pirates for ancestors. When did he fall out of love with me?

The sounds of sobbing replaced Adele's screams and her hand became too shaky to continue writing. It was time to calm down and catch her breath. Once the visceral anger began to subside, she sadly started to think about what she had lost. For more than four years Adele had shared a life with a man she thought she knew, but in reality didn't know at all. At times he seemed immature and self-centered, but what man wasn't? *He gave me confidence and support and I loved him unconditionally, never digging too deeply into his background and shady business deals. Was it all just an act? I don't believe it.*

At the breaking point, she sat in her car for almost an hour, swiping at tears, looking at the view, and fiddling with the radio scan which brought everything from "Put a Ring On It" to "Girl, You'll Be a Woman Soon." Her brain addled, her heart aching, she tried to think of what to do next.

Adele thought back to the *advice* from her mother about Curtis. Babs had warned her not to marry Curtis—especially when she found out he had been investing in an illegal lobster harvesting company. *I should have listened!* Adele chided herself. But at thirty-four and looking for love, even in all the wrong places, she had succumbed to Curtis' admiration of her moves, promises of a bit of a pirate life of adventure, and a great pair of wing-tip shoes.

How was I to know four years later the pirate would be my Great Aunt Anne Bonny and my husband would now have the family loot? Her ears were ringing so painfully, whimpers replaced her sobbing.

Finally gathering herself together enough to drive back across town and towards Cable Beach, Adele knew the police were not done looking for evidence in her condo, so she decided to go for some fortification—the liquid kind. She angrily ground through all four gears before stopping in front of an old and moderately battered-looking building about a quarter mile from home. She parked across the street, made her way through the sweet-smelling tropical park and headed towards her favorite haunt, The Very Berry Bar. She checked her watch. *It's not quite one. I shouldn't be doing this. One drink, then I'm leaving.*

But ten minutes later she was throwing down Cruzan Rum and a potpourri of fresh fruit. Slipping in her ear buds, she hit Play on her iPod and began listening to Fergie's "Big Girls Don't Cry." That's when the tears began again. *Oh, great, so attractive.*

Glancing around to see who might be watching her, she took

in the details of The Very Berry—a neighborhood haunt you couldn't make up even if you tried. Looking like an old, tin, one-story stable, painted yellow and orange, with crate-like windows from an antiquated horse barn, it was funky, quirky, and odd. From the rafters hung plastic replicas: bunches of bananas, melons, and parrots. *It's the definition of kitsch. But they do serve the best fresh fruit daiquiris on the islands.*

Adele watched a parade of drinkers—from businessmen in suits and slacks, to three-tattooed bikers—jockeying up for position at the sixteen-stool bar. The first biker ordered a strawberry-blueberry daiquiri while his bar mate chose something more traditional, a piña colada. She tried reading a tattooed arm. *That has to be my favorite: "I Love Singapore Sluts." Boy, I like a man with something to say.*

The friendly bartender had long, peroxide-orange dreadlocks that looked stiff enough to use for swivel sticks. Giving her a come-hither smile, he showed the gold tooth gleaming smack in the middle of his overbite.

As if I'd be interested, Adele thought, hitting Play on her next tune. The iPod slipped from her hand, yanking the ear buds from the connection port. Now her personal music was blasting full volume, loud enough to be heard by several other guzzlers around the bar. No one seemed to mind her playlist, so she retrieved her iPod and placed it on the bar in front of her.

She glanced around the room. *What a cast of characters!* A strung-out blonde was filing her fingernails and leaving the residue on the countertop. A stressed-looking man with a buzz-cut was downing a coconut-kiwi daiquiri while he was cooing to someone on his cell phone. Adele then spotted the black-haired Smee, who had added a three-cornered hat to his pirate pants ensemble and was drinking his rum straight.

"Fancy meeting you here, my dear," said Smee. "I don't believe I've ever seen you outside of class. Care for a cocktail?"

"Absolutely, with double rum."

After ordering her a pineapple-pomegranate daiquiri, Smee

settled in to chat. "Has anyone ever told you, Adele, that you look a lot like Wendy in *Peter Pan*?"

"No, and I'm kind of off men today."

"You are? Oh, tragic. It took me a long time to find my darling Woody, but I would trust him with my life. We have a little business here in midtown called Pirate's Plunder, and we have fun hunting down modern-day pirates to retrieve the stolen boats and their loot."

"You've got to be kidding me, Smee. I never knew what you did for a living. I thought Pirates of the Caribbean finished off with Johnny Depp and *At World's End*."

"Pardon me, my dear." Smee settled in to explain. "Pirates still roam the high seas doing their dirty work, and are costing billions of dollars in lost cargo and other loot. There were more than three hundred attacks and ship seizures last year alone. Most pirates have moved down to Africa to do their pillaging and plundering in open waters, but several luxury yachts have been stolen around the Bahamas in the last few months."

"Pirate attacks have been all over the news lately," mused Adele, "but I thought the reports were way overblown."

"No, no, no." Smee shook his head emphatically, the tricornered hat waggling as if it couldn't keep up with his movement. "These pirates are not like the ones you see on Turner Classic Movies, swinging through the rigging with cutlasses in their teeth, but well-armed militia men, equipped with high-powered weapons and high-speed motorboats. There are still a few renegade buccaneers who are killing for buried treasure, and salvaging ships that have gone down during the last three hundred years can yield tremendously rare and valuable cargo."

As a Sheryl Crow tune ended, one of Curtis' favorites started to play. She fiercely killed the music.

I really don't need to hear this, thought Adele. "Well, enough pirate lore for me. So much of middle school history was all about the pirates of the Caribbean. I got sick of boys pretending to be Blackbeard and trying to stab the girls with rubber swords."

She got up to leave, and just then her ears started to buzz again.

For a moment Smee seemed not to notice, and he started a long diatribe on how pirating was costing insurance companies and individuals more than fifty-five billion dollars a year. Then he turned his gaze on her. "You don't look so well, my dear. Can't I buy you another little drink?" He helped her sit back down on her bar stool, then added, "You need your strength. You look like the plum/passion fruit type and I haven't seen so much fruit since my last visit to South Beach, if you know what I mean?"

"I guess you could call me the passionate type, especially right now," said Adele, as the buzzing in her head began to recede. "But I'm filled up with fruit . . . no offense meant. I don't need another drink. But you can tell me a little bit about how you have the wherewithal to retrieve items stolen by assholes . . . or by maritime marauders, I mean."

Smee explained that Woody was the one who did most of the research work at Pirate's Plunder, while Smee did mostly sales. His expertise was landing business and assessing the value of the jewels and other stolen cargo. This being the case, he was not really sure what went on with the computers and GPS systems, but he relished the occasional visits when cute Coast Guard officers and Navy SEALs came to learn new systems Woody had developed.

"Sounds interesting," Adele lied, "but I gotta run. Or should I say 'adieu'?"

Adele headed down the block and then across the street to The Pink Flamingo. Walking carelessly through the busy intersection, she provoked honking horns and flashing headlights. Exhausted from the emotional energy she had expended, Adele drooped against the wall in the elevator up to the eighth floor.

The policeman and his investigator were leaving as she entered the hallway. Wanting to hear what they had discovered, she hid behind a tall plant and listened to their conversation.

"Let's go back to headquarters, Erskine, and file a report," said the policeman.

"Not much to go on," Erskine muttered. "Maybe one of her ancestors came back from the grave and took back the treasure."

Dejectedly, Adele noticed the police tape slumped down on the floor—and they hadn't even bothered to close her door. *No point now*, she thought sadly. She walked into her bedroom and over to her elegant desk that looked like an antique "what's what" of navigational artifacts. *Thank God these weren't stolen with the other things.* Fondly she touched the sextant, the map case, the spyglass. . . . Then, picking up the spyglass, she looked through the eyepiece, surveying the aqua-colored seascape below.

"Daddy, you were one hell of a sailor," she murmured.

Taking the pieces-of-eight coin out of her back pocket, she rubbed it with her t-shirt front until it gleamed. She then gently replaced this tiny treasure—all that was left of her family's cache—into her small pocket. *What a mess*, she thought, going into the living room. With a deep sigh she slowly started to clean up the papers and boxes, picking up a ripped note from Babs and stopping to read it: "Hi, Adele. Well, here it is—all that Anne and Jack put their lives on the line for. Have it polished up real pretty and perhaps we can start selling it off after the show. Merry Christmas! Love, Mom."

Sitting down hard on a lovely coral linen sofa, she reached underneath herself and found a ragged piece of glass. *Great, the broken bottom of a champagne flute.*

"Well, isn't this just perfect," Adele bit out. She sank down into the sofa, closed her eyes, and started to assess a life that would never be the same again. Even after she found the treasure, she would lose her husband and one of them would have to leave Nassau forever—but not before some sort of payback. She dozed off and on for the next several hours.

Adele finally blinked herself awake. She stood and picked up an oversized towel covered with yellow and green palm trees. *Maybe a swim will clear my head*, she thought, listlessly changing into her new blue and black tankini and heading downstairs. Unfortunately the pool was not heated, so after immersing just one foot in the 68-degree water she wrapped herself in her beach towel, sat down in a lounge chair, and started to doze again.

Sleeping way too many hours in the uncomfortable rattan chair, Adele woke up at the crack of dawn stiff, cranky, and covered in mosquito bites. Standing, she felt the ache of sore muscles, heard the pop of stiff joints. *The only cure for this is a workout.* She hoped exercise might work the kinks out of both her soul and psyche. Knowing she couldn't go back to The Rendezvous Fitness Center for dance class right now, she headed over to join Marvin Reed's early morning water aerobics class taking place in a cove on the resort property.

The sound of squealing seniors reached her ears before the sight of Marvin, standing shoulder-deep in the still waters. Marvin motioned her over and soon she had joined several salty 65-plus-year-old swimmers jogging in place and doing weightless shoulder presses. A handsome Bahamian in his early seventies, but looking much younger, he made Adele jog double-time, pointing out she was half the age of the men and women participating in this morning ritual.

"Hey, Delly," he called out to her, "how about putting some muscle into those movements?"

She thought of objecting to the babyish nickname, but she knew from long experience it wouldn't do any good with Marvin. And then Adele's thoughts were on anything but aerobics when she stubbed her toe hard on a piece of coral and submerged briefly underwater. Marvin took the "in place" out of his jogging and water-marched over to the injured Adele who was cradling her bloody foot in the bend of her waist.

"Whoa, Delly." Marvin steadied her with a strong arm and supportive glance. "Salt water's good for the outside of your body but you're not supposed to slurp it." He then gave her a wet hug.

"I guess my brain is just not into all this bouncing today, Marvin," Adele said glumly as she started to leave the water. "Think I'll go down to my *Bonny*, she'll clear my head."

Marvin held her elbow for an extra moment. "Now, Delly—

as you know, the fitness center can be a chatty place. I've heard that Mandy hasn't been flaunting her figure there since Friday and that no one has seen Curtis lately either. I'm always available if you feel like a Marvin moment."

Adele smiled at her old friend gratefully. "Thanks, Marvin, and I know how many of those moments Babs had with you."

"Are you ever going to call her 'mother'?"

"Not in this lifetime." Adele trudged to shore.

Towel drying her ruby red hair, she wrapped the bath sheet around her like a sarong and headed to the front of the resort to grab a cab. After a less than three-minute wait she got impatient and jumped onto the local #10 bus headed to Boat Harbour. Although she had seen this same view for more than three years, she still marveled at the majesty of the water. The baby blue color gave way to a turquoise tint and then turned into aqua hues as the drink of life calmly headed out of the harbor and into the open sea. She stopped in front of a wooden sign reading "The *Beautiful Bonny*" but then remembered her boat was at the end of the dock. Squinting into the sun, she didn't see the last slip was empty until she almost fell into the water. A bit confused, Adele rushed back to her original slip, but it was empty as well.

"They took her out for a test drive late yesterday afternoon and haven't been back." Adele heard Grant's deep voice and watched as he stepped out of the cabin of his boat.

"You mean Curtis and our boat girl?" asked Adele.

"No, this was another girl, much younger than Gracie."

"Did he by any chance tell you where he was going?"

"Well, you know Curtis, Adele. It took all of his concentration to be able to steer out of the harbor. He does more zigs and zags than a zipper and his bumpers hit quite a few boats heading out, so his direction was all off-kilter when he finally reached open water."

"I'm thinking the young girl could have been his little sister? About nineteen with auburn hair and dark eyes?"

"Ah, his *sister*," Grant said with an all-too-knowing inflection. “I was wondering who she was. I did find it strange that in addition to filling the *Bonny*’s tank he took three five-gallon fuel containers on board as well. I’ve never known you and Curtis to stay out longer than a night.” Grant started to rub down the mahogany trim on his flashy 43-foot FARR Fingulf sailing yacht. “And I did notice one other oddity.”

“I’m all ears,” Adele mocked.

“Curtis and his . . . sister . . . filled the cabin up with junk food as well. It’s amazing how trim her figure is with all the Twinkies, Ding Dongs and donuts she was stacking in the galley.”

Adele felt herself turning as red as a lobster being lowered into a boiling pot, but Grant didn’t seem to notice. She finally got it. The text message on Mandy’s phone was to Curtis and “BB” was the *Beautiful Bonny*—their assigned meeting place.

“And say, the new bronze mast looks pretty classy,” he remarked pleasantly.

“Are you sure you’re talking about the *Beautiful Bonny*? All Curtis did was clean it, but the *Bonny*’s mast has always been silver.”

“Well . . . not anymore,” stated Grant, matter of fact, and went back on to his boat.

“Son of a bitch,” said Adele. “No wonder he had the mast covered with canvas for three days—the bastard had it painted!” A pitiful meow interrupted her anger. In her panic she had completely forgotten about her cat. “My God, Gilligan, where are you?” Frantically she looked around the dock. The meowing continued and Adele finally found Gilligan tied to a wooden step near where the *Beautiful Bonny* had been anchored.

“That ass-bite!” she exclaimed. Untying Gilligan and picking him up gently, she petted his wet and rumpled fur. They quietly purred to each other.

Gazing at the empty mooring, she realized the reason Curtis had moved her boat to dock’s end was so he and Mandy could do a faster departure from the marina. Her fabulous 42-foot Hunter Passage was gone along with everything else that up to now had been important in her life. Not only had Curtis run away with the baubles and Mandy—he had stolen her boat as well.

"Well, Gilligan," she crooned, "at least he left you on the dock and didn't drown you. We wouldn't want that. No, we wouldn't."

Lying down on the hard wooden dock and cradling the cat, Adele started to doze. "That bacon-fed bamboozler," she heard in the deep recesses of her mind. Gilligan burbled deep in his throat and jumped away from Adele, and she settled deeper. "When we find Curtis and his strumpet, we'll hang them by the yardarm, my pretty, we'll make them dance the Tyburn jig and break their scurvy necks."

"Aunt Anne," mumbled Adele.

Chapter 3

Adele sat up straight on the dock next to her empty slip, her legs bent unnaturally in the Lotus position. Gilligan had abandoned her and was sleeping on one of the deck's tackle boxes. Had she really heard the voice of her Aunt Anne Bonny? *Snap out of it. Aunt Anne's been dead for almost three hundred years.* She tried to center both her body and soul. No use. Untangling her legs, she massaged her now throbbing ankle, which served as a barometer of her stress level, and dropped her feet into the dirty, oil-slicked water under the dock. Sludge began to stain her ankles but she hardly noticed as she started to flail her feet faster and faster. Within minutes she was wet to her upper thighs.

She vividly remembered the first time she'd spotted the *Beautiful Bonny*—then so aptly named the *Survivor*. It was three days after a hurricane had decimated much of the outskirts of Nassau in 2009, and the side streets were almost impassible. Not because of the usual relentless streams of traffic, but from the super-sized litter that had blown across the island. At the center of the traffic jam was the *Survivor*—catapulted from a nearby private marina by a 180-mile-an-hour wind gust and thrust into the middle of the road.

She'd always wanted a boat and jumped at the outrageous possibility of capturing one. She decided that possession was nine-tenths of the law, found two local dockworkers with a trailer, and enticed them to move the damaged boat to the dry dock. *What a year that was*, she thought wistfully. An added plus was finding Gilligan, then skin and bones with a badly cut right ear, cowering in a small cupboard on the boat. She named him after the television show her father used to watch—it seemed fitting to name a castaway after a castaway—and took him home to meet Curtis. Her husband eyed the cat with horror as his eyes turned red and he started to sneeze. It was a good thing Gilligan felt so at home on the *Bonny*, as Curtis insisted on his living there and not with them.

She thought deeply about why she never took sailing lessons from Gracie, her boat girl, after the *Bonny* was restored. When she was a young girl, her dad told her she was a natural. "You could sail a two-by-four, Delly," he used to say. *Dancing . . . sailing . . . they were sometimes interchangeable. I would sail across the dance floor and dance on the water.* Those happy days were before the *incident*, which happened when she was just twelve years old. On that day she decided she never wanted to sail again.

But she still loved her *Bonny* boat and when warm nights and bad dreams caused insomnia, she would leave the condo and drive down to the marina, sleeping better with Gilligan on an uncomfortable bench under the bounty of stars in the sky than in a plush mattress bed with Curtis.

And now the *Beautiful Bonny* was gone, and there was a chance she would never learn how to sail her. *What a bad decision*, she chided herself.

Getting up sadly and awkwardly, Adele picked up the sleepy Gilligan and deposited him into her messenger bag. Surprisingly, he didn't make a fuss but just curled into another sleep position. Moving off the dock, she decided she would walk the four miles back to The Pink Flamingo to at least dry off her dirty legs. At about the three and a half mile marker, she could feel an edge of irritation and hostility roiling in her mind. *The usual signal . . . I'm ready for a drink. Maybe a sickly sweet strawberry-pomegranate cocktail would be just the thing to mellow out my mood*, she thought. The Very Berry Bar came into her seaside view and seemed the perfect place to quench her thirst.

Forgetting that Gilligan was in her bag, she walked up the three rickety steps and saw the small bar area was standing room only, as usual. She didn't spot any of the first-time friends she'd seen the day before. The same bartender, however, still grinned at her with his gold-toothed smile. *Peachy,* she groused to herself. *I probably could get lucky tonight.* But perhaps lucky wasn't the word for it.

Gilligan started to scratch at the canvas, so Adele unzipped the bag a few inches to let him pop his head out. When the battle-scarred black cat meowed loudly, the bartender grinned and poured an ounce of rum into a saucer, placing it on the bar in front of Adele. "Maybe this'll keep him quiet."

Gilligan reached a paw out of the bag and quickly dipped it into the rum. He then put a claw into his mouth, sneezed, coughed, and snuggled back into the bag. Adele laughed and started to leave, but then she spied Smee slumped at the bar staring at a wrinkled note. When Adele walked over to him, he dramatically thrust the paper at her.

Before she had a chance to read it herself, he moaned, "Woody's disappeared! He just left a little note—read it!—'I've gone to find my smile,' he says. But I always thought I gave him something to smile about, if you get my drift."

"Ah, Smee, that's tough. I know how it feels to be left for the competition." Adele joined him at the bar.

Another festive-looking and very friendly "pirate" tried to put his arm around Smee, but the distraught First Mate would have nothing to do with him. So with a hearty "shiver my timbers and full speed ahead" he left The Very Berry, looking for a more compatible companion. Smee downed his drink and stood by Adele glumly.

"Trust me, he's already found another captain at a different port who's giving him plenty to smile about," said the cheerless Adele.

"Rub salt in my open wounds, why don't you? Oh, my. We have three open cases and this means I'll have to really do some work." Smee muttered to himself, "What would the captain do? Delegate, delegate, delegate."

Adele patted him on the arm. "Do you realize we both lost

our loves yesterday?" Smee blinked in surprise. "We need to have a heart-to-heart, but not here. And not—" she hiked her messenger bag more securely on her shoulder—"with so much of an audience. You come with me."

Adele left Gilligan at the condo and led the drunken pirate wannabe back to Coconut Joe's, her favorite local fish fry, for some conch fritters and a cup of dark black coffee. Sitting at a table for two, she took his arm and asked to hear all about Woody. Smee was starting to dish to Adele about his lover's golden Peter Pan good looks when their table was jostled by four gorgeous men, dressed in traditional metallic silver and royal blue feathers and frilly pants, who came dancing into the restaurant.

"I forgot," said Adele. "Tonight is a Junkanoo performance." Reminiscent of New Orleans' Mardi Gras and Rio de Janeiro's Carnival, Junkanoo was distinctly Bahamian and existed nowhere else. Any excuse for a parade—and Bahamians took them seriously. Participating groups were judged on best music, costume, floats, and overall group presentation. Junkanoo took place on Boxing Day—December 26—and New Year's Day, but Bahamians loved to practice all year long. It was believed that the festival originated in West Africa during the seventeenth century when slaves were temporarily "set free" for a day after Christmas to party-hardy with music, costumes and dance.

One of the very bright and shiny revelers brought a sparkling silver limbo pole from the back of the restaurant and set it up to the right of the bar, about three feet from where Adele and Smee were trying to carry on their conversation.

"Ah, my Woody," sighed Smee. "I met him at a Junkanoo Festival when he was doing the limbo. Had the flexibility of Gumby and the looks of a god. Gosh, does that pole bring back memories—Woody was the only man who could get me to bend back that far."

"Really?"

"I was usually not the one looking up at the ceiling, but seeing the stars with Woody was worth it," Smee confided.

Adele patted his hand. "TMI, my friend."

A large man got up from the bar and lumbered over to the limbo pole. He started to bend back and shuffle underneath, but his large stomach knocked the stick to the ground. Not deterred, the large man put the pole back parallel and started under again. This time he picked the limbo stick up, held it above his stomach, and shuffled across the bar floor amid angry "boos."

"I hate cheaters," said Smee as he left his chair. "There is a right and wrong way to limbo and I hate when someone pollutes the pole. Woody was such a wonder at the sport, and I wasn't too bad myself."

One of the revelers, a beautiful and buxom latte-colored woman, seized Smee by the arm and pulled him towards the limbo stick.

"You're wasting your time, honey," Adele whispered.

But Smee's dexterity surprised Adele as he slid down low and under the pole like a snake, shuffling under and through at a ninety-degree angle at a height of less than three feet. He'd captured the attention of the whole room with those low, smooth moves.

Adele was duly impressed and clapped with appreciation as Smee rejoined her. "You know I've lived on this island for three years and have never attended a Junkanoo. I guess I have a phobia of floats and hate getting dressed up. My husband wanted me to wear a frilly white corset and white satin pantaloons for our wedding—keeping in the style of my ancestors. And you know *that* wasn't going to happen."

"Sounds like my kind of man. You don't know what you're missing, Adele. I used to dress up like a matador and Woody was the bull, but I did draw the line at the use of more than one sword."

Reflecting on this last comment, Adele retorted, "You so have a wrong impression of Curtis. He's definitely not your kind of man. He's a liar and a louse and more into his designer briefs than he was into me."

Smee looked deeply into Adele's eyes and then patted her on the knee. "Well, my dear, why did you choose him for your life partner? Sounds like it was a wrong mix from the beginning."

"A very good question," said Adele, taking a deep breath. "There's always been a part of our relationship that wasn't quite right, but I wanted to make it work."

"Why?"

Adele sighed, thinking back to the attraction that'd meant so much to her. Tracking her down after the parking lot information swap, Curtis started attending her spinning class, wearing perfectly matched black bicycle tights and black t-shirt. Six weeks and a dozen classes later he had lost five pounds and gifted Adele with the pink leotard and fuchsia leggings, insisting she should lose the sweat pants she wore down to the soles of her feet to cover up her scarred and lifelong purple ankle; and he hardly blinked when she revealed her imperfection.

"He liked what he saw, and I had to admit the reflection in the mirror wasn't so bad. Twirling me around the room after class one night, he grabbed my butt firmly and we had a *Dirty Dancing* moment.

"It was such an exciting time," she confided to Smee. "I'd gotten a bit of an inheritance from my mom, Babs, but was still living like a pauper. After coming to my modern dance recital, Curtis decided I was way too talented to teach for twenty dollars a class. Somehow we had to open a dance studio."

Adele went on to relate that when she turned thirty-three, Babs had gifted her with valuable family heirlooms, but she decided not to tell Smee the source of the inheritance—the sale of several rare Anne Bonny and Calico Jack coins. She'd cashed in two of the coins and had ten thousand dollars—literally in hundred-dollar bills—under the tiny apartment's futon mattress. Madly and deeply in love—or so she thought—they made the investment: the ten grand staked them to a well-equipped 800-square-foot dance studio in Nassau and they rented an apartment nearby.

"That was the best year of my life. We had more than seventy students at first and Curtis would watch me from the back of the studio. I felt like the star, playing to my own personal fan club. I'm not sure what happened then. Students started to drop out, the landlord doubled our rent and we had to close down. This was two years ago and then Curtis started to change. Or maybe he started to show a different side of himself, I don't know."

Smee tilted his head like a curious sparrow. "Do you think he was doing the dance with some of your students?"

"No—Oh, you know, it never crossed my mind back then, but it does make sense now. He was always working at the studio late, doing the books or so he said, whenever the local high school drill team was practicing there. The landlord's daughter was part of the team as well."

She took a ragged breath. "I'm going to be sick. I think he's left the island with that teenybopper Mandy, if you can believe it, and my just-restored 42-foot Hunter Passage."

"Oh, honey, no wonder you're so devastated."

"And now I think back, he could have been putting the moves on our students! *My* students! It's horrible. I should've listened to my head and not my heart, especially when Curtis started studying boat charts."

Curtis was a passable sailor but so not very water savvy she'd bought him a pair of water wings and children's fins for their first anniversary. He was not amused. To him, swimming meant trying to tread water for more than several seconds before he sank like a stone.

Smee patted Adele paternally on the knee. "Not a very compatible couple, I'd say. But I guess love is one of the mysteries of life and marriage must be the most mysterious mating of all." She shook her head numbly. He held up an admonishing finger. "Now, my dear, it's your turn to earn some applause."

She looked up to see heading in their direction a hunk all glammed-up in silver sequins and fabulous feathers belying his masculinity. With turquoise feathers attached to his well developed pectoral muscles this male/female dichotomy attracted admiration from all the women sitting around the bar.

The hunk sidled up to Adele and motioned for her to come out on the floor. *He has no idea*, Adele thought, giving the man a smile. *This is what I've done all my life! And Curtis is not going to stop me now.* She motioned for him to lower the pole two more notches. Adele then swept under it, barely brushing her back on the ground or noticing the crimp in her ankle, and emerged victorious on the other side. This achievement reminded her of her high school days, when she was a standout on the dance team. She'd been so flexible that when the teacher asked her to do the splits, instead of going down to the ground she lifted her right leg and stretched it out high, doing the splits from the standing position.

As she raised a Rocky-like fist in victory, the revelers started to cheer and a man at the side of the restaurant applauded loudly. Incredibly handsome with brown-gold eyes and closely cropped hair, he was facing the limbo pole while his companion, a rough-looking character sporting scruffy chin-stubble and a glistening hoop earring, hunched over his drink and never looked towards the festivities.

"Impressive," he called out, turning towards Adele and smiling broadly, downing a tequila shooter.

Shrugging off what was meant to be a compliment, she rejoined Smee at their table.

"I'm not the only one admiring your moves." Smee smiled in appreciation.

"Trust me, I have moves you've never seen . . . and probably never will."

"Boy, did Curtis decide to sail on the wrong ship!"

As the cheers subsided and the revelers' attention moved on, Smee looked at Adele with a new speculation in his eyes. "I don't know what your financial situation is, my dear, and this suggestion may be a bit beneath you, but I need an office manager and it sounds like you might be able to use a job over the holidays if only to get Curtis off your mind." He paused. "Of course, this is short term. I'm sure my Woody will return home within the week, as soon as he realizes I'm the only one who can really make him smile, don't you think? Meanwhile it might be nice to have a woman around the office during the holidays, especially if you know how to type."

Adele drank deeply before responding. "Okay. You have another member of the crew, but for just one sailing as I go back to the Academy in early January."

She kept to herself any qualms about the computer part of the bargain, as no one had asked her about her typing skills since she was a senior in high school. "I do use a computer as long as it's a Mac—I've always loved that cute little apple. I'm not programmed to learn a new system at this point in my life."

"Picky, picky, picky. Nevertheless, see you tomorrow at ten. The address is 313 Lower Dagger Drive. This is so perfect, my dear, as we do use Apples at the office, and they make it so easy even my nephew Ignacious Quince —IQ for short—can input a brief letter."

"Well, I better go and brush up on my skills," remarked Adele sarcastically as she left Coconut Joe's. Turning to say "thank you" to Smee, she decided against it as a purple-plumed fellow had already taken her place at the bar.

Almost ready for what the day had to offer, Adele checked herself in the mirror, admiring the fresh t-shirt with the motto "It's Better in the Bahamas." Among her less valuable but highly prized possessions was her t-shirt collection. She had been partial to message t-shirts ever since her dad, Darryl, gave her one advertising *A Is for Action*, an old and very cheesy action adventure television series. He was a boat captain for hire in Florida back in the early '80s and had taken the giant jewelry-wearing star of the show on a three-day deep-sea fishing trip through the Keys. The combination of actor's girth and a neck heavy with gold chains almost sank his small boat. Part of the memory brought a smile, but she sadly remembered that the t-shirt was her dad's final gift to her.

Adele blew a kiss to Gilligan, left the condo, drove downtown, parked, and then cruised on foot down East Bay Street, looking for Pirate's Plunder at 313 Dagger Drive, knowing it was a small side street off the main drag. She stopped to admire several small, beautifully refurbished row style buildings; she found 312 and 314 but no 313, so she called Smee on his cell.

"No, dear, you're on Upper Dagger Drive—313 is on Lower Dagger next to the Cigars, Souvenirs, and Cuban Cuisine store," said Smee.

Adele gingerly walked down a dirty brick sidewalk lined with mom and pop stores that had seen better days and finally spotted the motley melon-colored building with a skull and cross-swords above the door. Walking inside, she immediately saw a sign at the foot of a narrow stairway with an arrow: "Candles and Cappuccino 12 steps up." Deciding to leave her coffee break until later, she turned left into a narrow foyer and heard voices straight ahead. A young man with flowing curly hair, wearing a bright turquoise shirt, was sitting in an alcove in the front office with two computers on his desk and piles of files all around him. There was a can of mousse on his desk and he was intently styling his brown curly hair. Assuming he was IQ, Adele did not interrupt his fervent hair reveries. Walking right by him, she moved into what she assumed was Smee's office. There were cutlasses, swords and muskets mounted on the walls and the whole Peter Pan family set of miniatures proudly positioned just so on his coffee table.

Inside, Smee sat with Billy, a blond, pimply-faced, hysterical teenaged boy, and Mr. Brill, a gray-haired insurance agent wearing a three-piece suit and seeming to be as brusque as his name implied. Spotting Adele, Brill stood up ramrod straight, informing her that she was thirteen minutes late. The ensuing silence stretched out until Smee asked Billy to continue with his tale of woe.

With sniffles and hiccups, Billy related how his small motor-driven Chris-Craft had been boarded in local waters the day before and the two thieves had made off with his mother's canary-yellow double diamond dolphin necklace. Billy had "borrowed" the necklace as part of an initiation to a gemstone club, but then the thieves came aboard and spoiled his plans. Now the dolphins were gone, he didn't get accepted into the club, and his mother was going to kill him if she found out.

Adele slid comfortingly into the conversation. "I know a bit about angry moms. Where was your boat boarded and do you have a photo of the piece?"

All eyes turned to Mr. Brill, who pulled out several snapshots of a very flashy white- and rose-gold double dolphin necklace. The two mammals touched noses, staring at each other with gem-encrusted eyes.

"Lucy in the sky with diamonds!" marveled Adele.

"This is a very valuable piece," reproved Mr. Brill, "and my goal is to have it returned before Billy's mother gets home from Bora Bora. The only clue we have to the culprit's identity is the sound of his laugh. It's described as sounding like a donkey on drugs—an absolutely obnoxious hee-haw. Are you up to the job, Reginald? I've heard Woody has gone wandering again."

"Only my mother calls me Reginald, Mr. Brill, and Woody will be returning soon. Until then I have my able Adele and my nephew Ignacious to assist me."

Adele rolled her eyes.

"My team is ready to engage, I assure you. I assume that the usual twenty percent cut is still your standard. And if my memory serves me correctly, those dolls are insured for thirty-five thousand dollars?"

Firm but not threatening, Mr. Brill informed the Pirate's Plunder "team" that they had five days to find the necklace. "I'm sure Woody would have returned the dolphins in less than forty-eight hours," he said pompously. "Billy will be graduating from high school this spring and the necklace is needed to pay for his college. I know his mother has one of the Ivy Leagues all lined up for him."

"Please, Mr. Reginald and Ms. Adele," implored the pathetic Billy, "my ass will be grass if my mom doesn't find the necklace back in her panties drawer when she comes home!"

After the meeting was adjourned, Adele sat at a small corner desk and started to go through the files at the Pirate's Plunder office, while on the phone with the curator of the Provocative Pirates of the Bahamas Museum. Neither participant in the phone call seemed very happy—Adele's trapped feeling had started at the sound of the sweet, sappy ring tone Curtis had chosen for her, before she'd even accepted the call. Adele was caught between a rock and a hard place. The museum curator asked her to bring over the showiest of Captain Jack's medallions to put on display for a little bit of pre-exhibit publicity. *Bite me*, thought Adele, concocting the excuse that the pieces were still being polished up at the jewelers. Well, the curator said, she just wanted to make sure the "Romantic Relics of the Caribbean" exhibit was still planned for set-up on January third. She once again reminded Adele she was beginning to book groups starting on the fifth, and the party planners had guests who couldn't wait to see the ruby and gold dagger Anne had used to kill her pirate nemesis, Bully Hayes. That piece had better be front and center. An historian was counting the days until his eyes could feast upon the collection of gold doubloons and pieces of eight looted from that Spanish ship. A collector couldn't wait to evaluate Calico Jack's gigantic and jewel-encrusted captain's medallion.

"Yes, it's all on the island and will be ready to be seen. See you in three weeks—and I would appreciate you sending a guard to escort me to the museum." *Nice touch*, thought Adele. *The best defense is a good offense.* She hung up the phone and stared out into the street. A shop sign reading "Almost Authentic Pirate Coins and Daggers For Sale Here" caught her eye.

Umm . . . she pondered. *Do you think they would know the difference?*

Chapter 4

Adele left Lower Dagger Drive and headed back to The Pink Flamingo. The cleaning service had done their job right and there was not even a vestige of the mess Adele had walked into two days earlier. A clean place was certainly a comfort, but when she moved into her bedroom all the beauty was gone. She did not even find solace in looking out of the eight-story window and down at the beautiful surf below. Adele didn't see the majesty of the coastline and high-rise skyline of Cable Beach—so named as this was the area where the first cable was laid in the Bahamas, linking the more than seven hundred small islands and cays with the U.S. mainland. She gazed out at the water and spied a young couple on a Sun Chaser, a peppy little sailboat contraption composed of a large surfboard attached to a small, brightly colored sail. The couple was steadying each other on the board while smooching at the same time, as it skimmed through the sea.

Just a few months ago this was the two of us, Adele thought, looking down at her windowsill and picking up the framed photograph of her and Curtis striking the identical pose. *This was the day he nicknamed me Boots, loving the way my booty stuck out from behind the little sail.* But none of it mattered now. Adele allowed one lonely tear to trickle down her cheek before smashing the photo to the floor. Glass exploded all around her. *Well, I guess I showed him!*

Hopping gingerly around the broken glass, she barely managed to avoid stepping on a sharp shard and gingerly headed to the living room. She closed the bedroom door to keep Gilligan away from the broken glass, and continued out the front door.

She found an envelope taped to the door's peephole. *What's this?* The stationery was a soothing sea-foam green and textured in a lovely laid finish, so she hoped for good news—but no such luck. What she opened was a not-so-nice legal letter stating that the condo was in foreclosure and as she was legally married to Curtis, his debts were her debts. She had three days to vacate the premises. This was more than a bad dream, nightmare, or Friday the thirteenth. This was a life gone bad—terribly, horribly wrong.

Adele walked back into the condo and plopped her purse down. What she needed now was a good endorphin rush. Running on the beach was her best shot at clearing her head fast, leaving both her bad memories and future anxieties in footprints on the sand. Putting on her Pumas and lacing them tightly enough to stop blood flow, Adele went for a fast beachfront run. She ended up sitting in the sand, talking to Marvin in between his renting out boogie boards and small sailboats to resort guests.

Well past middle age, Marvin had the physique of a forty-year-old, and several female beachgoers were keeping an eye on more than just his beach balls. He had quite the Cable Beach network going on, providing him with information as well as pleasant company. Now it pained Marvin to have to tell his goddaughter what he'd just found out—that her husband had mortgaged the condo to its hilt, borrowing an additional two hundred thousand dollars against their residence. He'd tried to revive the Abaco citrus groves he had invested in, but they were plagued with citrus canker and the trees didn't make it.

"I knew it was bad, Delly, when you were taking my swim class yesterday, but I didn't find out how bad until this morning," sympathized Marvin. "Maybe it's time to move back to West Palm with Babs until you get your bearings back. Nassau can be a lonely and dangerous place for single women."

"You know that is not going to happen, Marvin. She couldn't take care of Dad and definitely can't take care of me. Besides, I'm deathly allergic to Sheldon's stogies and can't stand to hear Babs say, 'told you so.' "

"It seems easy to judge other people, Delly. Little girls can create about any story they want to believe, especially when they love their dad as much as you and Alli did. You were just twelve when he died."

"It's not a *story*. I remember what happened like it was this morning's horoscope. Babs was fooling around on the boat, not paying attention to the fact that he had been drinking again. I don't think she ever loved him."

Marvin reminded her that taking care of her dad was no easy task and Babs had given up her career to take watch over him. Adele would have none of it, denying that working as a flight attendant and then lipstick tester in her thirties was much of a career. Not waiting for Marvin's reply, she dropped the subject. Her immediate problem was to find a place to live so she could quickly move on with her life. She already had a job for the holidays and needed a place close to work.

"Besides, how could I believe Babs' feeling about Curtis? Her relationship radar is usually so off-kilter." Babs had never trusted Curtis and early into the relationship mother had told daughter that he was plain and simple—a gold digger. A huge fight ensued, and Babs called Curtis "a failed farmer who was after the Bonny treasure." Adele ran out of the West Palm Beach cottage in a rage, flew to Nassau, and married Curtis three months later. Babs did not attend the wedding.

Marvin started to respond, but instead took the conversation a different way. "Don't be so hard on her, she's always loved you. As to a place to live—What about finding that pretty little Catalina your parents sailed in the early '80s? You know, the one your mother . . . well."

Adele picked up the conversation. "The boat she put in dry dock after the accident?"

"Yes, it should still be in the dry dock area of the marina you keep the *Bonny* in."

"Kept," Adele corrected acidly.

"Just a thought," said Marvin kindly, "and, by the way,

does Babs know about Curtis sailing away with the treasure as well?"

Adele gasped as the tears welled up. "How did you know?"

"I went to the appraisers yesterday to get the value of a trinket one of the tender young things at the hotel gifted me with and heard from Agnes that you never brought the pieces into her shop. Also, word is that Mandy was bragging at the Spa about her boyfriend who was going to give her more jewelry than we've seen on the young heiress who had her own television show."

Grief morphed into rage. Adele turned livid and shrieked, "There is no way in hell that Mandy's going to get her hands on my family's collection!" If Adele had her way, the only thing Mandy would have in common with the heiress was prison time.

Waiting for Adele to calm down, Marvin suggested they contact the authorities about the thefts. Adele was ready with a response: already done that, and she was now working for a pirate loot retrieval expert and expected to apprehend Curtis within the week.

Adele then asked her old friend for a favor, to drive her in one of The Rendezvous boat rentals to the dry dock to look for the Bonny family's old boat. Of course he would. Marvin knew the Catalina had been there for decades. Babs never wanted to see it again but was too sentimental to get rid of it. "If it's sailable, you might want to go to The Anchorage, on the far side of Marsh Harbour. I believe your mother befriended the current dock master's dad, and he might cut you some slack on the rental, at least until you're back on your feet."

"Thanks, Marvin, and I guess I know what you mean by befriended . . . fornicated with is more like it."

"Watch your mouth, girl," Marvin admonished Adele, as he reached for her hand.

Telling his young assistant to take over for thirty minutes, Marvin led her down to the water and into a small powerboat that was shore anchored in very shallow water. Just like the salty dog he'd been for most of his life, he smoothly tillered the little boat out into the shoreline waters.

"I forgot how comforting this was," remarked Adele, facing the brisk breeze. "My sister and I used to love it when we lived in Palm Beach and you and Daddy would take us out into the shallows."

Adele had a sister—one she'd barely spoken to in three years. Alli was considered the "brain" of the family, where Adele was considered the "heart." *Not a bad designation, really. Too bad I used to resent it.* Adele tended to have strong instincts and go with them. But Alli was the type who drew up lists and charts before making any kind of decision. Always the pragmatist, Alli cashed in the coins that Babs gave to her when she turned thirty-one and received a good twenty thousand dollars from an antiques dealer. The money became her share of a down payment on a small American Craftsman house in the stylish outskirts of Miami, soon after she and Stephen were married. Two kids later Alli was still living in the same house, while Adele had lived in two, soon to be three, different places in the same length of time. No wonder the high-tech world suited her so perfectly. It was all about logic for Alli, and sometimes the sisters were like oil and water.

"Your mother came with us as well," Marvin reminded her about the boat trips, but all Adele did was shrug her shoulders.

Their little journey ended much too soon and Marvin dropped Adele off at a seedy-looking dock area covered with all kinds of boats that looked as if they hadn't seen water since the days of Captain Kidd.

"Thanks, Marvin."

"Good luck. I hope you find what you're looking for, Delly." Marvin watched Adele square her thin shoulders and head towards the warehouse. He remembered the day when Adele turned nine years old and was part of such a happy family. Adele's dad Darryl had just purchased *The Pirate Pair* and brought Babs, Alli, Adele, and Marvin down to this exact warehouse to parade the sailboat proudly.

Adele and her mother have been walking on eggshells with each other for more than twenty-five years, thought Marvin. After Darryl's death, Adele seemed to shut down as far as her mother was concerned. Marvin knew she blamed Babs for her dad's death, but she was so young, only twelve years old at the time, and he couldn't understand how Adele could harbor such strong feelings for so long. It was Marvin who had persuaded Babs, with much cajoling, to send the clan's treasure to Adele on Nassau for cleaning and a professional appraisal in advance of the exhibit at The Pirates Museum. Now it was gone. *My fault? Delly's fault? How much could we have predicted, or prevented, before Curtis Albury pulled this stunt?* Sighing softly, Marvin putted away from Adele and her problems.

Picking her way cautiously among the debris at her feet, Adele realized this was just a hop, skip, and jump away from the upscale side of the marina where the *Beautiful Bonny* had been housed. Making her way into the old dockside warehouse, she stumbled through cobwebs and peered at dozens of vessels, listing on their stands and evidencing various states of decay. After ingesting way too much of that sticky spidery stuff, she finally found the old family boat, a 1972 27-foot Catalina. But what used to be *The Pirate Pair* had lost its two capital *P*s and was now *The irate air*.

Sneaking inside, she remembered the boat was her mother's decorator's last gig—and what a doozy it was. Inspired by the psychedelic early seventies, the colorful décor hadn't faded one bit. The cabin was full of hot pink and bright orange shag on both the seat cushions and V-berth, a narrow V-shaped bed at the front of the small cabin. Now she hoped to be able to renovate *The irate air* enough for a temporary living quarters. Shuddering a bit, she felt cramped in the small cabin space with its stale atmosphere. It had always made her feel claustrophobic, especially when her dad, Babs, Alli, and herself were all on board. *Well, any port in a storm.*

Hopping deckside, she found two boat rats hanging around the old boats and offered them one of her last fifty-dollar bills to move the intrepid vessel down to the water so she could try to maneuver it back to the Cable Beach Marina. They readily agreed. Adele disregarded the warehouse manager's warning that the guys had dropped smaller boats than hers . . . not an encouraging statement. But the rats managed to load *The irate air* down onto a small boat trailer with the help of a makeshift pulley. With a minimum of banging and splashing, they got the boat into the bay and Adele gingerly boarded her floating fiasco. She saw that the boat didn't have a working motor but at least the rats had tied up *The irate air* facing the wind for an easier getaway. *Shit, I'm going to have to row, instead of motoring the boat out of the harbor.* Finding one oar, she eventually managed to steer her boat over to the right side of the tracks and into the *Beautiful Bonny*'s empty slip. But *The irate air* was so much smaller and less luxurious than the *Bonny*, it looked like a child trying to wear her mother's clothes.

The cabin of *The irate air* didn't improve with further acquaintance. It had been bad enough when it was new and fresh, but now a musty smell added to its Da-Glo charms. The ceiling was covered with hot pink carpeting, the deck with fluorescent orange. And the accent pillows added a bilious chartreuse to the mix. The only item Adele found worth saving was a beautiful and centuries-old leather pirate chest hidden under a stack of decaying newspapers and *Cosmo* magazines. The chest invited further investigation, but first things first.

Adele was just starting to clean the cobwebs, and pull out the tattered glow-in-the-dark posters, from the cabin of *The irate air* when the marina manager gave her another dose of not such good news. The marina rent for the *Beautiful Bonny* was now more than sixty days past due and at ninety cents a day, per foot, the *Bonny* bill was $2,280.00 and rising thirty-eight dollars a day.

"You're going to have to take a rain check on the rent until I go back to work."

"I have a better solution," he told her. "There's a Saudi

Arabian prince and seven of his wives sailing in on Saturday—they'll pay big money for this space. So how about if you vacate the slip now?" The dock master went on to explain the reason for the windfall was that the sun rises in just the right spot for their daily prayers and meditations to Mecca. He was willing to cut the back rent payment in half if she would give up the space by week's end.

"Do I have a choice?" she asked him. Not really.

Adele walked up to the only pay phone on the dock and made the dreaded call to Dexter, the current dock master at The Anchorage in Marsh Harbour. He was surprisingly warm and cordial, and told her that Babs had dominated the place for three summers in a row. He would be more than happy to have any daughter of hers drop anchor for as long as she liked. He then asked her if she was going to bring her sister Alli along as well. Adele told Dexter she'd be the only Bonny making the trip—but the move would just be temporary. She would be traveling back between Nassau and Marsh Harbour during the holidays until she started back at the private Academy in early January.

Marsh Harbour, home to more than nine thousand residents, was the third largest town in the Bahamas. Though it was still a shipbuilding center, tourism accounted for most of its revenues and very wealthy men who wanted to be sailors for a week sailed down from Florida to participate in annual fishing competitions and bathing suit viewings. Not nearly as commercial or crowded as Nassau, Mermaid's Reef and Beach offered some of the best snorkeling around the islands and there was not a high rise in sight. With enough decent restaurants and dockside activities, this was the perfect location for Adele to regroup and chill out.

Except for quick visits to the condo for food and catbox duty, Adele had been holed up on *The irate air* for twenty-four hours while the boat rats cleaned and reconditioned the motor.

Aye, yi, yi, she thought, finally finishing scrubbing the almost three decades of grime from the bulkheads. Flashing back to when the boat was called *The Pirate Pair,* she thought about how she and her sister Alli had giggled all night long when Babs unveiled her design disaster to the family. Babs had spent three months working with "Mr. Frank" making sure that the hot pink and orange were the exact same colors as her old stewardess uniform was when she was flying the very friendly skies. The chartreuse had been Mr. Frank's idea.

Those were the days. Coming back to reality, she still had no idea how she was going to sail the broken-down boat across ninety miles of the Atlantic Ocean. There was only one solution: she had to call Gracie. Knowing now that Curtis had never paid her for the trip she took them on in November, Adele was reluctant to make this call. But she dialed the phone one number at a time and Gracie answered on the sixth ring. Adele stammered out her request.

"Hmm," Gracie replied. "I, uh, hate to say this, but I've known what has been going on with that white Bahamian husband of yours for almost a year. Curtis hit on me when I was hoisting the mainsail and I couldn't get away from his gross grab. My butt was black and blue for a week. I managed to avoid a second butt grab ever since, but I never trusted a man who pressed his cotton pants."

Adele laughed in spite of the licentious report on her husband. "You're one cool cucumber for someone so young, Gracie."

"That man tried one time too many for my booty call," said Gracie. "You've always been square with me, Ms. Bonny, and besides, I have a man who needs visiting in Marsh Harbour. But what are we sailing on?"

Adele explained about *The Pirate Pair,* now *The irate air,* and warned Gracie that this was a whole flight of stairs down in stature from the *Beautiful Bonny.*

"No problem," she responded. The boat girl's favorite sail was five years before on a vintage 27-foot Catalina, and she declared she was ready for this adventure. There was one condition, though—this trip was going to be a sailing lesson and Adele would be doing most of the work. Adele readily agreed. They decided to meet at the dock the next morning at six a.m.

Looking around the condo one last time on Wednesday morning, Adele put the sextant, spyglass, and mini-life vest into her canvas messenger bag, along with a touristy hula-girl halogen pocket light that had seemed amusing when Curtis bought it. The sextant, used to measure the altitude of a celestial object above the horizon, was brass and weighed several pounds, dragging her shoulder down.

Adele arrived at Boat Harbour at five a.m. with Gilligan comfortable in a plaid cat carrier, and she began to prepare the dauntless vessel to set sail to The Anchorage, a lovely little marina on the north side of Marsh Harbour. This was where Babs, Adele was sure, had an "up close and personal" encounter BS (before Sheldon Morton, the current and respectable attorney husband) with Dexter's father. Unpacking her messenger bag, she lovingly pulled out her father's sextant and spyglass, leaving the charts and halogen light inside.

Unzipping the carrier and giving Gilligan a gentle hug, she opened up her messenger bag and pulled out the pint-sized life jacket. He waited expectantly while she dressed him with the flotation device. This was a cat who was absolutely at home on a boat.

Adele smiled at her soon to be sailing companion. *Who knows how this day is going to turn out and I don't want you going overboard.*

Digging back into a cupboard, she pulled out an old and tightly sealed coffee can with seven hundred bucks inside—just enough money for gas and a bit of boat remodeling once she sailed to The Anchorage.

Putting the cash back in the can, she returned to her scrubbing. An hour later Gracie, a foxy 22-year-old Bahamian with braided hair pulled neatly back into a ponytail, arrived and pulled Adele away from her planning.

"There ain't no way we're gonna use that thing for navigation," asserted Gracie, looking at the sextant. "Looks more like an object of medieval torture to me."

"My dad taught me how to use a sextant when I was a kid," Adele replied, "but I haven't picked it up for years."

As Gracie opened her charts, she was all business. Under her expert guidance it took our plucky sailor just over an hour to rig and prepare *The irate air* for sailing. Up until now, Gracie had always prepped the *Beautiful Bonny* for launch while Adele watched from the comfort of a boatside cocktail. She had never actually done the work, which included attaching all the necessary parts—such as rigging the mainsail, the sail that actually made the boat move. As a little girl, she had had the job of taking the sail out of its bag and laying it on the dock. She now remembered her father's simple rule: *If you play on the boat, you learn the boat.* She had also helped her dad out a bit on *The Pirate Pair* years before, and she'd taken the wheel of the *Beautiful Bonny* once in deep water, but luckily she now found a one-page list of typed instructions left by Marvin as well as a drawn diagram of the mainsail.

Adele started to read. "My God, how did Marvin learn Spanish?" she joked to Gracie, but the boat girl didn't get her humor.

"This is really English, Ms. Bonny," Gracie informed her seriously. "It's just boat talk and you need to understand it. Looks like this guy Marvin has written down some pretty good information."

Adele began to read out loud to Gracie. "'Battens—Make sure the mainsail has empty batten pockets. (Babs and Adele, battens are the wood slats that slide into the pockets on the sail's back edge.) Insert the most flexible end first and secure really strong.' I guess I'm going to have to unfold this damn thing first," murmured Adele.

This is not good, she thought. The mainsail looked nothing like the pristine white canvas sail belonging to the *Beautiful Bonny*. This large sail was yucky and yellowed, and it had dark beige stains on it. She continued to read and Gracie interpreted the nautical terms. A fast learner with a distant childhood memory of boating with her father, Adele managed to attach all three corners and bottom edge of the mainsail to the back and front edge of the rickety boom while only breaking two of her polish-free fingernails.

She was too stoked to care about the fingernails. "It's all coming back to me! I think we're ready."

"Not quite. We need to check the charts first," said Gracie. "These waters can be pretty dicey, especially at this time of year."

Laying the charts out flat on the boat's one small table, Gracie showed her how to chart a line on the wind so they could track the time the trip would take. They then figured out they were about to embark on a twelve-hour sail.

Thirty minutes later Adele, remembering she had to point the bow of her boat slightly sideways moving into the wind, hoisted the sail, easily leaving the end mooring, and began her first adult high seas adventure on *The irate air.*

Gracie reminded her that the boom, the horizontal pole supporting the bottom edge of the mainsail, swings from side to side when the boat is turned more or less parallel and towards the wind. But Adele was not paying attention to this warning as she started to sail out of the harbor. Swinging sharply to the left, she ducked just in time to avoid the pole hitting her hard on the head. Good, her sailor's timing was coming back.

As they finally headed out of the harbor, Adele felt her spirits rise with the familiar thrill of open water.

The boat was equipped with a tiller instead of a wheel like what was on the *Beautiful Bonny*. A wheel has the wonderful advantage of turning in the direction you want to go and, through mechanical linkage, controlling the position of your rudder (the little below-the-water fin-like object that pivots from side to side) to push the boat one way or another. The tiller is also used for steering, but it's more like an arm that turns the rudder directly, thus giving direction to the boat. The trick with a tiller is that it goes by opposites: move it left and the boat goes right, move it right and the boat goes left.

Theoretically this all makes sense, but—*Damn*, thought a distracted Adele, when she hit a directional buoy in the harbor and almost capsized a small Chris-Craft. *I've got to remember—right is left and left is right. I guess I never steered while sailing with my dad . . . and no wonder.* Adele and *The irate air* finally wobbled out into open water. Gracie was laughing so hard she almost fell overboard.

When Adele and Gracie sailed into the shallow waters of The Anchorage Marina under darkness, it had been a long twelve-hour day and a challenging, yet invigorating experience for the novice sailor. She hadn't realized hoisting the sails up and down, attaching the battens and tillering the boat all day long would give her as much exercise as an aerobics class. Getting a whiff of something not so nice, the green sailor sniffed under her armpits—they were much sweatier and stinkier than any dance workout would cause. *Holy moly, get me to a sink and some soap.* She eyed several open slips at the end of a dock, and tiredly glided towards one. Gracie gave Adele a firm pat on the back for actually making it to their destination. The Anchorage was not nearly as flashy as Boat Harbour and the other marinas in the area, but it had a very down-home and comfortable feeling, housing more modest boats with upper middle-income owners.

Dexter Hull greeted the two women when they pulled up to the empty slip and he helped Adele tie off her boat while Gracie dropped the mainsail. His English accent was more pronounced in person and he seemed like a bit of a dandy in his Lacoste alligator polo shirt and Bermuda shorts. Dexter's mother Diana was all proper English, with silky, almost translucent, skin and Adele imagined she still enjoyed tea at three in the back of the Family First Store, the Hulls' other business. His father, Luther, was

Haitian-Bahamian with skin the color of coffee and hands callused from his backbreaking work on the lobster and crawfish lines. Dexter took after his mother. He was wearing a very wide-brimmed hat to protect his pale-skinned face from the harmful UV rays, even though there were stars in the sky.

"Boy, do you look just like your mom. I hope you're just as much fun. I remember her sitting up at the bar in an outrageous bikini, entertaining groups of boaters. She was really good for business and I hope you'll be the same."

"Not a chance, Dexter," growled Adele as she climbed back onto the boat deck, "and if your charity only extends to your private parts, I'll sail back to Nassau right now. I don't need another personal problem."

Dexter backed down a bit. "My heavens, Adele, Dad told me to tell you that The Anchorage is your home free of charge for as long as you need it. It was because of Babs and her brazen-babe attitude that Dad was really able to put the marina on the map."

"Yes, I know, she was quite the party girl and now if you don't mind, I need to unwind and exhale after my rough ride. And if you're looking for another bikini bod to take Babs' place, you'll have to search the beach."

Dexter next turned his charms on Gracie. "Would you like to take a walk with me? I know of a great surfside bar that gets pretty rowdy after ten."

"You need to cut bait while you're ahead," she replied. "I have a man waiting for me at the Sugar Shack. Bye, Ms. Bonny, and good luck."

Gracie walked purposefully up the dock and into the parking lot.

"Too bad," Dexter said wistfully.

"Good night, Dexter." Adele flexed her tired arms.

Bushed, yet exhilarated from her day-long sail, Adele lit two old kerosene lamps that she found on deck and carried them down into the cabin. She noted the initials "AB" etched in the glass. *I'll be damned. Anne Bonny is everywhere.* Looking around at what was now her living quarters, she opened the lovely old pirate chest and pulled out a bottle of vintage brandy and two silver cups that rested on top of several historic-looking documents and drawings. She poured three fingers of brandy into one of the goblets and drank deeply. Adele released Gilligan from his carrier, where she'd stowed him during the docking procedure, and started to doze. Falling into a fitful sleep due to the heat emanating from the lamps, she lapsed into a restless, dream-like state, envisioning a red-haired pirate beauty dressed like a man in purple pantaloons and flowing green satin shirt. Gilligan's insistent hiss brought her partially out of her reveries.

"Aunt Anne!" she murmured.

"What a fop-doodle that pretend pirate mate is," declared Aunt Anne, as plain as day. "Took his name from a story about a boy who didn't want to grow up. Hobbledehoy, neither man nor boy! Reminds me of Pierre in me day—couldn't tell if he was a lad or a lassie."

"So it really is you, Aunt Anne," sighed Adele. "How can this be happening? It doesn't seem like I'm dreaming."

Anne went on as if her niece hadn't spoken. "The loot can be found between two mountainous mounds of sweaty, jiggling flesh, so look lively, my lovely."

Adele woke up with a start. "Holy shit!"

Chapter 5

Adele spent her entire first day at The Anchorage hard at work on her boat, having just repainted the letters of *The irate air* dark purple to read more clearly. The boat's bumpers were badly cracked, the metal railings were so rusted they were the color of root beer, and the mahogany wooden bow and helm trim were scuffed and chipped. She even found some badly peeling paint and deep gouges below the water line. "Brandy" by The Looking Glass was blaring on Adele's boom box as she laid into one of the cruddy railings with some brawn and a giant Brillo pad. "The sailors say Brandy," sang Adele in a painful falsetto, setting off a rush of seagull wings when a flock of birds took flight to get out of ear-reach of the awful screeching.

With her long red hair piled up under a hairnet, spider web remnants on her cheeks, and tattered cut-off short-shorts, she looked and felt a bit like the mermaid Ariel when she thought she'd never get her shore legs. There wasn't much headroom in the cabin, so Adele had to bend over slightly while carrying the old and, as evidenced by her grimace, used chemical toilet up to the deck. Going back into the cabin, Adele decided to reward herself by doing something she'd been putting off. She removed her red leather Day Planner from the top of the leather pirate chest she had lovingly scrubbed clean, opened the ancient lid, and started rifling through the contents. She'd halfway reached the bottom when she found some brown, cracked, and decaying parchment papers with what looked like dried blood on their borders. A faint smile crossed her lips. *So, Curtis didn't steal all the treasure. These historic documents must be worth a fortune.*

Unrolling one, Adele saw a very lifelike drawing of her Aunt Anne brandishing a cutlass, in traditional pirate garb that didn't hide her seemingly pregnant belly. *She was a bit of a fox,* thought Adele, feeling that perhaps being compared to her wasn't such a bad thing after all. Unrolling another drawing, she saw in this one Anne was all smiles, wearing a saucy-looking dress and holding a tiny infant in her arms. But the third and final drawing told a much sadder story: the light had left Anne's eyes and her face was filled with sadness as she cradled a lifeless little baby body wrapped in a black shroud. Adele quickly dropped the papers and gripped her right ear when a stabbing pain traveled from the left side of her jaw into the opposite ear canal. *Damn,* she thought and reached for her Day Planner. Flipping to the back she found the last date in the book was December 31. There she made a note to order next year's calendar insert and another to call for an ear appointment the first week of January.

Suddenly the musical voice of Smee pulled Adele back to present time. "What a total wreck, my dear," fluted Smee as he climbed down into the cabin.

Adele quickly closed her Day Planner and pushed the tattered papers back into the chest.

"Oh, my God, what a mod mess," he blurted as he peered at the bright plush cushions and carpet. "You can't possibly live here, I'm getting dizzy just trying to digest these digs."

Smee stepped down gingerly into the small cluttered cabin and rubbed his hand across the orange carpet, then wiped his fingers fastidiously. Looking up at the ceiling, he saw it was also covered with hot pink shag. He shuddered, and offered her the hammock in his loft if she could get back to Pirate's Plunder this week as the several open cases were not going to get solved by themselves.

"I can see why you needed a week to work on this wreck, but I'm not sure even that will help," he smirked. Stepping gingerly over Gilligan's litter box, he questioned her about the boat having a bathroom.

"It's called a head when it's on board a boat, and cut me some slack, Smee!" Adele aggressively started to slap the yellow-green cushions. The resulting clouds of dust made the putrid green even less palatable. "This is fine for now and green brings out the color of my eyes and goes with my hair. Hopefully, I'll be sailing it back to Nassau soon. Besides, I'm sure your hammock has found more smiles than I care to think about. What are you doing on this island anyway?"

"Got a ride on a private biplane, and no, that's not a description of his lifestyle," said Smee. "Although I wish it were, as Marc has this sexy Speedo thing going on—any excuse to swim in his pool. I came to take you to lunch, but you have to get the yucky gray stuff out of your hair first."

Never one to turn down a free lunch, especially now, Adele used the sink for a quick sponge bath and hair wash, leaving Smee to continue criticizing her dive of a boat. Thirty minutes later they were munching on crab claws at the upscale Papayas Restaurant overlooking the marina at Marsh Harbour and all the multi-million-dollar boats anchored there. Marsh Harbour was the capitol of the Abacos, a 130-mile long archipelago of islets and cays in the northern Bahamas, settled by Loyalists of British heritage who left the United States during the Revolutionary War. Determined to remain loyal to the Crown, they fled New England and the Carolinas, bringing their culture and architecture with them. Main Street in Marsh Harbour reflected this Loyalist look more than two hundred years later and was lined with plantation and clapboard style houses and brightly colored shops and sidewalks.

Cracking a claw and dropping a piece of shell into the pristine water below them, Adele lamented her current situation. "I can't believe the turn my life has taken. I had a boat that used to belong there, a beautiful 42-foot Hunter Passage that really sailed the seas. And now look at the pathetic little firetrap I'm living on! The *Beautiful Bonny* means the world to me and I must get her back."

Adele took a bite of her crab and continued to rant. "And running away with Mandy . . . I just can't believe it. Maybe she'll exercise him to death."

"Highly doubtful," contributed Smee, "even if dancing is a better workout than calisthenics. Maybe Mandy has talents you've never dreamed of. But as to your beloved boat, interventions are what we specialize in at Pirate's Plunder and Smee will find it."

"I sure hope so. It seemed like we were finally hitting our stride, Curtis and I, but how wrong I was. It's so ironic. . . . He felt I was too good to just be a dance teacher for hire and now he's sailed away with a girl who is just that. Perhaps it's Mandy's perfectly matched leotards and leg warmers that turned him on. Me, I've never been much into fashion and took after my dad more than my mom."

Looking pointedly at her dull gray "Bikinis Never Die" t-shirt, Smee refrained from commenting on the obvious.

"They say opposites attract and it sounds like it holds true for you two," trilled Smee kindly. "But I have a great t-shirt saying. How about 'Come Out, Come Out, Wherever You Are'?"

"Very funny," replied Adele. "Let's walk." Smee left a fifty and didn't wait for the change. Adele tried not to feel envious.

"You know," mused Smee sadly, "Woody had a little place somewhere in Marsh Harbour. He never showed me where it was, but whenever we got into a fight, he'd fly over here for a day or two."

Adele took Smee's arm as they moseyed down the street. "With all your sleuthing ability, you didn't have him followed?"

"I thought about it, but 'we all need our alone time,' or so he said. Just didn't think it would be forever."

"I know what you mean," agreed Adele.

Adele stopped at a thatch-roofed cabana where Francis was preparing fresh conch salad. The waterfront chef brandished a knife almost the size of a cutlass, and sliced and diced green and hot peppers, and ripe red tomatoes, at a spectacular speed.

"I have never appreciated the appeal of conch, it's so tough," observed Smee. "I prefer to *wear* my rubbers. Guess it's just one of those island tastes that has eluded me."

Stopping at an open jewelry booth, Adele gasped at the sight of a salmon-colored conch tip and black pearl necklace. *Boy, does this look familiar*, she thought and picked up the piece, quickly turning it over as if looking for something. The conch tips were the same rosy pink color she remembered from her own necklace, but these pearls were blacker in color than deep purple. Not seeing what she was hoping to find, Adele finally put the necklace back in its dark velvet case, under the watchful eye of the attendant.

"Goodness, my dear," rebuked Smee as he picked up her hand and pretended to slap it. "I never figured you for a sidewalk thief! If you really want the pearls I can give you an advance on your first paycheck, but that doesn't seem too wise as your work hasn't even started yet, and it's costume besides . . . cultured not fresh water pearls."

Adele felt irritated at the constantly chattering "First Mate."

"Smee, enough is enough. You sound just like Curtis, always telling me what to do. When I want your *advice* I'll ask for it."

Smee started to sputter. "That's hardly called for, my not so dear!"

Adele relented a little bit. "I'm sorry, Smee. Just still a bit touchy, I guess."

"I know you are, Adele, and don't worry—we'll find your boat."

She smiled at him ruefully.

Looking at his watch, Smee exclaimed, "Three o'clock already!" He told Adele Marc was flying out at four p.m. so he had to go to the airport.

Not wanting to lose his company quite yet, she hailed a cab and together they headed for the Marsh Harbour Airport just three miles away. As the two friends arrived at the rustic and small, one-story outbuilding that served as a holding area, Smee complained to Adele that he didn't understand why Marc wouldn't fly in and out of the much more upscale Cherokee Terminal just a quarter of a mile away. The waiting room seats were real leather and passengers could have a leisurely cocktail at the private bar. This was where all the corporate jets and truly important people arrived. However, things were about to change. A new international airport was under construction and by Christmas 2012 it would be giving Cherokee Terminal a run for their money, as planes would be able to fly directly from the southeastern part of the U.S. into Marsh Harbour.

When they walked out on to the tarmac—no Jet Ways here—Smee facetiously held his nose and boarded Marc's vintage biplane. "*Bon voyage*, my dear!" He waved gaily and donned an old pilot scarf and pair of goggles, looking a little like Howard Hughes when the aviator first piloted his self-designed 1933 Hughes U-1 Racer.

"You think you're going to find my boat?" Adele shouted glumly, but she couldn't be heard over the loud and uneven drone of the engine. She waved valiantly, watching the plane manage a very wobbly take-off and disappear into the azure blue sky above.

Catching a cab back to The Anchorage, Adele was greeted by the marina mailman who handed her a certified letter, redirected from Cable Beach. It must have arrived the very day she left. Jumping on her deck, she read the return address: "The Island High School Academy." Tearing it open, she read . . . gasped and read some more.

Dear Adele,

It is with deep regret that I have to inform you the Academy is unable to renew your contract for next semester. With the faltering economy, school enrollment is down 20% and alumni donations have dropped 30%. The parent steering committee has decided to cut most of the arts classes and as you were the last teacher hired, we have no choice but to let you go. I am so sorry and would be very happy to write you a glowing letter of recommendation. Please call me. I would love to take you out to lunch and do some brainstorming.

Susan Arnold,
Vice Principal

Adele was shocked at what she'd just read. Falling apart, she started to sob uncontrollably. First her husband and family inheritance, then the condo, her boat, and now her livelihood. There was nothing else for her to lose.

I can't dwell on this or I'll go crazy. Trying to clear her head, she started to play catnip catch with the always willing Gilligan, and thirty minutes later decided to call the vice principal. Susan was very well connected and might have some ideas for private students.

When she dialed her cell, Susan was more than sympathetic, having heard about Curtis and the condo. As a bit of good luck would have it, she was in Marsh Harbour visiting the area's public high school, and free for coffee.

Leaving The Anchorage, Adele walked the fifteen minutes to Marsh Harbour's only coffee shop and found Susan already drinking a latte, deep in thought. Handing Adele a coffee drink as well, she gave her a heartfelt hug.

"I know you like vanilla lattes so I ordered for you. Listen, I already have an idea. When I visited the vice principal at the public high school here in Marsh Harbour, I found out they're looking for an instructor to teach modern dance at their continuing education school after the holidays. Not the student income you're used to, but these are adults who really want to learn how to dance. Evenings, only six hours a week to start. . . ."

"You're awesome, Susan. Thanks so much."

"Now I've got to catch a flight back to Nassau. And here's a small parting gift." Susan handed Adele a severance check for fifteen hundred dollars. Adele looked at her gratefully. "Don't say a thing," ordered Susan as she left the coffee shop.

Once again aboard *The irate air*, Adele held onto the halyard line and strutted some easy modern dance moves, already creating several three-step routines for next month's new students. Swaying from side to side, she made small precise circles on the bow. Thinking about a new start at the Marsh Harbour high school, she hoped these less affluent adult students would really embrace her dance class the way the girls did at the private studio. *It's never been about teaching dance to the "right" people for me, it was about seeing the light in the eyes of students who realized they could move freely.* Stepping a bit too ambitiously, she caught her right foot on a rope and landed hard on the deck. *Ouch, just keep moving and power through the pain*, she told herself sarcastically.

Chapter 6

Adele could think of nothing more exciting than taking a sail today, especially as she had started to get her sailor's groove back. She fastened Gilligan's life preserver on tight. Motoring out of the marina, she raised the mainsail and headed out to Great Guana Cay, a once sleepy enclave just a nine-mile trip from The Anchorage.

Two hours and four wrong turns later, she laid anchor at Kidd's Cove, joining several sailboats and brightly painted dinghies in the calm marina waters. But two blocks into the island there was a very different reality. *Oh, great,* thought Adele. *I've hit Guana Cay on Friday Night Grouper Fest at Crabbers.* Specializing in rum drinks, ocean-view ambience and a sheltered boardwalk bar, the hangout felt like a Jimmy Buffett experience. *Yes, the place could get wild.* Vivid memories returned of her last night there, which had turned into a grope fest. She and Elaine had taken a charter flight to Marsh Harbour and hopped the local ferry to Crabbers. Since she'd worn a t-shirt with the motto "Doesn't Play Well With Others," every college boy there took it as a challenge and tried to get her to play with him. This included dumping a *Miami Vice* fruit-flavored cocktail down her blue bikini bottoms when she took off her board shorts. Trying to compete with her friend, Elaine had taken off her shorts as well, but no boys wanted to play with her thunder thighs. Adele and Elaine never mentioned the trip again.

The mini fun center was multi-tiered with three swimming pools and two waterfalls, and a hot tub bubbling over with boys and girls who were giggling and trying to get better acquainted.

Tonight the sound system was cranked up to a deafening decibel level and the dance floor was crowded and sweaty. It was past eight p.m.; the bikini tops were beginning to fly off and the cocktails were cheap and continuous.

It might have been a mistake to dance with the older dude who looked as if the chronic abuse of sea, salt, sun, and rum had taken their toll on a body now displaying man-breasts and drooping abs. So Adele headed into the "mermaid" room for a hand wash and hair check. She passed by two thuggish looking guys at the end of the bar. They were dressed in bright Billabong trunks, wrap-around sunglasses and torn muscle t-shirts. Perhaps the only two at Crabbers drinking iced tea, the thugs gave Adele the once-over as she walked away from them, before continuing their low-voiced conversation.

"He's really acting like an ass," growled Thug One. "He thinks he's so cool dangling the ice around like bait. We're in this fifty-fifty and I don't want his trying for some tail to get in the way of finally making some serious dough."

"You better believe it, bro," agreed Thug Two. "That's why we're here—to make sure he doesn't screw this up."

Thug Two was the more menacing of the pair and perhaps it was the dozen or so acne scars on his face that put him in a perpetual bad mood. He let Thug One know the fence would be there in thirty minutes. "So if Andy wants some action he needs to make it fast. But I have no problem taking him out of the loop and making you my only partner, if you get my drift."

The thug's none-too-friendly gaze locked onto a teen in a red Crabbers t-shirt at the other end of the bar, talking animatedly and moving in close to a rotund older woman. All three made eye contact for an instant and the teen squirmed visibly before going back to the work at hand.

Once inside the mermaid room, Adele chuckled when she saw two young women trying on tremendously tight Crabbers t-shirts and deciding which color looked the best with their bright blonde and coppery red tresses, both undoubtedly many shades removed from the colors they were born with. *A plus in my column*, she thought. For better or worse her hair was still *au naturale.*

"Did you see the old hag with the kid young enough to be her son?" gushed the bright blonde. "She's all over him. He's a real cutie and what a turn-on it must be when he slides that dolphins necklace in between her two almost bare breasts."

Red strutted around the ladies room, making loud fun of the woman out in the bar. Thrusting her chest out, she told her bright blond friend, "She has these mountainous mounds of jiggling flesh, and they're kind of gross. But I guess there's something to be said for riding the high seas and he seemed to be enjoying himself. . . ."

Adele snapped to attention and thought, *dolphins . . . mounds of jiggling flesh*, before quickly moving out of the mermaid room into a crowd of less than seaworthy souls. Her eyes came to rest on a full-figured fuchsia V-neck tank top glittering in the golden moonlight. A young teen in a red t-shirt had her cornered up at the bar. They had gotten very cozy and he was dipping the diamond dolphin necklace into a frozen Blue Marlin cocktail and dragging the piece up and down between her very ample bosoms.

"Do you like my girls, Andy?" she cooed suggestively.

"I love your girls," replied Andy. "I think my boys have found a home."

"These fish are so beautiful," she purred while stroking a golden tail. "Can you anchor them around my neck, Andy?"

The woman tried to take the necklace from Andy but he defensively pulled the piece back to him, in their escalating tussle making a red burn mark across her cleavage.

"Son of a bitch," yelped the woman as she covered the chafed area and ran from the bar. Meanwhile the music was pumped up even louder until a bar-sitter had to use sign language to buy another round for everyone standing there. Andy downed a Captain Morgan and ordered another, before turning his attention to look for his next hoped-for conquest, dolphins tight in hand, as if getting ready to leverage the loot.

Adele quietly stepped in behind him. Trying his previous pick-up line, Andy once again scoped out another middle-aged female with cleavage and hinted, "I think my boys have found a home."

"Not even a temporary one," exclaimed Adele as she hooked the dolphins out of his hand. "These boys belong to Billy's mom and I'm taking them home."

Damn, I should have planned my escape route, she thought in a panic. The party had gotten much heartier and she had nowhere to go. *Got it*, thought Adele, preparing to brace her lower body against the bar. Years of dance and extreme workouts had made her legs and arms as strong as an ox and she was able to swing her body to the other side of the counter. *I'll roundhouse him with a kick to his cojones.* She smiled to herself when she remembered a few words of Spanish from her tenth grade language class. Muscles flexed and body taut, she was almost there—until Andy took her by the throat. All at once the two thugs, along with several other patrons, caught hold of her elbows and hoisted her above the sea of bobbing heads, suspending her body, as if by magic, as flat as a board. With legs and arms held snugly against her torso, she was constricted like a mummy and unable to move. Andy saw his opportunity and steered the boys over towards the edge of the platform and swimming pool below. But the two thugs took danger in a different direction and guided the group beyond the pool, to the thirty-foot drop and sharp rocks and raging water below.

Adele screamed, but her hollering couldn't be heard above the din of the music as hundreds of voices belted out "We will, we will rock you. . ." in every tone and tenor possible. Her heart was racing and forehead wet, but not from the impending sea spray misting up from the rocks. She was being held down terrifyingly tight, feeling as if she were in a coffin. *Oh, my God*—she could see the waves crashing below and closed her eyes to accept her fate.

"Woman overboard," yelled Andy, as he grabbed the necklace from her hand. Out of the mayhem a well-muscled arm appeared and the two thugs received hard jabs to the ribs. Then a pair of strong hands grappled Adele in mid-air and, in a move that made her look like a member of the Cirque de Soleil performing complicated acrobatics, they deftly pulled her back to the platform and laid her gently on the wooden floor. The injured thugs crawled away from the bar. The magic hands then decked Andy cold with a roundhouse to the side of his head. When she could finally sit up and get the hair from her eyes, Adele saw her rescuer.

"Hi," he said. "I'm Ricardo Rodriguez."

"Hi, hi," she stuttered. "I recognize you from Coconut Joe's." With his closely cropped black hair and green eyes flecked with gold, this macho man looked as if he could be Mr. December in the Hot Dudes Calendar.

"Yep." He smiled. "And you're Lady Limbo. I may have had one too many tequilas that night, but I remember that much."

Adele sat at the bar wrapped in a giant white Crabbers beach towel. Still shaken up by her first and only encounter with near death, she looked fish-belly pale but she had enough savvy to remember that white always makes a woman look fat and was grateful she'd lost those last three pounds.

Mr. December picked up the still unconscious Andy and carefully placed him on the ledge behind the bar. Neither he nor Adele saw the two thugs slink down the stairs.

He then turned his attention to Adele. "Lose something?" he inquired, as he handed her the necklace. "Call me Rocky. What was that all about?"

Shaking, Adele took a firm hold on the diamond dolphins necklace. "The little shit tried to kill me . . . and you . . . you saved my life. . . . Oh, my God . . . I could be dead."

"If you were we wouldn't be talking," Rocky pointed out. "Just take a deep breath, and tell me your name and why that punk tried to toss you over the edge."

"My name is Adele Bonny and thanks again for saving my

life," she croaked, fiddling with the necklace. "The punk thought these dolphins should be swimming where they don't belong, and I was just trying to bring them back to their rightful owner."

"An interesting story but I think we should take off before he wakes up," said Rocky. "He's going to have one hell of a headache."

Adele and Rocky left Crabbers very quickly and then high-tailed it down to where his motorboat was supposed to be anchored. When they reached the little marina and cove, Rocky discovered that his friends had already powered away and he was landlocked until morning. Adele offered to take him back to The Anchorage and from there on he'd be on his own.

Once aboard *The irate air*, Adele shut down like a clam and started to shake. Rocky took charge. "You're in shock. Let me sail back to The Anchorage."

"S-sounds like a plan," she stuttered. "C-can you sail?"

Rocky grinned. "To be honest, I'm used to power-boats, but I love a good sail."

"W-well, you saved my life—and you d-didn't even muss your shirt. I s-suppose I can trust you with my b-boat."

Rocky was stoked to be actually sailing again as he usually used powerboats up and down the coast. *Oh, man,* he thought when he saw the scratched wood and gouges below the boat's water line. He then checked the lines. A man who knew his knots, he was impressed to find she had tied *The irate air* up with a perfect cleat hitch. A couple of minutes later, the keelboat was free of its bondage.

He took command like the *mas macho* guy he was and began to sail the nine miles in full moonlight while Adele was still jumpy. Taking to the tiller like a horse to the track, he deftly maneuvered her out of the marina and into the Sea of Abaco. His smooth hand came to an end, though, when a large, black, furry object jumped onto his shoulder. Gilligan had a found the perfect perch.

"It's a cat!" Rocky said. "You've got to be kidding me. Is this your version of a parrot?"

Adele's eyes opened wide. "He doesn't usually do that—you're favored. Just pay attention to where you're sailing."

"Yes, ma'am. Boy, I love the feel of this tiller. Reminds me of swinging a golf club and so light to the touch. When you're on wave runners or powerboats you can't feel the water flow beneath the surface like you can with a tiller. This is totally awesome."

Adele finally started to relax as the boat caught the wind and she shook her head, breeze and sea mist blowing her hair. Rocky smiled as he watched her. He'd always been partial to redheads. "You look like a mermaid."

"Well, you're nothing like a merman and I learned the hard way that you can bring a man to water, but you're never sure where he's going to drink."

She then turned her head into the wind and away from the grinning Rocky.

Adele and Rocky moored *The irate air* at The Anchorage. Climbing down into the cabin, she tried to light the kerosene lamps, but set the tablecloth on fire instead. Rocky efficiently removed his immaculate white shirt and the t-shirt underneath to smother the flames, and our girl got a first-hand look at what was behind his knockout punch. *He has shoulders to die for and the rest of him isn't too bad either.*

Rocky guided her over to the sitting area, wrapped her in a woolly throw and started to rub her shoulders to keep her chattering teeth from chomping down on her lips. He then lit the lamps, illuminating the small area with soft yellow light.

"Who are you, anyway?" asked Adele. "You saved my life and now you're working on my sanity. Men are kind of off my list right now but you might be able to change my mind. So let's hear your story and it better be good. How did you get so deadly with that right hand of yours? Andy literally didn't know what hit him."

Rocky told her he was a Navy Commander and Navy SEAL on a thirty-day leave; with his well-built body and no-nonsense attitude he'd been trained to take care of problems much bigger than Andy. His full name was Ricardo Rodriguez and the Latin streak in his lineage seemed to partner perfectly with his line of work.

Adele opened up the old chest and pulled out the small bottle of Napoleon brandy and the remaining boxed pieces of the Godiva extra dark chocolate, raspberry-filled truffles.

"I like Rocky better and would you like a brandy and chocolate? My Napoleon and Godiva are only for my best friends, and, of course, those who rescue me from certain death or at least a very expensive trip to the cosmetic surgeon."

Rocky passed on the chocolate but Adele placed a healthy pour into two grog mugs and she then drank deeply, getting warm all over and just about shaking her shakes. She wanted to know from Rocky what exactly Navy SEALs did as she had heard about them ever since her cousin contemplated leaving the mainstream Navy and joining what he was told were the elite warriors of naval warfare. At thirty-three, he was four years too old to start the extensive training, but Adele had been fascinated with this fine specimen of military man ever since she'd eyed the posters of them on her cousin's wall.

"I guess we are all young, but very well trained bucks—and I'm a few years older than twenty-nine," said Rocky. "My team is tactical experts who are usually assigned to secret missions. I'm a member of a Naval Combat Demolition Unit off the coast of Florida and if I tell you more. . . ."

"Yes, I know the drill. . . . You'll have to kill me. No wonder you're so good at tying knots."

"You don't know the half of it," laughed Rocky.

Taking a chance and not entirely kidding, Adele told Rocky that she did have someone she would like him to do away with—". . . my soon to be ex-husband and his Lolita girl friend. He stole my 42-foot Hunter Passage; he drove our condo into foreclosure;

he disappeared with a babe barely old enough to vote. Thus my present not-so-sweet surroundings." Adele concentrated on her next swallow of brandy and didn't see the gold flecks in his fabulous green eyes darken to amber.

"Sounds like a real prick," commented Rocky. "Do you have any idea where he might be hiding? It seems like he could use more than a little straightening out. What did the police have to say? Too bad about the Hunter, those sloops are real beauties."

"Tell me about it," sighed Adele, "and Curtis has no idea how to sail her. Gets seasick at the sound of rough waters and has fallen overboard more than once. The useless police have no clues to his whereabouts yet, and I don't even know how hard they're trying. Please tell me pirating is still punishable by death."

"Not exactly," replied Rocky. "But I could make his life pretty miserable and arrange for some hard prison time for him as it's called pirating on the high seas."

Adele took another gulp of brandy and sleepily cuddled in the crook of Rocky's rock-hard bicep.

The irate air was again unusually toasty and Adele started to stir under a heavy blanket. She reached for Rocky but all she felt was a warm Gilligan and a soft spot where her Navy SEAL was once resting. *Oh, well*, she sighed.

"Ahoy, there! Look alive!" Aunt Anne's strident voice raised her from her brandy-heavy head and Gilligan from under the covers, where he clawed out into space. Anne was dressed in a ruby red vest and thigh-high black leather boots, looking like a very stylin' pirate.

"Control that black bag of bones or I'll boil him in oil!" Adele shoved Gilligan back under her wool blanket, trying to come to her senses. Of course he struggled, but he eventually allowed Adele to win this argument.

"So you listened to your aunt and captured both the loot and the heart of a worthy privateer," commended Anne. "A man of quality he is. My Jack used to fight like that but he turned into a drunken louse and I had to take matters into my own hands when we were boarded by a British Navy sloop off the coast of Jamaica."

Anne went on to tell Adele about her less than courageous—and more than drunk—crewmembers, who put up no resistance when their ship was boarded and cowered like curs in the hold. But using wits and guile, she and one shipmate fought back against the Royal Navy who came aboard to capture them. Anne told her greater-than-great niece they had been angry over being the only ones in a condition to put up a fight so they killed one of their own shipmates and injured many others before the Royal Navy eventually prevailed. Anne admitted she would have shot more men, but the hold was locked down tight so she was shooting blind between the grates.

"But I'm not a pirate and I could have been killed," complained Adele.

"But you're my flesh and blood and it's time for you to get back what belongs to our family, even if it takes hard-fought battles."

Adele breathed deeply before replying. "You may be right. How did you know about mountainous mounds of giggling flesh? Your clue led me to where the necklace was. But you died almost three hundred years ago!"

"Don't rub it in, you wench," said Anne. "I didn't tell you where to find it, just what to look for. And let me tell you, those giant heaving breasts reminded me of Jack's doxy before I ran her through with my cutlass."

"He took everything, Aunt Anne—the diamonds, emeralds, pieces of eight, your little sapphire and ruby dagger pistol and even that chastity belt your dad locked you into after bringing you back to South Carolina. Curtis has it all."

"The dagger was a peace offering from Jack after I found him heaped with a Spanish noblewoman," remarked Anne.

Daggers were usually gifted to noblemen from their wives or lovers as a sign of affection, but after Jack stole the nine-inch bejeweled piece from a Spanish nobleman and then bedded his lady, he had no choice but to give the beautiful blade to Anne. Most were worn for jewelry, but Anne used hers as a weapon and frequently poor Jack would greet his crew with a new cut across his chest or gash in his shoulder.

"And my da couldn't keep me locked in for long," continued Anne. "Jack taught me how to pick most any lock known to pirates and landlubbers alike. Mark me, I made sure Jack didn't spend all our plunder on drink and debauchery, and I left behind a tidy treasure trove for my family. If you have to fight to get it back from that bamboozler, so be it. Then Curtis should be keelhauled and his little strumpet, Mandy, tied to the figurehead. We will get revenge. But remember, poppet, jewelry is not always what it seems."

Adele was now almost fully awake. "Oh, Aunt Anne, I have no idea where to even look," she wailed. "And don't talk to me about jewelry. Every single stolen piece is etched in my brain."

"But this piece of jewelry is unique," teased Anne as she began to fade into the now emerging sunrise, "and can help you in your quest."

"What does the piece look like?" asked Adele.

Anne's voice gradually faded away. "It's an old gold coin, but its true value has to do with modern times, my pretty."

Chapter 7

Adele sat at The Very Berry Bar with Mr. Brill and Smee, celebrating the return of the double diamond dolphin necklace. *It's good to be back on Nassau*, she thought, *and even better to have solved my first case.* Mr. Brill, looking happy, was drinking a virgin strawberry daiquiri. He apparently didn't need the Cruzan rum in his drink. As this was a celebration, Adele made sure she and Smee had plenty in theirs. Adele looked around the bar. Patrons had doubled up in between the bar stools and no one seemed to be next to the person they'd arrived with. Two steel-drummers were beating furiously outside the doublewide trailer parked next to the bar, so Smee wedged in between Mr. Brill and Adele, in order to try to carry on a conversation.

Flush from her success as an amateur sleuth, Adele checked out the sea of unfamiliar faces. She smiled when a well-heeled looking yachtsman tenderly caught the wedding-ringed hand of a designer-clad woman and kissed it gently. *How nice to see a husband who actually seems to be in love with his wife.* With great concentration, she turned back to the conversation at hand.

"Congratulations, Reginald," applauded Mr. Brill, sipping his strawberry drink. "You brought back the double dolphins with almost a full day to spare. Billy's mother isn't home until tomorrow. How did you find them without Woody the Wonder Boy following the scent?"

Shaking his head with deep appreciation, Mr. Brill added, "I've never known you to work so hard over three months, much less four days. How did you do it?"

Huffily Smee informed Mr. Brill that while he'd allowed

Woody to take all the glory, the wonder boy was really still an apprentice. The young man had learned all about bling and boat retrieval under the tutelage of the First Mate, who worked overtime training him in the subtle aspects of tracking. "He's such a sensitive soul and I thought it was important for him to feel part of the Pirate's Plunder family, but truly I've been the brains all along."

Irritated at Smee's taking credit for finding the necklace, Adele accidentally-on-purpose spilled her sticky frozen mango-papaya-coconut cocktail across Smee's crotch and smiled gleefully when he gasped and grabbed at his balls.

"Oh gosh, I'm so sorry, Reginald," she gushed apologetically. "These drinks are dangerously slippery. I guess I've been out of the loop a bit. How *did* you track down the dolphins?"

Smee looked daggers at Adele, then turned to his client and put on his best smile. "Well, Mr. Brill, I do have to give some credit where credit is due. My trusty Adele has the ability of a bloodhound and she locked onto the necklace at the Crabbers Grouper Fest. That little whippersnapper didn't stand a chance with Ms. Bonny on the scent."

"So, Ms. Bonny, tell all," said Mr. Brill.

Putting off her reply—because anyway, how could she explain casually that a long-dead pirate was her source?—Adele turned her gaze back to the yachtsman. When his wife left their table to go to the restroom, he caught the eye of a young woman in the bar, giving her a million-dollar smile and a sly wink.

What games people play, Adele thought. Curtis loved to play the *advice* game and gave her sister Alli plenty of it when she and her husband decided to have a second child. Curtis was a firm believer in population control and advised Alli to stop at one child. After all, he lectured, her young son was such a handful and she did work nine long hours a day at the Department of Defense. Why would she want to bring another resource-using human being into the world? Feeling it was none of his business how many children she wanted to have, Alli couldn't ignore Curtis' *advice* the way Adele was usually able to do, and the sisters hadn't seen much of each other since the birth of her second son. *My loss.*

Hiding her momentary abstraction, she stepped back into the conversation with Mr. Brill. "Nothing really to tell, Mr. Brill," she responded. "Things got a bit hairy when Billy and his cohorts tried to throw me over the railing at Crabbers, but no biggie."

Both Mr. Bill and Smee cried out in unison, "Oh, my God!"

Adele continued with hardly a break. "Andy had those mammals anchored in a pair of pretty serious breasts and it took some strategic positioning to pry them loose. But they swam home with me and into an ocean of Billy's mother's panties, so all's well that ends well."

"You bet, and thank goodness you weren't hurt," interrupted Smee. "But all doesn't end well until I have the seven thousand dollars in my hot little hands."

Mr. Brill dug deeply into the vest of his three-piece suit, pulled out a cashier's check in the amount of seven thousand dollars made out to Pirate's Plunder, and slowly handed it over to the very eager Smee.

"Good job, Reginald. Partnering with you has been a good move and I shall ever be grateful to the Lucky Strike Casino on St. Lucia for our partnership. Can't believe we've worked together for almost five years."

It all started when Mr. Brill was losing at blackjack at the Casino on St. Lucia and Smee came in to play the quarter slot machines. For eighteen years Brill had been living the high life as a senior investigative agent for the FBI in the Miami Field Office, but he was nailed by a senior assistant for padding his expenses to the tune of ten thousand dollars. Twenty months short of his retirement, he had to return his all-access agency card and company car. At the age of fifty-two he moved to Nassau and started Brill's Insurance Agency with the lump sum he'd received to leave the Company quietly.

As dumb luck would have it, one of Mr. Brill's clients was on the island as well when his 61-foot catamaran, valued at

$375,000, was literally stolen dockside from The Harbour, a resort marina. An expert in insurance but not retrieval, he enlisted the help of Smee who, with the help of his Woody of the moment, solved the St. Lucia hijacking in three days. A drunken sailor who wanted to make an impression on his lover had commandeered the catamaran. The twenty percent finders fee bought them both what they wanted. Smee turned Pirate's Plunder into a real business and Mr. Brill gambled away his share.

As Brill walked away Adele commented, "He's a strange one."

"You have no idea, dear. But your dedication truly amazes me. You tracked down that kid like it was personal. I've only really known you a week, but what a seven days it's been! Don't tell me you were dumped by that kind of dude in your younger years."

Adele didn't appreciate the remark. What made him think her early love life was anything less than perfect? He was soon to hit fifty and even all the Botox, Restylane, hair dye, and laser resurfacing in the world doesn't turn back the clock for more than a decade. Flipping her hair so far to the side that she got a crook in her neck, she relaxed her V-neck lime green t-shirt and smiled brilliantly at the bartender.

"The big Hawaii 5-0 isn't far behind you if I'm not mistaken?"

"Eight long months until I'm fifty," he countered, "and it will be a celebration from sea to shining sea."

"Sounds like great times," shrugged Adele. "Whatever floats your boat."

Smee sighed, his mood shifting. Granted, he had a crisp new check in his pocket. But he had a bigger problem to consider. Adele had solved this case for him. Was she the answer to his bigger problem? It was time to find out. "I've never seen a woman this motivated in my entire life. Except of course for my NaNa, who insisted upon naming me Reginald after my father and grandfather, Reginald A. Stocking the first and second.

"But seriously, I'm dying to know—other than cold cash, what gave you the motivation to pursue what was an obviously dangerous situation? I get goose bumps just thinking about it." Smee shuddered artistically and ordered another blueberry-banana daiquiri, giving the bartender a saucy butt pinch when he came around to the other side of the bar. "I mean, that little brat at Crabbers could have broken your pretty little neck, much less given you facial lacerations not even my plastic surgeon Dr. Poudy could fix."

He then went on to lament her return to the Island High School Academy in less than three weeks.

"Why do you say that, Smee?" Adele had been too embarrassed after confiding in Smee about Curtis stealing her boat and driving her condo into foreclosure to admit that she had lost her job as well.

"Well, actually, Woody has put me in a bit of a pinch. Mr. Brill told me something confidentially, not to be repeated. Last October, Woody brought in a beautiful busty blonde wearing a sheer and barely-there blue blouse, and her even more beautiful yacht, into the marina for him to appraise and insure.

"He's usually a very smart businessman, but this woman used her cleavage to cloud his judgment and he insured her yacht for twice as much as he appraised it for. Last Tuesday it was boarded, the captain killed, and the boat stolen. If it is not retrieved, Mr. Brill will go bankrupt and our cash cow will stop giving milk."

Adele considered the story and started to put two and two together. *What's wrong with this picture?* Perhaps Woody was not such a wonder boy after all. Why had he wanted this yacht appraised for twice its value? Perhaps he was hoping Mr. Brill would cover the insurance payout in order to save face and he would get part of the money. Perhaps he used the busty blonde and her barely-there blouse to cloud Mr. Brill's judgment. She turned her focus back to Smee and asked, "What kind of a yacht was hijacked and what is the supposed payout?"

"My goodness, Adele, you've become so professional. The yummy bright green yacht is a 51-foot twenty-year-old Hinckley Sou'wester, the *Hygia*—you know, named for the Goddess of Water. She's valued at four hundred thousand dollars, but the policy payout is eight hundred fifty thousand. Supposed to be pretty spectacular with a six-foot-tall figurehead of an intricately carved wooden sculpture of the water goddess herself on the bow."

Opening up his man-bag, he pulled out a photograph of the beautiful green boat with the white and gold hand-carved Hygia attached to the bow. "Not many of those figureheads are around anymore as they cost thousands of dollars to carve and can really weigh the boat down."

"What a beauty!" She duly admired the yacht's craftsmanship. "So if the *Hygia* is found and returned, does Pirate's Plunder receive twenty percent of the four hundred thousand or the eight hundred fifty thousand? Big difference, I'd say."

"I'm not greedy, my dear. We receive a retrieval fee of eighty thousand dollars and the lucky agent gets a windfall of twenty grand; not bad for a couple of weeks' worth of work."

"But you split the finders fee fifty-fifty with me for the double diamond dolphins. What gives?"

Smee explained that the fifty-fifty deal only pertained to jobs netting under fifteen thousand dollars and he felt this was a very generous offer. Assuming Adele's only experience as a retrieval expert came from a single event as fortuitous as it was fortunate, he wasn't sure she had the talent or stick-to-it-iveness to bust this case wide open and he doubted that she could find the *Hygia* during her holiday break.

Adele was more than a bit interested in Smee's proposition and decided to let him in on more of her troubles. "There's some more news I haven't shared with you," she admitted. "Unfortunately I lost my job two days ago. Got laid off as enrollment is way down at the Academy."

"Perfect timing," crowed Smee. He did, however, ask her what her motivation was and why she was willing to put her life in danger.

I guess if Smee and I are going to be partners in the game of pirated retrieval, it's better to come clean than to continue my concealment. "I'm playing the revenge game, Smee, as my boat and abode are not the only things Curtis has stolen from me. He also pirated away my family's possessions . . . the Bonny jewels, ancient coins and other irreplaceable treasures I have to get back before the fourth of January when my family expects to see our dynasty displayed at The Pirates Museum here on the island."

Smee's reaction was not exactly what Adele had expected. He was delighted with his good fortune to be connected with buried treasure, and he was flabbergasted to find himself in business with a true Bonny relative. For years he'd heard the rumors on the island that the great-great niece, thirteen times removed, of Anne Bonny lived here locally, but Smee had never thought he would get the chance to meet a relative in person. This marvelous news had Smee beaming and babbling brightly.

Chiding her for not revealing this relationship sooner, he insisted she should embrace it and polish the pirate that was in her blood. All he had ever wanted since he was a little lad was to be a pirate and assisting Mr. Brill capture bad guys was as close as he had come—at least until now.

"You have to embrace your hidden corsair and I will help you dig deep inside to find it." Smee shuddered. "I just can't believe it. This is so exciting!

"When I was eight I so wanted a cowboy cake for my birthday, you know, all those whips and spurs going on, but my NaNa and mom and dad surprised me with a small pirate party."

His family had hired a long-haired hottie to dress up like Captain Hook and the hottie made Smee's heart beat faster than he could imagine. The breathtaking brocade full-skirted coat and frilly blouse, lustrous black curls, and shiny silver hook just put him over the top. That was how Smee's love for a pirate's life came about.

Smee had created a disconnect between the pirates of yore, including the fancy costumed man who had so entranced him at his birthday party, and the pirates of today who he thought were mercenaries and had to be stopped. These renegades were not like his beloved eighteenth-century icons who plundered and pillaged to survive, but robbers pure and simple. They didn't wear elegant brocades and fancy pants, but were style clueless, dressed in smelly t-shirts and torn cargo pants. They had to be stopped. He vividly remembered one of his first cases with Mr. Brill, where they captured the Bimini bandits, three scurvy men who had terrorized the tiny island, robbing all the local gift stores. Once they were in custody, Smee and his pre-Woody partner were appalled to see the leader wearing a filthy *orange* shirt and *red* shorts. He so needed to be arrested, even if it wasn't by the fashion police. Adele might wear t-shirts but at least they were usually clean.

"Just think, you come by it naturally," he moaned, almost swooning.

"Stop hyperventilating, Smee. You sound just like my mother, Babs. She was on my case for years to *embrace* my Bonny blood. So, of course, I went the other way. And now the loot is all gone and I'm hoping that with the help of Pirate's Plunder I can get it back. I would love to be your partner for a thirty-seventy split. I promise I'll be available 24/7 as long as some of my time can be spent on tracking down Curtis. Well, no, I do have one other commitment—teaching a couple of dance classes at the Marsh Harbour high school. But you'll have all the rest of my time, for sure."

Adele considered how high the stakes were in this revenge game of hers. Her mother was counting on that booty for her retirement, and she and her sister Alli had been promised a portion of the ultimate sales as well. "The sale of the Bonny treasure would have taken care of the family for the rest of our lives."

Smee reacted to her last comment with horror. "You can't possibly consider breaking up the collection. I've read that even when Calico Jack—too bad about his lack of brocades—was getting ready to be hanged 'like a dog' he never gave up the location of his and Anne's loot."

Adele told Smee that this was a discussion for a different day, and promised she would find the *Hygia* and the *Beautiful Bonny* and both of the scalawags responsible would be brought to justice . . . or even better . . . to the end of a sword. She could feel herself begin to embrace her inner pirate and dramatically suggested signing with a blood promise. In a flash the Bonny girl pulled out a pocket knife from her purse and pricked her pinky finger. Several drops of blood welled out onto her other hand. Smee again looked as if he would faint, but this time not with delight.

"We have a deal, but please, no more blood. I have a real aversion to that red, gooey stuff so can we just do Rock, Paper, Scissors competition and whoever wins draws up the agreement?"

The new partners did the best two out of three, and Smee covered Adele's rock with his paper twice in a row.

"Now let me down the last tiny sip of my daiquiri as we have a very busy day tomorrow," trilled Smee. "Do you mind working on Sunday? There's no time to lose!"

Seeing a dark curly hair floating in his drink, she suggested they should leave the bar without delay and Smee saucily placed three twenties in the back of the bartender's pants on their way out. With much internal debate, Adele decided to spend one night, and one night only, in his much-touted "Fly Me to the Moon" loft before flying to Marsh Harbour and sailing *The irate air* back to Nassau.

Adele was more than surprised to see the elaborate abode Smee called home. He owned one of the row houses situated under the massive bridge that takes visitors and fun seekers over to Paradise Island and all that the multi-multi-million-dollar Atlantis resort had to offer. A series of a dozen or more houses and small local food establishments and other stores looked like fragile shelter against the monolithic high rise. Smee had an end house next to the bay and once she stepped inside—across a plank, no less—Adele was truly in another world. An old, dark-iron cannon greeted her as she entered the great room. The area was filled full of luxurious and rich silk and brocade-covered chairs and settees in warm and wonderful hues, flowering tropical plants, and a giant saltwater aquarium.

Traveling to the bedroom, she found a massive mahogany four-poster bed swaddled with see-through silk canopies and satin bedding. Smee must have some sort of whole house diffuser as each room had the inviting aroma of cinnamon, cloves, and ginger. Adele sank down into the ultimate pillow top mattress and Smee brought in two glass mugs brimming with steaming hot Jasmine tea.

"And Woody couldn't find his smile here?" asked Adele incredulously.

"I think he was a little bit allergic to all these scents. His eyes watered whenever the diffuser would fill up the rooms with the smell of the Spice Islands. I offered more than once to change to sage and juniper berry, but the cloves drove him crazy."

"Sounds like a very sensual kind of guy." Adele thought back to Curtis once again, and how he too was allergic to so many of the scents and senses of the islands. She hoped he still had that nasty plumeria-caused rash on his back. *Snap out of it*, she reproved herself.

"He was very sensual," Smee agreed, bringing Adele out of her reverie. "Have I ever showed you his photograph?"

Not waiting for an answer, Smee went over to what looked like a real Ming Dynasty dresser and removed a very posed photo of a platinum blond, pink-cheeked and red-lipped young man reclining suggestively against a black fake-fur throw.

"Wow, he's a package."

"I know," cooed Smee wistfully, "and only twenty-three. I miss that package. But no time to mourn, we have a busy day tomorrow and I need you to turn all your angst and anger into finding the *Hygia* or we will both be singing for our supper."

"Will do, boss." Adele snapped to attention. "But first let me experience your lecherous loft."

Smee led Adele up a steep teak wood staircase into a lovely

sky-lit loft, which was furnished with one giant white rope hammock and a small gold-threaded duvet and matching fluffy down feather pillows, placed just so.

"You've got to be kidding me, Smee. How do you expect me to sleep in this thing?"

"Well, my dear, Woody and I never actually slept here. Remember me telling you that he was as agile as Gumby. . . ?"

"TMI again," said Adele as she pushed him towards the stairs.

As dawn broke Adele dragged her very sore self up to Smee's roof top deck for some leg lifts and knee bends.

Surprised at feeling happy and hopeful, she fiddled with her cell phone, shopping for a ring tone better suited to her new combative lifestyle. She tried the *Superman* theme and "Colonel Bogey March," but was happiest with her final choice.

There was a book up on the deck in easy reach, an old island guide, and she picked it up and started to read about legendary pirating in the Bahamas. She lit up at the mention of Calico Jack Rackham and how he and other pirates found it easy to clean and repair their ships due to the shallow areas existing in the Abacos. A clean ship would glide through the waters more easily, which made it much simpler for outlaws to outrun the authorities.

The local archipelago consisted of several hundred tiny islands and cays spread out over thousands of square miles, the layout of these islands making the area an ideal location for the pirates to set up their headquarters as well. There were plenty of places to hide ships and treasure, and there was a natural harbor, well protected at both entrances, between New Providence and Hog Island (now Paradise Island). This made it impossible for a single military ship to corner a wanted vessel. It was easy for a freebooter to escape to the other side of the harbor and out into open water. Inexperienced captains were also run aground in the shallow waters surrounding the Abacos, making it a simple science for the buccaneers to climb aboard and take whatever they wanted. They would then hide the loot in some remote coastal cavern. *Fascinating*, she thought, continuing to read.

Anne Bonny took up with Calico Jack after she became bored with her husband, James Bonny. The pirate wooed her with expensive gifts and the promise of a sea rover's life, providing her with several years of unbelievably exciting adventures at sea. Up to now, Adele had had no idea how interesting pirates really were. Smee, and even Babs, were right; she did indeed need to get in touch with her inner buccaneer. Adele began to doze off again and sleepily thought about what Aunt Anne's few years on the high seas were really like. She wondered if she could be happy with a hunk like the cotton-clad Calico Jack Rackham. He sounded so manly and a take-charge kind of guy, not a lying and cheating pantywaist like Curtis. *Jack was kind of like Rocky, only better. Lucky Aunt Anne.*

"Now don't get any high-flyin' ideas about my man," she heard in her head as the now all-too-familiar ringing in her ears started to subside. "Remember he was a here-and-thereian, much too fond of the drink and the dollies. I'll never forgive me Jack for bein' hammer-headed enough to get himself hanged."

Chapter 8

Adele awoke to the sound of Smee's voice. "Good morning, my dear. Hope you slept well. Cappuccino is waiting!"

Be right down, Smee, she thought to herself. *But somehow you're not the swashbuckler I'd like to share cappuccino with.*

As the partners left the safety of Smee's sizzling sanctuary, Adele breathed in the neighborhood she found so different from Cable Beach and glamorous downtown. For one thing, there were very few cars—bicycles were the most common form of transportation of the indigenous population. Getting into her brightly colored Bug, she noticed all the outdoor clothing and accessories kiosks where you could pay thirty bucks for a pair of "Chanel" shades and walk away with change, or luxuriate in a Kate Spade bag, still in the soft cover, for a fraction of the cost of the goods found on West Bay Street. The food courts were rough and tough with sometimes exotic and indefinable delicacies, but with enough spices and basting everything tasted good under the bridge to the Emerald Forest, better known as Paradise Island. Adele ignored the locals who stared at her rapidly whirling daisy wheels as she zoomed off towards Pirate's Plunder. Once she was inside the building, Smee pulled her into Woody's section of his overly decorated office and started to explain how to use their Global Positioning Satellites tracking unit mapping system. It was like the blind leading the blind.

"There's a power button on one of these three small boxes," he told Adele. "It hasn't been turned on since my Woody went smile searching. But he did tell me there are little mapping systems units located on the satellites up in space. Or did the unit use the satellite to give the location? I'm just not sure."

Adele didn't get it and questioned if those satellites were launched from the Kennedy Space Center or like *Apollo 13*, paraphrasing the line that had a country locked to their television sets, "Houston, we have a problem." Smee turned the GPS system on and the screen read, "acquiring GPS units that are transmitting location."

"Acquiring GPS units? What does that mean? Do we have to buy them?" she asked. "I didn't know satellites were available for purchase to the general public."

"No, no, no," sputtered Smee with exasperation in his voice. "It was hard for me to understand, too. Woody was the real wonder with gadgets. Oh, Woody, where are you when we need you?"

Smee went on to explain how Woody would use satellite links to track and locate lost objects including boats and their cargo. Last month he somehow found two yachts and a missing person by monitoring this device. Unfortunately Woody had never showed him how to use it.

"Stop sniveling, Smee. My sister Alli is the scientist among the Bonnys and I remember her talking about GPS at one of our few family dinners, if you can believe it. She works for AMAZON . . . no, AUTEC . . . hold on . . . I have her 4-1-1 written on a piece of paper somewhere in my purse."

Adele fished down deep into her messenger bag and found a crumpled old card. She read out loud to Smee. Alli Lithgow was a "Sonar Testing Range Scientist at the Atlantic Undersea Test and Evaluation Center," and she bounced between Andros Island in the Bahamas and West Palm Beach. AUTEC centered around accurate underwater, surface, and in-air tracking data on ships, submarines, aircraft, and weapons systems, and it supported the Navy and other undersea research programs. The instrumented test facility was located in a place called "The Tongue of the Ocean," east of Andros, but it was not really as mysterious as the name and location suggested.

"I think it's kind of like Area 51, although Alli swears no UFO work goes on there. Her drill is that AUTEC is involved with undersea, *simulated* warfare *only* and its vital mission is to assist in establishing and maintaining naval supremacy in the world. Sort of like *Mission: Impossible*, if you ask me."

"Well, call her, my dear. Hopefully, you have a very short learning curve as high technology is definitely not my strength."

Adele watched Smee walk into the other office and then sat in front of the tracking unit, feeling absolutely dumbfounded when the GPS screen asked her to "STU." After ninety seconds of stone cold silence the system displayed "Select Tracking Unit." Since her cell phone, iPod, CD player, and blow dryer were the only mechanical things she had been able to master, she closed the door of her small closet of an office and got to work on her phone.

Alli was everything that Adele was not. At the age of thirty-six (two years younger than Adele—Babs constantly reminded her), she had been married to Stephen Lithgow for six blissful years and had two perfect boys, aged two and four. She had stayed her career course for almost a decade, having earned her PhD from the University of Florida at the age of twenty-four.

Adele, on the other hand, had dropped out of Miami Junior College where she had studied modern dance for five semesters. Next she worked as a hand and accessories model for a local women's store in Miami for several years before transferring to State and finally graduating with a major in dance. She then started teaching dance at a local semi-pro studio. One problem, she was way too honest and if she didn't feel that her students had any promise she told them the truth. Four years later Adele wasn't working there anymore and, after she met Curtis, he convinced her they should open up their own studio.

The first year the studio was a huge success and Curtis encouraged her to teach seven days a week. As they became more successful, early in the second year it was all about the money and he landed a large agricultural contract due to Adele's growing contacts. She was teaching her moves to the daughters of the wealthy business people on Nassau and their parents were very grateful. *I should have started to figure it out,* she chided herself. As Curtis started to spend more time at the studio, the student enrollment dropped off dramatically and she had to cancel several classes that initially had a waiting list. Year's end became a disaster, and after she lost the studio Curtis used his bit of remaining community clout to land her the position at the Island Academy. *That didn't last long either*, Adele thought ruefully. *I've been an under-achiever most of my life.*

Alli was a different story; she was making a high five-figure salary in her late twenties. With this phone call Adele felt every degree of their differences.

"Hey, Alli, it's Adele. How are things in the world of bombs and bullets?"

"I work in the computer center and lab simulator and haven't seen either bombs or bullets in days."

"That's good, I think. How's everything else?"

"Everything else?—Covers a lot of territory. You basically never call me, Delly, so what's up?"

"I'm sorry it's been so long, Alli, just working on my marriage and I need your help," Adele admitted. "I recently made a new and very professional career move and need to be able to understand and use GPS tracking units—whatever they are."

"That's a piece of cake," Alli assured her. "But first tell me about the Academy. Curtis was thrilled when he landed you a job there, teaching all of those daughters of multi-millionaires. Isn't it just your third semester?"

"My so-called husband was more thrilled than I was about the Academy job—"

"So-called? Do I detect trouble in paradise?"

"Oh, don't ask. What I was going to say is that I was just laid off—the economy, you know. But don't worry, I always land on my feet and already have this other job lined up."

"I'm so sorry, Adele," Alli sympathized, "and I know technology is not your long suit." Adele did not respond, so her sister continued. "The GPS system is really easy to use. All you have to do is type in the tracking unit number or address you're looking for, and based on the unit's current location, the system will give directions to its position."

"Wow, that seems easy, but what about if you're looking for a boat?"

"A boat? Care to elaborate, sis?"

"Not quite yet, but suffice to say, our ancestors would be proud," boasted Adele.

"Oh-kay, well—" Alli informed Adele that this kind of tracking is a little bit trickier. The unit must be located on the boat and able to track satellites, and the GPS satellites broadcast precise timing signals from their on-board atomic clocks. Picking up signals from several satellites simultaneously can determine the position of the GPS unit in global coordinates. Commonly carried by boaters, the unit enables users to precisely track and then retrace their movements anywhere on earth.

"For those who don't have a scientific mind, that's latitude and longitude," explained Alli. "Most of these systems broadcast every hour or whatever the reporting time is set to." Adele could tell by her sister's voice that this was really elementary stuff, but Alli knew Adele had trouble setting the cruise control on her Bug. "Honestly, Adele, this seems a little bit beyond your depth. What does Curtis think about this radical career change? After all, he always gives you *advice* on how to live your life."

"Well, not anymore." Adele paused for a moment before deciding to unload the whole, horrible past six days on her sister's strong and sensible shoulders. It all came out in a nearly incoherent gush—the pirate treasure, the *Bonny*, the infidelity, the job loss, the condo mortgage, the black hole of unsuccessful investments.

"So that's it. What can I do? Mom's going to strangle you," Alli mustered to say after a long and awful pause.

"I know," moaned Adele. "You were so right about him, Alli, and I'm so ashamed I let his lies and deception hurt our relationship. Can you help me track the bastard? I have to get the *Beautiful Bonny* and family property back before Babs and Sheldon fly over for the Pirates Museum opening."

Little sister might just be able to assist big sister in that situation. Alli had strongly opposed Adele's intention to give Curtis a pieces-of-eight coin from the family treasure for his fortieth birthday, but in the end she had offered to prepare the gift herself. Adele had thought—hoped—that meant Alli had come around. But she now revealed to her older sister that she had added a little something extra. When creating the necklace from the coin, she had tucked a small tracking device inside the silver band that encased the coin and looped to the necklace chain. As Curtis had never learned how to swim—and since he had fallen overboard twice while trying to show off his sailing skills—she programmed the personal locator beacon to activate if he hit the water.

"What in God's name is a personal locator beacon?" asked Adele. "Sounds very James Bond-like to me."

"It's known as a Man-Overboard System—very apropos, wouldn't you say? It's a tracking system with a radio frequency transmitter and receiver. I installed it on the *Bonny* the last night I visited you and Curtis. If he hits the water the beacon will be activated and I'll be able to find where he is, and the boat will be nearby. Our AUTEC frequency location system can track the system frequency channel I set and I can give you the location. There's also a receiver on the boat for anyone who can figure out how it works, so they could go and pick up the bastard before he drowns." Alli paused. "You know, it feels good to call him that out loud! It's too bad the *Beautiful Bonny* doesn't have the system on all the time but if Curtis has the brains to turn it on we can track him."

"You were always the smart one, Alli," complimented Adele.

"But you're the fun sister, Adele, and fun counts for a lot. Love you. I'll be in touch soon."

For the first time in several years, Adele told her sister, "I love you, too," and she hung up the phone with a smile.

Adele walked into Smee's pirate-gear-filled office, carrying the transmitter unit. She once again smiled at the cutlasses, swords and muskets mounted on the walls. The First Mate was softly stroking the ceramic head of Peter Pan. She watched Smee raise his eyebrows when she smiled at him, the first she imagined since they'd met.

"Once again Alli has managed to demystify the mysterious."

"Do tell, doll."

"I'm assuming the yacht has a unit placed somewhere on a covered deck, and this unit is able to track GPS satellites that 'broadcast precise timing signals from their on-board atomic clocks.'"

Adele strutted her stuff, using her newly acquired knowledge. According to Alli, picking up signals from several satellites simultaneously could determine its position in global coordinates. All she had to do was turn on the Pirate's Plunder tracking system and select the *Hygia*'s unit number to see if it was on and broadcasting.

Smee opened a small treasure chest on top of his desk and pulled out a list of pertinent information about the company's still open cases. He read out loud the tracking unit's numbers and their frequencies. Feeling like a high-tech teacher, Adele turned on the system, typed in the numbers, and waited breathlessly for sixty seconds, but then read on the screen, "tracking unit not activated."

"Now why wouldn't Woody have activated the unit on the *Hygia*? Especially when he convinced Mr. Brill to insure the yacht for twice its value." The new partners locked gazes and Adele could see by his eyes that he was pretty sure of the answer already.

"Something is rotten in Denmark and I'm afraid it's not the cheese. Could my Woody turn out to be a real rascal?"

"I'm sorry, but it looks like it, Smee, and perhaps lots of money is the one thing to keep Woody smiling. Guess I need to return to The Anchorage and quickly sail back here before you run yourself through with a sword."

"This makes me so sad, but I'm glad you'll be my new partner in solving crimes and capturing brigands. With your diligence and my charm we'll find both the *Hygia* and the *Beautiful Bonny* well before the New Year."

Smee opened a drawer in his antique desk and brought out his Pirate's Plunder checkbook. He seemed happy when he wrote Adele a check for $3,500 and placed it in her outstretched hand. "I have a good feeling about you, Ms. Bonny," he told Adele. "You have good pirate juju." Looking at the check with love, she kissed Smee soundly on the cheek, told him she knew hers were not the lips he was looking for, and headed out the front door and to the Nassau International Airport. She hoped this would be her last inter-island flight for a while. Sitting in the small terminal, she pulled her Day Planner out of her messenger bag and turned the pages to her December 19th To-Do List. At the top read: "Collect $3,500 check from Smee." She crossed out the sentence with a flourish and wrote "Deposit check in Scotia Bank" before being called for her flight.

Adele had a very bumpy flight back to Marsh Harbour airport, the airplane doing her ankle no good at all, and she was in a grumpy mood when she limped to the sidewalk and hailed a cab back to The Anchorage. Her driver didn't help matters much either. A stylin' forty-year-old Haitian, she introduced herself as "Dr. Kim" and proceeded to go the wrong direction in the one-way round-about, incurring the wrath of a dozen or so right-way drivers who had to scurry up on the shoulder of the road to keep from getting hit head-on.

"Hey, Kim," rebuked Adele, "slow down! This is Marsh Harbour, not the Indy Five Hundred. And you're a cab driver, not Dale Earnhardt Junior."

Correcting Adele that her name was *Doctor* Kim, the driver passed a slower car from the left and just barely avoided hitting a palm tree as she pulled an Indy Driving Course certificate from the back of her dashboard. "This is how I learned how to avoid all these maniacs," she chortled gleefully. She screeched onto Main Street going sixty in a thirty-five mile an hour zone, the one-mile stretch to the turn-off heading up to The Anchorage passed like a blur.

"My mistake. So, you're a physician as well as a race car driver? Do you heal your passengers' injuries after you bang them around in your car? Where did you earn your medical degree?" asked Adele as she was thrown against the back of the seat.

"None of your business," said Dr. Kim. Her erratic driving threw Adele first to one side of the car and then to the other, before she careened onto the waterfront drive and into The Anchorage.

Adele jumped out, holding her neck with her hand.

"That'll be twenty-two dollars."

"But it's only five miles!"

"Education is awfully expensive."

Adele handed her a twenty-dollar bill. "Let's call this even."

Dr. Kim peeled out of The Anchorage parking lot leaving burned rubber the whole way out to the street almost before Adele's feet had hit the pavement. Limping painfully to *The irate air*, the weary traveler climbed down the ladder and tripped over Gilligan, who was sprawled across the bottom step. Adele fell face down onto the deck. "Damn you, cat," she moaned. Contritely Gilligan started to rub his furry sides around and between her beginning-to-bruise legs, meowing softly.

Thirty minutes later Adele was relatively comfy on the couch, nursing a sore body with both Gilligan and a heating pad on her chest, watching *Pirates of the Caribbean: The Curse of the Black Pearl* by lantern light on her portable DVD player.

It helps to have a sense of humor about this, she reflected. In fact, she laughed out loud when Captain Jack Sparrow was trying to wean away the prison cell keys from the prison guard dog who was making him really work hard for his freedom. She dozed off an hour later during the scene where Johnny Depp danced crazily around in circles on the deserted island where he was marooned. Soon she was enveloped in a very warm and comfortable cloud.

"What a buccaneer that boy is," asserted Anne sharply. She was wearing chocolate brown leather pantaloons with a matching leather strip to hold back her wild red hair. "And I love the eye paint. I remember linin' my Jack's eyes with kohl one naughty night when I got him to dress up in my one petticoat. Lord knows he had a rounder arse than I ever had."

Adele started to rouse herself. "Aunt Anne, why are you here?"

"I was bored with the afterlife, which wasn't happily ever after, and lookin' for a new adventure. When you lit my lanterns I was reminded of my pirate times. Many a night Jack and I played at hey-gammer-cook by those come-hither lights. . . . We may've even conceived . . . never you mind. You looked like a mighty sad lass and family should always be here to help. Reminded me of when I was facin' the gallows and had to plead my pregnant belly in defense to keep from gettin' hanged."

"Sounds like a pretty exciting life. Listen, how did you know the pieces-of-eight medallion contained a tracking system? You hinted that some jewelry is not what it seems to be."

"Well, my pretty, I keep an eye on your sister as well, but I don't reckon she's ready to hear about me just yet. That one don't have much of an imagination, but she sure looks out for you. We never had such arsy-varsy rigs to track our ships. It was all about gumption—dead reckonin' and knowin' which way the winds blew."

"Well, I wish I had a GPS system to help me sail back to Nassau. I'm still trying to regain my sea legs."

"I want you to put down anchor here, Adele."

"In Marsh Harbour? Why, Aunt Anne?"

"This holds a special place in me heart as this is where Jack buried our firstborn. I named her Beatrice. Caused a broken heart that has never been mended."

"I'm so sorry about your baby, Aunt Anne. I've been meaning to say that."

"Did you know about her?"

"I found some drawings in the chest."

"Aye, yes, the bloody chest. Jack was in the middle of an attack on a Spanish merchant ship when my time came and he couldn't make for shore until the wee one had passed through my legs. I was becalmed on Cuba with only a servant girl to help me birth my babby, and me already fevered and weak. She came out of my loins fast and healthy at first, but she took sick a few days later. By the time Jack made shore, our daughter had already passed away and I was close to death myself. My Jack lay beside me for a fortnight until my fever broke and, finally being released from Davy Jones' locker, I was strong enough to board the *Treasure* again. He saved my life there on Cuba."

But Anne had found some closure in the passing of her firstborn and started to reminisce about how Jack traveled from Cuba to the Abacos, right around The Anchorage location, in fact, and laid the infant to rest on one of the most beautiful spots in the area.

"'Twas my fault, darlin', as I was sick while I carried her. . . ."

"But you got sick, how was it your fault?" protested Adele.

"You're kind to say that to me—but hark'ee, now you need a high stomach and not a soft heart. We have to put the wind in our sails and find that worthless Curtis."

"Oh, Curtis. I hope with all my heart he has another up-close-and-personal encounter with the water and I find him just before he drowns."

"That's the spirit! And his skin will be soft enough for keelhauling," said Anne gleefully.

"Please don't think I'm not ship savvy, but I don't really understand what keelhauling is and why it's supposed to hurt so much."

Keelhauling was a subject that Anne loved to discuss as she

had turned this form of torture into a science. She used it to extract information from those poor captured souls whose ships were boarded and who were not forthcoming as to the location of their treasures. She also used it to punish sailors and gentlemen-swells alike who did not respect her. A dozen sailors and noblemen ended up waterlogged, half-drowned, and scraped raw under the hull of the *Treasure*.

"Let me tell you a little story. I once saw a scurvy few tied by ropes and attached to the yardarms on each side o' the ship and thrown overboard. They were then dragged under the bottom from bow to stern. The lads didn't die by drowning or from barnacle bashing, but I wager they wished they'd never tried to have their way with me."

"How could anyone survive such a procedure?"

Anne shrugged. "You'd have to ask the ones who did."

"Ouch," winced Adele. "I love this kind of pirate justice."

"Keep a sharp eye out for men overboard as the seas can sometimes be full of non-seaworthy men. And watch out for the Crocs. The blue ones can be the most fearsome."

"I only need to find one man, Aunt Anne," murmured Adele as she started to fall into a deeper sleep. "And I've never seen crocodiles around here, especially blue ones."

"Pay heed, Adele, the Crocs are fraught with danger and can cause you great harm."

Oh, that Anne, thought Adele drowsily. *I wish she'd stop using metaphors and tell me what she really means.* But as Adele fell into a dreamless sleep, the shadow of her ancestor tiptoed off the boat.

Chapter 9

Adele woke up the next morning feeling remarkably rested and very close to her Aunt Anne. Trying not to disturb her sleeping cat, she slid awkwardly from the side of the daybed that doubled as a sofa in the small sitting area. She was again drawn to the coffee table chest and opened it carefully, pulling out the Anne Bonny/Calico Jack etchings. Staring at one of the last in the set and locking onto her aunt's soulful face, she decided she was going to stay moored at The Anchorage. Smee would just have to deal with it.

Realizing she'd never showered in her postage-stamp-sized head, Adele decided to stuff herself in the three-by-three-foot unit. The little shower had only one faucet handle so she had to be very careful to center it right in the middle before stepping in and lathering up or she would either be scalded or frozen, depending on the temperature. For five very unsatisfactory minutes, Adele struggled and cussed before wrapping herself in a short terry cloth robe and towel-drying her hair.

The new "Battle Hymn of the Republic" ring tone on her phone made her drop her cloth belt before it was totally tied and Adele was visible to all the fish in the sea. *Yes, that's the perfect music, all right.* It was Smee on the phone. He asked if she was planning on sailing back for good this morning. If not, Marc was on the island delivering some Captain Morgan—only rum, unfortunately—and would fly her back to Nassau. Not wanting to sail back permanently, she made up the excuse that the new seat covers and table top for *The irate air* would be arriving at Marsh Harbour the day after tomorrow and she had to be there when they were delivered. Adele would explain her decision to stay at The Anchorage after she had plied Smee with a cocktail or four.

Adele did, however, accept the offer to fly back with Marc as long as she could return for the fashion installation. After a beat, Adele made a vague promise to sail back permanently to Nassau within forty-eight hours, but she would be at the office tomorrow.

"I agree, those seat covers are really important for the aesthetics of your boat," Smee conceded. "I don't mind if you're not in the office much. What I do care about is you developing a plan to find the *Hygia*."

Terminating the call, Adele belted her robe securely and attacked the tiny head with scouring powder and sponge, determined that it wouldn't defeat her. "We'll rub her 'round and scrub her 'round with holystone and sand," she belted out. She couldn't remember the rest of the song, so she repeated that part, while Gilligan roused himself to go out on deck.

The flight back to Nassau International Airport was a white-knuckler and since she and Marc were the only people on board, Adele used his right arm as an anchor against the jumps and dips. His prop plane was a small seven-seater and each bump seemed like a major thirty-foot drop. Adele's stomach started to feel as if it would empty all over the seats. To make matters even worse, her ears started to first pop and then clog, and she began to get woozy.

"Does turbulence make you dizzy?" she asked. "My ears have been bothering me for weeks."

Not sure, Marc recommended a good audiologist in Miami and to keep her mind off the roughness told Adele about how he had met Smee. It was at an amateur fencing competition in Fort Lauderdale more than two decades ago—he was sixteen and Smee was twenty-eight, but they were both competing in the same class.

"My technical marks were hands down higher than his were," Marc recalled. "But he was all showmanship, literally running up the side of the small arena wall, landing the five-foot vertical jump-off in perfect form and making a beeline straight to my heart with his foil. I thought I was in an Errol Flynn movie."

Adele started to laugh and hiccup at the same time as Marc dropped quickly in altitude to fly beneath an ominously dark and rainy cloud. "I'm sure he was wearing something straight from the Captain Hook catalog . . . perhaps a silver embroidered gull wing shirt and bright blue sash?"

"You're close. The shirt I think was gold and the sash red. He won the competition and his nanny, named Nanette—she's his NaNa's niece so that makes her Smee's first cousin once removed, and she was still working for the family even though Smee was in his late twenties then—anyway, she tried to win me over with a French kiss." That didn't happen, but the two men became fast friends.

A good pilot, but not a great one, Marc landed a bit dog-eared on the runway. He and Adele made it through customs in record time. Finding her lime green Bug in the sea of cars in the airport parking lot, she headed towards Cable Beach.

The $3,500 check from Smee was figuratively burning a hole in her pocket—she'd been careful to deposit it before leaving Marsh Harbour—and Adele decided to give herself a well-deserved treat by booking a room with a full view of the water at The Rendezvous. However, once inside, she was filled with sad thoughts of her beautiful condo, now in foreclosure, and of the happy-sexy times she'd spent there with Curtis. She couldn't help but laugh at one memory—last month's rose-petal disaster. *Plumeria wasn't the only pollen he was allergic to*, she thought, remembering his swollen eyes and throat.

"Served him right," she declared to herself as she put on a skull and crossbones t-shirt and thought about Aunt Anne.

Taking out her cell, she called Inspector Erskine who was assigned to her case. After putting her on hold for ten minutes, the dispatcher came on the line and informed her, "Inspector Erskine has been out sick all week. Can someone else help you?" She then asked for Cantrell, the sergeant she'd first met at the police station when reporting the apparent break-in and stolen treasure. After another long hold, Adele was disconnected. *Screw this*, she thought. *I'll call back tomorrow.*

It was mid-afternoon when Adele walked down to the beach hoping to run into Marvin. She just caught him as he was putting a waterproof cover over a Sun Chaser. This was the last small boat in the amateur fleet he had been presiding over as captain ever since the sun came up. Adele noticed a new garnet ring on his index finger and questioned him about the flashy acquisition.

"Always the ladies' man, Marvin. Whose jewelry box did this come from?"

"A lovely lady from Louisiana, whose husband landed a multi-million-dollar business deal. She gifted him with the garnet, but he hates rings, including his wedding band, so she gave it to me instead of returning it to the jeweler."

Adele helped Marvin move the little sailboat to the side of a sand bank serving as the end-of-day gathering place for the resort's rentals. "Tell me something, did you ever really care for Babs?"

Marvin stood up straight and shook the remaining sand from his body. "She was the love of my life and still is, Delly. We were always faced with bad timing. When Angela and I split up she had just married your dad, and when he died I was involved with Suzanne. She left me for a South African captain and your mom went through her boat boy period before settling down with Sheldon."

Telling Adele that he had some work to do, Marvin walked down to the small dock and Adele followed. Meeting Tim, the tattooed and very buff crewmember from the 32-foot McGregor sailboat *Bodacious Ta Tas*, Marvin handed him a brand new, high-tech wireless wind direction system. "Tim, this is Delly Bonny."

"Pleased to meet you, ma'am. You must be Babs Bonny's daughter," he said, holding out an oil-stained hand.

Adele replied with a limp handshake and one word, "Right."

Marvin jumped on deck of the boat and the men got down to the work at hand. Marvin slipped into a small rope harness and strapped on a tool belt, and Tim started to hoist him up the rigging with an electric winch. With the crewmember's strength and Marvin's agility that belied his seventy years, Marvin was hoisted up the thirty feet to the top of the mast in a matter of seconds.

"Wow, Marvin, you look like you're flying."

The salty sailor smiled down at her. He took a screwdriver out of his tool belt and loosened one of the clamps that held the rusty, old wind director anchored at the top of the mast. Next Tim hoisted up a loosely wrapped package containing the high-tech version of all sailors' "must-have." The handy little upgraded device was composed of several small lidless boxes built to register wind speed and direction, and it replaced the old and elementary wind director Marvin was disconnecting.

"The old system looks like a torpedo with a small windmill on the end," observed Adele, shading her eyes as she looked up at Marvin.

"Nothing wrong with it at all." Marvin tied it to the rope and sent it down to Tim. "But knowing Captain Clancy, he just wants all the newest bells and whistles."

This new wireless system boasted an outdoor and indoor temperature reader, a relative humidity tracker, and a wind speed and direction device, and it even measured perceptible rainfall. On the descent down the mast, Marvin removed the old wire, feeding it smoothly into the inside of the mast to where Tim disconnected it.

"Man, thanks, Marvin," he said. "Captain Clancy thinks I'm much handier than I really am."

"No problem," responded Marvin. "The only stipulation is that I get to keep the old device to give to a special friend."

"No problem," echoed Tim, handing the system Adele had described as a torpedo to him.

"You and your harems," reprimanded Adele. "I didn't know you were so handy either."

Marvin stepped away from the bow of the *Bodacious Ta Tas.* "Your mom always said I was great with my hands . . . when I was around."

"Was Babs really worth all this angst?" asked Adele.

"Is she really worth all your anger?" parried Marvin.

"Maybe love is blind, Marvin, but she was never very nice to you. Why are you always defending her?"

"It was more my fault than hers. I guess I just have the soul of a sailor and never wanted to be tied down. This three-year stint at The Rendezvous has been the longest time I've spent anywhere, and if you want to have a family you have to put down some roots—somewhere."

Realizing that conversations with Marvin about Babs always ended in an impasse, Adele headed back to the resort lobby and decided to buy herself a drink in the beautiful Island Bar. But something about all the marble and elegance made her feel uncomfortable, so she ordered a glass of chardonnay to go and took the elevator up to her room. Somehow that didn't make her happy either. Looking down at her skull and crossbones t-shirt, she thought about Aunt Anne. How would she track the *Hygia*? *Would she sail the sea of Abaco without Jack? Damn right she would.* Adele decided to visit The Provocative Pirates Museum to find some inspiration. In addition to the rather cheesy historical displays, the museum had the best set of navigational charts on the island, with detailed maps of dozens of inlets and coves around the area as well as their local topography. Leaving her half-full glass of chardonnay on the bed stand, she headed out the door, down to the lobby, and into the street.

Adele knew that Aunt Anne and Calico Jack commanded very different types of ships in those days, but they managed to find the ships hidden in the coves and caves across the hundreds of Bahamian islands when they only had compasses, sextants, and navigation charts to work with. Perhaps some of their "ship-dar" would rub off on her.

The glaring mural on the side of the museum was as garish

in the afternoon sun as it had been the last time Adele looked at it. Once again her ears started to ring, competing with the music being played over the sound system. Paying the ten-dollar admission, she entered a dark and narrow wooden hallway and got an eyeful of a full-sized pirate ship replica inside the building. This was Blackbeard's ship, the *Revenge*. Continuing to walk, she lowered her head as she passed by the gift shop so she wouldn't have to answer any questions regarding the state of the family treasure. Unfortunately the navigation room was closed for the day, so she decided to enjoy the exhibits before leaving the museum.

She walked by a family of four listening intently to piped-in music, representing the sounds of the handmade instruments that were played aboard ships in the eighteenth century.

Adele overheard a twelve-year-old boy read: "It was a short life, but a merry one."

How hokey can you get? she asked herself.

Moving on ahead of them, she spied a pair of familiar shoulders framed in a yellow tank top. Rocky seemed mesmerized, reading a plaque about life in the Merchant Navy. Walking up quietly behind him, she read about crew members frequently working eighteen hours a shift, heaving ropes in all kinds of weather.

"And when was the last time you went aloft in a gale?" asked Adele.

Rocky jumped a little before turning to face Adele. Then he smiled. "I'm just a tourist on this island. What's your excuse for wasting an afternoon?"

Adele passed in front of an oil painting of Anne Bonny. "Notice a resemblance?"

"Well, let's see. You both have red hair, green eyes, and I'm thinking a bad attitude."

They continued to walk down the darkened corridors and past two charcoal drawings of Anne and Calico Jack, washed with colors. Anne looked bold and brazen wearing a battered, three-cornered hat and navy blue silk shirt, complete with flashing eyes and flowing hair. Jack seemed to somehow be looking over at his lover out of the corner of one eye, with a calm, affectionate glance, his sword placed quietly at his side.

"We have more in common than you think," said Adele. "She's a blood relation . . . my Aunt Anne, thirteen times removed."

Rocky stopped in his tracks. "Now this starts to make sense. I should have gotten it when you told me your last name was Bonny and you were in the treasure retrieval business, but I was focused in on saving your life. Does your family have any idea what happened to the rumored Bonny/Calico Jack stolen loot?"

"Oh, no, does everyone know about the theft?"

"I wouldn't think so," replied Rocky. "Remember, I'm a SEAL. Even when I'm on leave I have my sources." He waggled his eyebrows like Groucho Marx.

They walked into the Coins Room and, in addition to the display of every kind of money ever known to pirate-kind, Adele and Rocky came into full view of the hokiest of all the Anne Bonny displays—a movie poster for *Anne of the Indies*, the saga of history's most famous pirate queen, with a boast that the film could be seen in fabulous Technicolor.

Adele confessed to Rocky that the family's stockpile was probably aboard the *Beautiful Bonny* along with Curtis and Mandy. "It was sent to me to get appraised before the exhibit at the Pirates Museum in January. But that ass-bite stole it all the moment the treasure arrived at our condo."

Rocky turned to face her. "Man, that really sucks. Are the jewelry and coins insured?"

Adele thought about this hard before finally understanding what this theft really meant to her family, and ultimately to her. Babs was right. "Damn it. That doesn't matter. This is my family history and heritage; it's important to me as a Bonny, an indirect descendant of the most famous female pirate who ever lived, to actually have some of these pieces and to understand and appreciate where I came from."

Adele leaned on the Navy SEAL, who did his best to comfort her. "My friend Smee is right, it's time I should embrace this wonderful woman and try to save and protect what Calico Jack gave up his life for."

"You're absolutely right, Adele. Now what are you going to do about it?"

Adele felt her spirits drop back down to earth, thinking about the difficult task at hand. Should she ask him for advice and help? Could she trust someone who'd saved her life? *But I wouldn't know where to begin describing the Man-Overboard satellite system and my hope that Curtis will activate it. Too soon for trust,* she decided.

"Hmm, let's just say I have the beginning of a plan," she cryptically revealed to Rocky.

Walking out into the museum grounds, Adele and Rocky found a series of silly plywood cutouts of both male and female pirates with Calico Jack's Skull and Cross-Swords flag blowing in the background. "Speak of the devil," she laughed, snagging Rocky's arm and jumping up to the cutout of Anne. As the family of four had just arrived in the courtyard, Adele asked the dad to shoot a photo of them with their heads inside of the cutouts. Adele's "Anne" two-dimensional character was waving a cutlass, while Rocky's "Calico Jack" cutout was brandishing an ax. The cutlass, hung from a belt around the waist, was used to back and slash in close-quarters fighting. It was one of the most violent weapons used by pirates and, once mastered, was the most murderous tool in the Caribbean.

Adele flashed back to the image of Aunt Anne when she had first visited just over a week ago. The devilish take-no-prisoners grin and flaming red hair were so much more fabulous in person. Her ears started to ring again and she felt herself drift back into her other pirate world. *Not now, Aunt Anne!* But the pull of the fantasy, or alternate universe—or whatever it was—gripped her so purposefully there was nothing she could do to stop it. Adele imagined being on board the *Treasure* with her Aunt Anne and

Jack Rackham. The trio was doing battle with several jaw-snapping, teeth-gnashing blue crocodiles slithering their way up on deck. Anne and Jack were fighting with their cutlass and axe head. Poor Adele. All she had to defend herself with was her canvas messenger bag. She hit one of the blue crocs hard on the head, but the reptile bit off the strap, leaving her defenseless as it continued to aim its slimy, powerful body in her direction.

Chapter 10

"Are you alright, Adele? You just looked like you were ready to pass out on me." Adele heard Rocky's voice and began to open her eyes.

Adele came back to the present just as her cell once again blasted out "The Battle Hymn of the Republic." "I guess I'm just overly tired."

"You've got to get another ring tone. This song always makes me want to snap to attention," complained Rocky.

"At ease, sailor," she laughed, answering her phone. She heard a very excited Alli on the other end of her line, so she put her sister on speaker. The same MOB frequency Curtis' necklace was tuned to had just been activated. Alli explained that her friend Petey's personal locator beacon was still not perfect, but there was a good chance Curtis had gone overboard and the medallion turned on its tracking system, and if so, the radio frequency transmitter would be sending longitude and latitude data. The AUTEC frequency location system had just tracked the location and if she had a pencil handy, Alli would give her the coordinates.

"The signal is emanating from the northeast side of Cat Island, over a hundred miles away. The exact coordinates are 24.31531 Latitude and 75.457777 Longitude. Did you get that, Adele? It looks like the yacht is anchored somewhere near Smokey Point."

"I know just where it is. Remember when Babs was obsessed with Sidney Poitier and sailed over to Cat to try and find where he lived?"

Alli sidestepped the question. "Do you have a boat you can borrow? I don't think *The irate air* can travel that fast."

Adele looked at Rocky, who gave a strong affirmative nod. "Yes, I do."

"And do you understand the coordinates I gave you?"

Adele looked at Rocky and saw another strong affirmative nod.

"Got them both and gotta go. Thanks so much, Alli, and I love you."

"Go get him, Adele, and be careful. Do you have someone who can go with you?"

Adele looked at Rocky, who gave yet another strong affirmative nod.

"Three for three. Don't worry about me. I can take care of myself and I do have a little bit of military backup."

"What military backup, Adele?"

"I'll call you after we board the *Bonny.*"

Adele hung up and turned to Rocky. "I learned about longitude and latitude with Gracie's help and it's all coming back to me. But I could sure use a refresher course. Do you really have a boat I can borrow?"

"Not borrow exactly, but you can join me for the search." They began walking towards her car. "Longitude and latitude are imaginary lines that grid the earth to help find a specific location. I can brush you up on it once we get moving."

"Sounds good!—I mean. . . . Isn't Cat Island about a ten-hour sail from here? If Alli has really found Curtis, he will be long gone by the time we get to the boat."

"Not at my speed, but we had better get going. By the way, who was that energetic woman on the phone?"

"My sister Alli. She's a Sonar Range Testing Scientist at AUTEC and somehow she was able to get a locator beacon on Curtis' body."

"So that's the plan you mentioned. How cool is that? Your sister must be a really interesting woman."

Adele thought for an instant. "She is."

They took Adele's Bug across town to the marina—Rocky

sat sideways in the back seat—then Rocky ran down to an outer slip with Adele close on his heels. He jumped into a 32-foot high-performance "cigarette" speedboat seemingly tailor-made for James Bond and looked incredibly comfortable behind the wheel. Adele climbed onboard and Rocky left the marina before she got her lifejacket snapped. Heading for open water, he really cranked up the Sunsation Dominator SS, soon speeding crazily at fifty miles an hour towards Cat Island, definitely dominating the waves.

"How could those drug runners get caught in this boat?" asked Rocky impishly. "But they're in Fulton County Prison and we're sightseeing across open water. Sucks to be them."

Cat Island was thought to be Columbus' original landing site in the New World. Rumor had it that the island was named after pirate Arthur Catt who used to frequent the area, and it was where the Loyalists forged the first permanent settlement in 1783. Historic ruins of their fabulous plantation houses, built more than two hundred and twenty years ago, still remain today.

Just two hours later they passed Arthur's Town, turned towards the top of Cat Island and headed northeast around the tip to Smokey Point. Off in the distance Adele spied a sparkling stern, accented with double navy and marine blue striping. As Rocky approached broadside, she saw it was a 42-foot Hunter Passage.

As Rocky pulled closer Adele read the name on the stern—*Dead End*. "Damn! This boat could be the *Beautiful Bonny*'s twin."

Approaching port side, Adele and Rocky saw this was a party boat with a celebration in full swing. Two bikini-clad babes were slathering on the sunscreen, while a third with long black hair was in the cabin blending up frozen cocktails, woozily pushing a red button in and out. Two leather-skinned men were making great progress on a Kalik Keg, the beer of the Bahamas. Pouring a full pint over his sun-soaked body, one of the sailors—who was wearing jams so low the very tops of his privates were peering out into the bright sunlight—invited them to come aboard. This was

Diego. Barefooted, with dirty, callused feet, he was wearing a giant shark tooth necklace, which he rubbed with great care. He looked like one mean hombre with a five-day growth of beard and way too much neck and arm hair.

Helping to tie the cigarette boat to the *Dead End*, Diego hoisted Adele aboard and gave her thin white t-shirt—and what was underneath it—the once-over, while leaving Rocky to come across from one hull to the other by himself. Once on board, Adele saw the differences between this and her own boat. The wood was much deeper in color, and it had not been taken care of very well. There were several charred cigarette burns near the rigging lines, and scratches and scrapes covered the back benches. The wooden wheel was covered in tattered leather and there was trash scattered everywhere. *What a waste of a beautiful boat*, Adele thought.

Rocky made the three-foot, slightly vertical jump from one boat to the other effortlessly. One of the sunbathers took notice, jumping up from her lounge chair and walking over to him.

"Well, hello there, I'm Suzi," cooed the bikini babe as she swayed her hips subtly. "Care for a cocktail?"

"I'm Rocky. 'No, thanks' on the cocktail. How about you, Adele?"

Feeling that she had no time for chitchat, she shook her head and turned her attention to the sailor who had brought her aboard and the more put-together-looking man standing next to him.

"Sorry to disturb you. We had reason to believe this boat was the *Beautiful Bonny* and, based on its tracking system, that my husband had fallen overboard. He doesn't know how to swim very well so we came out to investigate."

"I'm the one who fell overboard," said the put-together man.

He showed her the tracking system attached to his belt, raising his eyebrows at seeing the red, blinking light.

"Didn't know it was on, actually. We were playing Walk the Plank and I took the game too far. I guess your husband and I are on the same frequency." He gave a halfbaked leer at that, but then continued to maunder vaguely. "This is a great spot to party. Picked up the girls at Fernandez Bay Village. They were a bit bored there. My name's Winston. Where are you coming from? Do join us for a drink."

"We powered over from Nassau, and since the lady's husband isn't here I guess we're headed right back." Rocky sounded aggressively sober in comparison.

"Oh, stay and play." Suzi sidled up to Rocky. "Walking the Plank is not the only game we know, if you get my meaning. My friend Coco makes one mean Mai Tai."

She walked over to the cabin where the black-haired Coco had just finished blending up another pitcher of frozen cocktails. "Hi, have a drink," she said, handing a giant tumbler to Rocky.

"No, thanks—I'm driving."

"But I'm not." Disappointed not to have gleaned any information about the *Bonny*, Adele took the glass out of Rocky's hand—surprising him, to judge by his expression. "How long have you been anchored here, Winston?" Adele took a sip, then two, of the cocktail. "This is fabulous."

"Thanks," responded Coco. "Three kinds of rum, but who's counting?"

"And what a party it's been!" Suzi started to rub Rocky's shoulder. "But it could be better, if you know what I mean?"

"Back off, Suzi," admonished Winston as he and Rocky exchanged glances.

Adele took another sip and finished the glass, shaking off a brain freeze. "Yep, I taste all three rums. Hey, you haven't by any chance seen a yacht with, believe it or not, a figurehead on its helm? I know this sounds strange, but it's a 51-foot beauty named *Hygia*, and seems to have wandered off without permission."

Winston looked at Diego, who smiled before answering. "Haven't seen it. Where did it go missing?"

"In the water between Nassau and Eleuthera. With the Goddess of Water figurehead, it should be pretty easy to spot."

"Belong to a friend of yours?"

"Well, not exactly," returned Adele, slurring her words a bit. "A guy by the name of Mr. Bri-"

Rocky took Adele by the shoulder and spun her around towards him. "Well, thanks for the drink, but we've got to head back. Rented boat, you know."

The cocktail had really gone to Adele's head as she stumbled towards the side of the *Dead End*, and Diego watched her carefully as Rocky strong-armed her into the cigarette boat.

As they powered away, Diego slipped down the ladder to the back berth and made a quiet phone call. "Hey, BJ, it's me, Diego. There was some broad just on the boat asking about the *Hygia*, and some guy with her. Sounds like she was hired by the insurance company to track it down. Name's Adele and she's a hot little number. . . . Will do. Later, dude."

Going back on deck, Diego saw Coco in the cabin, still playing with the red button in a puzzled sort of way. He grabbed her arm so tight that tears welled in her eyes.

"What the hell are you doing? You stupid cow—you turned on the beacon and brought them here!" With a full sweep of his muscled arms, Diego then knocked her into the water. "Oops."

As Winston and the girls rushed to the side of the boat to throw a life preserver towards the thrashing Coco, Diego informed the drunken group that he was going to take the small seaplane out for a flight around the cay. No one questioned him further. Grabbing a wide-brimmed flop hat and pair of blue clogs, he untied the dinghy and motored slowly over to a little cove where the plane was waiting.

Tying the dinghy to a large rock, Diego climbed up into the cockpit like a seasoned professional and started the two engines. Gliding into open water, he took off with a thud and bounce, soon catching up with Adele and Rocky. Keeping his distance and positioning the plane between the cigarette boat and the sun, he watched effortlessly from the comfort of the cockpit and started to follow them back to Nassau.

Behind the wheel of the speeding cigarette boat, Rocky checked on an irritatingly noisy ball-bearing. Not able to eliminate the sound, he had to shout as he unloaded on Adele once they were away from the *Dead End.* He scolded her for being so amateurish as to reveal the purpose of her mission to perfect strangers. "You call yourself a retrieval expert, you need to start acting like one. Perhaps you should have filled me in on your other case before talking to total strangers."

Adele turned on Rocky. "What gives you the right to push me around?" she retorted angrily. "You're not the boss of me and you're not in charge of this operation. I got all the *advice* I ever needed from Curtis. My other cases are none of your business. What I was doing was asking strategic questions, not revealing my mission!"

"No, you were also getting ready to tell them your exact job title and who hired you. *Not* strategic. You'll make my job a lot easier if you just learn to keep quiet."

Adele could feel her blood beginning to boil. "*Your* job? Is that so? Fine. You're welcome to leave my company, *any time.*"

"We're on a boat, if you haven't noticed—my boat."

"Your very noisy boat!"

"Look who's talking, when your car is pinging like mad!"

Adele drew a long breath through clenched teeth. "Well, I'd say the boat we just visited had a very appropriate name. It seems we've hit a dead end in more ways than one!"

Adele and Rocky traveled the rest of the distance to the small private marina next to The Rendezvous in stone cold silence. Looking at Adele's firm jaw line, Rocky thought back to his last, and only, serious relationship. He'd always had a soft spot for redheads and the beautiful strawberry blonde named Madeline just about broke his heart. Twenty-nine at the time, he had just completed a six-month mission in Afghanistan and wanted to surprise Madeline when he returned to Tampa twenty-four hours earlier than scheduled. Bursting open the door to their shared apartment with a giant bouquet of pink carnations, he found her on the couch straddling a junior officer. He used his clout to get the JG transferred out of country, and Rocky had played the field for the last four years. *Maybe brunettes would treat me better*, he mused to himself. *But I'm really turned on by that crimson head of hair*, he thought as he stared at Adele's blowing and beautiful red locks.

The loud noise of the bad bearing brought him out of his reveries. Rocky pulled up to the dock, Adele sullenly jumped out, and neither one said goodbye.

Diego had landed in the water near the end of one of the empty slips, to see what Adele and Rocky were going to do before deciding whether or not to leave the plane. He saw her climb angrily out of the cigarette boat and Rocky power away almost immediately, so he glided as close to the dock as he could get. He jumped into someone else's keelboat and motored it to the dock, not bothering to tie it up. Rocky was already long gone and Diego followed Adele, whom he had named *that Adele woman*, back to the resort.

I need a drink, Adele thought as she parked her car at The Rendezvous, so before going up to her room she went into the Tropical Bar. There she saw the back of a perfectly coiffed dark honey blonde standing next to the open sliding glass doors. She recognized Elaine, who was just putting her iPhone into her purse and giving a goodbye hug and tight squeeze to a man who had long dark hair and a large gold hoop earring. His back was to her, so Adele did not get a good look at him as he slipped out the door.

Adele went up to her friend. "Wow, Elaine, who is that? Looks a bit like a pirate."

Blushing faintly, Elaine told her he was her new friend Bobby. She then threw her arms around Adele and said how sorry she was, for everything.

"How did you know?"

"I'm sorry, Adele, everyone at the club knows, especially

when Carlos boasted he's now the big kahuna in dance as Mandy wasn't coming back. I can't stand his classes; all we do now is exercise . . . and hard. Can I buy you a drink?"

Unhappy over the day's events and her fight with Rocky, Adele quickly agreed one cocktail couldn't hurt. "Sure, I'll have a Blue Marlin." They bellied up to the bar.

"Ditto," Elaine called to the bartender. "They're saying you moved out of your condo too. So what are you going to do?"

Elaine's eyes widened in amazement when Adele told her about Smee, Pirate's Plunder, and tracking down the double dolphins necklace. "What happened to your teaching position?"

Adele had to review what had happened since she'd last talked to Elaine. "Well, the Academy set me loose because they're cutting all their arts classes, but I'll be teaching an adult-ed class part-time after the holidays. Meantime, I'm now a retrieval expert," she boasted, and confidently predicted one of the first things she would retrieve was her own boat. In addition, she'd just got her second assignment: to find the *Hygia*, a fifty-one classic sloop that had disappeared west of Eleuthera.

"I don't believe in the Bermuda triangle and it couldn't have just disappeared, especially displaying a figurehead of the Goddess of Water on the hull. It was hand-carved in England and must weigh several hundred pounds."

"What does the figurehead look like?" asked Elaine, a slight frown on her face.

"She's about six feet tall with golden enamel hair and is wearing painted white and gold robes. She's really pretty, from the photo Smee showed me."

As they finished their Blue Marlin cocktails, Elaine started to bite her red-enameled finger nails and a little bit of red debris landed in her empty glass. "This sounds awfully dangerous, Adele. And drastic. Why this sudden change? Babs has plenty of money for you both."

"And for Curtis' debts too? No, I'm not going to live on her charity. Oh, I'm also making a change in the scenery and moving to The Anchorage at Marsh Harbour." Adele stared at Elaine's ragged nails.

"But isn't that a marina? I didn't think you had a boat anymore."

"Oh, that. I found Babs' 27-foot 1972 Catalina, did a little 9-1-1 and sailed it back to The Anchorage and think I'll stay there for a while." She told some anecdotes about redecorating and refitting *The irate air*, but Elaine wasn't a receptive audience. "Anyway, it gets me away from Cable Beach and a life I'm trying to forget. Did I tell you I'll be teaching in Marsh Harbour?"

"But it must be a wreck. How could you live on a little thing like that? I've never seen you like this, Adele. You need to snap out of it," Elaine urged with great trepidation.

I need to snap out of it? You're the one biting your nails! "Thanks for your concern, Elaine, but I know what I've got to do and the police haven't been any help yet. I've got to find the *Bonny.*"

At four a.m. Adele was tossing and turning in bed. At six a.m. she was counting the threads in her 600-ply Egyptian cotton sheets. Something was not right and she couldn't fall asleep until she figured out what the problem was. She struggled to sit up, experiencing the worst ringing in her ears yet. Suddenly she got it: it was hard to go to sleep without a visit from Aunt Anne. Deciding to put her insomnia to good use, she got dressed and, after an infusion of coffee, checked out of the resort and walked downstairs to the spa, hoping one of the fitness teachers might have overheard Mandy and her big mouth talking about Curtis and the *Beautiful Bonny.*

She watched as Melissa finished leading a ninety-minute yoga class and mimicked the last sun salutation, bending backwards into a graceful bow. She smiled to herself, realizing that she was still more flexible than the twenty-year-old instructress at the front of the room. Melissa was toweling off when Adele approached her. "Hi, Mel. How's it going?"

Melissa looked at her warily. "Fine. What's up, Adele?"

"I wondered if you knew where Mandy and Curtis were sailing to as you girls share more than fitness tips."

"No, Adele. I didn't know Mandy was with Curtis," Melissa lied glibly. "I just thought she was taking a week off."

"Well, if you happen to hear from her during her vacation, please give me a call as there's a reward involved. The spa has my cell number."

"Sure will," promised Melissa.

Adele walked away, circling around the spa's front desk and hiding behind a pole a few feet away from the yoga teacher. Her hunch was right. Ninety seconds later, Melissa was on the phone. "Well, Adele paid me a visit. No, Mandy, I didn't tell her a thing. . . . Where are you? . . . Wow. So you stayed within sixty miles of Nassau, isn't that near Gov-" The loud speaker interrupted their conversation, calling Melissa to her next yoga class. "Gotta go."

Who needs the police? Adele silently crowed. Feeling very proud of her sleuthing ability, Adele had her first clue to the whereabouts of her boat and felt relieved that the *Bonny* was still in local waters. *Melissa said Gov-, must be Governor's Harbour, only a four-hour sail from Marsh Harbour. I'm going to fly back today and head out early tomorrow*, she thought as she headed away from the spa.

She felt very independent and competent—until she stopped and asked Marvin to please have her Bug checked out.

Diego Hidalgo had taken off the shark's tooth necklace, dressed in a stained t-shirt and donned the flop hat that he now wore low over his forehead. He'd followed the *Adele woman* from the resort and down the beach as she talked to that old guy, handed him something, and then headed northeast away from Cable Beach and towards East Bay Street and the downtown area of Nassau. Cutting through to the lobby of another marble-floored and high-beamed hotel, with Diego discreetly behind her, she arrived outside just in time for scattered showers. As it started to rain harder, she shifted her fat messenger bag to her other shoulder.

The *Adele woman* was in plain sight half a block away in front of him when she looked up and down the street and called out, "Taxi!" Diego turned aside momentarily. But, fortunately for him, she had no luck.

He found himself amused that she was not a particularly patient person, judging from her fidgeting during the ten minutes she tried to find a cab. He had plenty of time to make a phone call, and then to see the boss' car pull up nearby in case she did score a taxi after all. She seemed to give up the taxi idea and flagged down a local bus painted all over with the Jamaican colors of the rainbow and flowers on each of the grimy windows. Well, the boss could follow a bus just as well as he could a taxi. The bus driver opened the door to more passengers than any code enforcement officer would have approved of. Putting his head down so as not to be seen by the *Adele woman*, he crowded in behind. What started out as simply a severely crowded bus turned into an accident waiting to happen when more and more locals crammed on the vehicle with the driver grinding gears at each half-mile stop.

The *Adele woman* was sitting on what was once an aisle seat, but was no longer even close to the aisle as a large man with bulging biceps pulled down the rumble seat next to her. He filled the narrow seat beyond capacity and she sat squashed up against a very angular man wearing glasses, her shoulders squeezed tight and her breaths shallow. The old bus continued to amble along.

Diego suppressed a laugh at the *Adele woman*'s growing discomfort. He watched when a cranky chicken, sitting on the lap of the woman behind her, zeroed in on Adele's tender neck and took a peck at her pink skin. She moved as if to raise a hand to the site of her injury, but she was pinned in too tightly. She scooted forward in her seat, still not looking at Diego sitting across from her. Once there was a narrow aisle separating the rows, but he pulled down the other jump seat and they were instantly just one seat apart. To hide his face, he took out his cell phone and pretended to make a call, periodically leaning forward to look past the large man and keep tabs on his prey.

He saw the angular man sitting next to Adele pull a small bottle of cologne from his breast shirt pocket and dab it liberally on to his sweating forehead and behind his ears. Two seats away, Diego could easily recognize it as Old Spice, a trigger for memories only he could find pleasant.

The pungent aroma hit Adele like an overflowing outhouse. She couldn't help thinking back to the subtle scent of Curtis' cologne. *Snap out of it.*

"Whoa," she objected as he started to pat another drop onto his chest. "More is not necessarily better."

The angular man raised his arms and offered her the bottle. His little movement set off the smell of body odor that had Adele covering her nose.

"Forgot to put on deodorant this morning and my girl Jenny thinks Old Spice smells like carnations. What do you think?"

"I think I'm going to be sick and have to get off this bus right now," gagged Adele.

"This is my stop too," he agreed pleasantly, putting on another dab of Old Spice and leaning down to collect his knapsack.

This was too much for Adele and, after pulling the chain to alert the driver that a passenger wanted to get off the bus, she reached down to the floor as well to gather up her bag. She head-butted the angular man, staggered a bit and fell into the lap of the man two seats over, who pulled his hat lower over his forehead. Adele's gaze traveled down to his legs, his hairy knees, and further down to a pair of dirty and callus-heeled feet. Feet in blue Crocs clogs. A flashbulb went off in Adele's mind.

"Watch out for the blue Crocs." Anne's voice came through loud and clear. Adele looked up at the man's face and stiffened in shock—she tried to get up, away from the pair of Crocs—but she was much too late. Adele felt a sharp prick on the back of her neck and then a severe burning sensation, before her body went limp.

Diego yelled, "My sister, she's passed out." Sweaty passengers made way the best they could for him as he carried the semiconscious Adele over his shoulder like a sack of potatoes, along the aisle and down the several bus steps. Winston hurried up from behind the bus and helped Diego carry Adele, softly moaning, to the boss' car.

Adele was still in a drug-induced stupor, but thought she was in a small powerboat and then heard the sound of a propeller plane starting up. Pulled roughly out of the dinghy, she was lifted into the seaplane where Diego was behind the controls. She started to struggle but another needle prick to the back of her neck quickly quieted her down. The sedative did its work and all Adele felt and heard was an airplane picking up speed in the water before once again being in the land of Nod.

Sometime later she woke up in a smoky warehouse, the smell both acrid and putrid in her nostrils. She painfully remembered seeing the guy from the *Dead End*—Diego, right?—just before everything went blooey. Her cheek hurt from lying on her lumpy messenger bag. She rose to her feet, hugging the bag to her as the only familiar item in a crazy world. As she tried to see through the deepening gray haze, her ears were roaring with pain when she bumped into a lone silver chariot without the horses. She clutched a flimsy gold leaf statue of King Tut to steady her balance. Flames were starting to flicker under a fortress-like door but Adele continued to investigate where she was and how to get out. All around her were bizarre props including several different sizes of false plywood boat hulls and sterns, an old metal helmet and ornate carved spear, a crossbow with a quiver of arrows, and a half dozen portable Andy Gump outhouses. She couldn't see a way out of the walls of a fake western fort that started to close in on her. *Breathe, silly*, she thought, but her breath was coming in gasps. A rat scurried across the floor and Adele heard a scream. *Who the hell . . . ?—Oh, my God, it was me.* As bad as things were in the fire, she felt in a way as if it were happening again. *It's as scary in here as it was in that shed,* she thought, going back in her life twenty-seven years and two months earlier.

Her sister hadn't meant to lock her in there, not really. She and Alli had just been playing a game of hide and seek as part of their Halloween fun. But in her eagerness to win, Adele had hidden herself in their backyard shed. And Alli, when she figured out where her sister was, had locked the door from the outside as a joke, going home for apple cider. Adele couldn't get out and waited in the dark as spiders started to crawl across her bare feet and silverfish darted down her neck. She still shuddered at the remembered squishy feeling of stepping on what proved to be a dead rat.

Back then she had pounded against the shed door, screaming, until her knuckles were black and blue. It finally opened. Facing her stood a skeleton. She didn't think she was dead, and definitely couldn't have gone to Heaven. The skeleton gave her a gap-toothed smile. Her taunting sister had tried on her Halloween costume a day early and had come back to the shed to find out what the screaming was about.

The warehouse was just as spooky as that old shed and, though Adele hated to admit it, she was still afraid of the dark. Add smoke and the potential to be burned alive and it was anything but a good night. She tried pounding now, willing to face a skeleton or any other creature inhabiting the warehouse. She slung her bag cross-body so she could pound with both hands while still holding her lifeline to normality. But no one came to her rescue. Scooping up the crossbow and leather strapped pouch with five metal arrows, which seemed to be the only useful items in the place, she tried to catch her breath behind several plastic palm trees but they were burning hot to the touch. She slung the pouch over one shoulder and clutched the bow as if she really knew how to use it. Facing her with white milky eyes and a mouth half full of broken rotted teeth was a Bruce-from-*Jaws* lookalike. The shark seemed ready to ravish her.

Falling back into a giant papier-mâché hand of King Kong, she was suddenly face to face with a dead body lying between Kong's thumb and middle finger. Adele gasped, and the stench gagged her. She coughed, her eyes ran, she swallowed to avoid puking, but she couldn't turn away. Hey, the dead man's face was familiar from Smee's loving photos—it was Woody! He was definitely not smiling now; his neck was broken, his face discolored, his head lying sideways in a ninety-degree, very uncomfortable-looking angle. His eyes and mouth were open and reminded Adele of the terrified man in Munch's painting, *The Scream*. His neck was covered with deep black and blue bite marks which were about the same size as Bruce's teeth. *Oh, my God*, she gasped. Woody had been dead for several days; his wounds were starting to rot and fester. Another whiff of the odor caught her at the back of her throat again. Panicky, she shoved at him with the crossbow, letting out a loud scream. But no one could hear her.

Moving away as quickly as possible, she slipped around several flaming boat helms and red-hot fort walls. Adele was beginning to panic. She felt herself start to lose consciousness.

In her stupor, Adele was suddenly thrust into Anne's world where her aunt was calmly sitting in front of a giant bonfire, stoking it with the same crossbow Adele was gripping in her hands.

"Follow the embers, my pretty."

"But I can't see anything!"

"Don't be afeard, Adele. Not all walls are solid and the crossbow will show you the way. Not exactly a cutlass, but it will do," whispered Anne. "Now follow the embers. Handsomely, handsomely. . . ."

Down on her hands and knees, trying to keep conscious, Adele saw a crumbling wall almost alive with red, burning embers. She rolled over on one elbow so she could load and crank and shoot the crossbow into the glowing target. The arrow easily went through the wall. Gathering her strength and composure, Adele scrambled to her feet and charged at the weakened spot. Ashes and sparks fell all around her, and she staggered back with a hurt shoulder, but the wall remained intact. *How do they do this in the movies?* Thinking for a second about the most effective dance kick she knew, she did a strong *jeté* leap through the air and charged the wall again, hitting it with all her might. Though Adele yelled in pain, this time the wall buckled, making a space just big enough for her to get through. Her bag caught at the burning wood for a frightening moment, but then she was free. She landed hard on a wooden surface.

Finding herself outside on a remote dock, she rolled off the wood and down onto the beach before most of the warehouse collapsed, engulfing the entire area in flames.

"I couldn't have done it better myself. I like your crossbow almost as much as my cutlass," praised Aunt Anne. "Now shiver your timbers and sail out of here."

Adele tried to stand up, but neither her bad ankle nor her shaky legs would cooperate.

"Get your land legs, lass, and hoof it. The red iron horses are on their way."

Chapter 11

Coughing and gasping, Adele tried to catch her breath in the damp dark of night. Looking at her watch, she saw it was five a.m. and pitch black, all except for the hellish fire she wanted to escape. *I lost a whole day! Checked out early in the morning, and now it's tomorrow already.* A dense cloud cover had obscured the usually astonishing array of stars. She made the mistake of trying to straighten her light-colored t-shirt, only succeeding in smearing it further with black soot. *I'm such a slob*, she thought. Looking down at her once beautiful and elegant hands, now a mass of grimy, red, fire-seared creases and cracked, dirt-encrusted fingernails, she started to cry. The injuries seemed to be only surface burns but they hurt like hell. Adele crawled down to the water and soaked them gently in the soothing salt water.

And just think I used to make a living with these hands. I'm going to find the bastards and when I figure out how to use my crossbow, I'm going to make them pay for a full spa manicure and fill. Adele laughed feebly as she realized the anticlimax of her thought.

Walking out to a deserted and dusty sidewalk flanking a narrow one-lane road, she finally recognized where she was—on the central Marsh Harbour docks. She hitched up her bag and quiver, shouldered the crossbow, and started to move slowly towards the center of Marsh Harbour and The Anchorage more than three miles away. Realizing that she must look like a bag lady or worse, Adele decided to stick to the shadows when the fire engines passed her.

Downtown Marsh Harbour had taken on a ghostly demeanor due to a very rare low cloud ceiling clinging to the tops of the buildings and occasional streetlights. Walking by a coral and green clapboard patio surrounded by several beach-type stores, Adele saw a beautiful sight. Instead of the traditional manger scene in celebration of Christmas, the area was aglow with crowned mermaids and mermen silhouetted in green, red and golden lights. Lighted palm tree silhouettes had replaced the evergreen trees, and the cornerstone of the display was a silver and gold glistening treasure chest filled with costume jewels overflowing onto the patio. The whole scene looked like a festive fantasy and feast for the eyes. But the lovely Christmas decorations only served as a reminder of her looming deadline.

Continuing her trek down Bay Front Road, she passed by a block of lovely little upscale shops, claiming "duty free" items such as designer watches and handbags, along with jewelry and perfumes. The less upscale kiosks boasted "Surrender the Booty" t-shirts and short-shorts. Her exhaustion turned what should have been a lovely nighttime walk into a terrifying trek. She imagined bad guys behind every building. A backfiring car was a bullet. A large stray dog, a small assailant. A headlight became a perceived searchlight. Jogging to the top of the hill, she finally saw the eerie reflection of the waterfront below and The Anchorage in plain sight.

Starting to feel sore and stiff, she hobbled the last fifteen hundred yards to the welcoming marina and limped down to the dock. Dawn was beginning to break and Adele saw a human obstacle just about the time she reached her boat. Dexter was hosing off the wooden walkways and stared at her suspiciously, stopping the water flow.

"Can I help you, ma'am?"

"It's me, Dexter . . . Adele."

"Adele! I know you were having problems with your shower, but this is ridiculous. What happened? You're a brown mess. Do you want a rinse-off?"

"Never mind what happened, and yes, I'd love a rinse-off. I don't think my shower could handle this. Wait a second." She tossed her things to one side.

Dexter turned on the hose and it was almost a fire-hydrant intensity of spray. The water stream rushing across the deck swept Adele across the sidewalk, and she barely missed an unintentional saltwater bath by taking hold of a mooring and anchoring herself down hard.

"Turn it down," Adele yelled to be heard over the loud water rush. "I want some skin left on my body."

Dexter turned down the hose level and Adele became clean in less than thirty seconds. The grime and ash were replaced by pink raw skin and her red hair was flattened against her scalp. Her muscles complaining, she leaned over to pick up the treasured remnants from the warehouse.

"Sorry, Adele," said Dexter. "But it looks like you took a bath in the local mud flats."

"Maybe I did." Adele limped down to *The irate air*, then turned to say one last thing. "Oh, Dexter—thanks for feeding Gilligan while I was gone." He waved back cheerfully.

Once on board, Adele dropped her things and broke down. Putting her hair in a tight ponytail, she unwrapped herself from her water-soaked jeans and t-shirt, opened the chest and brought out the brandy. Pouring several healthy ounces into a grog mug, she drank deeply, trying to shake off the last several hours. Lying down and breathing in rhythm to quiet her still raw nerves, she called Alli. It was the crack of dawn.

As soon as she heard her sister's voice, Adele went into a hysterical, hiccupping frenzy. "Someone tried to—*hic*—burn me—*hic*—alive, but Aunt Anne—*hic*—saved me."

"Holy shit, Adele. I never pegged you for a woman who had these types of enemies," exclaimed Alli with real fear in her voice. "Try and calm down. Hold your breath for fifteen seconds and take a sip of water. Do it now."

Adele held her breath for the ordered amount of time but took a gulp of brandy instead of a sip of water. Her hiccups did not stop. "I'm lucky—*hic*—to be alive."

"I said water, Adele."

Doing what she was told, Adele took a big sip of water and her hiccups started to subside.

"Now from the beginning, Adele," instructed Alli calmly.

Adele told Alli the whole terrifying story: about being drugged and abducted from a local bus in Nassau, and waking up in a burning warehouse on the Marsh Harbour docks. She couldn't find a way out until Aunt Anne told her to bust through a burning wall. Adele told her sister that she felt like she was in the Little Shop of Horrors with bizarre special effects, including finding a dead body in King Kong's severed hand.

"Get a grip, Adele. Did you say Aunt Anne? What have you been smoking?"

"Nothing, not even my salmon. The dead guy was Smee's sweetie, Woody, who disappeared two weeks ago to find his smile. But there wasn't a hint of a grin on his face when I found him. It was purplish-pink and I would have puked if he didn't look so scary."

"This is wild, sis. Why would someone want you dead? Have you called the police yet?"

"No reason to. Woody was definitely beyond resuscitating, the warehouse was already burned beyond saving. The Bahamian police don't do much anyway. Maybe it was Curtis—I wouldn't put it past him."

"But, Adele, you're not thinking straight. Someone tried to kill you. They may try it again. You have to go to the police. How about meeting tomorrow in Nassau and we can go to the station together?"

In denial that her abduction and the fire were serious crimes, Adele insisted there was no reason for her sister to hold her hand through this situation and besides, the crime took place in Marsh Harbour.

Alli told Adele she was planning to travel to Nassau anyway and they could go to the Bahamas main office then. She was up for a potential promotion and was stopping at the island the next day to attend a two-day conference and then would be on to Andros for a job interview regarding a more senior position. The meeting was at AUTEC's Test and Evaluation Range where she was currently a range scientist. The conference didn't begin until evening, and she could fly in early to go to the station with Adele, and meet Smee as well. This was perfect timing, Adele told her, as she had planned to fly back anyway and catch the ferry to bring her Bug back to Sandy Point, at the southern tip of Abaco Island. She would, however, visit the on-island police substation before leaving for Nassau. Then, changing the subject, Adele gave her sister the Pirate's Plunder address on Lower Dagger Drive. Alli wanted to know why she was carrying her car to Marsh Harbour when she lived in Nassau.

"Because Aunt Anne wants me to live here," explained Adele.

"You said Aunt Anne before. Do you mean the pirate one who's been dead for almost three hundred years?"

Knowing that Alli was going to think she was even crazier than she already thought, Adele told her sister about the nighttime visits from their aunt when she was in the twilight state of early sleep, and how she had received guidance in helping to retrieve stolen loot. In addition, Anne's first baby was buried somewhere around Marsh Harbour and their aunt wanted her to stay close to local waters.

"You've had a very stressful night," soothed Alli, trying to comfort her sister. "Where are you going to live?"

"I've resurrected *The Pirate Pair*—only now it's *The irate air*—and managed to sail back to The Anchorage."

"Are you sure you can stand the memories?"

"I don't have a choice."

"And the godawful shag carpet?"

All sorts of loudspeakers and sirens erupted on Alli's side of the conversation and she quickly said goodbye. "To be continued tomorrow."

Exhausted from her almost 24-hour ordeal, Adele fell asleep on the cushioned deck and slept for a scant six hours with Gilligan snoring on top of her head. Waking up sore and bruised, she tried to go back to sleep but her eyes refused to close again.

Her hair had dried all frizzy after Dexter's impromptu hosing-down, and it was flattened where she'd slept on it. After a minute of trying to pull a comb through it with hands dirty and shaking, she gave up and tied it back again in a bushy, lopsided ponytail. She pulled on clothes at random, and then read upside-down the t-shirt motto "Warning! Might Do Stupid Things at Any Time." She ate a meal bar and stared out to sea, and then she had a stupendous idea.

She decided to *power through the pain* and sail to Governor's Harbour, find Curtis, and take back her *Bonny. Alli will be so impressed when I tell her what I've done.* Walking up to the posting board, she read that seas would be calm today—three to four knots an hour maximum. *Perfect,* she thought, and she went back to her boat, looked over the day's sailing charts, and checked her supplies; she had oars, flares, flashlights, a life preserver, and several bottles of water. Pleased with her nautical knowledge, Adele put Gilligan into his tiny life preserver, untied her boat from the dock, and motored slowly out of the marina.

Adele expertly guided *The irate air* into the Sea of Abaco, concentrating on each task as she came to it, but just five miles out the wind became flat and our sailor gunned the engine. It sputtered and died. Never thinking she was going to have to rely on her motor to take her to Governor's Harbour, Adele hadn't checked the gas tank. She was completely out of gas. Six hours later, she paddled back into The Anchorage. Adele's well-toned muscles, now covered with sweat, glowed in the late afternoon light as she slowly glided into her berth and fell down exhausted into the tiny cabin.

She slept the clock around.

Adele got up at the crack of dawn, fed and watered Gilligan, and decided to go to the local police station before taking the nine-thirty Bahamas Air flight over to Nassau. Adele packed her now filthy messenger bag with her "Life Is Good" t-shirt, PJs, a pair of cotton hipsters, and a little Hello Kitty cosmetics kit which included tinted moisturizer, lip gloss, toothbrush, toothpaste, and compact hair brush, and she left her boat.

Walking the half-mile to the station, Adele went inside, finding one policeman behind a very tiny desk.

"I'm Officer Rolle. How can I help you?" he asked.

"I want to report a kidnapping."

Rolle looked skeptical. "Who was kidnapped?"

"Me." Adele then went on to tell the whole convoluted story about her being drugged on the Number 10 bus in Nassau and her vague impression of a plane and waking up in the burning special effects warehouse in Marsh Harbour. Looking at her incredulously, he went to his computer and typed something on the keyboard.

"Are you the Adele Bonny who claimed her condo was broken into and pirate treasure was stolen?" smirked the policeman.

"I didn't *claim* it, that happened too, and I was almost killed in the fire."

"Been a bad week, hasn't it? Perhaps you need to ask Blackbeard to help you out, but meantime I suppose I can take your statement."

"Screw you," cried Adele, running out the door shaken to her core.

She called over a cab idling across the street to take her to the airport. Just Adele's luck, the only driver out front was Dr. Kim. There was no other taxi on the horizon, so she reluctantly climbed in the back. The doctor might have been physically in, but not psychologically, refusing to speak to Adele. She wrote the word "AIRPORT?" on a piece of paper and held it up for Adele to read. Adele said "yes" and Kim sped away, bouncing off the sidewalk.

After an uneventful flight to Nassau, Adele found her Bug at the airport where Marvin had left it for her, and she reached into the wheel well to pull the keys out from the agreed-on hiding place. She drove to Pirate's Plunder, relishing the smooth sound of the engine.

Smee was in his office admiring the three different right-hand hooks he was trying on. One slid over his hand and wrist like a rubber glove with sharp curved aluminum hook protruding past his covered fingers. This was the $12.99 model. Adele told him it was really tacky, so he skipped over the middle one and tried on the Franklin Mint-type piece made from genuine leather with a molded steel hook. This was the $49.95 model and looked just like the real thing. Smee flashed the hook around for several seconds, seemed satisfied with the results, and started to order it online.

Sitting down, Adele said, "Listen, Smee. I have good news and bad."

"Oh, boy. Good news first."

Adele inhaled. "Okay. Woody didn't really leave you. . . ."

"But his note said. . . ."

"The bad news is—he's dead."

Deciding not to give him all the gory, hideous, horrible details, she didn't mention that his former lover looked like a beautiful broken Ken doll in the hand of King Kong. All she told Smee was that Woody had met with some kind of an accident in an old warehouse on Marsh Harbour.

"Can I see my lovely boy?" whimpered Smee, crying softly. "He knew he shouldn't wander. I can't believe that Woody is dead. He was such a sensitive soul and truly my life's partner. Who would do such a thing?"

Embracing Smee gently, she suggested that a viewing was not a good idea as he had been sitting in the warehouse for several days. She then told him about her near brush with death. Smee was absolutely flabbergasted. While his shaking hands—one covered with the best hook—fiddled with one of his Lost Boys figurines, Adele then asked him a hard question. "Do you think Woody's death could be connected in some way to the disappearance of the *Hygia*, and him insuring it for a crazy amount of money?"

"I hope not, dear, but it does make some sense. I don't think he would ever disappear on his own accord. Woody told me more than once that I was his true swashbuckling soulmate. Oh, me. I think I may need to disappear myself for a few days and visit my NaNa in West Palm. She always knows what to do. Besides, I don't do well in dangerous situations. I desperately need a serving of her pineapple upside-down cake." There was also another reason why Smee wanted to spend some time in South Florida. He had a second nephew, Stewart Stocking, who was seven years older than Ignacious and lived in the West Palm area. The uncle hadn't seen his nephew in more than five years, ever since he had graduated from college and enlisted in the Navy. He was a young lieutenant and planned to study submarine warfare.

Adele agreed that going to the mainland was just what he needed and, taking a deep breath, told Smee she was going to disappear as well—moving from Nassau to Marsh Harbour. She could spend nights with Elaine if need be, and she explained that she felt more like a true Bonny anchored in that part of the Bahamas. Smee surprised her with his response. He said he understood completely and was so pleased that she had decided to embrace her true pirate. But she had only fourteen days left to find the *Hygia*, or they would both be trying to survive on *The irate air*. Ignacious was at Pirate's Plunder to assist her and Smee was always available by cell phone and email.

"The Battle Hymn of the Republic" ring interrupted their little heart-to-heart. It was Alli and, like most visitors to the office, she was on Upper Dagger Drive and had fallen in love with the quaint shops and bistros, but could not find 313. Adele told her sister to head down Dagger Drive for a block and the office was next to a Cuban Cigars and Curios shop.

Alli arrived less than five minutes later and there was no mistaking the genetic connection. Alli was a bit more conservative than Adele, with chestnut hair swept back in a ponytail and no makeup other than mascara and lipstick. But the familial features were unmistakable, with her green eyes and prominent cheekbones; she was a Bonny through and through. However, Alli's signature bubble butt was covered with a pair of gabardine slacks, instead of short-shorts, and her silk shirt carried no slogans. She eyed Adele's tattered shorts and t-shirt before giving her a heavy-duty hug.

"Three months is way too long," reproached Alli, "and Curtis' fortieth was a lousy reason for our last family get-together."

Hugging her sister back, Adele introduced her to Smee, who "made a leg" in approved Captain Blood style. "Charmed, I'm sure." He reached to kiss her hand, but he'd forgotten he had the hook on his right hand and almost pierced her skin.

"Oh, my," said Alli. "I guess chivalry is not dead."

"It's the pirate code," Smee gushed. "No fair lady should be left unattended."

"Well, gee, thanks, Smee. The last time you took my hand was to slap it," objected Adele.

Smee sat back down in his chair and looked over at a silly shot of him and Woody wearing giant foam pirate hats that had to have been won at Disney World. "You girls must have lots of catching up to do, so go along and leave me with my grief."

"It was nice meeting you, Smee, but I'm sorry it wasn't under better circumstances," commiserated Alli.

"Amore, Amore," grieved Smee. "It's like Romeo and Juliet but I'll try not to end my life like they did."

"I'd rather you didn't, Smee, as you have a lot of living and loving to do before your fiftieth."

"Thank you both for being so understanding, girls. Now fly away like little butterflies. I'll have Marc bring me over to Marsh Harbour tomorrow, Adele, to bid adieu before heading on to West Palm Beach. Know that you can use the loft next week should the need arise."

"Not likely, but thanks for the offer." Adele led Alli out the door.

Walking next door to a coffee and cocktail lounge, Alli and Adele ordered double cappuccinos. What they were subjected to was espresso Caribbean style, strong enough to grow hair on a newborn baby's chest. Shuddering after the first sip, they found a bamboo bench and started to fill each other in on the last three months of scant emails and few telephone calls. Alli sternly told Adele they needed to go to the police about her abduction and the fire. Hedging the truth, Adele replied that she had visited the Marsh Harbour substation early in the morning before flying over to Nassau. Alli lightened up a bit and wanted to know about Curtis. She hadn't gotten a jubilant message from her sister, so assumed he was still missing, but wanted all the details firsthand from Adele.

"What I didn't realize is that there are many ignorant sailors who are channeling through the same signals," Adele told her sister. "It makes perfect sense. If there are thousands out there like Curtis who might depend on these tracking units for their safety, I can see why there are not enough frequencies to go around."

"It's something like that, Adele. So, what was the military backup you told me about when you were at the Pirates Museum?"

"Just Rocky Rodriguez, a Navy SEAL I met. No one important—so catch me up on your conference, Alli."

Her sister told her she was hosting a conference at The Wyndham on Cable Beach and meeting about a position with AUTEC that would enable her to spend a full week a month on Andros Island. The island was a naturalist's wonderland with its deserted beaches and birds galore, and Alli was looking forward to taking her young sons bird-watching.

"I don't want to be a downer," Adele interjected, "but the last time I visited Andros it was a mosquito-infested hole. The snorkeling is fantastic—if you don't mind swimming with a school of barracudas."

But Alli was very excited about this great opportunity. She would be involved with reef monitoring, conducting near shore environmental surveys, and assessing coral reef ecosystems.

"Why are you always so negative, Adele? I know you think

AUTEC is a Big Brother organization, but the Department of Defense actually does help to protect the indigenous environment around military training ranges and their facilities."

"I suppose missiles are indigenous to the area as well? Guess I'm negative today because my life has just about bottomed out and you're boasting about yet another career advancement."

"Sorry. I didn't mean to be talking about my career when your life has been threatened—not to mention the family assets. I guess it's just that, well, I haven't seen you for way too long."

"I've missed you too, Alli, and felt you never approved of Curtis and now I can see why."

"Let's not play the blame game, Adele." The sisters sat quietly for a moment and then Alli continued, "There were many times when I wanted your life, especially when you made the cheerleading squad. Maybe all sisters want to star in *The Parent Trap* and have the ability to swap lives at different times growing up. You were so mature and confident when you spent the weekend taking care of Mom's friend Clara after her tummy tuck. At fifteen I was still looking at micro-organisms through a microscope."

"Changing her bandages really grossed me out, but how do you think I made the cheerleading squad? Her grandson was captain of the football team." She decided not to mention to Alli that her becoming a cheerleader also had something to do with some kind of orgs as well, but Adele's discovery was not nearly as scientific as her sister's was.

"Always playing the angles, Adele," laughed Alli. "Now tell me about Aunt Anne?"

Adele squirmed as she wondered where to begin. "So, I've been having this problem with my ears. They'll just suddenly start buzzing, or ringing. At first I really thought I should see a doctor about it."

"Why didn't you?" Alli asked with concern.

"Let's just say I realized it had nothing to do with my ears and everything to do with our ancestor."

"I'm sure you're gonna make sense any minute."

"Bear with me. We have this pirate ancestor, right? She lived a long time ago and can't exactly make a phone call to get in touch, so she buzzes my ears."

Alli's eyes drifted out to the horizon. "We have our very own ghost!"

"Yeah, you could say that. Anyway, ghosts come back because they have unfinished business. That's the prevailing theory, right? I think that's why Aunt Anne is around again. And to help us recover the family valuables."

"I can see how losing all the spoils she fought so hard to win would make her turn over in her grave," Alli admitted. "So how does she communicate with you?"

Adele exhaled. "At first I would just hear her voice in my head. Now I can see her too. I thought I was having hallucinations, or maybe just making up these interludes because I felt so alone."

Alli put a hand over her sister's hand. "You could have called sooner, you know."

Adele patted her sister's forearm. "I know. Anyway, now I have these . . . conversations with Aunt Anne, these little chats. I'm getting to know her."

"What does she look like?" asked Alli. "Is she as feisty as her portraits? And what about Calico Jack?"

"She talks about her life with Jack, but I haven't seen him. It's so strange. She looks exactly like I have always pictured her. I never felt that Aunt Anne was ever a strumpet or even a siren, supposedly wearing all those sexy clothes. She's actually very sensible and wants me to succeed in my new line of work. She thinks of herself as my guide in this pirate life I've chosen."

"You, a modern day pirate hunter, pretty hard to believe."

"I guess necessity becomes the mother of invention, and the job also gives me the opportunity to try and track down Curtis and the *Beautiful Bonny.*"

Taking a final large sip of her cappuccino, Adele started to sweat and her conversation went into overdrive. "I've ruined our family and lost our fortune. I'm totally broke and drowning in debt, living on a boat so battered it wouldn't make it through a tropical storm, much less a hurricane. I've lost my husband to an underage bimbo and have a 300-year-old wraith trying to help me live my life and she's doing a better job of it than I can do. . . ."

Alli couldn't help but laugh and then sighed at what seemed like Adele's desperate and, at this moment, hopelessly sucky situation.

"Slow down, sis. You were always so susceptible to caffeine. Remember the night in the tenth grade when Mom asked you to bake cookies for her holiday cookie exchange but you forgot? You got up at six in the morning, drank two pots of Folgers, and had about two hundred snickerdoodles, sugar angels, and thumb prints done by ten a.m."

Adele smiled ruefully at the memory as her sister brought her out of her reveries with the power of positive thinking—something Adele hadn't had much of lately. They still did have fourteen days to find the *Hygia*, and with Alli's and Aunt Anne's help they had a good chance of finding the *Bonny* and booty as well.

Looking at her watch, Alli saw it was three p.m. and she had to be at the cocktail reception at five, so they rushed to Adele's Bug and made it to The Wyndham in fifteen minutes flat. Dropping her sister at the resort, Adele once again asked her for help to track the *Bonny*. "When I get back to headquarters, I'll nose around and see if any of the guys have spotted her in the area during their maneuvers," Alli assured her. "And besides, a third of the treasure belongs to me. Let me know what the police uncover."

Adele didn't skip a beat. "Absolutely! You're the best and thanks for checking with your team."

Chapter 12

Adele drove her Bug into the lower level of the crowded Bahamas Ferry, parked behind a Mini Cooper, and went up to the deck for the four-hour trip to Sandy Point. Grabbing a fish sandwich and vodka and lime, she sat down on a bench towards the front of the ferry and watched the two sailors cast off from the dock. Her thoughts turned back to Curtis and the *Beautiful Bonny. He was so supportive when I found the badly damaged boat in the street after the hurricane.* By selling the last coin Babs had gifted her with, she had just enough money to start renovations. And although Curtis didn't help her much with the repairs as he was much too busy overseeing the six thousand citrus trees he had invested in, when the last piece of wood was stained and head overhauled complete with a full-sized shower, he danced her around the deck with delight. *Perhaps he was so happy because he had planned to steal the Bonny all along.*

Emitting a sad sigh and taking a sip of her vodka and lime, she bent her head out into the cool breeze and was joined by a seventy-year-old man with a nose covered in zinc oxide, wearing a floppy hat and knee-length shorts.

He sat down next to her. "Pretty nice out here, huh?" Rolling up his shorts, he stretched out from the waist down, starting to capture a few rays at Adele's expense. Straightening his legs out as straight as a stick, the man literally pushed her into a hard-looking woman who was kneeling restfully, drinking a large Bahamian beer, and taking in the calm waters around the ferry. When the woman turned to look at her, Adele saw that she had a gray-flecked artichoke haircut and an exquisitely colored arm tattoo of an undulating wave peeking out of her t-shirt.

"Sorry about that," said Adele. "My seat partner wanted the whole bench, I guess."

"No problem." The woman finished her beer and clearly wanted to chat. "Looks like he can use the tan. My name's Courtney."

"I'm Adele." She held out her hand for what was a very firm handshake.

"You must be an American?" remarked Courtney. "A very distinct accent. I'm a native Bahamian, but I've been doing time for five years and I'm looking forward to going home to Guana. Where in the states are you from?"

"Oh, wow, I thought I'd lost my accent by now. I was born in Florida, but I have joint citizenship as I married a Bahamian." Adele took another sip of her drink. "Are you headed for Guana? Have you heard about all the brouhaha over the golf course and marina that Adventure LandCo is constructing over on the island?—Did you say you were doing time? You mean literally?"

"Yeah, literally. I forged one too many checks and my last one belonged to the Prime Minister's daughter. Got her signature down almost right, just forgot to curl the zeros."

Finishing her beer, Courtney told Adele she had a job on an Adventure LandCo construction crew and after checking in with the crew boss she had a three-day window to search for the man she left behind. He was quite a character and would sometimes even dress like a woman, but his kiss could pull the chrome off of a muffler. And what he could do with those hands of his, holy moly! He was just starting a tattoo business and she worked there for three months as his assistant. He did primo work as was evidenced by her right arm and when she flexed it just so, her muscle looked like an undulating wave. Unfortunately, she gave in to temptation and wrote a check for five thousand dollars on his business account, which almost caused him to go under. For five years she had been figuring out a way to make it right and hoped that now was the time.

"Prison hardens a gal up, but I still think I prefer guys," she commented to Adele.

"I've had just the opposite experience. It was my soon to be ex-husband who turned out to be the not-so-trustworthy one," confided Adele, loosening up after she finished her vodka. "When I signed up for aerobics, he was exercising horizontally after class with my teenybopper instructor. But let's talk about something that won't give me an itch."

As Courtney had been gone from the islands for five years she was anxious to know if the technology in the area had improved. The last time she'd spent a few weeks on Guana Cay, the island was trying to go to wireless Internet with the Coconut Express, but it was down more than it was up. Portable generators couldn't keep up with the constant electricity outages and Marsh Harbour Airport had one very bumpy runway. Adele informed her that things hadn't changed very much since then, but the Coconut Express was up and running at about seventy percent of speed and the runway had finally been resurfaced. However, a new international terminal was slated to open in late 2012.

Thinking back over the last few days, Adele realized she had really fallen in love with the Out Islands of the Bahamas. Gracie had taught her about navigation on the sail over to The Anchorage and she'd had the courage to solo sail over to Guana just two days later. When she was with Curtis she had been a passenger on her own boat, enjoying cocktails and admiring the view. She remembered one evening when they hit rough water on the *Bonny* and all she could do was to go down below and take a Dramamine—well, probably three. Two hours later the sun was shining, Gracie was exhausted, and even Curtis had helped steady the boat. All Adele could boast was an over-the-counter hangover—not nearly as rewarding as the crazy ride on a rocket-propelled speedboat with Rocky to Cat Island. But now she was able to captain a

27-foot Catalina and planned on being the master of the *Beautiful Bonny* once she got her back.

Exuma, Eleuthera, Andros, and Marsh Harbour—each had its own distinct personality and even the terrain and weather varied as the islands were scattered over a thousand square miles of ocean. She had visited Eleuthera on her honeymoon and loved the area's laid-back elegance, upscale resorts and pink sand beach. Gracie also sailed them to Exuma for a long weekend and Adele spent hours doing yoga on the miles of unpopulated shore line. Curtis, of course, suggested they should sail back to Nassau a day early, as he never wanted to stay away from the dance studio, or, she now guessed, the young girls dancing there, for more than three days. Then it was whatever he wanted to do, but now it was what Adele wanted and she planned to make the most of it.

She turned to look at Courtney who also looked lost in thought, until the ferry hit a wave that jostled them both. Courtney grasped her shoulder, probably nothing more than a friendly gesture, but Adele felt a bit uncomfortable with the sudden physical contact. She scarcely had time to worry about it, though, as just then a piercing alarm began to ring out across the deck.

"Where's that coming from?" shouted Courtney.

"Sounds like it's coming from the hold!" Adele shouted back. "Where they store the cars!"

Several crewmembers hurried below. Leaving Courtney behind, Adele decided to follow the crewmembers and found pandemonium down in the car lot. Windows had been broken on two cars, their sound systems stolen, and alarms were screaming at two-second intervals. A truck was without its front wheels and tipping down as if it were bowing. Adele's car was parked in front of the truck and her darling daisy rear wheels had been stripped and replaced with black-wall, over-sized radial tires—giving her sweet little Bug the look of *Herbie Fully Loaded.*

"Those are my wheels," accused a man who walked up to her.

"Obviously it wasn't intentional," Adele defended herself. "They don't exactly fit the Bug."

"I think they look kind of cute on your car," said Courtney as she walked up to Adele and the trucker.

"I want my tires back," roared the truck driver.

"You can have them back, but where are mine?" Adele walked around her car and saw a brief message scrawled on a piece of paper tucked beneath her left windshield wiper. "Stop tracking the *Hygia*, or your wheels won't be the only thing over the side." Adele snatched the note and stuffed it into her shorts pocket before Courtney or the trucker could see it. She then started to circle around the dozen or so other cars, but her daisy wheels were nowhere to be found. Not wanting to wait until the ferry reached Sandy Point, the trucker pulled a lug wrench from the back bed and started to remove the two rear tires from Adele's Bug. A crewmember told Adele they would have to push the car off the ferry and maybe she could find two tires at the junkyard close to the dock. Courtney promised to help her with the tires in exchange for a lift to the Guana Cay ferry. Seemed like a fair trade, and Adele and Courtney went topside for the remainder of the trip.

It was well into dusk by then. The water was smooth like glass when the ferry docked and a school of golden grouper fish greeted the group of boaters who climbed across to the wooden sidewalk. Adele and Courtney had stayed behind to push her car out of the hold with the help of two bulging bicep'd crewmen. It got stalled on the metal gangplank and took the full strength of all four in the group to push the car onto the sturdy dock. Next came the hard part, to get the vehicle over to the junkyard a block away. After fifteen minutes of swearing and sweat, it arrived at Junk Yard Dog, where the human dogs started to circle Adele and her short-shorts. Tires were at a premium at The Dog, but after a half hour the Bug was roadworthy with one white- and one black-wall tire. Neither did justice to the front daisy wheels. Adele gave the guys a fifty and she and Courtney wobbled towards Marsh

Harbour, where she dropped her passenger off in front of The Papayas Marina.

The Marsh Harbour docks were less than a mile away from where she dropped off Courtney, so Adele decided to inspect what was left of her Shop of Horrors prison. She was surprised to see a portion of the warehouse still standing, but her plan to break and enter was thwarted, as two security guards were guarding the building. When one of the guards took a stroll to the far west end, Adele pulled a flashlight out of her cup holder, opened the door, approached the other guard and hiked up her short-shorts even shorter. She then executed a hair flip to perfection.

"Excuse me, officer, I need to get into the warehouse. There's something important inside that I have to find."

"Sorry, miss, this is an official investigation, and besides the place isn't safe."

"But I left my pirate's wench bikini costume inside and I can't jump out of the cake tonight without it. My customer is a leg man, and the suit was especially made to please him," purred Adele. She coyly curled her right foot behind her left ankle to show her best side.

Looking as if he were about ready to swallow his tongue, the guard draped his arm around Adele and started to lead her towards the fire-damaged side door, but he stopped when the other guard called out, "Peter, where are you going? No one's allowed inside. Those walls could cave in at any moment."

"But I just need to get my costume," whined Adele.

"I don't care if you need to get your dildo, honey. This is off limits."

Taking his arm off of Adele's shoulder, Officer Peter walked her back to her car. "Save me a piece of cake if there's any left," he said.

Adele revved the engine and drove off with a jerky start-up due to those two mismatched back tires. Barely making it up and down the hill to The Anchorage, she parked on the flattest pad in the lot and walked towards her boat. The nighttime sky had come out, stars were beginning to twinkle and the water was a soft gray-blue color as she climbed onto *The irate air*.

Pouring the last couple of ounces of brandy into her grog cup, she looked around the cabin and decided she was too tired to put in another of her cleaning and redecorating sessions, so she opened her old lime-green Mac laptop to check her last twelve hours of emails. Only three had come in, and they were throw-aways anyhow. Shutting down her computer, she picked up a romance novel.

With Gilligan nestled comfortably on her chest, Adele read for a while and was starting to fall asleep right when the heroine and handsome stable hand were making hay in the haystack. Sleepily she was brought back to the eighteenth century, and Gilligan didn't like it one bit. This time he leaped towards Anne, falling hard onto the deck.

"Keep that nasty gib away from me," sputtered Anne.

"His name is Gilligan."

"No, it's a gib, the sorry guttersnipe lost his balls years ago and I'd like nothing better than to cut a V into his other ear."

"Lost his—Yeah, he has been neutered. . . ."

"Which you clearly have not," said Anne sternly. "Aren't you the coquette, darlin'? Reminds me a bit of myself and Mary Reade when I was, hum, let me see, twenty years younger than you. Guess I matured early." She was wearing a pair of chopstick-like hair ornaments to hold back her red ringlets.

"Great hair, Aunt Anne, but I don't want to talk about lovers, if any. By the way, thanks for saving me. The warning about the Crocs was a good one, but I thought you meant live crocodiles, not shoes."

"If I had meant crocodiles, I wouldn't have said Crocs. I remember when you were a wee one, you never listened to your mother, and when I tried to get involved, Babs just thought she was gettin' another one of her bloody headaches and closed her ears."

"That's so coincidental, Aunt Anne. I suffer from migraines

and ringing in my ears too and was telling Alli that you might be responsible for my head congestion."

"Well, missy, think where you are when they come on."

Adele dug down deep into her still foggy brain and came up with the answer, at least for the most recent ones. Most started around The Pirates Museum or when she was thinking about the problems in her life or, recently, about her aunt. More than a coincidence? You bet, so Adele questioned Anne further.

"Have you caused them, Aunt Anne?"

"Oh, Adele my girl, this was the only way I could hope to make you Bonny girls listen. But with your mom the ringin' fell on deaf ears."

Anne explained that this high frequency ringing in her and her mother's ears was caused when she tried to break through the time barrier and met with resistance. She had wanted a blood relative for a partner and confidant for generations and had thought Babs would be the one, but after Darryl drowned, she was not nearly as receptive as she'd been when Adele and Alli were young girls. Just like Adele, Babs closed down many of her feelings and didn't want to think about boats and the Bonny treasure for many years. Then it was too late, Anne had gone back to the nineteenth century for companionship.

Her aunt had almost connected with an East Coast riverboat gambler cousin in the 1880s, but the unfortunate card shark gave up her cheating game after a horrible roaring noise in her right ear and severe loss of her equilibrium. She was sure she was going deaf as penance for all the bad deeds she had done throughout her life. Holding the sides of her head tightly, she confessed to years of card counting. When Anne tried to calm her down, the distressed adventuress pulled out her derringer and discharged the tiny pistol into the ceiling. In the confusion, another gambler feared for his life and shot her dead. But thank goodness for Adele, now that she had embraced her inner Bonny, her hearing would be clear as a bell and Anne finally had her partner. Little did it matter that it took Anne almost three hundred years to find her.

"I get it, Aunt Anne, and I'm so glad you're here. I've been wanting to ask you, how did you and Jack track down ships back in your day? It's been nearly two weeks and other than having been almost burned to death, I'm no closer to finding either the *Hygia* or the *Beautiful Bonny* than I was at the start of my search."

"Just chart the right course, Adele. You may be gettin' closer than you imagine. Danger lurked when you were about to discover the double dolphins necklace. Hurry-durry, it's all about BJ and don't be afeard to explore where you've already been. Steady as she goes. . . ."

Anne started to fade away. Adele was too tired to wake up and began to dream about boarding the *Beautiful Bonny* and sailing into the colorful Caribbean sunset with Aunt Anne and Calico Jack at her side.

Gilligan woke Adele out of her reveries. The kitty chow was gone and the big cat was hungry. In a stupor, Adele filled his bowl to overflowing before falling back to sleep, continuing her dream from when she woke up.

Chapter 13

Adele woke up with a renewed sense of urgency, realizing Smee would be over later in the day to bid his goodbyes. Her concern was that she still had no idea where the *Hygia* had disappeared. Deciding to make another visit to the burned-out warehouse, she dressed in old cut-off Levis and a Crabbers Grouper Fest t-shirt. Driving down to the docks, she parked a good distance away from the crime scene and went around back to the one door still standing. The yellow police tape still surrounded the structure. Two security guards and a guard dog, along with Officer Rolle from the Marsh Harbour police station, moved away from her direction to the other side of the building.

"This is where that Bonny broad told me she was held captive," said Rolle. "She was right about the fire, but let's not look too closely. If this gets out, it's bad for tourism."

At least Rolle believed me enough to take a look inside the warehouse, thought Adele. *Why do men always give me such a hard time?*

Eyeing the canine that looked like a cross between a pit bull and a Rottweiler, and seeing it exercising its chops to no one in particular, Adele made a mental note to stay as far away from those teeth as possible.

Sneaking inside, she made her way through the remnants of burned props and charred curios. The police seemed to be finished with whatever investigations they were planning to do—where were the dedicated *CSI* team members when you needed them?—so it seemed the coast was clear for Adele to nose around. Woody was no longer held in the arms of King Kong. But then she heard male voices. *Cops?* She headed to a back room where a staircase was still intact. Creeping down the stairs, she saw a small studio apartment perfectly intact with a porcelain sign reading "Woody's Lair." Inside the small and very feminine sitting area stood Diego and Winston, the men she knew from the *Dead End*. And Diego, also from the Little Bus of Horrors, was thumbing through a bright pink cloth journal.

"Lucky the fire didn't get this far," said Winston. "Why'd you start it, anyway?"

"I told you, I didn't mean to. I must've dropped a burning butt when I left the Adele woman here, and all this stuff burns like kindling. You oughta know that."

"The trick is, whenever I'm working with props, I don't introduce any open flames."

"Keep talking to me that way and you'll find out what *my* trick is. Hey, I was right, that pansy Woody meant to screw us over. His 'accident' upstairs happened at the right time. Listen to this: 'Today's the day I confront them. Our deal for jacking up the insurance on the *Hygia* is 20K, but I had to leave my meal ticket. Besides, I know what's on board and it should be worth ten times that much for me to keep quiet.'—Guess our friend Bruce kept him quiet." Diego laughed nastily.

Oh, my God, they killed Woody. Adele's breath came in gasps.

Adele heard what sounded like canine footsteps, the pit bull started to bark furiously above her, and she climbed back into the stairwell, hiding behind an old wardrobe closet.

"Down here," came a voice. The stairs started to creak under the weight of the guards. She suddenly heard the sound of splintering wood.

"Shit," moaned a guard. "I think I broke my foot. Let's get out of here."

Their footsteps and the barking dog started to retreat and Adele breathed a sign of relief.

Climbing out of the stairwell, she heard a whispered conversation but couldn't make out either the words or the identities of the speakers.

Rocky spoke in low tones with a man who was shrouded in the shadows, only an earring glinting in the dim light. "The police are all over this place. I thought you worked alone," Rocky muttered, pointing towards Winston and Diego. "These are the two characters we ran into on the *Dead End*."

"This is too important of a job; I needed backup. Diego told me there was a dude with the Bonny broad, but I didn't know it was you."

Hearing his name, Diego joined the two men, seeming none too happy. "Weren't you with that Adele woman? The two of you looked mighty cozy."

"That's what playing both sides is all about," Rocky snapped back.

"How'd you hook up with Adele?" the man with the gold earring asked Rocky. "She's one nosy broad."

"Don't worry about her," said Rocky. "She's way far off the scent and won't be a problem."

"Are you sure?" asked the man, raising his voice up a notch to where Adele could hear the next part of the conversation. "We all have a lot riding on this score. Let's have the kid move the *Hygia* from Sea Spray soon."

Finally some information I can use, Adele thought. *As soon as I can get out of this warehouse I'll hop the ferry to Hope Town.* She quickly climbed up the stairs and hid behind a charred column in case the dog or the cops might come back, but she could still hear the muffled conversation. *Wish I could recognize the voices. . . .*

"I'd really like to see the merchandise," said Rocky.

"It's been less than three weeks, man," protested Winston. "Tell your buyer to just chill or the chip may end up in someone else's cookies."

Rocky walked outside the warehouse, got into an old Jeep Wrangler, and headed east on Main Street. Diego, Winston, and the man with the gold hoop jumped into an old truck. They drove right by Adele's lime green Bug with the mismatched wheels, hidden in the shadows of several large mangrove trees.

"This broad's way too busy digging into our business," growled the man with the gold hoop. "Losing two wheels wasn't enough to make her back off. Perhaps it's time for her to go missing as well."

"Will do, boss," Diego assented. "Sounds like fun. She's docked at The Anchorage and I think Santa should pay her a visit right after Christmas."

"If not sooner," said the man with the gold hoop. He pulled out a cell phone and hit a speed-dial number.

Adele crept out of the warehouse, streaked towards her Bug, and five minutes later was at the Albury Ferry dock, the central water transit system to the local islands. *Too bad Curtis wasn't that Albury*, she thought. *We could have been on Easy Street.* The ferry to Hope Town, the main town on Elbow Cay, was ready to depart, so she hopped on board. Forty minutes later Adele was on the local dock—renting a golf cart, as cars were prohibited on the island—and on her way to Sea Spray Resort and Marina. After traveling two miles on a narrow, bumpy road she arrived at the small resort and private marina. Not seeing the *Hygia*, she ran to the dock master's office, only to find out that the stolen boat had left the island thirty minutes earlier.

"It was traveling slow," the dock master told her. "That figurehead was mighty heavy. The young kid sailing her was talking about breaking her up and I offered to take her off his hands—to put in my mancave, if you get where I'm comin' from?"

"Do you know where the *Hygia* was headed?"

"Can't say I do—he wasn't very friendly."

Adele's initial euphoria over solving this case as easily as she had found the diamond dolphins necklace quickly came to an end. Slowly driving to the dock, she was able to catch the next ferry to Marsh Harbour and was back at The Anchorage just three hours after leaving the burned-out warehouse. Taking some bottled mint tea and wrapped deviled ham and tuna fish sandwiches out of the cooler, she changed her t-shirt for one that read "Surrender the Booty" and waited for Smee. He arrived with Marc in tow to say his goodbyes before going on to West Palm Beach. Going outside, she glumly greeted Smee. "I had my first real lead on locating the *Hygia*, but I was thirty minutes too late."

Putting his arm around her, Smee handed her three beautiful stems of fuchsia-colored tropical ginger.

He was thrilled over the great strides Adele had made in undoing her mother's last decorator's design disaster. *The irate air* had new blue and white striped cotton duck slip covers to hide the hideous hot pink cabin pillows. The galley now had a new microwave oven and compact refrigerator, and in the small stateroom she had just hooked up a 21-inch television and DVD combo.

For the first time since meeting Adele at The Very Berry, he seemed a bit like a tourist in his Tommy Bahama palmtree-patterned shirt and khaki cotton Bermuda shorts. Every vestige of pirate had been left in his bungalow in Nassau, as he started to prepare to see his grandmother NaNa for the first time in eight years and make nice after the *incident*.

Smee began to confide in Adele, telling her the *real* reason the two hadn't seen or spoken to each other in so many years. Loving a good dress-up, Smee was trying to jam his feet into her new high heels when NaNa walked into her bedroom and caught him. Furious after seeing the shoes stretched out at the sides, she kicked him out of her house, at the age of forty. Taking the small inheritance he'd received from his father's estate, Smee moved to Nassau and leased what was then a spice store. It took him two years to eliminate the scents of patchouli and pekoe tea. Not sure what he was going to do with the little storefront on Lower Dagger Drive, he investigated opening a tropical juice store before starting the short-lived Top Notch Tattoo Shop. He told Adele wistfully that he'd studied to become a master tattoo artist, learning how to incorporate subtle color in what up until then had been a primarily black and red graphic style. Unfortunately a woman he'd trusted embezzled most of his family's remaining funds. She then sneakily left the island after he'd gifted her with the shop's best work—an undulating blue wave tattoo on her right arm.

Oh, my God, Adele thought. The woman she had met on the ferry was the same one who'd ruined Smee's tattoo business. She let him continue his story. All was saved when in the depths of depression he had a dream about Austin Powers and his groovy little detective business. Then it came to him—a way to combine his love of pirates and interest in detective work. Thus Pirate's Plunder was born. At first the business did quite well as pirates were plundering the eastern and western areas of the Caribbean before heading down to Africa and especially Somalia. The southern waters were not as strongly patrolled and protected by the U.S. Coast Guard as the islands closer to the United States and around the shallow coastal shores. The scalawags also migrated down to South and Central America. But after a good year freelancing with the backload of cases from Mr. Brill, Pirate's Plunder almost went under again.

Business started to turn around three years earlier when Smee partnered fully with Mr. Brill. They flew down to St. Lucia after pirates had boarded a yacht there, beaten the captain into unconsciousness, and stolen his wife. She was wearing a perfectly flawless five-karat heart-shaped sapphire necklace crafted after *Titanic*'s Jewel of the Ocean. He and his previous Woody, a hot Latin named Antonio, found the wife and the $200,000 piece both being bedded by one of the pirates at a four-hundred-dollar-a-night resort on the island. Mr. Brill rewarded Smee with a $20,000 retrieval fee. The partnership had flourished ever since, even though good help had been hard to find.

Smee then breathed in deeply the ginger aroma. "I've always liked pink smells. But tell me about you."

"My story in a minute, Smee. I just want to know when during this time of your life you were locking lips with Courtney?"

Smee started to sputter, suddenly looking as if he might lose his lunch. "How did you find out about *her*?"

"Believe it or not, I met her yesterday on the ferry during my trip back to Sandy Point. She's quite the woman and actually wants to find you to make amends. I didn't know you swing both ways."

"I don't," asserted Smee. "Courtney was my one aberration and I paid for it dearly. She was so rough and tumble, there were times I was sure she was really a man. But no, she had all the indoor plumbing and it was the last time I ever went to the female side. What did *you* do early on that was wild and crazy?"

"Okay, fair enough. Well, as you might not know, I've been praised for my beautiful hands and worked as a hand and accessories model in my early twenties. They're very expressive, as you can see." Adele waved her hands elegantly in a hula-like dance.

"You were a hand model? What a coincidence, so was I."

Smee captured Adele's hands and gave them the once-over. "I'm sure they're delicious, so long and slender—or they will be, once they heal from that horrible warehouse ordeal. I didn't really have what it takes to be a success as my fingers have very short nail beds and my digits didn't stay unblemished for long. After dipping a French fry into boiling oil for a fast food commercial, my left hand broke out in hives that lasted for months."

Adele laughed. "Only you, Smee, would be my competition for hand jobs. My first was pouring gravy over a pork chop."

Smee started to laugh as well. "Hand jobs—I like the sound of that, my dear. On my second job my right hand was supposed to start a tractor. After ten takes my palms got all red and chapped and I couldn't grip the gearshift. But continue with your story."

"Not much else to tell. I met Curtis after quitting hand modeling when my manicures cost me more money than I was making at the shop. So I decided to go back to dance and you know the rest. But my goal while you're gone is to find the *Hygia*."

Smee perked up. "I have faith that an authentic Bonny can track her down." He didn't see the look of doubt on Adele's face.

"No more soul searching," declared Smee as he hugged Adele twice. "Ten days at the Gray Hair Gardens will be just what I need."

"I'm going to miss you, Smee, but have fun with NaNa and enjoy your comfort food, especially that pineapple upside-down cake."

"My hammock is your hammock while I'm away. Just be safe but never sorry, my dear," trilled Smee. He reached in his shorts pocket, produced a keychain with a brightly colored parrot and a door key, and handed it to her. "Oh, IQ told me yesterday he saw you at the Pirates Museum with a man who has shoulders to die for. Do tell?"

Blushing a bit, Adele admitted she was smitten with a Navy SEAL named Rocky Rodriguez, but wasn't sure if the initial infatuation would go any further. Giggling that broad shoulders made up for a myriad of sins, Smee left Adele on the bow of *The irate air* and rejoined Marc, waiting at the end of the dock.

Going back inside the boat, she decided to try out her cross-bow, the souvenir of her kidnapping adventure. She took it out of the chest and went up to the far side of the deck for a little target practice. Standing tall and erect like Athena, the warrior goddess, she aimed her bow at a buoy twenty feet away that had been painted with a funny clown face. *Zing* went the metal arrow, trailing its leather lead rope and making a resounding thump as it hit the mark, square in the clown's nose. *Awesome!* Who knew Adele could be such a sure shot? Certainly not Adele. Tugging the lead rope, Adele pulled the arrow out from the buoy and back to her bow. After two more bull's eyes she placed the weapon at the end of her berth with the arrow resting on the string, where it was ready for action.

Being drawn once again to her pirate chest, she lovingly shooed Gilligan from his now favorite place to sleep eighteen hours a day (or longer), opened it up, and dug down to the bottom. There she found a primitive pencil drawing of Anne, dressed in pirate garb. Berry dyes provided the color for the blue silk shirt and matching sash in her hair. Anne was brandishing a cutlass and proudly displayed her disheveled flowing red mane. There might have been an almost 300-year age difference, but resemblance between aunt and niece was unmistakable. *We've got a lot of work to do, Aunt Anne, and I really do need your help.* The newly found silence in her ears comforted Adele as she lay down on the plush berth cushions.

Chapter 14

Alli was in an Operations Room at AUTEC, having just finished a four-hour interview for the new position, and was ready for a beer. One of her co-workers popped two Kaliks and she drank deeply. "Say, Jeffrey. I know you were doing some sonar and optics testing a couple of days ago. Did you by any chance come across a 45-foot Hunter Passage with dark blue striping?"

Thinking for a moment, Jeffrey took off his glasses, rubbed his eyes, and pulled up a series of tracking images on his computer. After bringing up more than a dozen photos, he stopped at one of a somewhat unclear sailboat that looked as if it could be the *Beautiful Bonny*. Unfortunately it was too blurry to tell for sure.

"Where was this taken?" asked Alli.

"Near the Berrys."

"Thanks, Jeffrey," said Alli as she finished her beer, "and have a great Christmas." *Bingo*, she thought and headed out the door and to a military flight back to Florida, as tomorrow was Christmas Eve.

Adele had just finished a slow run around the marina. After unwrapping her now swollen ankle and giving her sweaty body a washcloth rinse-down, she dressed in her black tube-top sundress and painted her lips with Burgundy Bold lipstick. She then walked up to The Anchorage community bulletin board next to the bar and read a poster about a party that night at the end of Sandy Point near where the ferry comes in. Walking into the waterfront bar, she found a group of wasted women were doing the conga line to "I Will Follow Him," a song made famous by a girl vocalist in the early '60s. Adele sat down to watch the show. She didn't notice Dexter who had come into the bar just a minute or so after her. Moving up next to her, he caught her on a bare shoulder and she almost jumped out of her skin.

"Your hands are like ice," she complained. "What have you been handling?"

"Way too many wet bathing suits. A group of college girls from Miami University are staying on a parents' boat and they all decided to drop their suits at the same time. Three landed in the water. Luckily I have a long pole and hook just made for these kinds of occasions."

"Boys and their toys," muttered Adele.

"Your mom was the one who knew about boy toys. Babs would sunbathe topless on the marina deck and the local waters would turn into a traffic jam with captains of all ages trying to dock at the same time."

"Sounds like the same old, same old. I don't know how your dad put up with her for two years."

Sitting down next to Adele, Dexter told her Babs had really helped his father bring in boat owners from around the country to dock at The Anchorage. When they first met there were twenty-two full-time renters at the dock, and two years later there were fifty-three. She was a great businesswoman and would put flyers up at all the local bars, reaching out to resort owners and concierges promising to make referrals worth their while. Always assuming the worst, Adele gave off an air of disgust.

"It's not what you think, Adele. Babs would offer them free drinks at this bar and after-hours use of the pool and bathhouse. She always looked lovely and sometimes bootylicious, but she rarely behaved that way."

Dexter told her his dad really respected Babs, even more so when she rebuffed his awkward advances. He was fresh from a painful divorce and just wanted to have some fun, but Babs was still trying to heal from Darryl's death, more than five years earlier.

"Why do all the men who know Babs defend her? She must have the magic touch I didn't get."

"Not magic, just sweet." Dexter got up from the bar. "Gotta go and do a swimsuit count. It's a bit embarrassing, but the girls are waiting for me."

After one watered-down Bahama Mama, Adele applied a second layer of Burgundy Bold and headed to the parking lot. Deciding to make the drive out to Sandy Point, she put Fergie into her CD player and started to rock out, arriving at her destination an hour later. A typical Bahamian-style party was going full force, with a giant bonfire close to the water, a five-piece steel band playing Bob Marley favorites, and several amateur guitarists strumming along. One of the party hosts came up, offering her a beer and a plate of grilled fish. She sat down alone on a rock and started to move with the music.

Adele spotted Elaine, sitting on another rock about twenty-five feet away. Her tank top was at least two sizes too tight, but she was wearing a beautiful and bright floral-print skirt with it. Adele walked over and sat down on the sand in front of her. "Hi, Elaine. It's nice to see you. What a great skirt—love all the colors!"

"Thanks, it was a birthday gift from my new guy, Bobby."

Shit, thought Adele. *Elaine's fortieth birthday was more than a week ago and I didn't even send her a card.*

She made a date for a belated birthday lunch at Papayas on Christmas Eve Day, Adele's treat. Since Elaine was spending the night on Abaco, she enthusiastically agreed.

"You have a guy, Elaine. Wow. How great. Who is he?"

Looking self-conscious, Elaine admitted that he was there at the party but her parents didn't know anything about him because, as usual, they wouldn't approve.

"It's our little secret," promised Adele kindly.

Rocky and Diego emerged from behind a small, low stand of mangrove trees and walked along the beach, keeping clear of the beachside activities a short distance away. Winston and his boss were walking behind them in the shadows.

The four men then stopped for a moment and Diego gave Rocky a sealed envelope. "These are the specs," said Diego, "and the unit should be worth five million or more on the open market."

Rocky gave Diego a hard look and firm handshake. "I'll be in touch." As the four men parted company Rocky looked up the beach and spotted Adele by the bonfire. He carefully moved out of her eyesight and back among the mangrove trees.

Elaine splashed her feet in shallow water and looked up in time to see her boyfriend's gold earring glint in the moonlight. "My friend over on the rock really likes the skirt you gave me, Bobby," burbled Elaine, planting a sloppy kiss on his lips. Bobby looked around the party perimeter and spied Adele sitting alone on a rock.

"Is that her, with the red hair? Your friend looks lonely. Why don't we go over and keep her company?"

"Sure, but not yet. I want you all to myself." Elaine tried to nuzzle his ear.

Gripping Elaine firmly by the arm, he led her over to Adele and flashed his most charming smile.

"Hi. I'm Bobby, but I'm frequently mistaken for Blackbeard. I understand you're a friend of my lady here? Mind if we join you?" Bobby asked as he put his arm around Elaine.

"Great earring, Bobby. Nice to meet you," said Adele as she shook his hand. "I don't know much about Blackbeard the pirate, but you have a very pretty black beard thing going on around your chin." Elaine hung back a stride or two behind Bobby.

"Thank you kindly, Adele. It looks like you ladies need another beer." Bobby stepped away to one of the makeshift bars at the far end of the beach. As he turned his back towards them, Adele noticed the scorpion tattoo on his back.

"Is this the guy you met on Craigslist? He seems like quite the character."

"Oh, no, I met Bobby at Crabbers last week and things have been moving pretty fast. He's the guy you saw at the Rendezvous bar, and has seen me every day since." Elaine giggled and counted on her fingers. "That's Monday, Tuesday, Wednesday, Thursday, Friday. . . ."

"So what did you tell him about me?"

Elaine looked surprised. "Nothing."

"But he knew my name. . . ."

At the beachside bar, Bobby opened two Kalik Light beers and brought a small tablet out of his pocket. He broke it in half and dropped one piece into each bottle. He swirled the beer around gently and came back to Adele and Elaine, handing them each a bottle.

Adele was the first to take a long swig and then another one. Almost immediately she could feel her demeanor and expression start to change and she relaxed deeply. Though it wasn't exactly an out-of-body experience, Adele's muscles went fluid and she started to sway gently and without inhibitions. *Was it the beer or did Bobby spike it with something?* Within a minute, she experienced double vision and started to dance provocatively around the bonfire. The blond man standing fifteen feet away who smiled at her exhibitionism suddenly became Curtis. She moved towards him with clenched fists and a frozen smile on her face. Another wave of unreality hit her and she was alone, dancing on her own private stage. *The whole beach is mine, and I'm going to move across it all.*

But what the people at the party saw was something entirely different. Adele felt like an accomplished modern dancer as she threw her body around wildly on the sand. No such luck. Isadora Duncan be damned; she actually looked like someone who was trying to ride a kangaroo. She slipped to the ground, grabbed her now painful ankle and in the recess of her drugged mind heard her mother's old mantra, *power through the pain.* She slowly picked herself up.

Bobby watched Adele make a fool of herself while Elaine took three long swigs of her beer and finished the bottle, then started to tremble noticeably. Turning back to Elaine, Bobby helped her over to some remote rocks and left her there as her shakes turned into tremors and labored breathing. Seizing his moment, he hooked Adele around the waist, but our dancer wasn't done performing. She deftly moved away from him, garnering the applause of the partygoers.

Rocky heard the noise and headed towards the beach. The gold flecks in his eyes turned dark amber when he saw Bobby taking another beer and putting an unidentified substance into the bottle. But before Bobby had a chance to force-feed the drink to Adele, Rocky pretended he was drunk and stumbled into the wannabe Blackbeard, making him spill the beer all over himself. "Sorry, man," he said to Bobby.

Mission accomplished. Bobby was wet and smelled like a brewery. Looking angry and vulnerable, he left Adele behind and headed off from the party, picking up the unresisting Elaine on his way.

As Bobby moved out, Rocky moved in and picked Adele up from the sand, gently crooking her in his Popeye-the-Sailor-Man arms. He manhandled her back towards his old beat-up Jeep Wrangler.

"What are you doing here?" she asked.

"Following you."

"Damn good thing," she slurred. Rocky could tell she was definitely out of it but still coherent enough to insist that he drive her Bug back to The Anchorage. He loaded Adele in the passenger's seat and his duffle bag from the Jeep in the back seat, and locked the door. Struggling to get into the driver's seat of the Volkswagen, he found it was way too tight for his six foot, four inch frame. Opening up the sunroof, he half sat, half stood with his head and shoulders protruding up into the open air.

Ouch, thought Rocky as he managed to get back to The Anchorage with a minimum of leg cramps and shoulder strain. He helped Adele out of the car and walked her around the parking lot for a good twenty minutes before leading her down the dock and onto *The irate air*. Taking off her sandals, he rubbed the sand from her ankles and legs and then started to massage her arms and shoulders. Suddenly a big black cannonball shot out of an open cupboard and Gilligan was once again aloft on Rocky's shoulder. He jumped noticeably and placed the cat in Adele's lap. She started to stroke him randomly and hard. After a loud meow, Gilligan jumped back into the cupboard.

"Easy, girl," said Rocky gently. "That cat isn't stuffed." He then saw a package of NoDoz on the counter next to a photograph of Adele at the age of seven. In the picture she was standing next to Marvin, who had his arm proudly draped around a seven-foot sailfish. The photo was inscribed "To Delly, Love Marvin."

"Delly, huh?" Rocky mused, smiling slightly.

Adele was already starting to regain her senses, so Rocky assumed BJ hadn't given her anything too dangerous. He handed her two of the energy-infused tablets and she swallowed them hard. This was followed by a Jolt Energy drink Rocky found in the cooler.

Several minutes later, Adele had regained most of her equilibrium. Pushing Rocky away, she stared at him with still glassy eyes. "How'd I get back here? Were you at the party? I can't remember seeing you there."

Deciding not to tell Adele the truth, he said that the Kalik was spiked with Bacardi 151 and she'd started to spin out of control at Sandy Point.

Adele looked down at her scratched-up and reddened knees. "Somehow it seems like I was dancing. Was there a dance floor at the beach?"

"Not exactly. But you thought there was."

"Oh, my God. Did I make a complete fool of myself?"

"Not totally," said Rocky kindly.

"Thank you for bringing me back. Why do you bother with me?"

"You've had a tough couple of weeks, Adele. Don't be so hard on yourself." He then moved in more closely and gave her a kiss on the forehead. Tilting her head up to see his face, Adele uncharacteristically reached out and planted a firm kiss on his so-available lips. He pulled back a bit.

"Wow, that was unexpected. Nice, but unexpected."

Adele sat up a bit straighter. "How about if we start over, Rocky? I know Christmas Eve is usually family time, but it doesn't look like I have any next of kin here. What about you?"

"Me? Hey, I grew up in Pittsburgh's Southside. A Christmas without a drive-by shooting was a good day. We were real blue collar and never expected much in the way of presents. My dad was great with his hands and always carved me a wooden toy to put under the tree. Mom was a waitress and usually had to work on either Christmas Eve or Day, and she brought home cold cuts to share. Not exactly a full family dinner but it was okay. So any upgrade to the evening expectations would be nice."

"Let's not call it a date, but rather a very small gathering of unattached people. Should we gather here or on Nassau?"

"I'm not sure yet. I was alerted earlier today that I may be on call in Nassau tomorrow night. So much for Christmas vacation."

"Well, that could work. My boss—did I tell you about Smee?—gave me the key to his place. Wait'll you see his loft. . . ."

The stimulant was starting to wear off and Adele went into the head to straighten her hair and wash her hands and face. Next to the toilet was Rocky's SEAL-insignia duffle bag. She stroked it gently.

Then she lugged the heavy bag into the bow of the boat, asking Rocky why he had joined the Special Forces group.

"I got a free ride to Annapolis and felt I had to complete dad duty. No one was more surprised than me when being patriotic became appealing."

"What does 'dad duty' mean?" She blinked hard, trying to stay awake.

He explained that his grandfather was a low-level grunt in

the Navy but his dad, Frank, was the first man in the family who wanted to go to Annapolis. Unfortunately his dad was always late for everything and trying to get an appointment to the Naval Academy was no exception. After he finally got a meeting with Senator Constanza, an old boy from the neighborhood, he was literally a day late to be considered for an appointment to Annapolis. The Senator was allowed two appointments a year and he had just finalized his second cadet the day before Dad's visit. Even Grandpa Frankie's pleas and a promise of Grandma Connie's homemade Mexican wedding-cake cookies for life couldn't undo what had been done the day before. So his dad was forced to attend junior college for a year, study electronics, and then reapply. But he was hoodwinked by a sneaky Gunnery Sergeant at a local recruiting office who convinced him to enlist in the Navy when he thought he had been admitted to the Academy.

"Sometimes Dad wasn't the sharpest tool in the shed and he couldn't understand how his supposed freshman year turned into Boot Camp. It was a rude awakening when he found out he had actually been tricked to enlist in the Navy."

"Did he ever get into Annapolis?" asked Adele with great interest, leaning very close.

Not a man to give up easily, Frank befriended a commanding officer who helped him make it through Boot Camp as well as the required Prep School where he continued studying electronics. A year later, at the age of 20, he finally got accepted and was on his way to his life-long dream of "driving" ships.

"So you're second-generation Annapolis? That's really very sexy." Adele gave him butterfly kisses on the neck.

"Not exactly." Rocky met her kisses and returned them, then he cleared his throat and went back to his story. "Dad was just finishing his 'plebe' or freshman year when Mom got pregnant. Grandpa insisted on a shotgun wedding and eight months later yours truly came out of the womb. They don't allow married freshmen at the Academy so Dad had to quit."

"No wonder you're such a ball-buster," whispered Adele.

"I followed in the almost family tradition and joined the Navy right after high school as well, and I was recruited two years later to attend Annapolis. It was hell to have to go through the equivalent of Boot Camp twice."

It was the beginning of "May Week," the Annapolis version of the Navy's "Hell Week," the day he arrived at Academy. He was stripped of his enlisted man's uniform, had his head shaved, and became one in the sea of plebes. The goal of that week was to make the new freshmen blend in with the rest of their classmates.

"Well, I don't think you blend in, I think you're special," Adele said, "especially since you saved my life." She chuckled. "So you're first-generation Annapolis? That's *really* very sexy."

Rocky brushed his lips across her mouth and told her he'd be in touch by midday about their Christmas Eve celebration. But before he left he turned on the gas heater. "Wouldn't want you to catch cold before our private holiday."

"Wamblety-cropped, are you? Can't hold your liquor?" bellowed Aunt Anne stridently. "And that man you were chuggin' with, he's no Blackbeard in my book." She was wearing a white frilly man's pirate shirt and giant emerald earrings.

"What are you talking about, Aunt Anne?" mumbled Adele as she roused herself to a sitting position. "Hey, where do you get all those great clothes? Smee would love the shirt you're wearing."

"I've had three hundred years to find just the right fit and, trust me, goin' through all those old corpses, chests, and attics is certainly not pleasant. Why are we jawin' about my gussied-up silks and satins? I have somethin' to say to you.

"That hedge-bird who gave you the last beer, he don't know a hawk from a handsaw if he likens himself to Edward Teach—or Blackbeard, as he was known. Teach was as dangerous as they came when roaming the salty seas. Jack's friends called him BB. He was sailin' three years before we were on the *Treasure*, but I've been told he was brave and strong and more than a little bit wild, adonizin' himself in holiday silks and scarves."

"Sounds like I'm about to get another history lesson," Adele groaned. Sure enough, Aunt Anne went on to recount that Blackbeard was given the *Queen Anne's Revenge* in 1717 and converted her into the most powerful ship in American waters, able to carry a crew of up to two hundred sixty heavily armed pirates. He grounded her off Beaufort Inlet in 1718 but escaped with all her treasure.

Believing that a drunken ship was a happy ship, Blackbeard was perhaps the most famous of the early eighteenth-century pirates of the Caribbean. He was known for being very fond of the women he would find on his travels. Wooing them or not, he would kidnap the wives and daughters of planters and have his way with them. Legend says he was "married" to a dozen or more women scattered around various ports. Jack told Anne how one drunken night the two pirates decided to make a secret visit to a South Carolina plantation, as Blackbeard wanted to huddle with the owner's seventeen-year-old daughter. The young girl didn't seem to mind it when BB climbed up her trellis and through the open window. The flimsy wood broke when Jack tried to make the climb, however, so his only enjoyment came from the moans and groans he heard from the grass. Thirty minutes later BB jumped down the twenty feet to the ground, the dreamy-eyed teenager bidding him "adieu" from the window.

With a long black braid and chest-length beard, he would festoon his hat with slow-burning fuses, lighting them just before going into action. Blackbeard was truly a terrifying sight, which was part of the reason for his dastardly success.

Adele blinked at the mental picture. "Wow, why would anyone want to compare themselves to Blackbeard? He sounds like one gnarly character."

"In reality BB wasn't such a scabby soul, just greedy."

"Well, that's all fine, but listen, Aunt Anne, I went back to the warehouse just like you told me to and saw strange things: bows that weren't attached to boats and plastic plants and clowns and giant apes. What does this have to do with finding the *Hygia* and *Bonny*? Supposedly you and Jack were such great trackers, are you messing with my head?"

"Men have never been your strong point, Adele, especially landlubbers. Now, me on the other hand—but this conversation's about you. . . ."

Adele was finally becoming a bit more awake. "Thanks for noticing, Annie. I could really use some help here."

"Don't call me Annie, I've always hated the name. When one of Jack's hoity-toity mistresses called me Annie, I had the pleasure of hanging her by the knickers from the yardarm—and it wasn't my fault the flimsy fabric didn't hold."

"But as you said, Aunt Anne, the conversation's not about you."

"Well, it's time to listen and learn as every word is the truth, love. Men are never what they seem to be and that salty dog BJ holds the key."

Chapter 15

Adele woke up with a heavy head and rolled over on top of a crinkled hand-written note from Rocky: "Call you later, Delly."

She smiled, surprised to discover she didn't mind Rocky calling her by a childish nickname she usually resented. She turned over to get another thirty winks or so but the clock read 11:35. Realizing that she was meeting Elaine at Papayas around noon, she sat up suddenly in her berth, slamming her head hard on the very low ceiling. "Shit," she yelped, nursing a sore scalp and still slightly out-of-focus eyes. Finding one of her few unwrinkled t-shirts in a bunkside drawer, she slid it over her braless body. This one had no message, sort of summing up how she felt today. Unfortunately the khaki cargo pants weren't in as good shape as the shirt, but Adele pulled them over her ample bottom and crawled out of the bunk and into the very crowded common area, which was scattered with last night's clothes, the empty rum bottle, and several damp towels. Finding her red leather Day Planner under a pile of dirty t-shirts, she opened it up to the To-Do list section. She wrote: "Clean Up the Cabin. Change the Bed."

Stretching up tall to get last night's painful kinks out of her sore body, she slowly moved her feet into brown slides and ambled into the head where she combed her hair and splashed water over a puffy face. Trying to erase her sand burn, Adele powdered her cheeks with bronzer and added the Burgundy Bold lipstick.

Looking around the little area, she tried to think about what she could give to Elaine for this birthday brunch. "Perfect," she crowed as her gaze landed on four new unwrapped bars of ginger, verbena, lavender and amber scented Abaco Island bath soap. Next to the bars on the plastic vanity shelf was a piece of almost-new pink tissue paper and a roll of Scotch tape. She quickly wrapped up the bars, securing the ends with the tape.

Unfortunately she didn't have enough time to walk the thirty minutes it would take on foot, so she went up to the parking lot and unlocked the front door of the Bug, tuning out Dexter's smart-ass query: "Hard night, huh?" Inhaling the scented soaps deeply, she took the verbena bar and stuck it into her dashboard cubbyhole. *Better than perfume*, she thought, and headed towards Papayas. *Besides, Elaine can only use one bar at a time.* The loud sound of her "Battle Hymn of the Republic" ringtone brought her out of her reveries. Rocky was on the line.

"Hi, Delly. Sleep like a rock?"

"You can only call me that in private," she rebuked. "Why do I vaguely recall you saving my life again?"

"Probably not your life, but definitely your pride," said Rocky. "I stayed over at The Fig Tree last night, but I have to be in Nassau on the day after Christmas, so how about if I bum us a ride on a boat back to Smee's place this afternoon?"

"Sounds perfect. How about meeting me here at two?"

"Will do," Rocky agreed, then static took over the line.

Adele hit gold, a parking space square in front of Papayas. It was only twelve feet long, but she managed to maneuver her little car perfectly between a new T-bird and a tacky old truck. Elaine, as usual, was waiting for her friend with cocktail in hand. Today it was a frothy banana daiquiri.

"Why are you always twenty minutes late?" Elaine asked. "We all have schedules to keep, you know."

Adele sidestepped the reproach and handed her the bright package. "Happy belated birthday, Elaine."

Elaine unwrapped it with a smile on her face. "Maybe Bobby will find me irresistible tonight," she said, breathing in the amber-scented bar.

"Well, he better. Sorry I wasn't more original, Elaine, but as you know I've had a lot on my mind lately. I've lost everything important to me and don't know if I'll ever get it back."

"It's really sucky that Curtis turned out to be such an SOB. Maybe it hasn't been so bad being sheltered by my parents. But I don't know how to introduce them to Bobby. As you know, he's a little rough around the edges and I haven't been feeling so good either. Had a really bad headache this morning."

"No wonder, after last night."

Elaine looked at her blankly. "Last night? It was really fun, but I woke up about ten a.m. this morning on Bobby's boat with throbbing temples and no tampons."

"You don't remember someone spiking our beer?"

"No. I don't know what you're talking about."

Adele ordered a Coke with lots of ice from the hovering waiter and decided to change the subject. "So, are you and Bobby spending Christmas Eve together?"

"Yes, and it's going to be fabulous. But please don't tell my father." Adele didn't react, so Elaine continued. "It's been years since I've had a real boyfriend and don't want to blow it. Bobby's such a catch. I think he owns a whole fleet of boats. He brought me over from Nassau on a 42-foot Hunter Passage, almost a dead ringer for the *Beautiful Bonny*. Tomorrow he's taking me out into deep water on a yacht much bigger than Dad's catamaran."

Adele found this quite a coincidence and told Elaine about her experience boarding the *Dead End* and meeting up with two characters named Diego and Winston. Elaine examined her empty glass with seemingly rapt attention.

Interrupting their conversation, the waiter came back to their table and, after a beat, the ladies ordered crab cake appetizers. Adele then asked Elaine pointedly what her boyfriend's crewmembers looked like. Elaine glanced away with a stricken look on her face and quickly ordered another cocktail. "I'm sure there're dozens of boats in the Caribbean resembling the *Bonny*, and trust me, Bobby didn't steal your boat."

"I never said he did. But, honey, watch yourself. Wasn't Bobby the one who handed us our beers last night?"

Elaine then held Adele's hand firmly. "I'm sure you're mistaken. Bobby didn't do anything wrong. Adele—I really need Bobby to like me." Looking into her friend's tearing eyes, Adele decided not to pursue her growing feeling that boyfriend Bobby could really be very bad Bobby. She quickly turned the conversation to a discussion about how cool the weather had been on the islands this winter.

After they finished their crab cakes in silence, Adele left too much cash on the table, not waiting for change. When she went to her car, unfortunately, a full-sized Ford Explorer had replaced the T-bird, so it took several tries and a couple of fender nicks and bumper grinds to dislodge the Bug from the curb.

Driving back to The Anchorage, Adele thought about her eight-year friendship with Elaine. She was teaching dance in Palm Beach when Elaine and her mother Patrice came to class. They were on vacation from Nassau and the mom had obviously dragged her non-athlete daughter to step aerobics. Adele, liking the sparkle in Elaine's eyes, asked her if she wanted to take the next class. Patrice was delighted and insisted Elaine stay with Adele while her mom did some shopping, but Elaine was horrified over the thought of more exercise. As soon as Patrice left another instructor came in to teach the spinning class, and Elaine and Adele headed next door for the best mojito in the state. They really liked each other and became better friends after Adele married Curtis and moved to Nassau.

Now their relationship seemed to be in danger. *I hope my bluntness won't ruin our friendship*, she thought. *But I had to warn her about Bobby.*

While she drove back to the marina, her reveries were interrupted by a call from Marc. He said he was flying back to Marsh Harbour to pick up a small mast for Marvin, and he wanted to deliver a package to her. After she hung up, Adele gave herself a mental pat on the back. She loved being a *pirate loot retrieval ex-*

pert, had solved her first case in three days, and was hot on the trail of both the *Hygia* and the *Beautiful Bonny*; maybe she had finally found her next and last career.

Excited about her upcoming *non*-date with Rocky, she rummaged through the bunkside drawer, looking for a feminine outfit to wear—not too fancy, but something to show off her toned shoulders and firm bubble butt. She found a jean mini skirt and an off-the-shoulder white blouse, both just a little wrinkled and perfectly ready to be worn for Christmas Eve. Finding her tried-and-true messenger bag, she sighed over its singed state. *Not intended for use in dockside fires. . . .* But nonetheless, she stuffed it with a clean pair of panties, shorts, t-shirt, and, as an afterthought, a bright red silk teddy. She couldn't find the Hello Kitty cosmetics case, so she filled a plastic bag with the new makeup she'd been saving for a night like tonight, and loaded it into the pack as well. Her last addition was a half-pound box of Godiva chocolates, extra dark truffles with raspberry filling. *I could really fall for this guy.* She smiled to herself. *He's nothing like Curtis; he's a man who says what he means and means what he says. I like it.*

She heard Marc yell out a cheery "Hello" as he jumped aboard *The irate air*, carrying a large, slightly tattered cardboard box held together by duct tape. He handed Adele the box, and when she opened it she found it contained the old—but new to her—weather system Marvin had taken down from the *Bodacious Ta Tas* earlier in the week. After unpacking it carefully, she concluded she had no idea how to assemble the pieces. Marc told Adele to call Marvin and ask how to mount the system at the top of her mast. Remembering that Jack had needed a winch to hoist up Marvin, she looked inside an old locker on the dock next to *The irate air*, where Dexter had told her he stored "stuff." Sure enough, she found an old, rusty, cobweb-infested winch handle and a screwdriver, which she tucked in the waistband of her pants. She gave the winch handle to Marc on the deck of *The irate air*. He attached it to the onboard winch, and after Adele knocked the handle hard several times with the plastic end of the screwdriver it slowly started to turn. Feeling ready to tackle the task, she called Marvin on her cell.

"You old softie," she greeted him. "After I ribbed you about giving it to one of your harem!"

"Merry Christmas, Delly. You're right, this is the weather direction unit you saw me disable on Monday," said Marvin. "It's very simple to understand. Someone has to be winched up the mast to install the system by attaching the two clamps. The system wire then needs to be fed down through the mast pole and plugged into the outlet on the inside of the helm. I'll stay on the line to talk you through it."

Adele was deathly afraid of heights so Marc got into the harness and Adele wrapped the rope around the hand winch. She gave the old heave-ho, but Marc's feet didn't even leave the deck. Ten minutes later, and with all the help Adele's antiperspirant could muster, Marc was still grounded. They decided to change places, but Marc couldn't lift her up with *The irate air*'s small hand-turned winch either.

"I can't understand it," griped Adele. "Curtis would hoist Gracie, our boat girl, up the mast of the *Beautiful Bonny* as if she was as light as a feather."

"But *Bonny*'s a Hunter Passage and has the smoothest equipment out there," Marc pointed out.

"I'm smaller than Gracie," countered Adele petulantly.

Marvin's chuckle sounded through Adele's phone, left on the deck before she'd started her dubious adventure.

"With all the exercising you've been doing, I thought climbing up would be easy for you," grunted Marc, breaking a sweat.

"But this is a much bigger piece of equipment than I've used before and it's more difficult to get just the right grab. Try again."

Marc did try again and managed to get her hoisted four feet into the air, just high enough for him to be face to face—or face to fanny—with her ample posterior.

"I thought your butt would be smaller from all that exercise, not the other way around."

"It's a known fact that muscle weighs more than fat," lectured Adele.

Marc was starting to lower her down when Rocky arrived, wearing another one of his beautifully tailored white shirts.

Marc did a low whistle in admiration. "Man, I don't know how you do it. Even with a bucket of bleach, my white shirts are all tattletale gray."

Bypassing the compliment, Rocky surveyed the situation and asked Marc to step out of the way. With a few strong turns of the winch he had Adele up all twenty-eight feet and almost into orbit. Rocky looked at Adele from the bottom up. "Nice view," he approved.

"Don't talk to me right now or I'll lose my concentration," warned Adele.

Too late—the screwdriver came plummeting down, almost giving Rocky an unwanted flat top. "Yikes, you're dangerous when you're airborne!"

Marc sent up the weather unit and dented screwdriver on another rope before turning to Adele's squawking phone on the deck. "Delly, are you still there?" Marc picked up her phone and spoke into the receiver.

"That's an affirmative, Marvin. She's up at the top of the mast. Now what?"

"All she has to do is screw the two bolts into the metal plate in the box, attach the clamps to the mast and unit and send the wire down through the center of the mast pole."

"I love these little boxes," said Adele as she removed the wind detection system from the carton. "Makes me think of presents."

She was placing the unit up against the pole when a speedboat zoomed into the "no wake" zone and rocked *The irate air* so severely that Adele almost lost her grip. This was the reason for the "no wake" zone, which meant boats were legally supposed to slow down to five miles an hour within the posted distance of a marina so they wouldn't bounce and rock other boats that were either docked or close to shore. But this was the Bahamas and most boats were boy toys with captains who cruised by their own rules.

"Ass-bite," yelled Adele as the driver of the speedboat gave her the hard Italian arm and elbow upswing.

With the wind system firmly anchored aloft and wires feeding down the mast, Adele noticed that Rocky slowly wheeled her down to deck level and seemed to enjoy every minute of it.

"Wow, that was hard," grumbled Adele. "Remind me to never do it again."

Marvin had hung up when she'd assured him she knew what to do. He called back to leave a message while she was cleaning off her hands, and she played it back less than a minute later. It seemed her old friend was wondering if she was still alive. A small gust of wind started to move the system and Adele entered his number, getting very excited. "It works, Marvin, it really works!"

Marvin said something in private to her and she hung up the phone with a smile. "He doesn't think my butt is too big, Marc. He just doesn't think you know how to handle it."

"All packed, Adele?" asked Rocky, changing the subject. "Work is done. It's now the official start of Christmas Eve. Say, Marc, can Adele and I bum a ride back to Smee's place? I was going to get us a ride on a friend's boat, but your plane will be faster."

"Absolutely. I've already made the offer to Adele. Smee gave me a heads-up that you two might want to use his little den of iniquity. Good thing I didn't bring the biplane. Let's go."

"How many planes do you have?" asked Adele.

"Three that fly, two I'm working on."

Rocky and Adele got a ride from Marc to Smee's holiday house, and the flight over to Nassau was smooth and uneventful. Adele couldn't help smiling when she and Rocky entered Smee's lovely *pied-à-terre*. Since her last visit, he had decorated it with angels wearing red and green sashes, their rubber cutlasses hanging down the front of crisp gold voile gowns. His plants were topped with three-cornered hats, and colorful twinkle lights were celebrating the season. A bottle of Dom Pérignon was chilling in the refrigerator with a note from Smee: "Just in case, my dear."

"How thoughtful!" Adele popped the cork way too quickly and one of the angels lost a head and halo.

Rocky found three champagne flutes and put one underneath the flowing golden stream before an oriental rug was ruined as well. Marc drained his glass in thirty seconds flat and said goodbye.

"I'm going to let you two love birds coo in private. Besides, I need to get back to West Palm and then suffer through a family evening of dry turkey, wet stuffing, and gooey ambrosia."

"Better you than us." Adele hugged Marc. "Merry Christmas, Marc."

"And thanks for the lift, buddy." Rocky gave Marc such a firm handshake that he winced.

"Now, my little sugar plum," said Rocky as he shut the door, "show me Smee's much-talked-about loft."

Adele led the way up the narrow staircase carrying her messenger bag, while Rocky brought up the two champagne flutes and the bottle of the bubbly. He started to laugh in great guffaws when he saw the huge, tightly woven rope hammock with a reindeer-and-evergreen throw in place of the gold thread duvet. This was where Adele had tried to rest her weary bones a week earlier.

"Obviously not meant for sleeping!" Placing the glasses on the lovely polished cherry wood floor, Rocky threw Adele into the center of the hammock and jumped aboard as well. Thinking a hammock was pretty much like a trampoline, Adele got to her knees and jumped up to a standing position, thrusting herself higher and higher towards the ceiling. The hammock didn't rip, but they both started to bounce around wildly until Rocky was thrown to the ground. Although cherry wood is beautiful to look at, it made for a really hard landing. Adele started to laugh, bent down to the floor, and lightly massaged Rocky's lower back.

"I've been there," she commiserated, helping him stand.

"Just ouch," said Rocky as he gently put his arms around Adele and leaned her back into the rope netting. He kissed her eyes and nose before pouring the Dom into an awaiting glass and lifting it to her lips.

His soft "enjoy" was diluted by Adele's loud burp.

"Sorry," she mumbled and kissed him deeply.

Rocky reached for his glass and, after a long drink, emptied it, and then returned her embrace. The next twenty minutes were spent in soft caressing and blissful exploration of tender lips. Breaking free for a moment, she tried to untangle several strands of her red mane from the hammock ropes.

Rocky picked up *The Bahamas Pirates Guide* Adele had been reading during her first visit to Smee's loft. After telling her that pirate fact and fiction had not played much of a part in his life growing up in land-locked Pittsburgh, but that he started to research the life when he became a SEAL, he asked, "Mind if I read to you?" In answer, she settled deep into the crook of his arm. With a beautiful deep voice, Rocky read aloud to Adele the tale of the *Princess Galley* and her boarding by pirates off the coast of Barbados in 1721.

"My Aunt Anne was in New Providence then—I wonder if she knew the ship."

Adele had forgotten that Rocky knew nothing about her dockside chats with Anne Bonny; he looked at her quizzically. "Well, I don't think you'll ever find out, but according to this account, George Lowther was quite the pirate captain. He stripped the *Princess* of everything of value. Thank God there were no women on board. He then stole the slave cargo and several sailors, and made off to parts unknown. What a life."

"But you can't admire him—you're on the other side of the law," argued Adele.

"Not nearly as lucrative," Rocky remarked. "But I've promised to uphold the Navy SEAL Creed, for better or worse."

"Ah, yes, the Creed. 'In times of war and uncertainty, there is a special breed of Warrior ready to answer our Nation's call. . . .'"

"That be me," said Rocky, as he pinned her down hard on the hammock—with their combined weight it came close to touching the cherry wood floor. "Ready for a little plundering, wench?" asked Rocky, and he kissed her deeply enough to almost touch her tonsils. Making out turned into some heavy petting and our SEAL started to round second base.

"Do you mind slowing down a bit?" asked Adele, coming up for air. She thought she really liked this guy and didn't want to move too fast. Unbuckling her messenger bag, she pulled out the box of Godiva chocolates and opened it up, gingerly picking out two pieces.

"Got a little carried away," Rocky apologized. Moving away from Adele, he reached down for some more champagne but brought up an empty bottle.

"Damn. I need to really wet my whistle. How are you with the hard stuff?"

Adele made a face. "Well, too much Jack Daniels gives me the runs."

"Not a pretty picture," said Rocky, sitting up in the dangerously unstable hammock. Adele heard the buzz of the vibrating cell phone in his pocket. When he retrieved it and looked at the screen, he managed to fall out of the ropes onto his knees and stand up on wobbly legs.

"I really don't see what Smee finds so hot about all these ropes—getting tied up and tripped up does not really turn me on. Think I'll go down to Pete's Liquor Store and pick up a Jag."

"You're getting a new car now?" Adele also rolled out of the hammock.

Rocky just shook his head. He told Adele he was going to head down to Pete's Liquors for a bottle of Bacardi Rum and Jägermeister, a potent, dark green, 70-proof alcoholic beverage that tasted a bit like black licorice gone bad.

As he slowly made his way down the loft stairs, Adele got up and opened her messenger bag. Her RAZR was blinking, so she played back the message. "Merry Christmas, sis," sang out Alli merrily. "I told Mom it's too late to call, but my boys are still awake and we are as well. The boys love the new pajamas you sent them and they should fit in about two years. Love you and will call later today."

"Happy Holidays from Sheldon and me." How did Babs make that sound like a reproach? "Hopefully you didn't throw away our check. It was in an envelope in the express mail package. I would have sent a gift but you're so hard to please. Talk to you soon."

"A check! Another thing Curtis stole from me. And 'Happy Holidays,' how politically correct," muttered Adele, angrily punching the button to clear the phone just as Alli was saying "It's me again—" She dropped it onto a small side table and turned away from family contacts.

Adele smiled to herself coquettishly as she pulled out the impulsively packed red silk teddy from her bag and swirled in front of the mirror to admire the view. *This will really ring Rocky's Christmas bell,* she thought, her heart beating a little faster. Her SEAL got three gold stars today: one for helping with the winch, one for being fine with her request to take things slow, and the third one for actually wanting to share a bit of his life with her. How long had it been since she had found a non-gay guy to really talk to? Holding the piece of red silk up in front of an oval free-standing mirror, she thought about what Anne would have worn on Christmas Eve. She imagined her aunt wearing red silk pantaloons, lying lasciviously in the arms of Calico Jack, both drinking a good Chianti that had been pilfered from a Spanish galleon, all the while giving each other long, wet kisses into the wee hours of the morning. *That would have been one awesome night.* She dropped her skirt and slipped into the teddy.

Chapter 16

Rocky left Smee's place unable to stop thinking about Adele. *What a woman. It's going to be hell when the truth comes out, but she may be worth it.* He'd spent most of his manhood enjoying women, but he'd had only one committed relationship. Although he'd known Adele for just two weeks, the memory of faithless Madeline was fading. *Am I getting more involved than I should?*

Turning his thoughts to the task at hand, he raised his collar against the unseasonably cool breeze and light rain and walked towards the bridge leading to Paradise Island. Rocky shook his head over the repercussions of a long-ago event. It was a bad incident, though, almost twenty years earlier. BJ, Rocky, and their naval instructor had all had too much to drink that night. It was right after mid-term exams and all the cadets wanted to blow off some steam. Of course, the night ended in a fistfight when a comment about someone's mother was taken the wrong way, and Rocky got slammed. He punched back but hit their instructor instead. Then, while trying to stop the all-out brawl, he got blindsided in the right temple. As BJ and Rocky had been standing together, the top brass assumed that the plebe had landed the insubordinate punch while the upperclassman must be blameless.

BJ took the fall. Rocky later tried to repay him with a security guard recommendation, but BJ didn't land the job, and still traded on the guilt-trip that Rocky owed him one.

Knowing that BJ could easily lose his temper, he decided not to ruffle any feathers as he spotted his former Academy mate and Diego at a sidewalk food booth, munching on spicy jerk chicken skewers. Large gold hoop earring, scraggly black beard, and longish hair partly covering the tattoo of a scorpion . . . that was Bobby Jack Hunter, all right.

"Hey, Rock. How's your snuggly night going with Adele?" he asked. "Have you found out if she knows anything about where the microchip is stashed?"

"I don't think she knows where it is."

"Maybe she's just a nosy broad who needs to be taken down a notch or two," BJ continued nastily.

"And maybe she's an amateur and no threat to us. Listen, I only got involved with this to settle one last score. Consider my debt paid after we find the chip. You'll have more cash than you ever would have made in the cockpit of a Navy plane. Give me another couple days to find out for sure."

"Three days and then she's toast," rasped BJ.

"Toast?" Rocky asked softly.

BJ shrugged and laughed uneasily. "Hey, don't get excited!" He asked about Adele's light-in-the-shorts sidekick, but Rocky told them so far there was no sign of Smee's knowing the true value of the *Hygia* was much more than the insured amount of $850,000. It was just too bad the yacht's captain had found the microchip attached to the bottom of the compass, he said. Most skippers today used the onboard navigation system for direction.

"The compass was really a stupid place to hide five million dollars' worth of military secrets," Rocky told BJ. "But don't take your stupidity out on Adele. She has no idea the *Hygia* houses the microchip."

BJ watched his long-ago Academy mate leave, not so sure that Adele was as clueless as Rocky professed. Continuing to chew on his chicken skewer, he motioned for Diego to join him. "I want you to go back to the fairy's place and put the screws on that redhead when he leaves," said BJ. "I don't think I want her to celebrate another Christmas."

"I know what you mean." Diego and BJ watched Rocky slip into a store. "I still don't trust him."

Rocky hoofed it back to Pete's Liquors where the proprietor was just closing for the two-day holiday, Christmas and Boxing Day. Convincing Pete to keep his light on just a few minutes longer, Rocky hooked two Grouper-engraved shot glasses and small bottles of Bacardi rum and Jägermeister. He paid with cash to hurry up the process.

Arriving back at Smee's, he found Adele asleep on the floor next to the hammock, wearing the red silk teddy. He carefully picked her up and placed her back in the ropes, sitting down on the hammock as well.

"Mrs. Claus never looked so hot," he growled, gently stroking the red silk.

He watched as her eyelids fluttered and a soft smile curved her lips. When she motioned for him to crawl in with her, he bent over to take off his black boots. Adele's gaze locked on his back, where his shirt was gapping upwards; moving closer, she pulled his shirt up further and licked him lightly, in the small of his back just where his Navy anchor tattoo was. He couldn't help squirming as a tingle ran up his spine, and Adele chuckled delightedly.

"What made you decide to join the SEALs?" asked Adele. "The training must be incredibly hard."

"Well, not as hard as I am right now," said Rocky, as he leaned back into her body. "Truthfully, any real fancy flying made me air sick and I've always loved the romantic notion of sailing out to sea."

"Tell me more." She stroked his arm, then moaned. "You do make it *hard*," she teased. "But let's talk first. Do you mind? I want to hear more of your stories."

The year-plus of hard work was anything but romantic, Rocky remembered out loud. Before graduation he went to "the wall," a massive list of job opportunities. Students were grouped in order of their grades, test scores and other specialties. It was unusual to be chosen for good duty right out of Annapolis, but it did happen and he had a skill—make it two—they just couldn't refuse.

"I became a black belt in taekwondo as an enlisted man in the Navy, and I could do one fifty one-armed pushups in under two minutes."

"Wow, my own Popeye," admired Adele, gripping his right bicep.

"The training is worse than being a plebe during Hell Week at the Academy," he told her. After he'd returned to active military duty and passed a series of mental and physical aptitude tests, the real training began. The five-week indoctrination course was a breeze and Rocky thought the training wasn't going to be so hard. Then came the twenty-four weeks of Basic Underwater Demolition/SEAL training at the Naval Special Warfare Center in Coronado, California.

"From AK assault rifle training and parachute jumping practice to running an eleven-minute 1.5 mile in military boots and fatigues, I was one busy boy."

"No wonder you handled the bad situation at Crabbers like you were ballroom dancing," commented Adele.

Getting tired just thinking about that time of his life, Rocky took the two shot glasses and two small bottles and poured them each a shot of Bacardi. Rocky's was down the hatch in an instant, but Adele took several sips before starting to shiver. "Wow, there's a reason why I never drink my rum straight."

Smiling, Rocky unscrewed the bottle of Jägermeister and refilled the two shot glasses. "Wait until the Jag wallop." He then downed the greenish liquor in one smooth movement as well.

Adele took a big sip and started to see stars. "I've always thought the taste was kind of gross, sort of like a cross between stale cigarettes and licorice." She finished the shot. "But I do like it."

Rocky licked a drop of the elixir from the corner of her rapidly numbing mouth. "Does it taste better with Burgundy Bold lipstick?" she asked.

Before Rocky had a chance to answer her, his cell phone rang loud and clear, with a simple two-tone like an old-school doorbell.

"Gotta take this," he said, pulling a pen and pad of paper from his duffle bag before moving away from her and down several loft steps. "Rodriguez here. What's up?"

The official-sounding voice on the other end was Navy Admiral Bart Braverman, an officer with the U.S. Special Operations Command in Tampa, Florida. He informed "Rock" that a waterproof pouch was picked up off the coast of Fort Lauderdale by an older couple out for a quiet sail. There was an MP3 player inside with a return address. The couple was still in shock after dropping the player off at the police station, as floating next to the pouch was a dead body. After listening to the recorded message and determining it had something to do with the *Hygia* and national security in coastal waters, the police sent it up to Atlantic Command.

"A plane will be at Odyssey Airport at twenty-three hundred hours to fly you back to Tampa," said Admiral Braverman.

"I'll be there, sir." Rocky jotted down his last notes. "Don't let anything go down without me."

Rocky walked back up the stairs, shoving both the note pad and phone into his pants pocket. He heard a rustling. *Did she just jump back into bed? How much did she overhear?* Fortunately he'd been receiving information and not giving it. He watched her for a moment, her curves captured in the gentle swinging of the hammock. *She looks so vulnerable when she's sleepy . . . and probably a little drunk.* He felt the muscles around his heart tighten. "Adele, I've gotta go."

"The bathroom's downstairs," she mumbled, apparently drowsy as she snuggled more deeply into the hammock.

He grinned and bent to give her a hard kiss on the lips, pulling out a small silk pouch from his pocket. Inside the pouch was a very pretty rhinestone and black onyx skull and cutlass necklace. Unwinding its black silk cord, he put the necklace around Adele's neck. She touched it with delight, pulling him roughly into the hammock, covering his face with butterfly kisses and strongly caressing his shoulders. In the heat of the moment

Rocky didn't notice that his phone and note pad fell out of his pocket.

"Not exactly the caliber of a Bonny/Calico Jack piece," he shrugged ruefully. "But it might tide you over until the real loot is found."

"It's beautiful," said Adele sincerely, kissing him harder.

Resisting, he pushed her away gently and sat up straight. "I've got to get back to headquarters. A plane is picking me up at Odyssey in ninety minutes. Sorry I can't stay."

He read the disappointment in her eyes as she tried to edge away from him. "But you're on leave and I think it's Christmas morning."

"Not quite yet," equivocated Rocky. "Hey, don't pout. You know how Santa feels about pouting." Adele turned away from him, pulling the reindeer throw over her head. "I'll call you to-night . . . and Merry Christmas." Adele did not respond.

Fumbling in the dim light, he kicked the table on his way out. There was a rattle as something fell to the floor. It was a RAZR and Rocky picked it up, sticking it in his pocket.

Hurt and angry, Adele lay still under the covers until she heard the door close behind him. She then slid her fingers up and down the necklace cord, fast enough to get a rope burn. Sitting up quickly, she jumped out of the hammock, kicking a phone against the wall and skidding a bit on the note pad. Picking up the pad, she found the scribbled words "recorded message—dead sailor—*Hygia*—found cargo—not safe."

Trying to still her troubled mind, she wondered about the one-sided phone call and cryptic notes. She had followed Rocky to the entrance of the loft, still not trusting any man yet, but it was useless. Rocky hadn't said anything informative—*damn it.* What did it all mean? Was he working to assist her, or was he playing some game of his own? And who was the dead sailor? She was afraid of the answers and began to recite an old drinking rhyme, replacing the "ninety-nine bottles of beer on the wall" lyrics with ninety-nine pirate heads on the wall. At about sixty-four heads she finally started to doze. An echoed hiccup stirred her restless sleep, and she covered her mouth. Another hiccup, not her own, roused her more strongly.

"What are you doing in Nassau, Aunt Anne?"

Anne hiccupped again. "I was just rememberin' a favorite Christmas Eve night around here on New Providence. Jack and me commandeered a French ship, chock-full of Bordeaux barrels from a fine vineyard. We had to drop anchor for three days until Jack was sober enough to continue our course."

She was dressed in a bright green satin shirt with a crown of holly berries nestled in her hair, looking very festive.

Adele murmured a laugh. "Your Christmas Eve must have been better than mine. Rocky left me high and dry on my very favorite holiday."

"I'm not surprised. I never trusted privateers."

"What? I thought you liked Rocky. You called him 'worthy' and 'quality' and everything!"

"A privateer can be a good fighter but still have two faces under one hood. Not like your own shipmates. Don't you know the difference?" She explained that a privateer "let go an anchor to the windward of the law," but was frequently as violent and unscrupulous as his pirate brethren. Furnished with military commissions to fight against sworn enemies of their countries, privateers were authorized to capture both enemy ships and their loot, frequently under the guise of maritime warfare. Rocky seemed to be walking this thin line between legal and illegal activity, "holding with the hare and hunting with the hounds."

"I've always thought privateers were turncoats, like that hocus James Bonny for one, and they should be run through and hanged from the yardarm for the flies to eat," asserted Anne. "They hid behind government letters of marque that let them take and make prize of enemy ships. At least you know where you stand with an honest pirate."

"Pirate . . . privateer, whatever—I'm not sure I trust him,

Aunt Anne. He just had a very hush-hush phone call and left in a hurry."

"No man can be trusted," declared Anne. "Every mother's son'll betray you. I'm feelin' a bit howish, it bein' so early in the mornin' and me here on New Providence, so I'm not at my best. But I think BJ visited last night."

"No, Aunt Anne, Rocky left before any real action happened."

"Well, there's still a chance as the evenin' is late, but the mornin' is still very young. You cut a rare caper at Sandy Point the other night. With legs like those, who needs a cutlass or crossbow? Better than swingin' from ropes, and I wager you could get out of many a sticky situation with one long leap."

"Don't remind me, Aunt Anne. I guess I was quite the Sandy Point clown."

"Mark my words, pretty, you never know when an agile stummick and a swift kick amidships will come in handy." Anne hiccupped again and dissolved in the impending daylight. "Merry Christmas, Adele."

"Ho, ho, ho," Adele said to her aunt sarcastically, pulling the very festive holiday throw over her head. However, sleep eluded her so she continued her countdown of pirate heads on a wall. With only eighteen heads left, she swung her body over to the side of the hammock. Sitting up, she picked up the bottle of Bacardi and poured another shot. *Merry Christmas to me!* But something made her put down the glass midway to her mouth. She then picked up the bottle of Jägermeister and studied the label for several seconds. "B" for Bacardi and "J" for Jägermeister. *Oh, my God . . . BJ. Was Anne seriously trying to warn me about Rocky?* Crashing onto the wobbly hammock, she started to sway erratically and whimpered to herself, "Another one just can't bite the dust!"

Chapter 17

Rocky and three other men sat at a conference table and were deep into a "for your ears only" meeting at the U.S. Special Operations Command in Tampa, Florida. Behind the closed double doors there were only four people in the room, but enough military brass to make sunglasses mandatory. This meeting was about as covert as it could get. The Top Secret group comprised Admiral Bart Braverman, the Special Operations Officer; Lieutenant Commander Chad Wu, one of the members of Rocky's SEAL Team; Colonel and Delta Force leader Sheppard (Shep) Keating; and Commander Ricardo (Rocky) Rodriguez. All four men were dressed in their Navy and Army uniforms with Rocky looking especially handsome in his light brown suit with gold "scrambled eggs" on his shoulder epaulettes. National security was on the line. A dime-sized microchip had been hijacked by mercenaries and was loose on the *Hygia*.

Admiral Braverman informed the team that the Navy had been tracking the yacht ever since it left Solomon's Island off the Maryland coast. The boat's captain was a young lieutenant named Stewart Stocking, planted undercover by the Navy to try and pinpoint where on the vessel the stolen Micro Chip Descriptor that monitored the satellite control was hidden. This was a constellation of five satellites, built and sent up six years after 9/11 to watch the coast for potential terrorist activity. The chip had been stolen from the Patuxent River Research Lab six weeks earlier and was on its way to the Middle East via the Bahamas and the Dominican Republic. On the basis of his intel, Braverman then sent Rocky to the Bahamas on a mission to determine if the *Hygia* was still close to the Florida coast.

Until fifteen days ago Lieutenant Stocking's mission was classified as "need to know" and he was only told that there was a stolen Top Secret package onboard, but he didn't know what it contained. Stocking found the box, outfitted with a tracking device with the "T.S." label broken, and immediately hid it, Braverman told his elite team. But when he was shot, something happened to the tracking unit and it stopped transmitting. The last traceable destination was eighty miles northeast of Nassau, where the *Hygia* was last seen. The only other clue to the chip's whereabouts was the MP3 device, recently found floating in the water near Stocking's dead body and delivered to the Miami police station.

Braverman played the message out loud. "A Fast-Boat is approaching without slowing down. There are guns on board. I'm sure this has something to do with the package I just hid inside the head. I know it's Top Secret stuff and I don't trust my crew. I'll put this recorder in a pouch and throw it overboard." Some muffled sounds, then, "BJ, what are you doing? Are you nuts?" The sound of gunfire permeated the recording before it went silent.

"So there you are. The vital chip is hidden somewhere in the head of the *Hygia*. And we have further confirmation of what we'd suspected, that BJ was not only involved in the hijacking but that he was the one who killed Lieutenant Stocking." Braverman asked Rocky to fill them in on his surveillance in the Bahamas and what he had learned from his former Annapolis roommate Bobby Jack (BJ) Hunter.

"The *Hygia* is somewhere in the Cays around Nassau," Rocky responded. "BJ doesn't trust me well enough yet to reveal the precise location, but I do know that he and his mercenaries haven't located the chip yet. They're disguising the ship and plan to sail to the Dominican Republic after the first of the year."

Rocky went on to tell them about Adele and the work she was doing for Pirate's Plunder. "I'm playing a dangerous cat-and-mouse game with Adele's life and if we haven't found the chip in forty-eight hours I need to get her out of the area."

"When did we ever care about collateral damage?" asked Keating.

"Well, always. Besides, she's a very special lady and I don't want her to get hurt, Shep."

Colonel Shep Keating was a bit of a show-boater and thought the Army's Delta Force should take over *Operation Hygia.* "You and Team SIX have been tracking these guys for almost a month, Rodriguez, and have not made much headway. So how about letting the professionals take over?"

"But what if the mission has some passing and receiving?" Rocky taunted. "I doubt if the Army will be up to it." The previous year Annapolis had creamed West Point 31-17 at the annual Army-Navy football game, and Keating hadn't been civil to Rocky since.

"Up yours, Rodriguez," muttered Keating.

Braverman, not amused, asked Lieutenant Commander Wu and Rocky to leave the room. Wu was a casually tousled and handsome Hawaiian-Japanese who looked as if he would rather be surfing than participating in a high-security briefing. He had flown in from Dam Neck, Virginia and was under Naval Special Warfare Command. Like Rocky, he arrived early Christmas morning and was part of the Commander's 4-Man fire team. Wu was three years behind him at Annapolis and had treated Commander Rodriguez as his mentor, ever since they were stationed together in Somalia six years before. At that time Rocky, with his usual cool, took enemy fire so the young Lieutenant Commander could escape an African ambush with just a graze to his right shoulder.

"Mele Kalikimaka, Rock," greeted Wu, "even though being on assignment away from my folks does not exactly get me in the holiday spirit. What's up? I've been kept in the dark as usual and before today I didn't know where you were or anything about a microchip."

"Back at ya. I'm sorry, Wuze. Until today my assignment was on a need-to-know basis. Sometimes I think I'm back in

Mogadishu with Special Operations, everything is so Top Secret. But as you heard, we have a major Homeland Security breach and it's going to be up to us to find it and bring it home."

"Sounds like old times. I'd rather be tracking mercenaries here than Somalian guerrillas halfway around the world. But the way pirate attacks have flared up, that might be my next assignment."

Admiral Braverman opened the door and motioned for them to come back into the room. "Shep is going to take his lead from you, Rock. But make sure to call him in if you need backup."

"Will do," said Rocky, a bit smugly.

"That'll be all." Braverman waved them away. Rocky and Wu left the secured room.

Once out of the locked-down location, Rocky decided to call Adele and wish her a Merry Christmas before going back into the heavily guarded area. But when he took the cell phone from his pocket, Rocky saw it was a bright purple RAZR, not his own deep red one. *What happened? Oh, shit, I picked up a phone on the way out—guess it was Adele's—mine must have dropped when we were wrestling in the hammock.* He decided to call his cell hoping Adele would answer. He started to dial, but the phone rang in his hand.

Curtis Albury should have been happy but he was not. It was late Christmas morning and he was lolling on a nautical blue silk chair in the spacious cabin of the *Beautiful Bonny* anchored in sight of the Berry Islands, grimacing at the still perceived smell of dirty kitty litter, and talking on the phone. He enjoyed the view of Mandy stretched out on the deck in a revealing pink string bikini. But today the reality finally hit him. He had fenced Adele's conch-shell and pearl necklace for a quick thousand, but he now had millions of dollars' worth of antique treasure and no way to turn it into liquid currency. He was stuck on a luxury yacht, in the middle of a three-day holiday, with no ability to turn the loot into cash. To put it bluntly, he was a broke multi-millionaire.

Though he considered himself a master bull-shitter, he still couldn't convince his contact on the phone to purchase even a portion of the Anne Bonny/Calico Jack treasure. "What do you mean, you can't fence the pieces?" he asked. "I need money now. Six months is too long to wait, asshole!" A dead receiver was his only reply. He angrily threw his cell phone through the hatch and up on the deck.

Going to the small stateroom closet, he pulled out and put on a luxurious navy blue and burgundy brocade smoking jacket. These elegant threads made him think about Adele—because they were so unlike her. For the first two years of their marriage he had really loved her—the dancer's body, her hard-work ethic and free spirit. And knowing that she had a claim to part of the Bonny/ Calico Jack fortune didn't hurt either. Then her lack of caring about her appearance really started to bother him. She would wear a hot pink leotard with bright green leg warmers, or a wrinkled skirt with one of her endless signature t-shirts. *Not really appropriate attire for a woman in her thirties.* The straw that broke the camel's back was on their third anniversary. Curtis had made reservations at The Mansions, a members-only restaurant on Lyford Cay. He approved of the casual cocktail dress she wore, but the ballet flats did not jibe with her satin skirt. He knew then that he had made a mistake marrying her. It was time to move on.

Stroking his beautiful brocade jacket, he looked out to the deck where Mandy was sunning on a lounge chair. She had a few pieces of the Bonny treasure in her lap and was gently caressing them, draping Curtis' captain's medallion necklace around her neck.

Then she reached down to pick up his cell phone where it had landed on the deck. She punched some buttons and held the phone to her ear. "Hello, Adele?" she cooed.

"Mandy?" Curtis called to her in a minor panic.

Mandy waved a dismissive hand at him. "Well, I know who *I* am, sugar, but who are you? . . . Okay, just tell her Mandy loves the necklace. And thank her for being so generous." She hung up the phone.

"Mandy, what are you doing out there? Who are you talking to?"

"Nobody."

"But didn't I hear you say 'Adele'?"

"Well, she didn't answer. In fact, it sounds like she's been very busy." She gathered up the phone and the shiny things and went inside the cabin. "So everybody got lucky."

"A man answered her phone?"

"He sounded hot. But what do you care? You've got me, don't you?"

Curtis opened a small ice chest placed on the lovely teakwood table next to him. He took out a bottle of Dom Perignon, the same vintage Adele had found in Smee's refrigerator. He popped the cork and took a deep drink before passing it on to Mandy. After taking a swig, Mandy sashayed over to Curtis, opened the front of his smoking jacket, and started to rub across his nipples with the cold and hard antique coin necklace.

"Kind of like mine when you touch me," cooed Mandy suggestively. "And this bling looks soooo much betta' on me than on Adele."

"A bit of advice, Boots—I don't really feel like talking about my wife today." He playfully slapped her bikini-clad bottom.

"Ouch." She squirmed suggestively. "I wanna go for a ride."

When Curtis moved to pull her closer, she stood up. "Not that kind of ride—I mean in the boat!" She headed for the dinghy, her laughter trailing behind her.

"Wait for me!" Curtis got up and dressed hurriedly, slipping out of his satin smoking jacket and into a navy blue Burberry polo shirt and new topsider shoes.

For not being the brightest bulb in the chandelier, Mandy was a natural around boats and the water. She lightly jumped into the sixteen-foot rubber dinghy, untied it from the *Beautiful Bonny*, and started the motor up instantly. She took the tiller and began to move away from their mooring in the time it took Curtis to step into the small boat and sit himself down.

"Where to?" asked Mandy.

"We're not too far away from Giggling Girl, so head dead west, Skipper."

"Which way is west?"

Curtis hid a superior smile and pointed in the direction of a large thicket of tall trees about a mile away. Very excited over visiting a beach called Giggling Girl, Mandy gave the dinghy as much gas as it could handle, causing strong fumes and bluish smoke to pollute the pristine waters.

"Easy, girl," he scolded.

As the dinghy headed out into open water Mandy asked him about Giggling Girl and how it got its name. Not wanting to go into detail about the giggly time he and Adele had playing hide-the-salami on the beautiful beach, he told her about the very unusual wooden sign of a laughing mermaid on the shoreline. Curtis recounted that, as he didn't know where he was when the *Beautiful Bonny* was blown off track, he had named the beach after the wooden sign.

"If my memory serves me right, there's a beautiful, wide, pink sand beach, to the starboard of that grove of trees." Curtis pointed to a towering group of mangroves. "Right inside the cove there."

Mandy headed towards the silver trees with such a sudden wheel turn Curtis almost fell off the back of the boat.

Inside the partially hidden cove on Strawberry Cay, Elaine was wading into the water about fifty yards from the Giggling Mermaid wooden sculpture. The bright pink sand beach was one of the most beautiful areas in all of the Bahamas and had been featured in most of the travel magazines as a "must visit" in the Caribbean. The *Hygia*, minus her figurehead and name plate, and painted a deep burgundy, was anchored close to shore, so Elaine waded out to the boat and clumsily pulled herself up on board. Noticing several sea turtles swimming nearby, she found her phone, which was on board, and turning on the camera app she started to screech for them to come closer to the boat so she could snap a quick picture. "Come, turtles, come here, turtles. I won't hurt you."

Hearing her cries, BJ looked up from studying several charts laid out on the sand and yelled out, "They aren't dogs, Elaine!" Under his breath he continued, ". . . but you are."

The mangrove trees started to rustle near BJ, and Winston emerged. "Come look at my handiwork, boss."

Rolling up the charts, BJ crept quietly into the stand of trees and was greeted with the sight of a brand new six-foot boat hull extension, recently painted to match the stolen boat. "Great work, Winston!" whistled BJ. "You're a damn genius. Those three years at Magic and Miracles have paid off."

"Just like at the movies, set decoration and special effects can disguise anything. With this bow extension, burgundy color, and new name, not even her former captain would recognize her," said Winston with pride.

"And he's dead," BJ laughed nastily. "In another two days I'll ditch Elaine the rich bitch and we'll be able to sail the newly named *Gia* into any port and not be recognized. That's the time to tear her apart and find that damn microchip."

Elaine was angling for a good shot of the turtles when the sound of an approaching motor drew her attention to the bend in the cove. Horrified to recognize Mandy standing up at the tiller with her very small triangle top revealing her not-so-hidden treasures, Elaine dropped her cell phone on the deck and did a shallow dive off the side of the boat, swimming towards Bobby and Winston. Getting to the shore quickly, she saw Mandy showing off her skills as both a savvy sailor and swimwear model, flaunting her body to both men who definitely took notice.

Winston leaned down to pick up a pair of binoculars from where they were lying on the sand, to get a closer look. Mandy played for the lens.

"Holy shit," Winston blurted out. "We have a booty call."

Elaine didn't try to hide her irritation at this gathering. "I can't believe it," she exclaimed. "That's Mandy, Adele's and my dance teacher. She's with Curtis, Adele's husband. What a little tramp."

Bobby grinned. "Husband, huh? He should have the inside track." He urged Elaine to wave them towards the beach.

"But why? Inside track to what?" she asked, thinking that this was so not right.

"I could use a little bit of exercise. Now just do it."

Startled at Bobby's gruff tone, she started to wave wildly to Curtis and Mandy, urging them to shore. The small craft dropped anchor, and Curtis and Mandy started to wade to shore.

One of the baby turtles got curious and swam around Mandy's legs. Seeing bubbles in the water, she screamed. "Help! Curtis! There's a poisonous snake by me. Maybe it's a rattler." She tried to shoo the bubbles away.

Curtis started to laugh. "Rattlesnakes are only found in the West and never in the water. Besides, there're no poisonous snakes in these waters."

"It's he-ah, it's he-ah . . . I can feel it," she screamed, jumping up and down.

"They're just sea turtles, Mandy. You're safe. Fancy meeting you here," fluted Elaine in her best heiress airs as the couple approached her. "How do you like my boyfriend's boat?"

Mandy seemed to calm down but not before an ample breast fell out of the fabric triangle. "Not bad," replied Mandy, repositioning her left one. "But my boyfriend's boat is newer."

Elaine looked past her at the small dinghy. "Those tiny boats all look the same to me."

Mandy followed her gaze. "Not that boat! The *Beautiful Bonny*, silly."

Elaine did not miss a beat. "Oh, you mean Adele's boat. Where are you hiding it?"

Before Mandy could answer, Bobby stepped in between the women. "I understand you're a dance teacher? Your work has done wonders for my Elaine and her friend Adele. They both look great."

"Thanks—you've got awesome arms yourself," responded Mandy.

Curtis now stepped into the conversation. "I'm Curtis, bro." He held out his hand but Bobby, busy showing off his muscular arms for Mandy's admiring inspection, cold-shouldered him.

So he turned to Elaine, asking her what she was doing on Giggling Girl.

"Adele told me about this beautiful spot," said Elaine, looking at Mandy. "Shame on you, Curtis." She raised her voice and directed the next sentence toward Bobby and Mandy. "I'm not sure she's even eighteen. Have you spoken to your wife lately?"

"We've split up," he replied curtly.

"So I've heard."

"Now I'm havin' all the fun," bragged Mandy. "And I am too eighteen. I mean nineteen."

Elaine put her arm through Bobby's and pointedly told the group that Adele seemed to be having a pretty good time as well.

"She's awesome—turned into a pirate and is looking for lost treasure."

"Have you lost your mind, Elaine?" asked Curtis. "She's a school teacher."

"Not anymore she's not."

Curtis quizzed Elaine while Bobby listened respectfully, almost raptly. Smiling saucily and playing to her boyfriend, she relished this new celebrity status and started bragging on her friend's adventurous new life.

Mandy sighed deeply and ostentatiously, rolled her shoulders, and flipped her hair. But to Elaine's delight, Mandy was yesterday's news. Curtis and Bobby were too interested in Elaine's stories to react, and the only one who turned towards her was Bobby's employee, Winston—and who cared about him, anyway? Elaine's smile grew a little broader as Mandy walked away from the group and sat on the sand by herself. Winston joined her and whispered something in her ear, then he ran his hands through her chestnut brown curls and she smiled with pleasure.

Elaine shifted her position so neither of her listeners, facing her, could see Mandy's little sideshow. By this time, in her fertile mind Adele was brandishing a cutlass, wearing big slouchy boots, and taking down a half dozen pirates in less than two weeks. She knew she had gone too far with describing Adele's new life, but it was so exhilarating to have Bobby's complete attention for once. She saw Mandy rub some sort of necklace medallion over Winston's chest. Elaine sidled up to Curtis, to make sure she didn't lose his interest, and continued to talk about what a renegade Adele had become. Her friend was looking for mercenaries and had a strong lead, something about a boat with a carved figurehead on the helm.

"She's now living on some old boat in Marsh Harbour. It's so decrepit, it's even lost some of the letters in its name." Bobby looked away from her.

"Wow," said Curtis.

"Well, you didn't give her any good options, did you? You left the condo in arrears, and took the *Bonny.* Where's she supposed to live? Anyway, it gives her a good mobile platform for catching the bad guys, you know?"

"A regular superhero, huh?" Bobby murmured. "A ruthless pirate hunter. Good to know." He looked back toward Elaine. "In case I meet a pirate who needs to be hunted."

Mandy had rejoined the beachfront group, and she now leaned up close to Curtis and whispered to him, but loud enough for Elaine to overhear. "I've got cramps, lover—my period just started. Let's go back to the *Beautiful Bonny.*"

Curtis looked embarrassed and hurriedly said goodbye to the group. As they walked down to the beach, Elaine saw her turn around and wink saucily at Winston—and she saw him return the flirty gesture with a broad and knowing smile.

Chapter 18

Diego would be skipping today's big holiday. He would have a busy day, though, all carefully planned by his boss, BJ. First, he'd gathered his supplies: a bottle of a reliable knockout drug and a large piece of gauze to go with it, and some rope to tie the bitch up after he had sedated her. Check. All was ready. Now for the hunt.

Adele woke up with a start and looked at the clock. It was almost noon and Christmas day was close to half over. Getting up, she changed out of her teddy, putting on yesterday's jean skirt, white blouse, and a black hoodie as the holiday morning was still in the sixties. Grabbing her messenger bag and the RAZR phone from the floor, she climbed down the narrow loft stairs and headed out the front door, looking for any little shop or café that might be serving up some very strong, black coffee. The streets were almost deserted and there was not a java shop open on all of Bay Street. Continuing to stroll, she found herself on Lower Dagger Drive. Still halfway contemplating a break-in of the souvenir shop displaying the imitation pirate treasure, she tested the strength of the front window. Scrutinizing the dull swords and daggers, however, Adele realized not even her inebriated guests at the Provocative Pirates opening would think this dime-store stuff was the real thing. The next door was the main entrance to Pirate's Plunder. Surprisingly, it stood ajar. Creeping in cautiously, she saw the door to the office also standing open. Looking inside, she found IQ with all of Smee's figurines on his desk. He was dusting them carefully.

"Merry Christmas, IQ. What are you doing here today?"

IQ jumped at the sound of Adele's voice and he knocked over a figurine of one of the mermaids found in Neverland's Mermaid Lagoon, breaking her head off.

"Crap," bleated IQ. "I promised Smee I'd take good care of his Peter Pan family. He's going to be so disappointed with me."

"Nothing a little super glue can't fix. Don't you have family on the island?" she asked him.

"They're at Atlantis gambling, something I don't believe in on the day that Christ had risen."

Adele thought for a minute. It was kind of sad that IQ didn't know Christmas was the celebration of Jesus' birthday, but she decided to stay mute, as this was a conversation she didn't want to start. Telling IQ she had some work to catch up on while Smee was gone, she went into Woody's cubicle to search it thoroughly for any kind of clues. Getting extremely frustrated over her lack of success, she pulled out his computer table drawer and dumped the contents out on the floor. Sitting down low herself, she sifted through a myriad of photos with Woody in provocative positions with various other men.

Whatever. Adele also found three shades of lipstick and a pressed powder compact, but nothing to prove Woody's connection with the *Hygia* hijacking. She picked the drawer up and attempted to slide it back on its rollers, pushing it into the waiting slot; something was blocking the path. Reaching her hand inside, she pulled out a dusty day-planner calendar embossed with gold filigree lettering: "There's a little bit of pirate in everyone. Love, your First Mate forever."

Adele smiled a bit sadly as she turned to early December. She found a nail and hair appointment for the second and third and a note reading "Take Smee to meet Santa Claus" on Dec. 7. On December 9 there was a cryptic note, "*Gia*—1713 Bay. Bring drawings and paint chips."

Continuing her search, she opened the bottom drawer of his desk and found three architectural drawings labeled "*Gia*." She looked back in the drawer and picked up a burgundy paint chip.

Hmm. She carefully studied the renditions of the 51-foot twenty-year-old Hinckley Sou'wester. It was the same length and model the *Hygia* was. On the same sheet of paper was a small sketch of an add-on bow extension. With a burgundy paint job, a new bow elongated by five feet, and no figurehead, the yacht could be the hijacked boat and literally hidden in plain sight. Eliminate the *H* and *Y* on the starboard side and it would read *GIA*.

"Hot damn! Finally some progress," whispered Adele excitedly as she put the drawings back into the drawer. She was leaving the office when IQ stopped her before she reached the door.

"Hey, Adele, a group of us are taking a party boat over to Marsh Harbour tonight. Wanna join us? We're gonna' dock there for Junkanoo tomorrow night. Should be awesome."

Not paying any attention to IQ, Adele spoke absently. "Sounds great." She tried to get around him and out the door.

"We're gonna' leave the main dock at four. There're twelve confirmed and we have room for thirteen."

"Can't wait!" She scurried out the door.

"Party, party, party on. . . ." is what Adele heard as she headed up north on Dagger Drive to Bay Street. Concentrating on finding the street number 1713, she drove past a very touristy-looking man heading south.

The man stepped into the Pirate's Plunder doorframe, took off his flop hat, and went inside. Walking to his office, he saw Ignacious trying to use Krazy Glue to mend the mermaid's figurine head.

"Put that aside, IQ."

"Smee! I'm so sorry I broke—"

Shaking his head sorrowfully, he firmly embraced his nephew. "Stewart is gone," he said. "NaNa got the call a week ago that he was killed in the line of duty—an attack at sea aboard the *Hygia*."

"Killed! Why didn't she call us?" cried IQ.

"The Navy didn't find his body right away, and she wanted to tell me in person. I'm so sorry." After holding his grieving nephew tightly for several minutes, Smee asked him if he had seen Adele.

"You just missed her," sniffled IQ.

Walking by the Straw Market, usually bustling with vendors and visitors either trying to make or save a buck but now quiet, Adele saw that even the crazy cruise ship docks had taken the day off. There were no drunken conga lines weaving through the area and into Señor Swordfish's marathon margaritas establishment. *Is this what peace on earth looks like?* Shaking off her poor-me mood, Adele had no time to window-shop and she hurried past the Coach, Magellan, and John Bull shops lining the Rodeo Drive of the islands. Looking carefully at the street number, she found 1700 was at the corner of Bay Street and down a small recessed alleyway. There was a sign with an arrow pointing to 1713; it was located a little south of Bay. There was a sandwich board sign outside boasting "*Art With A Pulse*, the shop that tattooed Anna Nicole Smith."

Grimacing at the commercial use of the poor deceased actress' name, Adele shook her head sadly. Suddenly she was grabbed from behind. Though she tried to pull away hard, she was no match for her assailant. He put her into a chokehold and held a sickly-sweet-smelling cloth to her nostrils. This was the last thing she remembered. . . .

She woke up some time later with a heavy head and itchy eyes. Adele couldn't move the upper part of her body. She had a thick gag in her mouth and though she felt like throwing up, she didn't want to back flush. She swallowed a couple times, hard. Still not thinking or seeing straight, her primary fear was that somehow she was paralyzed from the waist up to her neck. In what seemed like the distant background she heard a man talking on the phone.

Diego had struggled to carry Adele up the rickety stairs into the tattoo parlor, as she quickly became a dead weight. He did, however, manage to tie her up to a support pole in the middle of the dusty room, and made a phone call.

"Aren't the Berry Islands a bit off of the beaten track?" he asked the person on the other end of his cell. "Do you really think we'll be able to leave in two days, BJ?"

"Yes, and a detour provides more time to find the chip," said BJ, on the other end of the phone. "Besides, I want to do a little bit of reconnaissance. Elaine's parents own a private cay there, near Great Harbour, I believe. It will give us time to scope it out in person. Elaine told me the most valuable special-order pieces of jewelry that ultimately end up at their Nassau shop are locked up in their home safe on Anchor Cay until the buyers are in town and able to pick up their loot at the store. Should just be a few hours' sail and we can fill our coffers up even more."

"I like your thinking, boss. The Berrys it is." Diego mouthed one of the dirty shark's teeth in the necklace around his neck. "This must be how the rich get richer."

The Berry Islands comprised more than two dozen small cays, most of them privately owned, and there were more millionaires here per square mile than most places on earth. It was believed that the thirty plus clusters of cays, dear to the hearts of sailors worldwide, were given their name because of the abundance of succulent thatch berry trees growing wild in the region.

"I'm planning on a very lucrative trip," said BJ. "Get rid of Adele and bring the plane back to Strawberry Cay."

Adele's brain and sight started to clear and she realized she was tied at her arms, neck and waist to a rusty pole running the height of the room. The cords were so tight there was no wiggle room at all, and her wrists stung while her hands were sticky. *Must be bleeding.* Listening to Diego's conversation, she realized that the Berry Islands were a very easy sail from Marsh Harbour as well. *Now all I have to do is get out of here and prepare* The irate air *to set sail the day after tomorrow.* Wanting to get Diego's attention, she started to moan, thrashing her head against the pole.

"She's awake. Gotta go." Diego hung up the phone and

lifted her chin. "Good morning, sister." He pulled the gag gently out of her mouth. Then he slapped her hard across the face. "Not a very Merry Christmas, is it?" Still pretending to be totally out of it, she let her head fall down uselessly towards her chest.

Diego untied the shark tooth necklace from around his neck. It was a monstrosity with the front three teeth almost two inches long and sharp as razors. Adele realized these must have been the teeth that did so much damage to Woody. She then looked through her lashes into the face of this predator, watching his eyes turn dead-looking without a hint of remorse.

The predator sized up its prey. "It's time to wake up," he crooned, giving her head a strong push, "and have some fun." Walking to Adele's backside, he started to rub her behind suggestively with his hand. Getting aroused quickly, his hard mound replaced his hard hand and he began to hump her buttocks.

"Feels good," he murmured. "Bet you like it from behind." He wrapped himself around her and started to massage her buttocks. Handling the largest protruding shark tooth with a sexual stroking, he rubbed it all over Adele. "Can't wait to start having fun," Diego smirked.

Pretending to be more drugged than she really was, Adele started to slowly move her legs to distract Diego's gaze down to the lower part of her anatomy.

"Gotta go pee . . . gotta go pee now," Adele mumbled.

"Wouldn't want a golden shower," croaked Diego nastily. "But if you try to get out of here your butt is going to burn."

Diego untied her hands, neck, and waist, and Adele almost fell to the ground. There was a painful red rope burn at her throat. Picking her up by the hair, he started to rub her neck with the shark tooth and got ready to lead her to the bathroom. But before they had moved two feet, Adele jumped back, grabbed the pole, and did a full, fast circle at right angles to the floor. She aimed with all her might at Diego's lower body and kicked him hard. His tanned face went white; he screamed and clutched his manhood. *Now it's time for that animal to feel some real pain.*

Not skipping a beat, she circled again, kicking him in the head, and he crashed down on the wood floor. The necklace flew up into the air and broke apart, and one of the dislodged teeth flew into the corner of Diego's right eye. Howling at the pain, he squirmed backwards, covering his eyes with both hands.

"Take that, shark eyes," she yelled, heading for the exit.

Adele used his momentary distraction to escape and took the unstable steps two at a time. Just inside the door she tripped over something. Getting up with a whimper, she realized it was her own much-abused messenger bag. She took a few seconds to throw the strap over her head, clutched the bag to her chest, and ran towards Pirate's Plunder. The door was locked and there was a roughly handwritten sign pasted to the front. "Gone to party on Marsh Harbour." She looked at her watch and saw it was 3:45. *What was it IQ said? Four o'clock?* If she could make it to the dock, the party boat would take her to the safety of Marsh Harbour. She had fifteen minutes to get to IQ's ferry and away from Diego.

Pulling her black hoodie up to hide her injured neck and the sleeves down over her bleeding wrists, Adele ran the half mile plus down to Boat Harbour, with her adrenaline in full gear. She made a flying leap, landing on the deck of the small and tacky-looking ferry—now doubling for a party boat—just as it was pulling away from the dock. She almost knocked over the island captain. "All Summer Long" by Kid Rock was screaming over the loud speakers, and a dozen young adults were rocking to the words.

"Awesome move, lady," said the captain, with admiration. "Were you a long-jumper in school?"

"Not exactly," she replied, looking around the ferry. "It's amazing what happens when you're facing primal fear. Where's IQ? I could really use a drink."

"He didn't make it, had a death in the family."

Adele got panicky. "Was it Smee?"

"Don't think so, it was some military man."

The captain pulled out a small tarnished silver flask, opened it, and took a sip before handing it to Adele. "Man, you never know when your time's up."

"I'll drink to that." Adele swallowed deeply. Sitting down on a bench, she turned her face to the wind and darkening skies, watching the gray water churn underneath the bottom of the ferry. The only thing keeping her going was the thought that the *Hygia* would soon be on its way to the Berrys and she would be in hot pursuit. But she couldn't leave too soon because she would need help from the local authorities and didn't want to contact them until the yacht had already docked. Perhaps an evening at Junkanoo would lift her spirits. Starting to miss Smee and his crazy costumes, she took what she thought was her cell phone out of her messenger bag but saw a red RAZR mobile—definitely not hers. Furious, Adele dialed a number and heard her own sweet voice: "Adele here and you know what to do." This was the last straw. The red RAZR belonged to Rocky and Adele had his cell.

"You have my phone, ass-bite!" she yelled into the receiver at the sound of the beep and hung up.

It was dark and still when the ferry started to land at the small marina next to Papayas. Everyone except Adele seemed to have had a really good time on the calm crossing. The captain told Adele he would meet her at The Anchorage tomorrow night for "Junkanooooooo. . . ."

Not able to find a taxi, Adele barely managed to drag her battered body back to her own little marina and onto her welcoming vessel. Tired, frightened and sore, she again thought about Smee and decided to call him, using Rocky's phone. After the third ring his voice answered loud and clear.

"Who's calling?" he asked politely.

"It's me, Smee," Adele quavered. "This is Rocky's phone and I think he has mine. I'm scared, Smee—the bad guys are coming after me." Gilligan jumped onto her lap and she hugged him, ignoring his protests at being held so tightly.

"Where are you, my dear? The bad guys killed my nephew. I'm back on island and at the office."

"I'm on *The irate air*—just."

Smee told Adele about Stewart's being shot aboard the *Hygia* while on some kind of undercover mission, and he wanted her help to track down the mercenaries. He'd heard from one of Stewart's navy buddies that these men were working out of the Bahamas and the nastiest one wore a shark tooth necklace.

Adele was now not the only one playing the revenge game.

"I'm so sorry, Smee. Stewart was the dead sailor?"

"What's that?"

Rocky knew about Stewart last night. And Diego was talking to BJ on the phone this afternoon. "Nothing, I'm sorry. Never mind. It sounds like the same gang that's trying to kill me. I've met those shark teeth! What are we going to do?"

"I want you to go someplace safe and I will fly to Marsh Harbour tomorrow and we can figure out the next move together. Get a room at a local hotel. I'm sure you could use a long shower and a longer sleep."

Adele smiled wryly. "Thanks for looking out for me."

"What are partners for?" Smee hung up the phone in his office and looked up to find a man standing in front of his desk. Smee was too preoccupied even to take a second look at the young and handsome sailor.

"Excuse me," said the man. "Does Adele Bonny work here?"

Smee immediately became wary of him. "It's Christmas night. Who are you and why do you want to know?"

"Back off, man. My name's Tim, I'm a friend of Marvin's. I met Adele last week when Marvin was helping me replace a wind system on my boss' boat, the *Bodacious Ta Tas.* I may have some info on the boat she's looking for."

"Adele's not here, but we're partners, so tell me what you know."

"Okay, well, my girlfriend Melissa works at The Rendezvous Spa. She's the yoga teacher there. So she got a call from her friend Mandy who used to work there. Supposedly she's on the *Bonny* with Adele's husband and anchored someplace with a laughing mermaid. I know it sounds kind of crazy, but I thought I'd pass on the info anyway. Heard something about a reward. Well—Marvin knows how to reach me." Looking around Smee's office at the Peter Pan décor and then pointedly at the hook on Smee's desk, Tim hurried out of the office.

Smee had always been more interested in the possibility of mermen than mermaids and he had no idea what Tim was talking about, but he would mention it to Adele when he saw her tomorrow.

The wind was howling outside when Adele checked into a local hotel. Going up to her room, she opened her bag and watched Gilligan streak out of it and under the chest of drawers, then she collapsed onto the white duvet-covered bed without removing her flip-flops, and started to doze.

"Pretty fancy footwork, missy, but I would have cooked him alive and eaten him. That's what I did with Hurricane Harry when he tried to have his way with me. Jack and me lived beyond the law, it's true, but eating is too good for such a huff-snuff."

Adele was still so tired she was barely able to open one eye to acknowledge that Aunt Anne had arrived. Every inch of her body ached and her elbows, knees, and ankles felt as though they had been pulled from their sockets.

"You're making that up," Adele managed to say. "You didn't really *eat* him, did you?" Anne's corset and purple pantaloons were too bright for her, and she winced her one eye shut again.

"Well, no, but it makes a good yarn, don't it? Truth is, I cut his head clean off and his body went overboard, so it was the sharks as ate him."

Adele groaned, "I'm sorry I asked."

"And who plundered your neck?" Anne changed the subject, smiling knowingly. "I see a hell-fire big love bite there."

"It's not a hickey, Aunt Anne, and you look like you just got out of bed. That bastard tied me up by the neck and almost raped me."

Anne was on a roll. "But he didn't rape you. You engaged him at close quarters, you took him aback, and then you cut and run. Your guggle's not bad hurt. It's now all about the Bonny revenge. I remember when one of Jack's morts tried to keep me a prisoner deep in the bottom of the hold. Although I was known for carrying cutlasses, Jack gave me that eight-inch jeweled dagger I always carried in the bodice of my shirt. Great for gutting both fish and merchant seamen who were grounded on the coast. I was out of the leather ties before rope burn set in and givin' Esmeralda a dozen lashes deckside. She never had the chance to indulge in my decadent purple articles she stole from our berth. As you can see, I'm still wearin' them today."

Anne cackled deeply, remembering Jack's partiality to purple. Esmeralda knew that removing a woman's pantaloons was second only to plundering. When Jack and his mates returned from New Providence, the rival for his affection was already leagues away from the *Treasure*, having been cast off the ship in a tiny rowboat.

Adele tried to rise, but fell back down in her bed. "I need your help, Aunt Anne."

"Balderdash," declared Anne. "You know where you have to go. Gettin' there is goin' to be the hard part."

"I've only sailed to the Berry Islands once before and Curtis was at the wheel. What if I get lost?"

"Then just pull into port and ask for directions. All we had were the stars and dead reckonin' to find our way. Remember that some of the most dangerous boats don't float on water, and embrace the mermaids."

"What do you mean, Aunt Anne? I think you've had too much ghostly grog and I'm getting tired of your riddles. Give it to me straight!"

"It's a tale of a tail and pay me heed, my pretty. Your course is going to be a rough one." Adele sank down into the comfortable bedding but did not fall asleep.

Rocky's two-tone cell phone ring brought her to full consciousness. By the time Adele answered the phone by instinct it had gone to voicemail. She punched hash and one to play the message back. A male voice she didn't recognize said, "It's me. Call me back about that Bonny broad. Thanks to my girlfriend's fat mouth, I hear that you're wrong and she's a real threat to us."

Oh, shit. Aunt Anne was right. Rocky is a hell-fire scurvy, hocus, bamboozling, hound-and-hare privateer!

Chapter 19

Rocky was back in his apartment in Tampa. *Damn,* he thought. *I was supposed to be waking up with Adele this morning, enjoying Boxing Day.* But there was no rest for Rocky this December 26. He was struggling over a lime green ironing board, pressing a white shirt, while three more remained in the laundry basket on the tile floor. Just nine hundred square feet, his apartment was extremely efficient but not very warm and inviting. The living room furniture was limited to a futon, a large particleboard double desk, and a medium-sized flat-screen television mounted on the wall. With no plants or paintings, the place looked as if it were rented by the week. Painted Navajo White, the bedroom wasn't much more personal, featuring an oak headboard and queen-sized bed dressed with a navy blue quilt and navy blue pillow shams. The double dresser was oak as well with the only decorations in the room being several brass-framed photos and three hand-carved wooden toys crafted by his father when he was a young boy. A small kitchen nook was outfitted with a three-quarter sized refrigerator, oven, dishwasher, and microwave. By the looks of the latter, it definitely got more use than the stove.

Rocky carefully put a freshly pressed white cotton shirt on a hanger and carried it into his bedroom. His closet was full of a dozen shirts looking exactly like the one he had just hung up. Not much of a selection to demand his attention in the morning. Stopping at the dresser, he smiled at a photo of himself with his arm around a giant golden retriever. The dog was slobbering happily on his bare and bronzed shoulder. He spoke to the photograph. "I really miss you, Max, even though you shed like crazy on my white shirts." *As soon as I settle down I'm going to look for one of your puppies*, Rocky thought wistfully.

He next glanced at the photograph of himself and a twelve-year-old girl screaming wildly as they careened down the Thunder Mountain roller coaster ride at Disney World in Orlando. The girl, who looked as if she could be Rocky's daughter, was clutching onto his bare arm tightly. They both seemed to be having a marvelous time. The old-fashioned Ma Bell phone stationed next to the photos pealed out and Rocky jumped slightly. Looking at the Caller ID unit under the phone, he answered enthusiastically.

"How's my favorite niece?"

"Awesome," she replied. "Did you have a fun Christmas?"

"Working as usual, but I guess I like it that way. How about you?"

"Awesome, but I wish you were here. Are you still hanging out with the redhead?

"Which one?" her uncle asked.

"The one after the one who was after Madeline?"

"Not any more," said Rocky. "How do you like the Nina, *My Twin* doll?"

"She looks just like me. It's kind of freaky."

A voice in the background yelled, "Nina is getting too old to play with dolls, especially her twin. There was a reason we only wanted one child, Ricardo." The voice belonged to Raquel, his older brother's third wife.

Nina started to laugh. "Mom and Dad have the Schwartzes over and they're on their third Bloody Mary." There was a beep on the line. "Gotta go, Uncle Rocky, I think my boyfriend's calling me."

"You're too young for a boyfriend," proclaimed Rocky. "When can I meet this jerk? He better be too young to drive."

"Of course he can't drive, Rocky. Going out in the seventh grade means he walks me to class."

"Whew, my kind of guy."

"Love you," called Nina, hanging up the phone.

"Love you, too," he said to the dead receiver. Moving out of his bedroom and back towards the ironing board, he saw a blinking light on Adele's phone. He picked up the RAZR and, pressing #1 on the phone, played back the message. What he heard caused a rueful grin—Adele's voice and her distinctive vocabulary. "You have my phone, ass-bite!"

He tried calling her back, but reached his own terse message after three rings. "Rodriguez here." Rocky decided not to leave a message. Disconnecting the iron, he went into his barren bedroom and picked up a pair of 35-pound steel dumbbells that were resting against the wall. He started doing bicep curls as fast as he could.

Adele was still tossing and turning in bed when the ring of the hotel room phone caused her to bolt upright. The wind was still as loud as it had been the night before and Smee was on the line. Unfortunately, the Nassau airport was closed for the day due to the sixty-mile-an-hour winds, so he would not be able to meet her until tomorrow. Feeling a bit safer in such secure and anonymous surroundings, Adele told him not to worry as she wobbled to her feet, feeling every bit of her sore body. The clock told her it was eleven a.m., checkout time, and she slowly got dressed.

Cautiously approaching *The irate air*, she was sure that danger lurked behind every palm tree as the blustery wind blew loudly in the fronds, and that Diego was hiding in the hibiscus bushes. The coast seemed clear so she stepped up on the bow of her boat. Just as she and Gilligan were settling in, she heard the sound of approaching footsteps. Snatching up her crossbow, she got into the crouch position, waiting for anticipated danger. The familiar voice of Marvin calmed the start of sweat trickling down her brow.

"Delly, are you here?"

"Oh, Marvin, you scared the crap out of me."

"I guess so." He eyed the crossbow. "Who were you expecting?"

"Not sure, but not you."

"Hopefully this wasn't for Curtis, as I don't have enough money to post a murder bond."

Adele decided not to share with Marvin the attempt made on her life, knowing he would insist she should move back in with Babs and Sheldon Morton. There was no way that was going to happen. "I just get a little bit hyper-vigilant living alone here. No biggie."

Jumping lightly onto *The irate air*, Marvin looked a bit beat. He explained that he had spent the previous night solo sailing a 31-foot McGregor over to the Abaco Beach Club. He had just delivered it to a couple who were staying there for a week and thought he would come see Adele. Going into the galley to get a drink of water while Adele went into the head to brush her teeth, he took a small package out of his pocket, opened it, and poured it into his glass. Marvin's wallet fell onto the deck and a photograph of him in his mid forties fell to the ground. All smiles for the camera, his arm was around another man several years younger than he was, who looked very unstable and skinny as a skeleton. Adele glanced at the photo before Marvin scooped it up off of the deck. He quickly drank his infused water.

"How's your heart?" she asked him with concern.

"About the same," he replied. "I'm okay when I drink this."

"I haven't seen that photo of Dad in years. He was such an alcoholic by then. Did he turn to drink because Babs was so hard to live with?"

Marvin turned the photo for her to see. "No, Adele, your father was really sick right before the accident happened."

"I guess you can call alcoholism a disease, so why didn't she get him some help?"

After several silent seconds contemplating the picture, Marvin unloaded on her.

"Your dad was never a drunk. He had a brain tumor and was very unstable the last year of his life. Your mother, bless her soul, spent that year shielding you and your sister from the truth because Darryl didn't want you and Alli to know how sick he really was. The tumor was untreatable and as he started to lose his equilibrium, everyone thought he was an alcoholic. Babs loved him so much that she honored his wishes and never told a soul about his degenerating illness except me.

"In retrospect this might not have been the right way to deal with his sickness, but you and Alli were only eleven and nine at the time, and she didn't want you to know your father was dying."

Although this was more than twenty-five years ago, Marvin remembered the last year leading up to Darryl's death as if it were yesterday. One day during that time, Adele was playing at a friend's house and her dad came home from an evening with the boys, drunk and disoriented. The man was exhibiting similar characteristics to Darryl: slurred speech, impaired vision and a bit of a stagger. Her friend told Adele her dad was *drunk* and in Adele's young mind her own dad became a *drunk*. When she went home, Marvin was attending to her dad and Babs was in the living room, trying to relax with a glass of wine. As absolutely positive as only an eleven-year-old could be, Adele told her mom she knew her dad was a *drunk* and what was she going to do about it? Exhausted, Babs replied, "Nothing." Adele stormed off to bed and a wall of resentment began to form between her and her mother.

"Darryl got worse and it was hard for Babs to get him on *The Pirate Pair*, the one place he felt at home. So I had to help your mom get him situated on board and then sail the boat, as she needed to keep her eyes on him all the time."

Adele still didn't understand why Babs couldn't talk to her daughters about his brain tumor instead of attributing the symptoms to alcoholism. "It made us, me especially, think that Mom didn't love Dad enough to get him help."

"Untrue. Babs was protecting you from knowing your dad didn't have long to live and wanted to have as much family time on the boat together as possible. It was a mistake, but we didn't know it then."

Marvin went on to tell Adele what had been in his heart for more than twenty-five years. "My eyes left Darryl for a few seconds when I went to the bow to view a school of jumping dolphins. That was all it took for him to fall overboard. Your mother heard the splash when she was in the middle of getting dressed and rushed topside. She and the boat boy jumped in after him. I was already in the water by then, but it was too late. Darryl didn't have his faculties intact, so he sank like a stone in the thirty-foot-deep water. We all three dove down into the dark water again and again, but we just couldn't find him.

"We called the shore patrol on our old walkie-talkies but it took them thirty minutes to locate us." There was great pain in Marvin's voice. "They brought bright outdoor lights and three scuba divers, but he was already on the bottom. Remember, Delly, this was before cell phones and satellite systems."

Marvin had tears in his eyes as he took Adele into his arms. "I'm so, so sorry, Delly," he keened. "Darryl was my best friend. If you need to blame anyone, make it me. There's not a day I don't think about the accident."

Adele felt a crushing weight on her heart. She had horribly misjudged her mother for almost three decades. *Babs wasn't a player, at least during those years—she was a protector.* Adele started to cry and Marvin hugged her tightly.

"Maybe it's time to make amends with your mother," urged Marvin.

Adele had a heartfelt question for her old friend. "How can I say I'm sorry?"

"Your mom doesn't want an apology, honey. She just wants her daughter back."

Thinking for a moment, Adele told Marvin she wanted their reconciliation to happen before the Provocative Pirates of the Bahamas Museum opening. But the family collection was still missing and Adele didn't have any idea where Curtis and Mandy might be hiding both the boat and the booty. According to Marvin, the word around The Rendezvous was they could have set off for Giggling Girl, just around the bend from the Berrys. Mandy had called Melissa at the fitness center last night and was bragging about this pink sand beach with a really lame-sounding wooden engraved happy mermaid sign.

"You know about Giggling Girl? I thought that was our private name for it."

"The rest of the world calls it Strawberry Cay. But Curtis has a big mouth, Delly. He told me how you got off course last year and found this beautiful hidden pink sand beach."

"That was the first and only time we tried to sail without Gracie," admitted Adele ruefully. "We screwed up big-time."

Marvin grinned. "And no, you're not the only ones who have 'rocked the boat' there in the surf. I was literally blown off course more than a decade ago, and the lovely lady and I ended up moored in those mangrove trees, which at the time hadn't been named Giggling Girl by Curtis."

"Way to go, Marv," said Adele proudly. Then, trying not to reveal too much, Adele hinted at the possibility the *Hygia* was on its way to the Berry Islands so perhaps she could capture both boats on the same day. Marvin looked at her as if she were crazy. There was no way in hell he would let her sail to the Berrys solo to do battle with hijackers, and then make her way to Giggling Girl to find Curtis. Adele was adamant. Once on the island she would alert the authorities, get professional backup, have the bad guys arrested, and be on her way to Giggling Girl. *I can certainly handle Mandy, and that pantywaist Curtis, by myself.*

Hugging her hard, Marvin stepped back aghast. "What happened to your neck?"

Adele reached instinctively to the raw rope burns, exposing her wrists.

"And your wrists?"

Adele looked down at her scabbed-over wrists. She shrugged.

"And you wanted to go alone?"

"Well, Smee's flying over here tomorrow morning, maybe he'll come with me."

"Smee? I don't think so. I'll meet you here at nine a.m. with a friend and the three of us will sail out together." He then pulled out several charts he had placed through his belt. "Take a look at these tonight. If everything goes well, no one will know the treasure was MIA for three weeks."

Adele thought about resisting the offer, but then she wised up. "I can see why Mom thinks the world of you."

He kissed her on the forehead and climbed out of the boat, saying under his breath, "Finally." Adele thought she saw Marvin stagger a bit, but he quickly regained his footing and she dismissed her concern.

Snagging a soda from the cooler, Adele sat down in the cabin and lovingly picked up Gilligan from the top of the old treasure chest. She nestled him into her lap before opening the lid.

Tucked neatly in a side pocket were three photos of Babs, Darryl, Alli, and Adele. Really looking at them for the first time, Adele saw that they were all onboard *The Pirate Pair* and seemed to span about four years. In the first photo, Adele looked about eight years old and was jauntily wearing a white captain's hat angled to the side. Babs had on a navy blue bikini and her body was taut. This was one happy family. In the next photo, Darryl looked a decade older, although Adele wasn't any more than ten or eleven. Babs was again in one of her infamous bikinis, but this time her body looked saggy and aging. Tension was reflected in all four faces. The last photo was the most telling. Adele was staring angrily at her mother, who had her arm on her father. Looking very out of it, Darryl was clutching tightly to Babs' right shoulder. Surrounding the foursome was the pristine *The Pirate Pair*.

She looked around the small Catalina, proud of making a great start on returning it to its former seaworthiness. The boat's dark wood now gleamed brightly and the new cushions were close to comfortable. Unfortunately, the jib that should have been stowed days ago was still spread across the dock, causing congestion at her berth. Turning a kind eye back to the photo, she saw a family clinging together by a thread.

Adele then made a very hard phone call. "Hi, Mom, it's me."

There was a short pause on the other end of the line. "Did you just call me Mom?"

"I love you, and I'm so sorry I didn't get it."

"Marvin told me he was going to talk with you, and I guess he did," murmured her mother.

Adele revealed that she had been terrified to be shut inside the boat's little cabin, especially with all the activity going on topside. By the time Marvin let them out of the locked room their father was gone, Babs was half-dressed and wringing wet, and Adele and Alli were sent back to shore with the Coast Guard. She had never gotten over the feeling of abandonment.

"You were never abandoned," said Babs. "I should've known you could handle the truth. I thought you'd think alcoholism was curable and not a death sentence like his tumor was. I felt I had to *power through the pain* for the sake of you girls."

"But, Mom, I didn't always want to power through life. Sometimes a hug would have helped."

"I know that now, Adele, but there were times powering through was the only way I could make it through the day."

Thirty minutes later, mother and daughter had finally made peace with each other—though Adele, still hoping to rectify the situation on her own, hadn't confessed to losing the Bonny heirlooms. Flopping down on the cushions, exhausted by this emotional outpouring, she reached out to Gilligan.

"This was way before your time, fella," she purred to him. "But I think you would have felt right at home with my family." As a reply, the affectionate black cat climbed up her chest and touched her nose to nose. Adele started to giggle and, placing him on the deck, began to dig more deeply, pulling out several old navigational charts of the waters around Jamaica. "AB" was scrawled across the bottom of the page.

Let's see how these 1720 charts match up with Marvin's twenty-first century ones, Adele commented to herself.

Chapter 20

Adele decided to call Alli and saw that she had just two bars left on Rocky's phone. Alli answered in her most professional voice.

"Lithgow speaking."

"It's me, Adele."

"What number is this? Don't tell me you lost another phone."

"Not exactly. It has been temporarily misplaced." With a very emotional voice, Adele told Alli about her conversation with Marvin and how their dad wasn't a drunk—he'd had a brain tumor. Their mother's last two years with him were really hard and she spent so much of her time and energy pretending everything was okay. Those wet panties had nothing to do with indiscretions. She was trying to dive for their dad in that dark, murky water.

"Maybe it's truce time," said Alli kindly.

"It is, and I just called her."

"Finally," Alli echoed Marvin's sentiment exactly.

"But I need your help, Alli. I have a lead on the whereabouts of both the *Beautiful Bonny* and the *Hygia* and want you to do a background check on a man named Ricardo Rodriguez. He's the Navy SEAL I mentioned and might be involved with the hijacking."

This request was way above Alli's pay grade but she thought aloud: her oldest son went to a playgroup and his little friend's mother had a Top Secret security clearance and maybe she would do some investigating. Alli was worried about Adele and hoped she was not involved in something dangerous. "And you know, you never called me back on Christmas Eve," Alli continued.

"I'm sorry, I just wasn't into talking to Babs, err, Mom that night."

"But I also called you again to let you know that one of my guys may have spotted the *Bonny* near the Berrys. Wasn't a clear image, but looked a lot like it."

"Damn, I guess yours was the message I deleted. Thanks for the heads-up. That goes along with Marvin's scuttlebutt about the *Bonny*'s possible location. We'll be on our way there tomorrow."

Alli promised she would do her best to get the skinny on Rodriguez and would call her at the new number when she heard back from her friend.

"You're the best," said Adele. "If anyone can find out about Rocky, you and your cronies can do it."

"I don't know who this Rodriguez guy is, Adele, but why do you always assume the worst in people?"

"Just because I never trusted Babs, ah, Mom. . . ."

"And me . . . and Rodriguez . . . you should have known Mom always loved you. Perhaps the one person you shouldn't have trusted was Curtis. You know, after your dance studio closed down, Mom talked to your landlord about why he doubled the rent. Why do you think? I found out years later that Curtis hit on his daughter."

Alli told Adele that when their mother heard about the studio's demise she went to meet the landlord and offered him a gold doubloon valued at over twelve thousand dollars to keep it open. Adele had told her sister that the monthly rent had been doubled to two thousand dollars, and it was Babs' plan to pay the other half for a year. She hoped Adele's talent would then entice additional students. But it wasn't about the money, it was about Curtis' inappropriate behavior. The landlord didn't want him around young girls.

"That ass-bite. Why didn't she tell me?"

"Would you have believed her?" asked Alli curtly. "Mom never felt Curtis was trustworthy and good enough for you. He had no family and no family values. When you were first dating and she discovered he was an embezzler, you didn't want to hear about it. So you married a man you hardly knew. Why? To teach her a lesson? It's hard for me to feel sorry for you, Delly."

"I don't want you to. It's just, I loved Dad so much. . . ."

"So did I. So did Mom. So did Marvin. But we never played the blame game. Dad was sick. It took me years to get over it. He fell overboard and drowned. It was more than twenty-five years ago. It's time to move on."

"I can't. I think about him every day."

"So do I. Your nephew's middle name is Darryl, in Dad's memory. There's so much of him in you, the love of the water and of sailing. Embrace it and stop feeling sad and resentful."

Adele started to sob loudly. "You're right. Do you think Mom can ever forgive me?"

"She already has. That's why she entrusted the collection to you. And we've got to get it back."

"We will," Adele promised.

The two sisters said goodbye and after rubbing her red, tear-filled eyes, Adele breathed deeply, closed her eyes, and did a half dozen very wide, almost contortionist-looking, neck rolls. She then sat on the deck to calm her racing mind, and visualized a flickering candle for more than twenty minutes. Finally standing up, she felt her painful neck where the rope marks from yesterday's assault had turned puffy and deep purple. She jumped at the sound of Dexter's voice.

"How about a little Junkanoo action tonight?" asked Dexter from the dock. "I bought a new British pith helmet especially for the evening."

"I already have a date." Adele lay down on the front cushioned bench. She drifted away into a restless sleep.

Adele woke up with a start. It was already dark outside and she hoped she hadn't missed Junkanoo. The clock read seven p.m., party time. But knowing Marsh Harbour, the party probably wouldn't start for at least an hour. Getting dressed in skinny jeans, a long-sleeved t-shirt that read "Bring It On," bright red hoodie, and a large sequined scarf to hide her bruised throat, Adele heard bells and saw flashing lights approaching *The irate air*. The raucousness was caused by yesterday's ferry captain, who was wearing the ultimate party hat. The garment looked as if it belonged to a court jester and was midnight blue with silver sparkles. Jester-like curls were topped with pink flashing lights and small bells, and the captain was swinging them around like crazy. His head truly looked like a firefly on steroids. His three buddies were wearing glow sticks around their necks and carrying blinking king-like scepters. Throwing on a bright pink and orange sequined crown, Adele put Gilligan into his cat carrier with a handful of cat-chow, hopped off her boat, and joined the group.

They passed by Dexter, who had changed into his pith helmet with light beige safari jacket and matching Bermuda shorts. He frowned at the twenty-something captain who had his arm draped across Adele's shoulder.

"I guess if they're old enough to shave. . . ." muttered Dexter. Adele made a face at him.

"What did he say?" asked the captain's buddy.

Thinking quickly, Adele translated, "Dexter thought I was going to dress up as a slave."

"That would be so cool," said the captain, as the foursome loaded into Adele's Bug and headed downtown. Her passengers found the mismatched tires and bumpy ride a source of further hilarity. Parking more than two blocks away from the parade route, the group immediately got separated as the three young men stopped to ogle five teenage girls getting ready to hop onto a float with the banner "Friggin' A." Their high school was nicknamed the Aquanauts and the girls were shimmying into skintight green spandex diving suits to show off every curve and cranny to their best advantage. After buying some sweet johnnycake from a street vendor, Adele lined up on the curb with the masses.

The downtown area of Marsh Harbour was an adrenaline rush of colors, costumes, and floats, driven by the beat of goatskin drums and Caribbean bands. Hundreds of locals and tourists alike lined the streets as Goombay drummers from Nassau marched proudly, looking like transplants from Great Britain in their high white hats, chrome buttons, and other brass-embellished red and black uniforms. Adele was mesmerized by their pomp and circumstance and was absolutely amazed when the drum leader turned his ramrod straight body towards her and gave a sly wink. Marching past her, he handed his staff and hat to a young boy on the side of the street, ran back to his marching group, and moved into a break dance that would have done Michael Jackson proud. He twirled around on one hand with both legs up in the air. Jumping up like an acrobat, the drum leader started to moon walk backwards, covering more than a half of a block. The crowd went wild and even Adele had to laugh with delight.

An announcer was up on a podium with a standing microphone and amplifier, trying to get the attention of at least a small portion of the wild revelers. This was a futile task.

"Ladies and gentlemen," he yelled. "Welcome to Junkanoo, a celebration that was brought to the island in the sixteenth and seventeenth centuries by African slaves."

The crowd yelled for him to speak up, so the technician turned up the amplifier.

"The exact origins are unknown. . . ." His next words were lost in a horrible squeal, so the technician turned the amp back down. "But the most popular version is that John Canoe, a benevolent plantation owner, allowed his slaves time off to celebrate on Boxing Day, as they had worked so hard on Christmas. Thus the slaves named the celebration in his honor."

Adele continued her walk down Main Street and his voice was now completely drowned out by the din of the crowd. Approaching her was the "Friggin' A" float—and what a monstrosity it was. *I guess this is the reason I've never been to Junkanoo before,* she thought. Sort of a cross between a pontoon boat and a giant raft, the float part covered the body and cab of a small Dodge Dakota truck and bounced precariously with every bump in the road.

Decorated like a party boat with a DJ playing island music, the body of the "boat" was filled with the five teenage Aquanauts clearly having a terrible time trying to move around in their unyielding suits as they had even added fish tails to their feet. There were giant papier-mâché fish and suspended sea turtles in danger of falling out of the truck's open back. This was one jammin' Junkanoo mess.

Diego tried not to touch his throbbing head, swathed in a white bandage that covered most of his forehead and all of his right eye. Standing at the front desk of a small medical clinic, he reached instead into his pocket for his wallet and paid the bill for the bandaging services he'd just received. The medical attendant handed him a small packet.

"These are pain patches and very strong," he warned Diego. "Only use them if you're in extreme discomfort and be sure to be lying down or you'll get disoriented."

"Uh-huh," agreed Diego, turning to limp out of the clinic.

"And a word of advice," the attendant called after him. "You were lucky this time, but if it should ever happen again—seek immediate medical attention and don't mess around with eye injuries, okay?"

"Okay," Diego ground out between gritted teeth and pushed out through the door, where he was caught up in the rush of Junkanoo. This was a man who had been hurt and was not happy about it. He aggressively shoved and shouldered his way to the curb. There he did a double take when he spotted Adele across the street, devouring her johnnycake. Circling around the back of the crowd, he jogged across the street a half block west of her, causing seven people to crash their festively decorated bicycles.

"Son of a bitch," he said, approaching Adele from behind while unwrapping all three medicine patches and stuffing them into his pocket. But when he saw her connecting with someone she knew, he decided to fade back into the crowd and wait for his opportunity.

Adele was walking backwards, getting a real kick from watching the female fish on the float taunting boys on the curb, trying to get the teens to reel them in. She saw the Aquanauts had now gotten their "sea" legs and were laughing and having a good time in their rubber-suited mermaid tails. Moving away from the float, she backed right into a woman with a traditional pirate hat, a patch over her left eye, and an eyebrow pencil drawn mustache.

"Hi there, Adele," hailed the woman.

Adele swallowed a mouthful of johnnycake. "I'm sorry, do I know you?"

She pulled up her eye patch and took off her three-cornered hat. "It's me—Courtney. Marsh Harbour Junkanoo never used to be this crazy."

"Great get-up, Courtney. How is going straight treating you?"

Courtney was very pleased with herself. She told Adele she'd been working at Adventure LandCo for less than a week, and two days ago, when the bookkeeper left the petty cash drawer open and within her eyesight, temptation raised its ugly head. But after massaging the money for a good ten minutes, she left the cash where it lay, put her hand back in her pants pocket and walked away. Adele gave her a fist-pump to show approval for that triumph. In addition, Courtney said she had been tracking the man she left behind and discovered that his tattoo parlor had been turned into Pirate's Plunder, a small retrieval business on Nassau, and she planned to start paying him back the money she owed him.

There would never be a better time to break the news to Courtney than right now. "He uses the name Smee, and I work for him."

First flabbergasted and then pissed off, Courtney asked Adele why she hadn't told her on the Sandy Point ferry.

"I didn't know then. Smee was telling me a bit of his history the next day and described the same embezzlement story I'd heard from you. Feelings are still hard, but I think he would love to see you again."

"When and where?" she asked.

Two very butch-looking gals, wearing leather and chains, interrupted their conversation by pushing them apart. "What's your email?" yelled Adele. Courtney's response was drowned out by the noise.

"Pirate's Plunder—call me there!" yelled Adele as she was rushed down the crowded street.

Adele paralleled another funky float. This was "Blackbeard's Bounty"—yet another buccaneer ship, with several teenage pirate wenches throwing candy treasure to the streetside crowd. Two young and dashing traditionally clad corsairs were embroiled in a spirited and clanking duel and she enjoyed the rather good swordsmanship.

Suddenly Diego grappled Adele by the arms, pulling them tightly behind her. Wrestling her to the ground, he pinned her with a strong elbow and shoulder, and brought out the opened medicine patches from his pocket. Yanking at her disguising scarf and pulling it down to her shoulders, he pasted all three patches on the back of her neck, and she immediately started to lose her equilibrium.

"Drunk woman coming through," yelled Diego as he flipped Adele over his shoulder. No one seemed to be paying any attention to him so he yanked open the truck cab door of "Blackbeard's Bounty," pulling out the driver. He threw Adele inside and climbed in, fighting off the driver with a stab of a dropped sword. Blood spewed across the bodices of the wenches on that side of the truck, who jumped off the still moving vehicle. He pulled a papier-mâché octopus down out of the way of the windshield. The truck was rolling erratically and Diego yanked the steering wheel hard, turning it sharply to the right before jumping out of the vehicle. Careening slowly down a side street, the truck started to pick up speed as it went down a steep hill. At the end of the road was a dense cluster of trees.

The noise ramped up even higher than before. Everybody was yelling, but half the nearby crowd members seemed to think they were still watching a planned entertainment. Applause mixed with cries of alarm.

One of the young wenches hadn't abandoned ship with the others, and she managed to crawl up into the front seat through the opened back window. She attempted to stop the float before it veered into the trees, but Adele's limp body was lying halfway off the seat and her legs covered both the gas and brake pedals. The teen tried to steer, but the car grazed the first several trees before taking dead aim at a trunk that was more than three feet wide. Swinging the passenger door open, the girl started to hang her body outside while firmly gripping Adele's legs. Anchoring herself against the dashboard, she got up enough force to catapult both herself and Adele out of the cab just seconds before the truck crashed into the huge tree trunk. Debris exploded all around them. The teen's constricting corset was torn from her exertions; she untied it the rest of the way and started to crawl up the hill when a taxi came to the rescue. Inside was Dr. Kim.

"Dr. Kim! It's me, Angela. We need your help. This lady is unconscious."

Dr. Kim jumped out of her cab and recognized the prone woman as Adele. "I'll go for help, Angela," she said, starting to get back into her car.

"But we need help now. Where's your medical bag?"

"Uh, I left my medical bag at the clinic," stammered Dr. Kim. "Help me get her into my taxi and I'll take her back there."

Unwrapping the scarf from Adele's shoulders, Dr. Kim quickly examined Adele, finding the three medicine patches behind her raw and bruised neck. She ripped them off quickly and Adele gave a jolting jerk. Angela winced at her pain.

"My beach boys have used these things to get high," noted Dr. Kim. "I hate it when the neck hair and skin come off as well."

Angela reported excitedly, "Some guy actually shoved her in the truck and sent it down this hill. I think he meant to kill her!"

Five minutes later they managed to load Adele into the taxi and Kim took off for the clinic that was just four blocks away. It was slow going and very frustrating for Kim, who was used to speeding way beyond the limit of the law. Swerving to avoid the jester-capped captain and his scepter-wielding group, she sideswiped the "Barnyard Boys" float, spraying feathers all over the crowd.

Adele regained consciousness when she felt a sharp jolt. Looking around, she saw she was in the front seat with her nemesis Dr. Kim. "Why are you here and where in the hell are you taking me?" asked Adele groggily.

"To the clinic. You might have a concussion," said Dr. Kim. "Who did this to you?"

Adele rubbed the back of her neck. "Well, I didn't see his face but I recognize his handiwork."

As Dr. Kim drove over a very deep pothole, Adele was jostled once again. "Lucky you're a doctor, because you're a terrible driver."

"Well, I'm not exactly a doctor, but I've learned to do a mean mouth-to-mouth."

"Yuck," gagged Adele. "I don't need that. I'm fine. I just want to go back to my boat."

Making an erratic U-turn, Dr. Kim headed away from Main Street and towards The Anchorage. She handed a small bottle over to Adele. "Smell this."

Adele did as she was told, gave a giant sneeze, and immediately felt her head clear. "Wow. What is it?" she marveled.

"My own concoction," boasted Dr. Kim. "Six different kinds of pepper and a dash of peppermint."

"It did the trick." Adele sneezed again. "Why are you pretending to be a doctor?"

Dr. Kim told Adele about her first mouth-to-mouth experience, with a blond college student after a stingray stung him in the shallow waters of Mermaid Reef. The teen knocked himself unconscious on a bed of coral and Kim, snorkeling nearby, pulled him out of the water. Watching him come awake was better than sex, so she gave him another dose of heavy breathing. He was so grateful that the word *doctor* just popped out of her mouth, and she had been giving mouth-to-mouth to cute blond boys for the last eighteen months. Most of the young people on the island now really thought she was a doctor and the label got her into all the hot local parties, whether she knew the hosts or not.

Adele really could not believe what she was hearing. Dr. Kim assured her that she didn't administer any real treatment; she drove anyone with a serious problem to the Main Street Clinic. Once they arrived at The Anchorage, Adele thanked Dr. Kim sincerely. The doctor smiled and invited her to do some party-hopping with her sometime, when she had fully recovered, promising she would leave her medical bag at home.

The only lights near The Anchorage were on the dock as all the boaters were downtown, still jamming at Junkanoo. Adele slid her battered body down onto the new cushions, opened up the pirate chest for the last swig of brandy, and realized the bottle was already empty. So she slowly lifted her Day Planner from the seat and turned the pages in next January's To-Do List. She painfully wrote "See doctor for complete physical" before carefully lying down and trying to sleep.

But Gilligan kept her from deep slumber with his insistent meowing.

"You've had an amazin' busy night, darlin'!" Aunt Anne stared at Gilligan warily. "I warned you about that bantlin' boat." She was dressed up for Junkanoo in a silver and gold bodice with matching hair combs and flowing black skirt. "Not a crack about this get-up. Jack liked me in petticoats every once in a while."

Adele decided it was wiser not to make a comment. "There were two boat floats, Aunt Anne. You could have been more specific."

"You should thank me, my pretty. My warnin' got your guard up and the would-be pirate puke didn't get his hands on you again."

"Maybe not his hands, but I sure as hell hurt my head."

"Avast, there. Stop feelin' sorry for your puny self and set sail for Gigglin' Girl. It's an area I know well as Jack and me had more than one huddle there. It's time to take back your boat and the family treasure. A key to your success is to trust the ship."

Adele told her aunt that *The irate air* was hardly a ship and she didn't remember how to find Giggling Girl as she and Curtis had discovered the hidden cove when they were blown off course. She planned on sailing for the Berrys as soon as Marvin arrived in the morning and then they would make their way to Giggling Girl, as he knew the way from there. Anne warned Adele not to depend on a man for her survival, no matter how tried and true of a friend he was.

Getting worked up, Anne revealed to her niece that, as usual, Jack and his male mates were celebrating their plunder in typical hard-drinking tradition when their ship was boarded by the governor of Jamaica and his soldiers, and the men didn't even put up a fight.

"They hid below deck," related Anne angrily, "leavin' only me and me mate Mary to defend our ship."

Adele had read a lot about Mary Read, the other female on Jack's ship. Anne and Mary, both cross-dressers, became fast friends on board the *Treasure*. Anne told Adele the rest of the story of their capture in Jamaica she had started to reveal to her a week and a half earlier.

"We were overwhelmed by the British soldiers and the entire crew was captured and taken to Jamaica to stand trial. As Mary and me were carryin' babies in our bellies, we weren't hanged, but Jack wasn't so lucky. Had he fought like a man, he wouldn't have been hanged like a dog—and so I told him." Anne's anger was mixed with tears.

The more Anne spoke about Jack's carelessness, the more she waved her arms and Gilligan's eyes were anchored to her every move. Suddenly he sprang like a cougar, getting a claw caught in mid-air, seemingly in Anne's hair comb. Cat and pirate lass both yowled and flailed.

"Ouch," shrieked Anne. "It may be time to string that gib up on the jib!"

Gilligan streaked into hiding, but his bottle-brush tail protruded from the cupboard.

"Wow, I wouldn't want to be your enemy," said Adele.

"You never will be, my pretty, as Bonny blood pumps through your veins. Now get back the *Beautiful Bonny* and find the family's portion. And don't forget to luff the sheets."

"I don't know what that means, but it sounds like untangling from a one-night stand to me. You know I've been sleeping solo for the last three weeks."

"It's going to be a dangerous day tomorrow and you have to remember to luff the sheets if you want to live to see another day." Anne started to fade away. "Remember to trust your ship, as puny as it may seem."

"I'm almost ready to set sail for Anne's revenge." Getting up slowly, Adele reached into the cupboard for the cat. Cuddling and petting him, she started to jog aggressively in place with Gilligan in her arms, paying no attention to her sore body or his protests; her psyche was finally ready for the challenges lying ahead. *You saw her, Gilligan, you really saw her!*

Chapter 21

For the first time in his life Smee had set his alarm clock for five-thirty in the morning. He was worried about Adele and took the early morning flight from Nassau to Abaco to try to talk some sense into his partner's pretty head. Marvin's boat assistant had called him late the night before, explaining that Marvin had had a minor heart attack and was being airlifted to Miami. Nothing to worry about, the doctors said, but Marvin insisted he must call Smee to make sure Adele did not set sail today in pursuit of the bad guys who had stolen a boat. *Isn't it just like a woman*, thought Smee, *getting in over your head and not even admitting it to yourself.* After landing in Marsh Harbour, he called her cell phone again, forgetting she'd told him it was in Rocky's possession, but it just rang and rang. He then grabbed a taxi to the marina, hoping he was not too late to stop her.

Adele tossed and turned all night in anticipation of the biggest adventure of her life. Finally getting out of bed as the sun started to raise a magnificent magenta color over the calm marina water, she began to get ready for retribution. Over the last several days Adele had made the final transformation of *The irate air* into a lovely and compact sailing vessel. She looked around at the indoor berth and outside sitting area with pride. The slipcovers had finally been comfortably broken in and were accented by canvas throw pillows with a palm tree design. The marred and dull oak cupboards and shelves were polished and repaired to their original luster, a small captain's chair had replaced her bench, and much of the rigging had been bleached a bright white. The jib that had spent too much time on the dock was now properly stowed. The chipped tiller had been replaced with a beautiful carved parrot handle and her father's antique spyglass was featured prominently on the cabin's bulkhead. Her small outboard motor had been cleaned and was ready to take over should the now nice breeze and flowing sea turn into still water. In addition she had filled a five-gallon container with fuel, just in case she needed it. The ropes and lines were either wound up precisely or on the deck in perfect order, ready for the day's adventure.

Dad would have been so proud, she reflected bitter-sweetly.

She carefully chose a t-shirt with the motto "I do all my own stunts" and pulled it on with a sense of ceremony. Doing some warm-up stretches and leg lifts, she stretched her right leg up to her outstretched hands and took hold of her always slightly red ankle. Grimacing a bit, she raised her foot up to the shoulder, standing in perfect balance. *I'm so ready for this sail.* Opening the small cupboard in the galley, she saw it was well stocked with water and a case of protein bars. Fresh fruits and vegetables had never been Adele's thing.

Scooping Gilligan out of the cupboard and holding him tight, she made a big decision. "This trip could end badly, and I don't want you to get hurt." She picked up Gilligan's brush and stuck it in the waistband of her shorts. Taking a short walk around the docks, she found Dexter and asked him to take care of Gilligan for several days.

"I'm not sure *The irate air* is seaworthy enough for a two-day sail," he responded with concern. "Is that Navy SEAL going with you?"

"How do you know about Rocky?" Adele asked him. "He's only been on board twice."

Dexter prided himself on knowing all the doings at The Anchorage. One of the college girls had seen a handsome man wearing a SEALs insignia cap, assisting Adele on board several days ago, and she'd marveled at his muscles.

"Well, it won't be Rocky, but I will have a First Mate sailing with me on the trip."

"All right, then." Dexter gently took Gilligan from Adele's arms. "I'll need that brush, as black hair is hell to get off of khaki."

"Sure thing," said Adele with a laugh. She then went up to The Anchorage billboard to read the Bahamas daily wind charts posted there. The winds were in her favor today. Checking the posted charts once again, she decided it looked like a great day to sail to Giggling Girl, near the Berrys, and get her life back.

The second largest of the Berry Islands, Chubb Cay, was known as the billfish capital of the Bahamas. Adele thought back to her one visit to the Berrys Great Harbour Cay fondly. Curtis caught his only sailfish ever at a local fishing tournament and even though the billfish was too tiny to keep, he nevertheless had taken pride in his reeling skills ever since. Adele had rented a kayak and rowed up a remote river, meeting a native moonshiner who'd given her an ample sample of regional homemade thatch berry whiskey. It wasn't until he saw stars in her eyes after the second sip that he told her the berry base came from refined ethanol.

Screeching to a halt on memory lane, she went up to the bow to check the rigging and ran into Smee who had come to find her.

"I'm so glad I found you, Adele." Smee gave her a big hug. He was carrying a Louis Vuitton knapsack across his shoulders.

"Well, I actually found you," Adele pointed out. "But I'm glad you're here. How did you get here so soon? I thought you never raised your pretty head until nine a.m. or later. Boy, have I missed you."

Smee put his arms around her shoulders. "We have some serious business to discuss. Marvin can't go with you today and he thinks you should call the police." He went on to tell her about his conversation with the sailor.

"Shit, is he going to be alright?"

"Sounds like it, Adele, but we need to get some professional help. And I have some more news for you. Mandy's girlfriend's boyfriend visited me yesterday. He told me Curtis and Mandy are moored someplace with chuckling mermaids. I had no idea what he was talking about, but he seemed to think there was a reward involved."

"Giggling Girl!" exclaimed Adele, snapping her fingers. "So Marvin was right. Of course that asshole would take his new girlfriend there. And Alli was also right about seeing the *Bonny* on satellite photos because the way I remember it, the cay is near the Berrys."

"Let's call the authorities right now. Should be an easy capture if both boats are in the same vicinity."

"I don't think so," said Adele. She went on to repeat almost verbatim what she had told Marvin. After sailing to the islands and seeing for themselves that the pirates were there, the partners would alert the police about the stolen boats and cargo as there was no way in hell she wasn't going to be there when they were apprehended. "Those mercenaries killed your nephew. And Woody, too. I overheard them actually laughing about Woody. Don't you want to be there to see justice done?"

Smee wasn't so sure, and he went down into the small head to both empty his bladder and contemplate the proposed mission. Two minutes later he came back with a decision. "From now on *Danger* is my middle name, Adele, and besides I've just taken a Dramamine—let's roll." Opening up his designer bag, he brought out a strong white net carrier with a large dark phone inside. "It's a satellite phone."

Adele looked at the phone blankly. "Why would I want to call a satellite?"

Hanging the satellite phone up on a galley cabinet door handle, she started to evaluate what safety gear was on board and didn't hear her maritime radio warning of a huge storm on the horizon. Finding a wet suit, fire extinguisher, and single escape oar in case the sails went down and the motor went out, along with a tattered copy of *Sailing 101*, she felt she was ready for the sailing adventure. She also did a final check to make sure her crossbow was ready to rumble should the need arise. The Berrys would be an easy sail and once she turned Diego and Winston over to the authorities, along with their boss BJ, Adele would take on some real provisions and head on to Giggling Girl. *I so hope "BJ" doesn't mean Rocky, but if it does, well, the daughter of Babs Bonny can power through the pain on that, too. Watch me!*

Adele knew the Berrys were a simple six- or seven-hour sail from Marsh Harbour. Giggling Girl was not far away from their northernmost point and she was sure she could find the giant mangrove trees to be her guide. As it was not mentioned on any map, the challenge would be to try and retrace that last merlot-induced hour, when she and Curtis were playing doctor instead of steering the boat. They'd taken a cruise to several of the more remote cays and when they'd had a few drinks and gone off track they ended up in this remote, pristine hideaway, an inlet and cove not visible from the sea. Being adventurous—or foolish—enough to pull up anchor and slowly sail into what they hoped was not shallow water, they found a naturally deep marina where they and the *Beautiful Bonny* could get lost in the lush, dense trees surrounding a pure pink sandy beach. The beach was marked by a small, hand-carved wooden sign of a lovely, happy young mermaid basking in the sunlight—so "Giggling Girl" was a natural name for the place. Marvin said that navigation was "more of an art than a science," she remembered. He also said that even the most modern sea charts could be inaccurate. *It's all about judgment,* she told herself. Making judgments had never been Adele's problem; she just hoped they'd be the right ones today. With great trepidation, she vowed to set sail and bring back the *Bonny* and family treasure trove.

Curtis poked his head out of the cabin and looked at the sky over Giggling Girl, feeling a bit insecure over the Christmas Day encounter with Bobby and Winston, so he removed his light-colored Tommy Bahama shorts. He then took a pair of well-pressed navy blue trousers out of the closet and put them on, breathing a sigh of relief. Dark clothing had always served to comfort him. Looking around the cabin, he glanced at one of the bigger pieces of loot—what looked like a wrought-iron instrument of torture. *This must be the much talked-about chastity belt.*

But before he could view it further, a high-pitched squeal greeted his ears. "What is *that*?" Mandy screamed as she placed the item on top of her head, wearing the flat band as a hat and the iron belt as chinstraps.

Curtis was repulsed and quickly grabbed it away from her. "Nothing you'll ever use," he told her.

"Ow," she complained.

Then, taking several pieces of the Anne Bonny/Calico Jack treasure from a black velvet bag, he removed his pirate's medallion from around her neck, replacing it with a deep gold and ruby encrusted chunky necklace.

Mandy squealed with excitement as she felt the heavy piece of jewelry settle between her breasts. She hadn't felt this much bling since she was fifteen. She remembered teaching aerobics to a group of middle-aged women at a luxurious resort in Freeport, the second largest city in the Bahamas, when she'd made eye contact with a man three times her age who was at the spa to pick up his wife. While the wife was taking a nap, Mandy and her soon-to-be sugar daddy were being anything but quiet in the "quiet room." Eye contact became lip contact and six weeks into the affair he gifted her with a three-carat, square cut emerald necklace. When she had the piece appraised, she was delighted to learn that something so small could be worth thirty-eight thousand dollars. Fine jewelry became her passion. Just a month later his bald head really began to bother her, so she and the necklace took off for Nassau. The sale of the necklace staked her to a one-bedroom condo and a very comfortable year—a nice rest after the precarious first two years away from home.

Jiminy Christmas, she thought, *this piece could be worth more than the emerald.* Stroking the heavy pendant, she started to unbutton Curtis' shirt and rubbed her breasts against his bare chest, moving closer to other pieces of the pirate treasure. She pulled out a small gentleman's dagger from the velvet bag and put it to Curtis' throat.

"It's time to go skin driving or I'll tie you up to the yardarm." She then unbuttoned and pulled off his navy blue slacks. Curtis folded them carefully over the back of a chair, while Mandy rolled her eyes and tried to be patient.

Curtis yanked off Mandy's bikini bottom roughly. "It's walking the plank time for you, Boots, and skin *diving* is one of my favorite things to do. Dive, dive, dive," he whooped and went down on her.

Mandy and Curtis started to rock the boat but with only limited success. Baffled, Mandy looked down below and discovered that his organ wasn't fully cooperating.

"What's up . . . or not?" Mandy taunted.

"Just shut up." He now seemed more determined than ever and redoubled his efforts but to no avail. *What the heck*, she thought. He must be thinking about Adele, not her. "This isn't exactly working for me either," whined Mandy.

"Hold on, babe, it'll come. Do you by any chance have any lavender hand lotion?"

"Maybe it will come, but I won't, and why are you askin' me about lotion? We used up the massage oil yesterday, and I'm tired of the smell of it anyway." Then she told her lover what every man hated to hear. "Don't worry, this can happen to anyone."

When she rolled off of him, the cold metallic pendant Mandy was wearing hit Curtis' chest painfully and clinched the dysfunction. His self-named Serendipity shriveled up completely.

"I guess not right now, Boots. Got too much on my mind."

"Well, it's obviously not me," reproved Mandy, as she got up and put on her bikini bottom. "I'm gonna go for a swim."

Before Curtis could get up, well . . . get out of bed, she had jumped overboard and into the twenty-foot-deep water, still wearing the necklace. Swimming strongly, Mandy headed back towards Giggling Girl.

Coming side by side with the sea turtle family, this time she swam with them, trying to stroke their little heads. Wanting none of this affection, the aquatic family took off for the open water. Rounding the rocky bend, Mandy saw the skyline of giant mangrove trees and soon sighted the beautiful pink beach, with Winston on the shore waiting for her. Behind him stood a finished new boat hull extension with freshly painted "GIA" on it. Mandy wondered if the smell of fresh paint would be a turn-on for him.

She bounced up to the sand. When she stumbled the heavy necklace flipped up, hitting her in the bottom lip, which immediately swelled up and looked better than a Botox injection.

"What took you so long?" asked Winston, looking at his watch.

"Curtis had an erectile function and I had to pretend I was interested," she complained, sucking his face hard with her swollen lip.

"I think you mean an erectile dysfunction," he said with a laugh.

Pretending to be nonchalant about the very visible bling around her neck, Winston asked her about the jewelry.

"It's really old." Mandy put the piece into her mouth and treated him to a sultry look she'd practiced many times in front of her mirror, then she spat it out so she could talk some more. "I think it came from a real pirate. Curtis' wife is somehow related to the Bonny family. Maybe it's Daniel Bonny—you know, that really cute guy on TV Land who wears animal skins *all over* his *body. . . .*"

"You're talking about Daniel Boone and he wasn't a pirate, honey, he was a pioneer."

"Pie—whatever." Mandy wrapped her leg around Winston's right thigh. She pushed him down on the sand where they started to get hot and heavy. Seemingly unable to stay on, the tiny bikini bottom again hit the sand, but poor Mandy experienced coitus interruptus when BJ and Elaine arrived in the dinghy.

"What are you doing, Winston?" asked BJ as they debarked onto the beach. "We've got work to do."

"I know, boss." Winston got up quickly and pulled on his pants. "I just thought you might be interested in seeing Mandy's necklace."

Elaine stared at the gold and ruby necklace. "That looks like one of Adele's pieces. She showed me photographs of the Anne Bonny/Calico Jack treasure last month. What are you doing with it?"

Pulling up her bottoms again, Mandy explained it was on loan from Curtis.

BJ suddenly showed much more interest in the teenager than he ever had before. "Elaine, you didn't tell me your friend owned a treasure."

"Didn't I? I'm sure I told you Curtis stole all her stuff."

"But, honey, you didn't mention *treasure*. Do you mind if I feel it?" he asked Mandy. And before she could answer him, BJ grabbed the piece tightly and brought it up so close to his face that it got caught in one of his large gold hoop earrings. Mandy was pulled roughly along with the chain.

"Ouch," she yelped.

"Bobby!" protested Elaine, but BJ shook her hand off his arm.

He untangled the piece from his earring in order to bring it to his mouth and bite at it ever so gently. "This is so soft . . . pure gold . . . no other metals to dilute it," he said with amazement. "Is there more where this came from?"

Mandy tried to move away from his gruff beard and glaring eyes, but BJ still had a tight hold on the medallion. "You're hurtin' me."

"Answer my question," he commanded.

"Only if you'll take me with you," Mandy squeaked.

"I don't think so," said Elaine.

But BJ had different plans. Turning towards Elaine, he slapped her hard across the face, telling her, "I'm running this operation. Shut up! You're as expendable as your superhero friend is, *honey.*"

"What?" Elaine cradled her cheek and cringed.

Pushing her away from him, he turned towards Mandy. Of course he would take her on their next sailing adventure, he promised. She could share a berth with Winston. Seeing the look of fear on her face, he gripped her hard by both arms, and she emitted a low whimper. Looking down at the necklace and raising his fist again, he demanded to know where it came from.

Mandy told all. Curtis had three velvet bags full of treasure stored on the *Beautiful Bonny.* She thought he had stolen the pieces from Adele, but Curtis had told her possession was eight-tenths of the law.

Not taking the time to correct her math, BJ asked if their boat was still anchored off the cove. Getting the answer he wanted to hear, he told the now cowering Elaine to keep Mandy on the beach while he and Winston paid Curtis a social call. Taking the necklace and turning away from the girls, he slid a small cutlass through his side belt loop.

"Let's get Adele's loot and then find her. I'm sure Curtis will talk with the right kind of persuasion," BJ said to Winston, as they took off in the dinghy. Turning back to the beach, he then yelled out, "You two girls have fun."

Nursing both a bruised ego and eye, Elaine frantically looked for her cell phone. "I got to warn Adele," she said, checking the pockets in her shorts, "but where's my phone?"

Curtis was taking stock of the *Bonny*, seeing if there was anything he could sell. Opening up cupboards, he found the small GPS system and red button. *Hope this is a stereo as I could really use some music.* He pushed and pulled the knob but, although a light started blinking on it, no music was forthcoming. He gave up on that and began polishing the two most elaborate ceremonial daggers. *How can I sell these?* he asked himself, as he needed money and right *now*. He'd made three calls to fences over the last week and his contacts were either on holiday break or thought the merchandise was too hot to handle. Maybe that Bobby character was the answer, despite his innocuous name; by the looks of him, he probably had contacts in the pirate underworld. He decided when he saw Bobby again not to reveal too much, but to subtly do a bit of probing to see if he'd be interested in helping get rid of some of the loot.

A speedboat passed by traveling way too fast; the choppy wake in its path caused the *Bonny* to rock-and-roll and Curtis to trip over a cord and hit his elbow hard on a wooden panel in the bulkhead. Much to his surprise, it slid open, revealing a cubbyhole he hadn't known was there. Cautiously putting his hand inside, he pulled out two pairs of Adele's black lace thongs. *What the hell—but it's a perfect place to hide the loot*, he thought. He located the captain's medallion that Adele had gifted to him and fastened it around his neck, then wrapped the velvet bags with the rest of the goods in the thongs and one of his freshly laundered polo shirts. He opened and closed the panel several times to make sure it slid easily. Both the panel and inside compartment were fortified with steel plates and would be almost impossible to force open. Satisfied with the maneuverability, he stuffed the three packages inside and did a final door slide. What he didn't realize was that a pair of Mandy's stiletto heels had been wedged up against the panel as well. When he removed them from the cushion, the small button sprang forward and locked the panel securely.

Hearing a motor in the not too far distance, Curtis walked to the helm and smiled at his luck. He saw Bobby and Winston powering up in the dinghy. Winston asked him to tie them off, so Curtis tied the dinghy to a cleat on the aft port side of the *Beautiful Bonny*.

"Hi, buds!" Curtis helped both men aboard. "Have you seen Mandy? She was swimming in your direction fifteen minutes ago."

"Yeah." Bobby started to look around the boat. "She and Elaine are stretching on the beach."

Sitting down on a blue silk cushion, he pretended to admire the newly refinished woodwork and opened up the panel above the hidden cubbyhole. "Nice wood. Looks like it was just refinished."

"It was," said Curtis. "Can I offer you guys a beer?"

"Sure." Bobby followed Curtis into the galley. Opening up several cupboards, he asked if there were any peanuts or pretzels to go with the beer. All he saw were two shelves of junk food, from Ding Dongs and Twinkies to Hot Tamales and Pork Rinds.

"You would think that little body would be showing the signs of eating all this crap," bragged Curtis. "But not Mandy. Help yourself." Winston reached for a Ding Dong and then thought again. Curtis closed the cupboard door and suggested they should go outside to drink their beers, where it was less crowded.

"I hear you're married to that Bonny broad," commented Bobby. "So what gives with Mandy?"

"Just a distraction," leered Curtis. "But a hot one."

Bobby continued to look around the *Beautiful Bonny.* His constant movement was beginning to bother Curtis.

"I hear that Adele is loaded," stated Bobby pointedly. "How much do you figure the Bonny/Calico Jack loot would be worth if it was cashed out in today's market?"

Curtis didn't like the way the conversation was going and gulped down his Kalik. He had never spoken to anyone except Mandy and the potential fences about the treasure and this guy seemed to know way too much about it. He decided these were *not* men he wanted to get into business with.

"I have no idea, but it must have been worth millions," he tossed off. "Adele had me sign a pre-nup when we got married and made sure most of the pieces were not part of community property."

Curtis went on to tell Bobby that all the valuable jewelry and daggers had been sold over the years, so there was not much left of the original treasure. This was his story and he was sticking to it, but the black-bearded pirate seemed not to buy the tale.

"All right, no more Mr. Nice Guy." Bobby pulled the cutlass from his belt loop, while Winston nailed Curtis from behind in a chokehold. He began to have an immediate gag reflex and a little bit of his regurgitated Kalik made its way onto Winston's hand. Raising the cutlass to Curtis' neck, Bobby sliced it ever so slightly. A thin line of blood started to trickle down the terrified man's Adam's apple.

"Tell me where the treasure is or I'll turn your throat inside-out."

All Curtis could think was that he'd never been so frightened.

Adele and Smee were getting ready for the most daring journey of their lives. Smee was on the bow practicing with the crossbow so she decided to infuse Aunt Anne into her brain one more time, but what she found did not exactly instill her with the courage she had hoped for. Inside the chest she pulled out the second-to-last of the Anne Bonny and Calico Jack historic papers. This sheet was a weathered, torn page from a journal entry.

> *My dear Jack: Yr goen to the Gallows today & without Me. Usen my Head—which yr about to Lose—I pleaded my Hans in Kelder in defense of not getten Hanged as the Magistret would be killen Two of us, & One an unborn Babe. I am Afeard that yr last Day has come, but I will live to fight another Day. Farewell, lover. Yr Anne.*

Right on, Aunt Anne, thought Adele. *Today's my day to fight and I won't let you down.*

Chapter 22

Adele and Smee powered slowly out of her slip two hours later than they planned. The sun was beginning to rise bright red in the sky as they slipped into the marina waters, making their way out to the Sea of Abaco. Turning off the maritime radio to save electricity, Adele slid "Smooth Operator" by Sade onto the screen of her iPod and turned the volume all the way up. The breeze had picked up a bit and the now choppy water was capped with what looked like whipped cream. She put on her blue hoodie and kind of shivered, even though the sun was still shining brightly, before cutting the engine. Now the teacher, she took great pride in giving Smee sailing lessons, showing him how to raise the mainsail and jib. She put him in front of the tiller with instructions—"left turns the boat right and right turns the boat left"—and they began to head southwest to the Berry Islands.

With his face to the wind, Smee drank in the responsibility of driving *The irate air*. Adele began to fantasize what life must have been like for her Aunt Anne, having to live in such a man's world, wearing a disguise on board ship to keep her gender a secret. Thinking about how Curtis and Mandy had robbed her of so much of her own identity, she started to dream that her aunt had the right idea. A woman once insinuated Anne wasn't worth knowing, so she proceeded to punch her in the mouth, knocking out two teeth. *Poetic justice*, Adele thought. *How would Mandy look without her front teeth?* Then there was the tale of how the pirate queen gutted a man who challenged her right to be aboard the *Treasure*. A bit messy for sure, as his insides spilled out all across the bow of the ship, but Adele could now finally imagine this kind of torture for her husband.

Dreaming about a blood-and-guts end to Curtis and Mandy, Adele slipped deeper into her reveries while *The irate air* sailed away from The Anchorage, soon about twenty-five miles south of their starting point. When the gentle breeze picked up to a twelve-knot west-northwest wind, Smee turned to Adele for some help.

"I'm getting sick to my stomach, Adele. Take over, I'm going inside for some more Dramamine." Holding his stomach, Smee carefully went below.

Bringing out her compass from the treasure chest, she glanced at the family photos and noticed some old drawings she didn't recognize underneath them. When she lifted the first page carefully from the old trunk, it started to crack. Laying it down gently on a cushion, she saw it was an historic and very detailed nautical chart. Just what a still-green sailor needed to get her through the day. New Providence was circled in what looked like blood. There were several routes marked all around the Bahamas, including the Berry Islands. Adele guessed where she was right now in the Atlantic and thought she had to travel less than forty miles almost due west to make her destination and then another mile or so to Giggling Girl. With the winds now a gusty eighteen knots, she figured they would arrive at the Berry Islands around seven p.m.

Calling out to Smee, she told him that seasickness was better dealt with on deck. "If you need to puke your guts out, I'd rather it be in the water."

Smee slowly came topside. "This is a real testament to how much I love you, Adele. I'd really rather be hunkered down in my house soaking in those fabulous scents and imagining when my next Woody will make the scene."

Adele looked at Smee tenderly and told him, all kidding aside, how much she appreciated his sailing with her. She felt that she now had a true partner, a man she could share both her inner thoughts and true adventures with.

Smiling wanly, Smee moved over to the side of *The irate air*, murmuring that he hoped the now energetic winds would calm down his queasy stomach. Watching her partner's discomfort for an instant as he went to the starboard side to get some air, Adele snagged a protein bar and bottle of water and *felt* how much she was enjoying the sailing trip. She thought about the amazing turn of events her life had taken over the last three-plus weeks. Multiple turns, really. She had gone from a comfortable condo, underwhelming job, and uneasy marriage to living on a sailboat, partnering with a pirate booty retriever, and serious smooching with a Navy SEAL. Even better, she was following in the footsteps of her Aunt Anne. If Anne could help command a five-masted ship with a crew of eighty men, Adele could certainly sail a 27-foot Catalina with a crew of Smee. It was in her blood and in her father's too. Her mother was right—she was a Bonny through and through.

Off the starboard side, the water turned darker and choppier. The skies began to cloud up and the temperature dropped dramatically. She zipped up her hoodie and decided she no longer liked the way this adventure was shaping up. As the water got more turbulent, she tried to remember the old nautical saying: "Red sky at night, sailors take flight" . . . or was it . . . "Red sky at night, sailors delight." But then what about during the day? *Oh, shit*, she thought to herself. It goes, "Red sky in the morning, sailors take warning." The sky this morning couldn't have been any redder.

The sky turned deeper in color and more ominous looking; reassuring Smee, Adele pulled her small outboard motor farther up the side of the boat. If the trip got rough and she had problems with her sails she could always drop it back down into the water and motor part of the way to the Berry Islands. But her sense of confidence diminished in mere minutes as the water around *The irate air* became more unsettled. Going from a breeze to almost a gale, the wind hit thirty knots and started to roar around her mast. The sky turned dark gray and a first crack of thunder rattled the flimsy porthole windows. Lightning struck on the horizon and waves formed around *The irate air* in the thirty-foot-deep seas. Adele instructed the green-faced Smee to go down into the cabin and stay there until she told him otherwise. He was glad to oblige.

Down came the rain, hard and unrelenting as if a dam had burst. Pummeled by a giant wave, Adele was tossed to the railing and just managed to grasp it, avoiding a nasty fall to the deck. When the boat hit some very rough water, the mainsail suddenly crashed across the boat from the starboard to the port and the old sail sustained a giant jagged rip. The boat rose high on its side and Adele held on tightly to keep from being tossed overboard. It was now pitching and rising like an enraged steer. She managed to tie off the tiller and climb below to check the hull's integrity and to her horror there was water in the stern of the cabin. Not good. Dipping her finger into the water, she tasted it. Thank goodness it was fresh and not salty. Several of her water bottles had burst open and were flowing across the deck. She wasn't going to sink—at least, not yet.

Frantically ripping everything out from underneath the seat, Adele found extra sails, the oar, snorkeling gear, protein bars, and the rest of the water. However, she had forgotten to pack flares, a flashlight, or a life jacket. If the electricity failed, she would be shit out of luck, even with the paddle. The renegade sail was now pointing dead north, flapping wildly due to the three-foot-long vertical tear. Its force was carrying *The irate air* along at breakneck speed. While she was trying to lower the mainsail a section broke free from its rigging and part of the ripped sail plummeted into the water. This was dangerous—the wet sail could pull the whole boat over and down.

All of a sudden Adele remembered one of the last sailing trips she had taken with her dad, when she was only eleven years old. They took off from West Palm under cloudy skies and he wasn't feeling very good. When he claimed to want some sea air to clear his foggy brain, she assumed her dad had been hitting the bottle, not suffering from a horribly painful brain tumor. Before they even got *The Pirate Pair* under sail he was swaying on the deck and then the wind speed picked up dramatically. Just able to lower the jib before falling down onto a seat, Darryl slurred that he needed her to take control of the tiller. Feeling very small and scared, Adele grabbed the helm and her dad started to tell her how to steer into the open water. She was a natural, he encouraged her, and soon she was *coming about*, or aiming into the wind to slow the boat down. The jib dipped into the water, but luckily Darryl had his wits about him and strength enough to pull it out. She remembered the loud slurp when it hit the air.

The young sailor was able to head back to the marina before all hell broke loose. And no, the real storm wasn't the weather. Babs was beside herself when they got home. She was dressed in her yellow LL Bean slicker over her eternal bikini, and ready to take the dinghy to the rescue. She took Darryl straight to bed and Adele heard her dad mumble, "She did good, Babs, helped me lift the sheet."

Adele now knew what she had to do.

"Thank you, Daddy," she cried. "You're the best."

Coming back to the situation at hand, Adele realized rest time was now over for Smee and she screamed that she needed some help, as she now had no control over the direction in which the mainsail was taking *The irate air*. Smee fought his way up on deck. Adele yelled for Smee to catch the ripped mainsail while she tried to lower it down. Before he got a good grip, though, the sail broke free from the rigging—throwing him to the bottom of the boat where he moaned in great pain—before a section of it crashed down into the water. It formed a suction cup that seemed unbreakable and wrapped under the hull, stressing the jib to the max.

"I think I broke my leg," he screamed out.

"Grab onto something solid," Adele screamed back. "I'm afraid we're going to capsize." Adele reached for a knife and began cutting the boat free from the sail. Smee managed to put his arms around some still secure rigging before a renegade wave loomed on the horizon. The wave caught the boat, breaking the tiller free, and she was thrown hard against the mast. Adele now moved forward and held on desperately to the boom, which was thrashing from one side to the other. As another giant wave hit the bow, it broke the suction on the sail and the bow. The boom careened back to the starboard side, knocking Adele with it. As she started to fly overboard into the dark, choppy water, an image of Mandy popped into her mind and she vowed that the little bitch would not be the co-owner of her family's inheritance. George Clooney was really hot in *The Perfect Storm*, but Adele had no desire to imitate him by going down with the ship.

Wrapping her leg through the safety line, she managed to hook her knee around the railing in perhaps the most important acrobatic move of her life. Putting on the snorkel mask and clutching her small knife, she lowered herself head first into the water. The safety line gave her another twelve feet, so she took a deep breath and swam along the bottom of the boat. Finding the sail, she hacked away at it until she ran out of air and struggled to the surface gasping for breath. After several dives she was finally able to cut the sail line free, relieving the pressure on the tiller.

Exhausted and visibly shaking, Adele slithered back into the boat but had no time to even catch her breath. By sheer dumb luck, her *Sailing 101* book floated by her. It was open to the page talking about "luffing the sails." "I'll be damned! Aunt Anne," said Adele out loud as she quickly read: "luffing refers to when a sailing vessel is steered far enough towards the direction of the wind, or the sheet controlling a sail is eased so far past optimal trim, that airflow over the surfaces of the sail is disrupted and the sail begins to 'flap' or 'luff.'" This was just what Adele had experienced.

The book floated away as quickly as it had appeared, like something in *Alice in Wonderland*, but Adele thought she got it. She needed to steer *The irate air* into the wind and do the exact opposite of what should be done when a sailor wanted to catch the strong breeze. Sailing directly into the wind made the sail flap so the boat would slow down. With Herculean effort, Adele regained her footing as the rain came pelting down. Gripping the tiller with all her strength, she tried to point the boat into the wind. But as it lacked a working mainsail, the current was too strong. The tiller swung at a ninety-degree angle and caught her deep in the stomach. She let go of the tiller to clutch her abdomen as the boat started to spin. Adele lost all control. She staggered to her feet, tried again, and braced her leg against the railing and used this traction as a body wedge. With her body strength fortified by a lifetime of strenuous workouts, she grabbed the end of the wooden parrot head with all her strength and pulled it starboard. *The irate air* turned sharply and headed straight into the wind. The mainsail immediately started to luff, slowing the boat so Adele could regain some control. She caught the rope and resheeted the sail, tightening it just enough so she could manage the tiller.

Remembering that Clooney turned into the rolling swells, Adele was finally able to sail *The irate air* on a diagonal, literally surfing the swells. Suddenly Aunt Anne's words to "trust the ship" came into her mind and she managed to maneuver the vessel as a seasoned sailor would and turned with the wind. *It's a miracle. No . . . it's my legacy. Aunt Anne is looking out for me.* When the rain tapered down and the skies began to clear, Adele took stock. *No electricity.* Turning towards Smee, she saw that he had let go of the rigging and was crawling towards her.

"Are you strong enough to take the tiller?" Adele asked him with concern after glancing at the swollen and discolored leg revealed beneath his torn pant leg.

"Aye, aye, captain," he whimpered weakly and pulled himself up to the tiller, taking it from Adele.

Adele stumbled to the front of the boat and found herself in six inches of water. She began to bale out the bottom of the boat. Thirty minutes later her arms were aching and the neck burns she had sustained when battling Diego were bright red and puffy. Lowering the outboard motor's shaft into the water, Adele gave the starter rope a tug. The motor fired up for a second and then abruptly stopped. Five tugs later it was still silent so with all her dwindling might, Adele tried to lift it back out of the swirling seas. But it would not budge. A school of swimming dolphins were now surrounding *The irate air* and it seemed as if they had churned up a mass of seaweed and fishing nets that had wrapped their way around the propeller. Giving up, at least for the time being, Adele sat down in the cockpit to clear her head and rest her body.

Four hours later, on the point of exhaustion, she was sure she must have been dreaming when she heard the eerie sound of whale song. The wind had died down and the clouds cleared away. A half moon was shining so Adele could see well enough to follow the sound to the galley. Walking around Smee, who was passed out across the tiller, she tracked it to the satellite phone he had brought on board. Adele looked at her watch—it was two a.m. Answering the phone, she heard Alli on the line. "Marvin called me from Miami this morning and told me what was going on, Adele. I've been calling you for hours. Is everything okay?"

"No," moaned Adele as she started to gasp. "I've been in a horrible storm and my electricity is out. Smee is with me, I think he has a broken leg, and I have no idea where I am."

Alli took control. "Listen to me, Adele. The moon is relatively bright, so go to the deck and see if you can spot land." Adele did what she was told. Tripping over the spyglass, she picked up the magnifying piece and put it to her right eye. Canvassing the horizon, she saw the signature group of magnificent mangrove trees and the *Gia*, a.k.a. the *Hygia*, anchored no more than a mile away from her. Turning her sight to the west, Adele then spotted the *Beautiful Bonny* on the horizon.

"Thank you, Aunt Anne!"

"What?"

"You're not going to believe this, Alli, but I somehow have ended up at Giggling Girl—I mean, Strawberry Cay. Both the *Bonny* and the *Hygia* are within my telescope sight as well!"

"Wow. Unbelievable. I'm going to call the Nassau police or the Coast Guard and get them to the Cay pronto."

"I'm going to investigate myself too."

"Stay where you are, Adele. I'm going to track down Rocky and have him send a medical helicopter to evacuate Smee as well."

"I don't trust him," her sister countered.

"Well, you should. I've been doing a bit of investigating and found out that Rocky is rock solid. He's working undercover for the Navy and on the trail to track down the ringleader, a man called Black Jack, and his mercenaries. The two men attended Annapolis together and the pirates were involved with the hijacking of the *Hygia*. There was some Top Secret item on board."

"Wow, Aunt Anne was right. I've hooked up with a real privateer. A partner just like Jack was to Anne. And you said 'Black Jack'? That's BJ! That's wonderful!"

"You're going off the deep end, Adele. I want you to stay on board until help arrives. Rocky should be able to get to you in a couple of hours."

Adele agreed with her sister, but her sixteen hours of battling the sea were kicking in. She dropped the mainsail and untied the tiller, throwing out the anchor. Checking on Smee to make sure he was just asleep and not dead, Adele could suddenly no longer keep her eyes open and, going down the ladder, she slumped onto the waterlogged cushions before calling the Coast Guard.

It was well before dawn when Aunt Anne raised Adele from what seemed like the dead. She was wrapped in a heavy wool cape.

"I could have hardly saved the ship any better than you did, my pretty," said Anne, giving her niece the most sincere compliment in this almost month-long relationship. "What a feat of sea-woman-ship. Even I decided to dress warmly for the inclement weather."

"Great cape, Aunt Anne. I sure could have used it last night. Oh, the charts were a real help. Thanks."

"No rest for the wicked—and the good don't need it. What

a tracker you turned out to be! I see you're close enough to the *Hygia* to send a shot across her bow. Who'd of thought you'd have both boats within range?"

"Yeah, when I thought I'd be too late to catch the *Hygia* again. They were planning to leave yesterday. Wonder why they didn't—the weather, you think?"

Anne waved away her question, warned her that this was going to be a dangerous day, and advised her to wait for her privateer and his crew. But patience was not one of her niece's virtues.

"I can't wait to get my hands on Mandy," Adele fumed. "She's going to wish she'd stayed at the spa working out in her spandex."

"Why don't we strip and skin that doxy?" proposed Anne. "I remember when I gutted Jack's First Mate Junior Jim. Junior found out I was of the female persuasion and thought I should leave the *Treasure* directly even though there was no land in sight. Came as a big surprise to him when he was the rogue who was thrown overboard . . . in pieces. What a bloody mess it was."

"I've heard that story. In fact I was just thinking about it yesterday, before the storm hit." Adele was pleased to be able to participate in her aunt's reminiscences for once.

"With two ships you have twice the risk, but also double the reward. That was always the position I wanted to be in. Having the loot hidden behind a panel of steel is surely a challenge."

Adele thought for a minute. She had to be able to decipher Anne's clues, before going deeper into danger. Where in the heck on the *Beautiful Bonny* was there any steel? She remembered doing a Google search once on boat building materials and finding fiberglass, plywood panels, and polyester resin. Aluminum was the metal of choice to reinforce the body of the boat, but rarely steel since it was much too heavy. She did a mental scan of her vessel. Then it came to her—the fortified steel cubbyhole hidden in one of the boat's side panels.

Suspecting Anne could read her mind, she wondered how Curtis had found it.

"Aye, lass, I knew you'd remember where your smallclothes was hid. That landlubber literally fell into it. He hurt his elbow when he hit the panel. Poor Curtis, he should have broken it and every other bone in his body, too."

Anne went on to curse that the bastard should be hung on the mast for all to see if Adele didn't want to keelhaul him. He would become a buzzard's banquet just like several of her mates and would-be mates had the pleasure of meeting their demise. It was well known that Anne had a jealousy problem and many ladies, be they peasant or proper, had discovered their fate at the end of her cutlass or even more cruelly.

"Don't forget the other girl as well."

"What other girl? What do you mean?" asked Adele. "Does that asshole have another woman on board? This is not going to be a pretty reunion."

"You've got to get inside of her head."

"I don't know what you're talking about, Aunt Anne. Mandy doesn't have much of a brain to invade and boats don't have heads unless you're talking about the bathroom."

"The answers lie in the head," repeated Anne as she wrapped herself up tightly in the coarse navy blue wool cape and swirled into thin air.

Chapter 23

Adele woke up at the crack of dawn and looked around at her damp and disheveled boat. It was truly the still after the storm and there was not a breath of wind on the water. Smee was starting to stir and she went over to attend to him. He was groaning loudly and his leg was now the color and size of a giant eggplant.

Cradling his head in her lap, she asked Smee if he could move his leg. In great pain and with tremendous effort, he moved it slowly from side to side. *Thank God*, she thought, *it isn't broken.* Collecting several wet towels from the cabin, she wrapped up his swollen leg carefully. "Now I want you to stay put until help comes," she told him, sounding a lot like his NaNa.

"No argument from me," Smee acquiesced weakly.

Picking up the spyglass, she scoured the area, barely able to find the *Beautiful Bonny* behind the slightly bronze-colored mangrove tree trunks. Now she got it—Curtis had planned to come here all along and had the mast repainted to blend in with the colors of the mangrove trunks.

Doing a series of sideways waist bends and toe touches to loosen up her body, Adele lowered herself down to the outboard motor and half-heartedly pulled the starter rope. It did not budge. After two more attempts she realized that something was caught around the propeller and that she would have to get up close and personal to find out what was causing the restraint. Adele was none too happy about having to take another plunge, but she gingerly lowered herself down into the now glassy water, knife in hand, and sawed away at the kelp and seaweed wrapped around the propeller.

Fifteen minutes and three broken nails later, it was free of the ties that bound it. Struggling to get back inside of *The irate air*, she lay on the deck for several exhausted minutes before tackling the next task at hand. After three good pulls the motor started and stayed going. Deciding to idle for ninety seconds just to make sure it would keep running, Adele picked up her crossbow and thought about the hard part. *Which boat should I try to board first and what am I going to do once on board?*

Hearing whales calling her again she picked up the ship-to-shore telephone. It was Alli saying that Rocky and his team, as well as a medevac helicopter, would be there in less than an hour. They had just landed in Nassau and would be launching two SEAL Dominator speedboats in just minutes. With a cruising speed of sixty miles an hour, they would be to the rescue before Adele had finished eating breakfast and changed into a dry t-shirt.

Sliding into the sopping wet galley, Adele reached down to the lower drawer and felt the small hula-girl waterproof flashlight, turning it on to illuminate the wet mess that was once the clean cabin. She spotted the soggy box of protein bars and, tearing it open, was ecstatic to find the foil wrappers had done their job and her breakfast was still crunchy. Adele offered one to Smee, but all he could manage was to ingest several gulps of water. Adele, on the other hand, chomped down three bars in a matter of minutes. She chased them with a bottle of water, and suddenly the world seemed like a brighter place.

Opening up the old pirate chest, she was amazed to find that the 300-year-old seal had held and her cherished photos and drawings were as dry as a bone. *Your work, Aunt Anne?* Digging to the bottom, she found an exquisite antique sapphire and diamond, sharp-ended hair comb wrapped in a delicate and yellowed lace scarf. On a whim she swept up her tangled red mane and secured it in a tight bun using the antique comb as an anchor. Now totally inspired by her Aunt Anne, she decided to head out. Rocky and his team would be there soon, but there was nothing wrong with a head start, she justified, calculating a course to motor slowly through the mangroves and up behind the *Beautiful Bonny*. She would then cut the engine and swim the last quarter mile, and hope to use the element of surprise against her absconding husband. What she didn't realize was that Diego had already commandeered the vessel and taken a hostage.

Had he been a sane man, Diego might have been disgusted by the degradation to which he'd stooped.

A filthy bandage adorned his forehead, a dead glint shone in his left eye, and a sick smile played over his lips. Cracking his neck and knuckles several times, Diego got ready for the work at hand. Curtis had been tied to the mast of the *Beautiful Bonny* and Diego had cut off his shirt, but it amused him to leave the captain's medallion hanging around Curtis' neck. As the preliminary punching and slapping had not convinced Curtis to reveal where the treasure was hidden, the mercenary decided to go another way and was using several shark teeth to create small cuts down both sides of the neck. He saw with delight a look of abject terror wash across Curtis' bulging eyes when tiny blood streams ran down his chest.

Little points of blood started to bubble up and Curtis shrieked in unimaginable pain. The longer the time between painful physical contacts, the more terrified Curtis seemed to become. He begged Diego to stop, but the mercenary enjoyed taking his own sweet time. He bent down for another hard prick. Turning white . . . then gray . . . then purple, Curtis pleaded for an end to his agony.

"I know where the treasure is," he cried. "Just please stop. I'd always planned to sell the loot, so let's make a deal! We can both be richer than we ever dreamed of."

Giving one more slice for good measure, Diego untied Curtis. The poor man grabbed the sides of his neck, moaned, and crawled over to the bench, sat down and hit the hidden panel. It did not budge. He hit it again and again and again, but it would not open. Curtis only stopped when Diego punched him out cold.

On the other side of Giggling Girl, three hundred feet off shore, the newly named *Gia* bobbed at anchor. She was almost completely unrecognizable as the 51-foot Hinckley Sou'wester that had arrived in these waters just two weeks earlier. Winston, the former engineer at Miracles and Magic, had seamlessly attached the balsa wood, burgundy-painted helm extension to the bow of the boat and the entire vessel had been painted the same color. The *Gia* now looked like a 56-foot, newly refurbished super yacht. A new pristine silver mast and white jib sail accented with two burgundy stripes had just been raised.

BJ was on board, breaking apart the wooden body of the Goddess of Water figurehead. He had opened a five-by-four-foot, 36-inch-deep footlocker and was placing the head, arms, legs, and torso inside. Next he closed the brass flap loosely over a brass horseshoe-shaped bar.

Mandy and Elaine had been alone together again on the beach this morning for way too long. Feeling sorry for Elaine, who was nursing a black eye, Mandy was trying to teach her how to do the Downward Dog yoga position on the sand. But she would have none of it. Elaine was holding her eye and way too tense to be interested in exercising.

"That Bobby's re-ah-lly mean," observed Mandy.

"You've got that right, but he's going to pay. I'd call Adele and warn her but my phone is on the *Gia*. They've disguised the boat, it must be the stolen one Adele was after, and I'm going to tell Adele all about it as soon as I see her. She's a pirate hunter and Bobby's definitely a pirate. I think he means to harm her. Do you have your phone, Mandy?"

"Curtis doesn't want me to have one—and he got mad at me when I used his phone to talk to my BFF Melissa. It's a control thing, ya know. I think all guys are the same. Curtis loves to use and abuse me, especially when I get into the chick's yoga pose."

"I think you mean the Child's Pose, Mandy. You've always seemed underage to me."

"Well, my driver's license says I'm nineteen," confided Mandy as she got back into the sitting position, bent her torso and head down to the sand and curved her body over her legs, moving into a tight, compact position.

Elaine shuddered, looking down at her own calves. "You look like a beetle. How can you get your body to look so small? That position is really freaky."

This was the last straw for Mandy. A criticism of her body was a criticism of her soul. Quickly unwrapping her legs she thrust them out at Elaine who was pacing by her. The older woman took a tumble, eating a mouthful of sand. Gagging and choking, Elaine retaliated with a hard grab to the ankles and the teen landed right on top of her.

Chick fight!

Mandy wrapped her legs around Elaine, who punched at her wildly and pulled at her bikini top. Mandy was once again topless on the beach. The sand flew and the punches landed. The women were in a full contact, violent beach bash.

As planned, Adele cut the engine when *The irate air* was about a quarter of a mile from the *Beautiful Bonny*. She decided to carry the crossbow on her back and the hula-girl flashlight in her jeans pocket when she swam over. She hoped to surprise Curtis and Mandy aboard her stolen boat. Giving Adele a hug for luck, Smee warned her to be careful as she lowered herself silently over the side. The water was cold and the crossbow weighed heavily on her shoulders, but the thought of revenge propelled her through the twelve-foot-deep surf. Arriving at her destination in a matter of minutes, she shimmied up the side and swung her very toned thighs over the helm and into the boat. Being careful not to clang the crossbow, she stopped moving entirely when she heard Curtis begging for his life.

"It'll open, I promise, I promise. Please don't hit me again."

Creeping down to the stern, she nearly stepped on a single, and very bloody, giant shark's tooth. There was no mistaking who was on board with Curtis. Sneaking into view, she saw Diego had her husband down on his knees next to the steel-enforced hidden cubbyhole Adele had so painstakingly installed last year. Her plan, so long ago it seemed like a folktale now, had been to put their valuables inside it once they started taking longer than overnight sails. She'd never told Curtis about the strongbox, but Aunt Anne had said that Curtis hurt his elbow when he fell into it. But why did both men so desperately want it open? All they had to do was push the button that was now hidden behind a pile of Curtis' clothes.

"I swear the loot's inside," croaked Curtis, gasping with fear. "I put it here less than twenty-four hours ago and the panel opened just fine." Curtis' bare butt had replaced his bare neck as the object of torture and Diego stabbed his crack hard. Adele winced.

"Please, please stop it," begged Curtis. "Let me call Adele and find another way to open it. Maybe we can be partners and steal all the treasure." Diego stabbed him again. Curtis gulped and attempted another tack. "It's worth millions of dollars."

What an ass-bite. Curtis has stolen my boat, stashed my treasure in my personal safe, and somehow he thinks I'm going to help him open it. That is so not going to happen.

"BJ would find and kill us both, asshole," barked Diego, picking up a blowtorch he'd brought on board. "This should open it just fine and next I'm using it on you."

"A blowtorch. . . ." gasped Curtis.

Reaching for her crossbow and taking aim, Adele shouted, "Hey!" and confronted the two men at the instant Diego stoked up the blowtorch into a full flame to use on the panel. Starting at sight of her, he dropped the tool, which skidded and made its way to the five-gallon container of gasoline Curtis had stored by the cabin. Realizing what was about to go down—and none of it good—Diego froze for a second. He then grabbed for the torch, but at that instant the flame came in contact with the red plastic.

"Fuck me!" yelled Diego as he shoved Adele out of the way and flung himself up the ladder and overboard.

Knowing how badly this scene was going to end, Adele and a screaming Curtis dove off of the boat right behind him. Less than fifteen seconds later fire ignited the fuel and the *Beautiful Bonny* exploded. The force of the water slammed Adele, stunning her for a moment. Diego was the strongest swimmer of the three so he was well on his way to the *Gia* as Adele surfaced. Curtis was nowhere to be found. Having to really think about it, Adele finally decided to dive down and rescue him. He came up gasping for air and glommed onto her as if she were a lifeboat. They both sank down again ten feet below the surface. With Curtis holding onto her shoulders, Adele had no traction to reach the life-giving air. There was no way she was going to let Curtis drown her. She forced his hands off of her shoulders. He panicked and seized her from behind around the chest. Since being buxom was never her problem, his arms easily slipped down to her waist. He was still kind of tangled up in her crossbow's straps, but now Adele summoned all the strength she had left, kicked as hard as she could, and swam them both to the surface.

About a hundred feet from shore Adele's strength gave out and she spotted Elaine on the beach, arms akimbo, looking at the smoke from the explosion. A large, seemingly inanimate object was lying next to her in the sand. It was Mandy. Adele then yelled out to Elaine for some help dragging her husband in to shore.

"Is that Curtis?" Elaine yelled back.

"Yes," answered Adele, gasping for breath, "help me."

Elaine waded out into the rough surf. Wincing when the salt water hit her sand-skinned knees, she evinced great pleasure while dragging the now unconscious Curtis in to shore and dumping him next to Mandy.

Adele laughed breathily, suddenly remembering the wish she had once expressed to Aunt Anne—that Curtis would have an "encounter" with the water and she would find him just before he drowned.

"I didn't know being a pirate hunter could be so much fun," Elaine chortled gleefully. "I'm so sorry I didn't believe you about Bobby."

"Is that what you're doing here? Bobby is BJ?"

"Yeah." Turning into the sun, Elaine revealed her black and blue eye to Adele and told her that Bobby had smacked her hard. He had hijacked the *Hygia*. She'd also found traces of what looked like blood outside the stern of the boat. He prided himself on comparisons to Blackbeard and maybe he was a murderer just as the historic pirate was.

Now it was time for payback. "I've been a lousy friend, and will probably go to jail for aiding and abetting a real pirate," cried Elaine. "You need to find Bobby before he hurts anyone else. If I had a weapon and knew how to use it I'd go with you."

Adele hugged Elaine lightly. "Right on. It's now time for some justice," she declared and headed back to the water.

"What are you going to do, Adele?" asked Elaine.

"Well it's obvious I can't get the *Beautiful Bonny* back—there's nothing left of it—but I'm close to finding the loot. I'm also going to recover the *Gia*, or whatever her new name is, and make some money for Smee."

"You've always been my most fun friend and I really screwed it up," mourned Elaine.

"Bygones."

Curtis started to stir as the medical helicopter approached. "Keep an eye on Curtis and Mandy until the Navy SEALs arrive and then send them over to the *Gia*. The SEALs, I mean. Also, once the helicopter lands have them power out to *The irate air*. Smee's onboard with a seriously injured leg."

"Will do, Adele. Do you think there will be a SEAL who's single?"

"I only know one, and he's mine," Adele yelled back as she reentered the water.

Approaching the stern of the *Gia*, she climbed onboard just as BJ walked back from the cabin. Adele managed to hide behind the old Navy footlocker without his seeing her. Winston was at the wheel and Diego had covered his singed head with a cold, wet towel. Behind him stood a loaded grenade launcher and three assault rifles ready to do battle.

"I'm going to kill that bitch when I get my hands on her," he announced. "She's been trouble since day one."

"She's beaten the crap out of you more than once, hasn't she? But you have to find her and make her open the panel first," ordered BJ, patting the towel harder than necessary. Diego winced in pain. "I can't believe she escaped from you four times. This is just one broad, Diego, and a kind of fat one at that."

His comment was more than Adele could stand. No one called her fat and got away with it. An ample ass, yes, but a fat body—absolutely not. Removing the crossbow from her back, she started to load it.

Winston put a pair of binoculars up to his eyes and adjusted them accordingly. Seeing a powerboat on the horizon, he turned the wheel sharply starboard to head towards some big rocks. The sudden shift made Adele lose her balance and crash against the chest. Diego heard the noise and moved in the direction of the footlocker, blinking painfully while looking for where the noise came from. Finding Adele, he pulled her up by her hair to a standing position.

Not noticing that Diego had found Adele, BJ steadied himself and hurried over to Winston. "What the hell was that?" he asked, slapping Winston across the face.

"We've got company," Winston said, handing the binoculars to BJ. "A Navy Dominator is about a mile and a half off portside."

"Damn it!" BJ looked through the binoculars. "Head over to the *Bonny*. We've got to find the loot before the Navy arrives."

"And I have just the woman who can help." Diego dragged

up Adele with both of her arms pinned behind her back. Adele kicked out at Diego, but a quick grab by BJ made her land hard on a wooden bench.

"Well, what do we have here?" asked BJ. "According to Elaine, you're the most dreaded pirate hunter to patrol the Bahamas."

Diego's smile was ugly. "Not when I get finished with her."

Diego pulled Adele up hard by the neck of her t-shirt and was about ready to punch her lights out when BJ gripped his arm. "Throw that bitch into the footlocker. We don't need her until we reach what remains of her goddamn boat. I'm going below to open the weapons cabinet." BJ snagged an assault weapon on the way down to the cabin.

"Think you can handle her?" he taunted.

"Yes, boss," replied Diego.

Grasping Adele by the neck, he pulled her over to the footlocker, opened it and stuffed Adele into the trunk, just like a rag doll, flinging her crossbow across the deck and forcing the old brass latch back into place. He then instructed Winston to motor towards the last few remaining burning embers marking what was left of the *Beautiful Bonny.*

Struggling in the dark and musty footlocker, Adele felt around for her flashlight as claustrophobia had attacked her and she desperately needed to find out what sharp objects were restraining her. Once it was switched on, the hula-girl started to jiggle as her halogen breasts lit up. *Oh, shit,* thought Adele, looking around at her confined space. She could see the head of the Goddess of Water and managed to catch hold of it. Using the piece as a battering ram, she banged the top of the trunk but it did not budge. Dust, dirt, and creepy crawlies fell down on top of her. Next she hit all four sides of the trunk, hoping to find a weakness, but they were tightly held together as well.

Getting a bit panicky, Adele gripped the head by the ear again for better leverage, but the ear gave way. The figurehead's pink and red garish mouth popped open, revealing a small package. It was a slick and tightly wrapped piece with a "Top Secret—Eyes Only" warning label wrapped around it. This was beyond creepy and entering the macabre as our goddess grinned brazenly at Adele. Pushing the small package into the pocket of her wet jeans, Adele knew she'd found something very important and wanted to get out of there fast. She banged against the lid with all her might but it still would not budge.

Rocky and his SEAL team arrived on the beach in the two kick-ass Dominator speedboats and saw the remains of a boat in the distance, burned beyond recognition. Rocky and Wu jumped out of the boat and found Elaine at water's edge looking out to the burning *Beautiful Bonny*. Curtis was on his knees attempting to expel all the water in his lungs.

Rocky grasped Curtis' arm. "Who are you? Where is Adele?"

Curtis stared at him as if he were from a different planet. "Who in the hell are you and why are you looking for my wife?"

"Oh, so you're the *husband*. Listen, pal, my intel says Adele's in these waters. Who was on that boat?" he asked, looking out at the still burning frame.

"None of your business."

"It is my business now, buddy. You gave up your claim when you went looking for a younger dolly."

"The only place Adele could be is on the *Gia*—anchored on the other side of these trees." He pointed in the direction of the small sheltered cove.

"She swam out to the *Gia* a few minutes ago," confirmed Elaine, eyeing Wu as if he were a peach to be eaten.

"Wuze, you're with me. You others, stay here on the beach." Rocky and Wu armed themselves with two assault rifles and new Glocks, and took off towards the cove.

As the Dominator approached the *Gia*, it was motoring towards the burning embers of the *Bonny* and the strongbox that had more than likely sunk to the bottom of the ocean, right underneath the red-hot mast.

Adele struggled harder to get out of the chest, trying to use the jeweled comb from her hair to pry the flap open. Oxygen was getting scarce in the padded, airtight trunk and she went into a dreamlike state.

"That's a mighty pretty piece," came the familiar voice. Adele was foggily amused to see that Aunt Anne was full-figure, but tiny enough to fit inside the trunk with her. The pirate lass was wearing a calico cotton shirt, black pantaloons, and battered three-cornered leather hat. She was dressed for business. "Glad you're not wastin' it in your hair. I pick-pocketed it from a very nasty lady-in-waitin' in New Providence who didn't need it after she was dead."

Adele chuckled. "Like this wasn't all your idea, like you didn't keep the contents of the chest dry and then point me to this comb. Focus, Aunt Anne."

Suddenly the inside of the trunk got warm and toasty and Adele had to shake off the feeling of wanting to sink down into a deep sleep. "The reason I came back was to help you, darlin'," explained Aunt Anne, "to guide you through my pirate world and help you reason out yours. It was all about me in those three years I was with Jack, and we both paid dearly for livin' outside of the law. I lost one daughter and I don't intend to lose another."

For the first time since her dad died, Adele began to feel that people close to her were watching her back and she embraced the womb-like safety of the trunk. Rocky was really a good guy and Smee made the dangerous trip for her when it was obvious that water, literally, made him sick. Alli gave her inspiration and information to track down the missing boats. She then remembered the nights when her dad would wrap her in a blanket up on the deck of *The Pirate Pair* and they would tell stories about the stars. His favorite was Orion and his belt. Made of three stars in a straight line, the belt was thought to be the core of Orion's strength and Darryl would compare himself to this mighty hunter as his strength started to leave him.

"I wish you had known my dad," Adele said wistfully.

"Trust me, darlin', I did. Darryl knew I was around. There was more than one night after takin' sick that your dad sailed with the freebooters, but now it's time for you to get busy, missy! Put the tooth comb. . . ."

"I can do this myself," Adele interrupted.

"You always could, my dear," crooned Anne softly. "You just didn't know it until now."

With renewed strength, Adele started to work the comb harder; one of the teeth caught just so and she felt the brass flap move away from the side of the footlocker. She tried to push the lid open, but it was too heavy for her. Having so little room to maneuver, she couldn't shove it far enough to count. It fell back down and the flap closed once again. Giving another heave ho, she leveraged herself against something that shifted. She knew the trunk was so well insulated no one on the outside would hear her scream, even if there had been a friend to call to. Hoisting with all her might, Adele finally pushed open the lid. She climbed out of the chest, spotted her crossbow lying on the deck, and readied herself for the next challenge.

Chapter 24

Rocky and Wu came up fast with the speedboat roaring at full throttle and they crossed behind the stern of the *Gia*, ramming it hard. The SEALs jumped from their speedboat to the *Gia*'s deck. Pulling out their Glocks, Rocky and Wu were locked and loaded, carrying their weapons down low so the mercenaries wouldn't see them. Winston was still behind the wheel but turned quickly to face the Navy men. He fired wildly with a small rifle, missing everyone and everything except the buoy in the distance. Wu took him down with one punch. The *Gia* began to thrash around wildly, as the motor was still going at high speed but no one was at the helm.

BJ came charging up from down below, clutching an assault rifle. He rushed to the already loaded spear gun he'd brought up from the weapons cabinet and fired at Rocky. It missed the commander but was dead on for Winston, who had just recovered from Wu's blow. The pathetic mercenary took the hit square in the chest and fell backwards into the churning waters below.

Adele did deep-breathing and worked to get her sea legs back, as she had been folded up in the tight trunk for more than an hour. Facing the water, she looked to the horizon for an instant, seeing the medical helicopter at *The irate air*, dropping a line for Smee. Hearing BJ charging up from the hold, she calmly loaded her crossbow and shot him in the arm just as he was reloading the bloody spear gun. Howling loudly, he dropped the weapon and looked around for his assailant, but Adele had crouched down behind her recent prison, the footlocker. He grabbed the assault rifle and fell back down the ladder and into the cabin below. Shots were fired up through the deck and Rocky and Wu dodged away from them. Rocky started to go down the ladder after BJ but suddenly turned in the other direction and drew his pistol. Wu picked up Rocky's slack and shot back through the deck at the mercenary.

"Son of a bitch—you betrayed me!" BJ yelled from down below and the firing stopped. Wu charged down into the cabin and pointed his rifle dead on at BJ's head. Radioing to the other Dominator on the beach, Wu called for backup.

"On my way," the voice on the other end of the radio fired back.

Adele's head was bent as she stood up to reload her crossbow and she didn't see Diego approaching her with a giant cutlass. "It helps if you have a cut man in your corner," he menaced her, and slashed wildly at Adele. The tip of the blade caught her on the leg and she stumbled. "Yummy," said Diego as he slashed again. This time all he cut was a lock of Adele's hair, so he kept coming at her.

"Maybe now I'll find out if you're red down below as well."

"I don't think so," asserted Adele as she finished reloading.

Diego slashed out again at the still-crouched Adele as she raised her crossbow. He struck with his cutlass, slicing down into her shoulder; she released the arrow at the same time there was an explosion behind her. The arrow found its mark precisely in his black heart, and a widening red spot appeared on Diego's chest. With a surprised look on his mangled face, Diego fell forward, hitting the deck hard, and Rocky moved in to support Adele—his gun still smoking.

The group of waterlogged survivors was on the beach at Giggling Girl trying to catch their breath and assess their wounds. Adele had given Rocky the Top-Secret package and he had hidden it with care. Rocky got out a first aid kit from one of the beached Dominators, and was using an antibiotic ointment and gauze bandages on all the battered parts of Adele's body. Lubricating her raw and sore neck, his hands managed to slide down the front of her body as well. She was enjoying the moment.

"I'm getting kind of tired of having to thank you for saving my life," she remarked.

"You don't need to thank me," responded Rocky, "and you kind of helped me along this time."

"But I love having a SEAL at my beck and call." Adele touched his face and looked into his eyes for a rare moment of tenderness. "Hey, I'll be back, but I really want to hear this." She moved away from him and over to another SEAL who was interrogating Curtis and Mandy.

"It's all his fault," claimed Mandy, clutching on to the SEAL's arm.

"Yeah, right," said Curtis. "I'm not talking until I get an attorney."

Adele stepped into the conversation. "Not many around here, Curtis." Looking at Curtis and Mandy with complete disgust, she pulled the captain's necklace off from around Curtis' neck.

"He gave that to me, Adele," cried Mandy, looking at Curtis.

"Can't we just let bygones?" asked Curtis. "Your new style and attitude is really a turn-on, Adele."

"Ew. What do I care? Listen, I didn't say this before, because I wanted to save our marriage—can't remember why—but you know? *Your* new bacon-fed gut style and what I now know about your same-old bamboozling attitude is *not* a turn-on. Hopefully, I won't be seeing either of your sorry faces for a long, long time."

"I'm not responsible," stated Mandy. "My last boyfriend got me a fake MD. I'm only seventeen."

"I think you meant ID," translated the SEAL. He went on to tell Adele that if this was true, Curtis would be put away for many years. He'd be facing a charge of statutory rape along with grand larceny.

Smiling with satisfaction, Adele walked away from the two men and looked over to Elaine and BJ. Wu had the injured mercenary in handcuffs and Elaine was giving him a piece of her mind.

"You're just a stupid old pirate!" She slapped his face. "And I was stupid to believe anything you had to say."

"Yes, you were stupid, you fat cow," snarled BJ. "But that just made it easy for me."

Elaine raised her hand to slap him again, but Wu caught her by the forearm.

"Oh, that felt really good," she said to the SEAL, looking deeply into his eyes.

Wu grinned back at her before moving towards Rocky and Adele.

Down the beach another SEAL had put on his diving equipment and jumped into the Dominator, heading out towards the burning embers of the *Beautiful Bonny*. Her mast was just starting to go under the water. Adele and Rocky watched him dive into the still smoking sea and bring up the steel box thirty seconds later.

"I sure loved that boat," lamented Adele with tears in her eyes.

"All you need to do is sell a piece of your Aunt Anne's ill-gotten gains and you can buy a boat a big as the *Titanic*," Rocky reminded her.

"I don't think so," said Adele wistfully. "*The irate air* kind of feels like home to me now."

The Dominator landed back on the beach and the diver jumped out, carrying the steel-enforced compartment. Bringing out a small hammer and chisel, he broke the box open. Curtis' polo shirt had kept the pieces safe and sound. However, several gold doubloons were clinging to Adele's lace panties and Rocky whistled softly. "So this is what's underneath your shorts!"

"Ass-bite," she replied with great affection.

Rocky called Admiral Braverman and gave him a status report. The microchip had been found and he needed a recovery crew to be dispatched to Strawberry Cay ASAP as there were two bodies in the water. Rocky and his team would be bringing back the survivors.

Adele was alone on her boat, as Rocky and his team had powered back to Nassau after the previous day's battle, and on to headquarters for a debriefing. She had not yet pulled up the anchor and was enjoying the beautiful and balmy Bahamas morning. Opening the chest, the one that had miraculously remained watertight through Adele's horrible ordeal, she pulled out the battered box of dark chocolate Godiva truffles and the last historical document. Fittingly it was a "Warrant," written in a flowery black ink script.

WARRANT
For the Arrest of Jack Rackham and Anne Bonny
Last seen in New Providence
Or on board The Revenge
REWARD—5,000 Pieces of Eight

Laughing out loud, Adele lay down on her deck and looked up at the azure blue sky. She started to doze.

"Mayhap we should find you a cutlass and ax," mused Aunt Anne. "True hand-to-hand combat stirs the blood better than usin' a crossbow. You can really feel the severin' of limbs."

"I've had a good teacher." Adele sat up on the deck. "But violence isn't really my style, Aunt Anne."

"Well, shiver my timbers and this old boat, too. I never could have guessed that by the pirates you've taken on."

"It has been kind of a fun month, Aunt Anne," admitted Adele, looking at her roughened hands and broken nails. "But now I think it's time for a manicure."

"You can't get rid of me this easily," said Anne. "There are more than a scurvy few out there who need to come to justice, one way or another. We'll chat tonight."

With a renewed burst of energy, Adele popped the last truffle into her mouth, then used her gnarly hands to raise the repaired mainsail in record time and lift the anchor. A ten-knot wind was softly blowing as she set sail for The Anchorage.

Epilogue

"Psychedelic," murmured Adele, when colors, one brighter than the next, started to raise her from a very deep sleep. Anne Bonny was wearing the most elaborate pair of royal blue embroidered pantaloons her niece had ever seen. Her bright green puffy sleeved silk shirt and neon orange sash powered her niece out of her plush, cotton sheets like a giant adrenaline rush. Finally it was January fourth, and tonight was the opening of the "Romantic Relics of the Caribbean" exhibit at The Provocative Pirates Museum on Nassau. Almost awake now, Adele felt annoyed that Aunt Anne was already dressed.

"It's my party," she mumbled to her aunt, but Anne was starting to fade away.

Adele looked out the wet windowpane of her spacious room at The Rendezvous Hotel and Spa and finally felt comfortable again at the resort. *Gee, another day of rain*, she thought, sitting down at a small desk and pulling her red Day Planner out of the faithful messenger bag, now cleaned and lovingly though inexpertly mended. She turned the pages to January third and her To-Do List. A broad smile crossed her face. The To-Do List included: Replacing daisy wheels; Watching Curtis go to jail; Calling Mandy's mom to let her know where her wandering daughter had washed ashore; Rocky taking BJ back to Tampa for trial; Getting the treasure to the museum. "Well, I'll be damned," she murmured with great satisfaction, "the To-Do List is already done."

To make the day even sweeter, Adele had sailed over to Nassau yesterday where two great-looking guards had escorted her and the Anne Bonny/Calico Jack treasure to the museum. The two young men both looked mighty fine when making Adele the center of their attention. Hearing her phone hum, she saw she had two text messages. Smee would be able to hobble to the party and was so looking forward to the Bonny Bahama Mamas bust tonight. Alli was touching base about their late flight so she and Babs would meet Adele at the museum. She also wanted to give Adele a heads-up not to ask Babs why Sheldon wasn't there. It seemed they were on the outs, and Alli promised to fill her in later, in person. *Like Aunt Anne said, every mother's son'll betray you. Hope they're not too late. I really can't wait to see my mom. Rocky will be in from Tampa momentarily and all I have to do now is take a hot shower and get dressed.*

The driver stopped in front of a brightly lit building where well-dressed people were entering in droves. Stepping out gingerly, Adele landed right in the middle of a puddle, splashing up wet brown spots on her tan, bare ankles, but managing to avoid splattering her blue brocade skirt. "Isn't justice sweet?" she muttered, heedless of the muddy mess.

Stepping through the front door, she adjusted her two bright orange sashes, one in her flaming red hair and the other covering her still-bruised neck and bandaged shoulder. *I'm fashionably late to my own party, but maybe being late wasn't such a great idea.* She viewed the pandemonium as two hundred fifty eager partygoers tried to move and mingle inside a space designed for a hundred twenty people at best. This was *the* place to be tonight. She watched with amusement at how seriously the six armed guards were taking their evening's assignment. *Clearly the treasure's safe from another theft.* Big and burly, the men were placed strategically in front of five fortified glass cases full of pirate plunder glistening in the subdued party light. Edging towards the cases, she looked up at the nearest brawny man, gave him a beguiling grin, and glanced through the glass. Arranged on felt-lined shelves was a collection of rare coins from the eighteenth century: solid silver pieces of eight and gold doubloons, their etchings depicting monarchs clearly visible, along with a distinctive square cross at the center of each. Before them, reclining on burgundy velvet, lay the cast-iron chastity belt with the shield and personal hygiene slot visible for all to view. Adele chuckled. *Awkward!* But the *pièce de résistance* was the display of half a dozen gleaming captain's medallions lovingly placed on the elegant folds of velvet.

Seeing some of her favorite people huddled in the least crowded corner, she made her way towards her mother, Alli, and Rocky, while glancing down at a case full of her family's loot. Smee joined them, leaning on a picturesque single crutch like Long John Silver while IQ carried a tray with cocktails. They toasted the Bonny women. Adele embraced her mother warmly for the first time in almost fifteen years, and whispered that she loved her.

Adele then looked up at a woman who stepped up to the podium. Blowing a shrill whistle, this was the curator of the Pirates Museum—the very woman who'd made her life miserable for the last three-plus weeks. *Hope she enjoys that Bully Hayes dagger she was bugging me about.*

"Thank you all for coming," the curator whinnied. "Now may I have your attention? We are all here to preview the Anne Bonny/Calico Jack treasure that has so generously been loaned to New Providence's very own pirate museum by the Bonny family.

"Although this collection comprises fewer than forty pieces, its value has been assessed at many millions of dollars." The curator paused dramatically to acknowledge the gasps in the room. "I'd like to share with you several of the most spectacular pieces," she continued. Turning to a pedestal behind her, she picked up a sixteen-inch 300-year-old ornately carved dagger pistol.

"This weapon was both a knife, with eleven-inch embossed blade, and a fully functioning pistol. Encased in solid yellow gold and polished to perfection, the pistol part had a flintlock mechanism, which fired exactly like the rifles of the day. The handle, as you see, is carved in the shape of a mermaid with flowing enamel red hair and small red garnets accentuating her shapely breasts."

Some of the guests tittered at the scholarly curator's choice of words. Adele waved to Elaine and her parents, across the room. She sighed, sorely missing Marvin who was still in the hospital. The curator resumed her lecture. "The dagger pistol offered a pirate double protection and proved very handy in battle, which included hand-to-hand combat with the very sharp blade as well as the firing pistol to use at a greater distance.

"It is thought that Anne Bonny had this piece commissioned for Calico Jack to honor him as one of the most notorious pirate captains to sail the Caribbean seas," exclaimed the curator dramatically.

Several guests exhaled envious sighs. Looking around, Adele saw a man with a hoodie emerging from the men's room with almost a furtive look, but then she focused again on the speaker when she continued. "This type of dagger was frequently worn at the waist of wealthy and distinguished European gentlemen."

Suddenly an ear-shattering alarm went off, and the museum steel doors slammed closed immediately, forcing all the revelers into a lock-down of instant hubbub and confusion. Ducking down low, the man wearing the hoodie tried to push his way through the locked and barred doors. The guards didn't see him, and no one made a move in his direction.

In an instant, Adele lunged towards the sweaty man, yanking back his hood and wrestling him to the ground. She caught his hands and arms and roughly dragged them behind his back.

"Hell, no. Not again," she muttered.

Pulling away from her, he put up his hands to protect his face and cried out. "Don't hurt me! It was my pacemaker that triggered the alarm. I was going to the outside restroom. Rush call—and the indoor john won't flush."

Rocky came up behind her. "I think you have to let him go, Tiger," he said.

Chagrined, Adele released the hoodie wearer immediately and apologized as the security gate was lifted.

"Now you're startin' to think like a pirate!" boomed the all-too-familiar voice in her head.

Glossary

adonize. to beautify, dandify; from the mythological Adonis

arsy-varsy. backwards, mixed-up, preposterous

articles. trousers

bacon-fed. fat, greasy

balderdash. nonsense

bamboozle. to deceive by elaborate scheming. Also adjective (bamboozling) or noun (bamboozler)

bantling. a young child or brat, sometimes with an implication of illegitimacy (a baby conceived on a bench)

crossbow. a medieval bow fixed crosswise on a wooden stock having a trigger mechanism to fire sticks or arrows

Cross-Swords. a pirate flag design attributed to Jack Rackham

cutlass. a short, heavy sword with a curved single-edged blade, used by pirates

dance the Tyburn jig. to be executed by hanging

dolly. a childish and beautiful young woman

doxy. a whore, a prostitute

fop-doodle. (c.18) a man who is much concerned with his dress or appearance; an insignificant fellow

freebooter. a person who pillages and plunders, especially a pirate

gib. a male cat, especially a castrated one; probably short for the personal name Gilbert

guggle. throat, windpipe

gumption. (British usage) common sense

hammer-headed. dense, stupid, or thick-headed

Hans-in-Kelder. an unborn child

have two faces under one hood. to be deceitful

heaped. (adjective) coupling

hedge-bird. a scoundrel or sorry fellow, or a wanton woman

hell-fire. (adverb) extremely

here-and-thereian. an unreliable person, a vagabond, a rolling stone

high stomach. courage

hobbledehoy. an awkward, bad-mannered adolescent boy; a work-shy young oaf

hocus. to fool or deceive; to befuddle, often with drugged liquor. Also used as an adjective

hoity-toity. (current) pretentious; (c.18) wanton, quarrelsome

howish. vaguely indisposed

huff-snuff. a bully

hurry-durry. an impatient or indignant exclamation

keelhauling. a form of punishment meted out to sailors at sea. The sailor was tied to a line that looped beneath the vessel, thrown overboard on one side of the ship and dragged under the keel or bottom of the ship

landlubber. a person unfamiliar with the sea or seamanship

let go an anchor to windward of the law. to keep within the letter of the law

letter of marque. a government commission granting the authority to attack and capture vessels of an enemy nation

mort. a woman; sometimes a harlot or near-harlot

pirate. one who robs at sea or plunders the land from the sea without commission from a sovereign nation

play at hey-gammer-cook. to couple

poppet. a term of extreme endearment; a sweetheart or doll-baby

privateer. a private person or ship authorized by a government by letters of marque to attack foreign ships

scurvy. low in quality; from the disease, common to sailors on long voyages, caused by vitamin C deficiency

smallclothes. small articles of clothing such as underclothing or handkerchiefs

strumpet. a promiscuous woman

yardarm. the horizontal timbers or spars mounted to the masts of a sailing ship

wamblety-cropped. nauseous, sick to one's stomach, hung over

wench. a girl; originally, though this was used to address someone of inferior standing, it had no other insulting connotation

Return soon to

the world of Adele Bonny!

Coming in 2014

Wendy Wilkinson's

Pirate's Plunder:

In Search of the Bermuda Triangle

Book Two
in the adventures of Adele Bonny

Here's an excerpt from
Chapter 1 . . .

Chapter 1

Six months can seem like a lifetime, thought Adele Bonny, looking over at her mother, Babs, who sat next to her in their rented red, white, and blue Mini-Cooper. And perhaps it was. During the last one hundred and eighty days she'd been abandoned by her husband; had the Bonny family fortune stolen and found; uncovered the hint of a new romance; and changed careers—from teaching dance at a private high school to chasing down pirates, retrieving stolen loot. Not bad for an almost forty-year-old with wild red hair, small breasts, and a big butt.

Driving across the long suspension bridge from downtown Nassau to Paradise Island and the mega Atlantis resort and surrounding super-wealthy beachfront properties, Adele momentarily locked eyes with her mother who had been applying way too much powder to her still beautiful 62-year-old face.

"I'll be so relieved when the treasure's off the island," commented Adele. "Hiding it under my bed wasn't an option."

"I know what you mean, honey," said Babs, applying two coats of Burgundy Bold lipstick to her lovely lips. "I'm excited to hear what the appraisers think about the collection. Being a wealthy woman is the best revenge."

"Do you still miss Sheldon?" Adele asked. "He was *not* my favorite stepdad. Always telling you what to do—just like Curtis did with me."

Adele grimaced at the thought of her ex-husband, now doing hard time for peeling off the panties of her seventeen-year-old exotic dance teacher, along with many other crimes. *I may not have my cheating husband or beautiful boat, but, like Mom,*

I'm a wealthy woman, and I even have a hunky Navy SEAL circling me.

Babs' resolute *no,* in answer to the question about her third husband, brought Adele out of her reveries. "Marvin and I are trying to ramp up our romance one more time. We're both finally between marriages and have to grab the moment—fast."

Adele smiled as she slowly snaked her way through the throngs of cruise ship tourists, Bahamian locals, and elegantly dressed business people, to the end of the island and private Paradise Island Airport.

"He would definitely be my favorite stepdad so far. I say go for it."

In the middle of the runway, with engines humming and propellers whirling, stood a three-million-dollar Pilatus, an eight-seat luxury plane, ready for takeoff. Killing her own engine, Adele reached behind her mother to the back seat and pulled out a large and heavy navy blue canvas duffle bag, with discreet Ralph Lauren insignia, lugging it out of the car.

"Just like you, Adele," chided Babs, rolling down the window. "Stuffing the treasure in one bag, when two would be so much easier."

"I'll be right back, Mom," she called as she trudged toward the plane.

The distinguished-looking captain greeted Adele at the bottom of the plane steps while First Officer Butch Dupree stayed in the cockpit, running his hands across his blond buzz cut. Dupree reached under his seat and pulled out a navy canvas bag, almost identical to the one Adele was carrying, and placed it behind the captain's seat.

"I'm Michael Gleeson. Let me help you with that." The captain lifted the heavy bag from Adele's shoulder, noticeably straining under its weight. "Jesus. What's inside? Rocks?"

"My mom's makeup," she replied glibly.

Looking around Adele, Gleeson stared into the front seat of Adele's Mini. "I *thought* that was Babs," he said, waving at Adele's mother. "She still looks great."

Adele started to laugh. "Another notch on my mother's belt, huh?"

Blushing, Gleeson told Adele that he would call her after landing in Miami. She watched as the captain closed the door, placed the Bonny bag next to the other blue satchel, and taxied toward the runway. Not waiting until the Pilatus was in the air, she jumped into the rental car and started to tease her mother.

"Nice looking man, Mom. Was he before Sheldon and after Marvin?"

"Neither, Adele. I met him ten or fifteen years ago at The Anchorage. He had a small sailboat docked there and was a great friend after your father died." She paused for a moment and mother and daughter both felt the pain from the loss of a wonderful man. "What did you tell Michael about the cargo?"

"Not a thing. He's on a need-to-know basis, and I decided he didn't need to know." What she hadn't revealed to the captain was that he was flying more than eight million dollars' worth of rare historical pirate treasure to Miami. After a very successful six-month museum show in Nassau, Adele and Babs had packed up the family loot and were shipping it to Miami for an appraisal by Christie's, before beginning a national tour. The collection included emerald and diamond encrusted crucifixes, ruby jeweled daggers, several emerald brooches, solid gold dinnerware, and several dozen gold and silver doubloons and pieces of eight coins—the legacy of Anne Bonny and Calico Jack.

At the end of the runway, the Pilatus was flagged down by an overall-wearing airport worker. When Captain Gleeson got out of the plane, he was immediately grappled by an incredibly handsome man who zapped him with a stun gun, then dragged the unconscious Gleeson into a storage room and emerged ninety seconds later dressed in his uniform.

Dupree broke the lock on the Ralph Lauren bag behind his seat, amazed at what he found in it. He hurriedly pocketed three pieces of eight, one gold doubloon coin, and a small emerald and pearl brooch, watching for the attacker to join him.

The now uniformed "captain" ran to the plane and jumped inside next to Dupree. He glanced at the pilot's paperwork, reading that a representative from Christie's and a Brinks guard would be meeting the plane at the Jet Way in Miami. Grabbing the controls, he taxied down the runway and took off smoothly.

"You still have the touch, Francis," approved Dupree. "Hasn't it been three years since you last flew?"

Francis gently moved the controls and the Pilatus turned towards southern Florida. "My hands still have the memory, even though all those skin grafts were torture."

Several minutes later Francis and Dupree were flying over the fabled Bermuda Triangle, an area that ran from Bermuda south to Puerto Rico, northwest to Miami and back east to Bermuda.

"Your face looks unbelievable," marveled Dupree, staring at the fifty-year-old's smooth-as-a-baby-bottom skin. "Not even your own mother would recognize you. I especially like how much firmer your chin and cheeks are."

"Thanks. You sound like Janice, but it seems a little wrong coming from a guy. It's amazing what drug money can buy." Francis then looked behind his seat at the Bonny bag, not noticing its designer insignia or the other dark blue satchel wedged beside it. "I'll be able to get a full body lift after this next drop," he gloated. A red beacon that started to flash on the dashboard interrupted their conversation.

"Drop straight ahead," said Dupree, squinting at the sea below.

Francis dropped down to several hundred feet, turned on the homing device, and deftly pulled the heavy bag from behind his seat. "Jesus, I didn't know cocaine was so heavy." He passed it to Dupree and slowed their speed down to almost an idle. Dupree opened his window and pushed out the satchel. As the Pilatus flew on and away, the bag hit the small orange canvas raft tied to the buoy below. But the weight of the treasure broke it in half, and the raft, part of the buoy, and the loot sank into the water.

"That should keep Dr. Strickland's patients content for the next three months," said Francis as the plane picked up speed and altitude, now in sight of the Miami airport. He got onto the radio for landing instructions, using his most professional and commanding voice. "This is XYZ123 requesting permission to land?"

"Cleared to land on West runway," the air traffic controller shot back.

Making a less than smooth landing, the Pilatus hit down hard and skidded to a stop at a remote runway, just steps away from the edge of the Everglades. Cutting the engines, they pulled out the other satchel from behind the captain's chair.

"Shit, shit, shit," screamed Dupree as he found the ten bags of uncut cocaine inside. "We've got to go back to the drop site. We threw out the Bonny bag by mistake." He turned angrily in his seat, snagging and disconnecting the wire to the tracking device. It lodged in the back of his seat, turning the unit off.

"You've got that right," Francis bit out icily as he restarted the plane's engine and began to taxi back down the remote runway, not paying any attention to the Bahamas Air plane on approach. Francis ignored the frantic calls from the tower. Avoiding what could have been a disaster, the other plane lifted its wing and began to circle until the Pilatus was in the air.

"Holy Christ," panted Dupree. "What was that all about?"

"That was about saving our ass." Flying fast and low, Francis arrived in the area in twenty minutes and tried to turn on the beacon. It did not light up. They flew aimlessly for a few minutes, spotting a Dominator speedboat circling the area as well.

"Adele and Babs will think we've stolen whatever was in that satchel," said Francis in a panic. "It must be valuable if a guard is supposed to meet the plane. We've got to land somewhere else and get in touch with Strickland and lay low for a while."

Dupree didn't share his knowledge of the satchel's contents with Francis. Thinking as deeply as a man with a blond buzz cut and tenth-grade education could, Dupree came up with another idea. Watching the Dominator's wake bounce part of the broken buoy to the surface, he told Francis to drop down as low as he could once the speedboat had powered away.

Pulling one of the cocaine bags from the satchel, he then dropped the half-zipped canvas bag dead on into the buoy where it flew open, revealing more than a million dollars' worth of packaged white powder. "What's to say the buoy didn't break when the cocaine hit it and one of the bags sank to the bottom of the Atlantic? Should be worth about ninety thousand dollars on the open market."

"You're a damn genius, Dupree," grinned Francis.

Once again flying back to Miami International, now in dusk, Francis circled around an outer runway till he saw two moving flashlights guiding him to land. After coming to a halt at the end of an old, unused, and badly patched stretch of blacktop, Francis killed the Pilatus's engine and wrenched the door open, jumping out. Dupree followed. Both men quickly removed their uniforms and Dupree was draped with a three-sizes-too-big white tee shirt and baggy bright green sweatpants. Gripping the back of the plane, they slowly pushed it off the runway and into an overgrown, jungle-like thicket on the edge of a patch of the Everglades. Dupree jumped at the sound of a snapping alligator.

"It'll take a bloodhound to sniff out this baby!" Dupree patted the side of the plane as its tires started to sink down into a mud flat. Unfortunately the bottom of his very baggy pant leg got caught under the moving wheel and he started to go down into the mud. "Francis, I'm goin' under," he screamed as that snapping gator took a swipe across his face. Suddenly his buzz cut was bloodied.

"Pull back, dick-head," yelled back Francis, clutching Dupree with all his might. After a ten-second mud and man standoff, Francis pulled him out but his green sweats stayed behind.

"White briefs," chuckled Francis. "Who would have thought it?"

Dupree didn't catch the humor as he nursed his badly scratched face.

Reading Group Topics for Discussion

1. What makes a pirate's life seem glamorous? Is the reality just the opposite? Do pirates have any redeeming qualities?
2. Do modern pirates have anything in common with their predecessors? Do you consider them to be more dangerous than the pirates of yore?
3. Why do smart women sometimes allow unscrupulous men to take advantage of them? Can a woman be receptive to romance while at the same time protecting herself?
4. What are the key elements for a woman to find herself? Do most of these elements come from within? Or from outside herself? What do you consider to be one of the most important aspects of your own development?
5. What is the nature of Adele's relationship with her ancestor Anne Bonny? Is it purely fanciful? Does Adele actually "hear voices"? Is there a legitimate sense of guidance in what she hears, or is she in danger of losing her mind?
6. Wendy Wilkinson did extensive historical research to create her novel. Why do you think women in history ever became pirates? Was it because they had very few choices? Or were they too brazen and unruly to have normal lives?
7. Is Adele's romantic relationship one that you feel will continue through the Adele Bonny trilogy? Or do you feel it's a frivolous entanglement? What works in the relationship? What does not?
8. How do you feel Wendy Wilkinson's non-fiction writing (collaborating on three *New York Times* Best Seller books) influences her fiction?
9. Why is this book called *Pirate's Plunder*? Ultimately, do you feel what Adele recovers is plunder? Or is it actually something that was rightfully hers?

To share or print these discussion points please visit:
http://www.BellekeepBooks.com

About the Author

Wendy Wilkinson, *New York Times* Best Seller nonfiction author, takes her work in a new direction with her debut novel *Pirate's Plunder, An Adele Bonny Adventure.*

Stories and tales of the Caribbean and high seas are in Wendy's blood. She grew up near the beaches of Southern California, and now Wendy and her husband spend many weeks a year at their cottage in the Bahamas, sailing aboard their 28-foot Sabre sailboat. She recently partnered with Morgan Freeman on the acclaimed celebrity lifestyle cookbook *Morgan Freeman & Friends: Caribbean Cooking for a Cause.*

A horse owner and horse lover for more than thirty years, Wendy is the co-author of the *New York Times* Best Seller *People We Know, Horses They Love*, the first book of its kind to reveal through personal stories and intimate photographs the ties that bind notables in the film, music, television, literary, and equine world.

A freelance writer for more than a decade with a Master's degree in Journalism, she has seen her work published in many national and regional publications, including the *Los Angeles Times*, *Los Angeles* magazine, *Fit* and *Fit Yoga*, *Travel & Leisure Caribbean (online)*, and *Colorado Springs Style* magazine. Ms. Wilkinson is currently crafting cover stories for *Cowboys and Indians* magazine, profiling such celebrities as Jeff Bridges, Christie Brinkley, Mark Harmon, and Morgan Freeman.

Wendy is married to Dennis Caffery; their daughter Alexandra attends college in Boulder. They divide their time between Colorado and the Bahamas.